W9-BTI-392

Cult &
Canon

HELMUT MARTIN

Cult & Canon

THE ORIGINS AND DEVELOPMENT OF STATE MAOISM

M.E. Sharpe INC. Armonk, New York
London

80 Business Park Drive, Armonk, New York 10504

This book is a translation of *China ohne Maoismus?: Wandlungen einer Staatsideologie*, published in Reinbek bei Hamburg in 1980 by Rowohlt Taschenbuch Verlag GmbH. This edition has been revised and edited by the author.

Translated by Michel Vale.

Library of Congress Cataloging in Publication Data

Martin, Helmut, 1940-
Cult & canon.

Translation of: China ohne Maoismus?
Includes bibliographical references
1. China—Politics and government—1976-
I. Title. II. Title: Cult and canon.
DS779.26.M3713 1982 951.05′7 82-16811
ISBN 0-87332-150-2

Printed in the United States of America

For Liao Tienchi

廖天琪

Contents

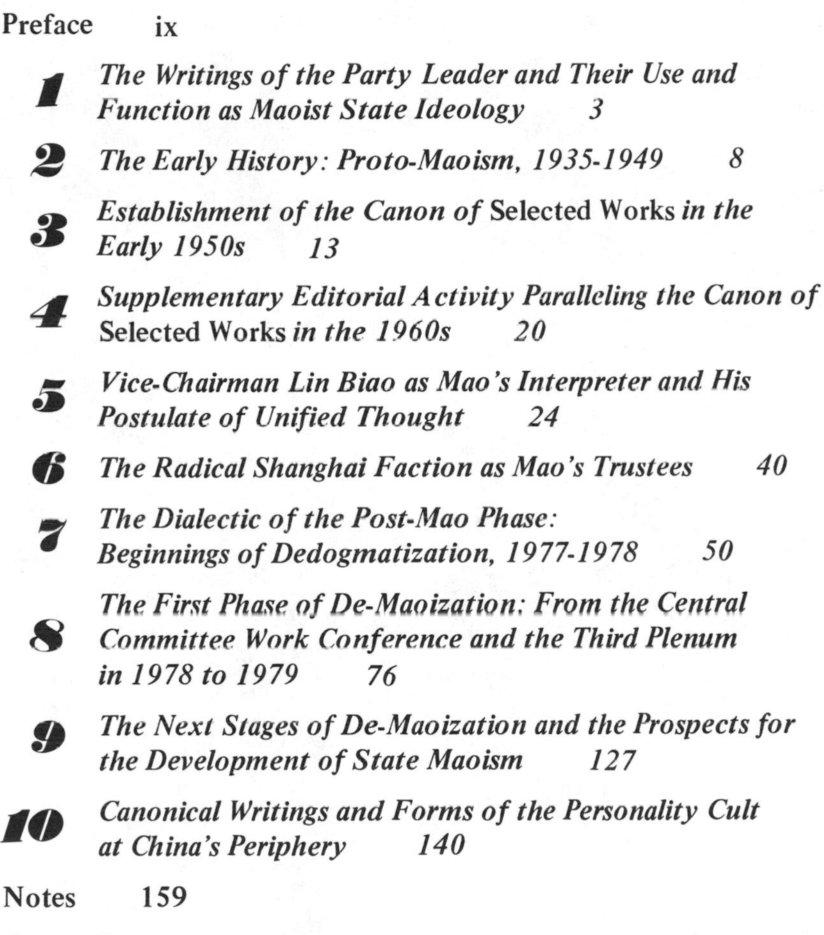

Preface

This book is the fruit of several years I spent studying Chinese Maoism at the Institute of Asian Affairs in Hamburg (1972–1979) as an observer of Chinese domestic politics; the final draft of the manuscript was completed at the Department of East Asian Studies at Ruhr-Universität, Bochum, West Germany. Originally interested in the Wansui volumes of unofficial Mao texts which came into circulation during the Cultural Revolution, I became fascinated by the idea of describing "Mao Zedong Thought" from the perspective of "state Maoism" when I was writing the introduction to our comprehensive seven-volume bilingual German-Chinese edition of Mao's post-1949 works, published by Carl Hanser Verlag, Munich, in 1979-1982.

A research sojourn of several months in 1978-79 at the Center for Chinese Studies at the University of Michigan, one of the most stimulating American institutions for the study of Chinese affairs, happened to coincide with a renewed outbreak of tensions and heated debate within the Chinese leadership and attempts by Deng Xiaoping, the architect of post-Mao era policy, to neutralize the Maoist minority around Hua Guofeng and Wang Donxing, which was engaged in delaying tactics within the party and the government. This development gave me the opportunity to include in this study the first clearly defined phase of the de-Maoization process (a constituent part of the "Beijing Spring," as it has been called), which covers events until mid-1979, following a precursory phase of struggle between the opposing forces of Maoist orthodoxy and a tentative de-Maoization which lasted from 1976 to early 1978.

I decided to undertake a measured survey of the main lines of this development without becoming caught up in the arcane details of Chinese power struggles and without, of course, assuming that the current state of knowledge among Western specialists is shared by the general reader. Nonetheless, the phase of final struggle for the Mao legacy and the years that immediately followed are described at close range and in great detail in my account, in view of the current interest in this new chapter of the People's Republic's political and social life subsequent to the death of China's great leader and the fascinating official debate on the restructuring of his teachings. In addition, since Chinese developments demand comparison with the corresponding periods in the Soviet Union (Stalinism, Khrushchev's de-Stalinization, etc.), I have provided some points of reference for such a comparison together with a short commentary on the situation in Vietnam and Korea.

Important developments up to early 1982, especially the attenuation of de-Maoization and the 1980 rehabilitation of Liu Shaoqi, the former state president and "public enemy number one" during the Cultural Revolution, could only be touched upon summarily. The show trial of the "Gang of Four," the skillfully staged dismantling of Hua Guofeng's power, and the conflict-ridden discussions that led up to the key document in the de-Maoization process, the resolution "On Questions of Party History" adopted in 1981 by the Sixth Plenum, have not been covered adequately. However, in view of the continuing fluctuation of values and evaluations in China, this official statement, comparable in some ways to Khrushchev's de-Stalinization speech, seemed to me to be the most reasonable cutting-off point for the book, and the document has therefore been included here as an appendix. I believe the reader will be surprised to see how accurately the crucial points and "final" judgments contained in the party statement could be anticipated in 1978-79 by observing the situation and fitting together the pieces of information then available.

The resolution, styled as an abridged history of the Chinese Communist movement and its successes before and after 1949, is in fact a devastating attack on the theory of "continuing revolution" and on Mao's subjectivism, his arrogance and personal arbitrariness. The mass campaigns are condemned as disastrous radical deviations, as Mao's personal "tragedy." The compilers took great pains to disentangle the cult around Mao — there ends the party's self-criticism — from "Mao Zedong Thought," which remains the cornerstone of the "superiority of the socialist system" in China. Certainly the process of de-Maoization is continuing: the recasting of Mao's image did not come to an end with the Resolution of the 1981 plenum. The perspective that comes with the passage of time will undoubtedly necessitate additions to the study — changes in emphasis and somewhat altered conclusions. This, of course, is an inescapable problem for an author commenting on recent events. To cite but one example of information recently come to light pertaining to questions treated in this book: We know today from party documents that Deng Xiaoping and the moderate leadership considered two decisions made in 1976, immediately after the removal of the radical "Gang of Four," to have been grave political errors. Hua Guofeng and his collaborators are now accused of not having followed Mao's 1956 instructions concerning cremation and his reported comments rejecting the compilation of an edition of his Complete Works. In other words, a final chapter in the personality cult, the decision to place Mao's embalmed body in the mausoleum in Tiananmen Square and the publication of Volume V of the Selected Works, which were both criticized internally by Deng and his supporters, are now openly condemned.

Today the emphasis is on the collective wisdom of the top leadership. Accordingly, a "Central Committee Editorial Department on Party Literature" has compiled and published the first volumes of Selected Writings from Zhou Enlai and Liu Shaoqi, and these have been defined as an integral part of the abstract system of Mao Zedong Thought.

* * *

My thanks go to Professor Albert Feuerwerker, Director of the Center for Chinese Studies at the University of Michigan, and to Dr. Werner Draguhn, Director of the Hamburg Institute of Asian Affairs, for the concern and support they have shown for my work. I must furthermore express thanks to the experienced editors of this volume, Doug Merwin and Patricia Kolb of M. E. Sharpe, Inc., who patiently reduced the cumbersome German sentences to manageable proportions.

I should like to dedicate this book to my wife, Liao Tienchi, who has been my best friend, critic, and colleague in numerous research projects during the last decade.

Helmut Martin
Tokyo University
February 1982

1

The Writings of the Party Leader and Their Use and Function as Maoist State Ideology

It will be yet some time before we are able to assess Mao Zedong's real influence on China, Asia, and world politics on the basis of a relatively comprehensive or complete critical edition of his writings (whether in the Chinese original or in translation), much less to trace all the ramifications of that influence down through the most detailed aspects of day-to-day political work. However, thanks to the considerable efforts Sinologists have devoted to the study of Mao's writings over the past decade our knowledge in this area has expanded rapidly, particularly our knowledge of Mao's writings in their more or less original versions, and as a result the role of the historical Mao[1] as a central figure in Chinese politics has become clearer.

Over the years, however, Chinese society (and to a lesser degree, those countries that are close observers of China) has been subjected to a relentless bombardment of state propaganda — propaganda constituting the official Mao ideology. At its most intense, especially during the great mass campaigns, this propaganda must have reached the absolute saturation point many times over in its total pervasion and direction of that society. However, the official writings of state Maoism, on which this propaganda is based, are selected writings, chosen for political motives and often altered by editors. These official writings function on a distinctly different plane from the Mao texts in more original form, which document the activities of the party chairman.

Accordingly, a discussion of Mao's texts at these two levels must first focus on the historical Mao as he appears in his writings and in the commentaries of eyewitnesses at particular moments in time. Such documents are roughly of three kinds: accounts from Mao's private life, accounts of day-to-day political activity, and finally, statements of principle by Mao Zedong, the revolutionary and political leader. Considering the reverence in which Mao is held in China generally and the cult that Mao and the party built up around the chairman, and in light of the simple fact that Mao as no other has stood at the center of political events in the People's Republic of China (PRC), it is not surprising that the accounts of his workaday political activity – from the routine memoranda requiring his signature to the hundreds of stenographic notes and tape recordings of talks, conferences, or receptions – fill giant archives. This archival material has not even begun to be properly assembled, let alone adequately and definitively edited, even in China itself. The October 1976 appeal of the Central Committee of the Chinese Communist Party (CCP) is testimony to this: the call went out to gather together all material from within the country and abroad to complete the archives in preparation for an eventual edition of Mao's complete works.

Second, alongside the historical Mao and his writings we must distinguish the ideological Mao canon, which by no means covers the same territory. By the term "canon" we refer to writings that at various times were promulgated by the Chinese leadership as "Mao Zedong Thought" (Mao Zedong's ideas)[2] – i.e., as the ideological foundations of the state – via the media and the device of the general campaign with its techniques for promoting participation and study. Such a distinction would seem to be crucial. The "canonical" Mao texts with their political function as an instrument of ideological control have left deep marks on the People's Republic. Even during Mao's lifetime the texts often functioned almost independently of him[3] and they will probably continue to serve as an ideological linchpin of the Chinese nation well into the future.

In examining the writings of "state Maoism," a term suggested by analogy with "Soviet ideology," it is helpful to effect a clear breakdown into successive stages, each marked out by specific constellations of texts corresponding to the political objectives that happened to enjoy priority at the time. The ideological orientation adopted at any particular moment drew its legitimation from an orthodox theory, proclaimed to be eternal and immutable, which denied the contradictory developments or controversial about-faces that had in fact taken place and, indeed, had produced the given situation. Moreover, on closer inspection one finds that each of the various stages of "valid" Mao text constellations is enmeshed in a network of sundry interpretations by party theoreticians or top-level functionaries who were invested as ideological "spokesmen" or who as a faction collectively seized upon this ex cathedra function quite instinctively as their power grew.

Since a tension exists at many levels between those texts reflecting the historical Mao, i.e., Mao the thinker and politician, and those that primarily document the ideological coinage of the state at some moment, it has understandably been the historical Mao and the development of his thought, or the reconstruction of the original writings as opposed to their later canonical forms, which has constituted the primary concern of scholars in the West. Stuart Schram's analyses[4] have given us a broader sense of the difference between the original Mao writings and their later edited versions and political function. Minoru Takeuchi's critical edition[5] of the texts has provided a solid foundation for reconstructing the historical Mao of the period prior to the founding of the PRC. Finally, the numerous publications of so-called internal Wansui writings,[6] which were circulated within the PRC and abroad during the Cultural Revolution, have put permanent holes in the orthodox view of the Mao canon. In the pages that follow we shall attempt to sketch out the development of the Mao ideology in its state function from the formal perspective of its successive outwardly manifest stages. This constitutes the history of the various editions of the texts of the Mao canon in China, at least in its most essential features, though we have made no attempt to exhaust this voluminous material.

The propagation of the Mao ideology by means of obligatory study of specific perspectives of the historical Mao or his writings reflects a concept of orthodoxy prevailing among the Chinese leadership that does not derive solely from the Soviet ideology of Stalinism. The traditional state Confucianism with its canonical writings, commentaries, and subcommentaries had given rise to a notion of orthodoxy (by no means restricted to the purely political) as early as the Han period at the beginning of our era and again under the Song dynasty (tenth–thirteenth centuries), which undoubtedly preshaped the modern doctrine. Only if the party is assumed to be infallible must its political course always be "correct," as the tirelessly repeated slogan[7] will have it. Thus, every conflict within the leadership concerning the party's course could subsequently be depicted in the PRC only schematically, as a struggle between two lines, with the rejected alternative dismissed as either an ultra-left or, even better, a right-wing deviation from the correct line — that is, as revisionism.

To complete our picture of the basic evolution of state Maoism, based on such notions of orthodoxy and taking the form of a Mao canon and a Mao cult, we may distinguish the following phases. A Mao cult and a proto-state Maoism had actually been established before the founding of the PRC — a sort of prehistory, as it were. Scarcely a decade later came a second stage, in which the Mao canon was definitely established in a three- and then a four-volume selection and disseminated, uncontested, for the first time, on a national scale. Then came an interim stage in which an attempt was made to expand the four-volume canon by the compilation of official parallel volumes of collected writings. This stage eventuated in the Cultural Revolution which was to permanently remold Chinese society. In the course of this mass campaign a multitude of unorthodox collections of Mao texts burst upon the scene, distributed by inexperienced activists and approved or at least tolerated by the leadership as a necessary weapon in the ideological struggle. At this time the cult of Mao reached its height, and ideological interpretations were being shaped largely by Lin Biao, who was grasping for power as Mao's successor. The Red Book of Quotations from Chairman Mao Zedong became the symbol of a conscious mass dissemination of Mao ideology. In an interregnum before Mao's death, the radicals in the Shanghai group[8] established themselves in the ideological domain, largely unchallenged as interpreters of the canon, while behind the scenes a power struggle between the two factions was coming to a climax.

Finally, the early post-Mao phase resulted in the expansion of the four-volume Mao canon by one more volume, a fifth dealing with the period following the founding of the PRC, after an uneasy consensus was reached among the leadership. Once the reunified collective leadership around Hua Guofeng had decided not to permit the open break that a complete de-Maoization would entail (although a profound reorientation of political goals and methods had already been undertaken), this phase was marked by a reinterpretation of party history and of the canon, and by the appearance at tactically opportune moments of hitherto officially unpublished Mao writings used to legitimate the new Realpolitik. Eventually Deng Xiaoping drove the party into an initial phase of limited de-Maoization during which the "mistakes" of the late Mao were aired on wall posters and in the Hong Kong left press. In 1979 there were signs of an impending broadening of criticism wherein Mao — although still acknowledged as the leader of the Chinese Revolution — would be held to account for the "left-opportunist" politics that since 1957 had unleashed upon the country successive waves of mass campaigns. But not until 1980 was Deng able to accomplish the elimination of the Maoist opposition from the leadership as well as the official rehabilitation of Liu Shaoqi, the preamble to an ever more pointed repudiation of Mao's policies.

The formal charges leveled against the Gang of Four in their 1979 trial served to justify what would ultimately be a wholesale condemnation of Mao's Cultural Revolution and to legitimate Deng Xiaoping's "new course" for the future development of the PRC. The new perspective was later formalized in the official de-Maoization document of 1981, the resolution "On Questions of Party History" (see Appendix). Hua Guofeng's relinquishing of the premiership to Deng's man Zhao Ziyang in 1980, followed by his ouster from the party chairmanship in favor of Deng's long-time ally Hu Yaobang, should be understood as the final outcome of the behind-the-scenes power struggle that will be analyzed in the chapters that follow, the culmination of Deng's cautious maneuvering toward his goal of unchallenged power — the power to mold the policy directions and the ideology of post-Mao China.

The Early History: Proto-Maoism, 1935-1949

1. MAO'S POSITION IN THE PARTY BEFORE 1945

Fourteen years after the founding of the CCP, Mao had consolidated his position in the party to such an extent that he could begin to lay the foundations for his unchallenged ideological leadership, which was to begin with the establishment of a codex of writings and the first elements of a personality cult in the mid-1940s.

As the story goes, in July 1921 Mao (then twenty-seven years old) was among the twelve founders of the CCP in Shanghai. At the Third Party Congress, in June 1923 in Guangzhou, which established cooperation with the Guomindang, he became a member of the Central Committee — then consisting of only nine full members and five alternate members. At the Fifth Party Congress, in May 1927, Mao came into conflict with the leadership because he had advocated radical agitation among the peasants, as is set forth in his well-known investigation report[9] of that year. In parallel with the rebellions led by other CCP leaders, he organized the Autumn Harvest Uprising, as it was called, in his home province of Hunan at the beginning of September. The uprising miscarried. As a consequence, in November 1927 Mao lost all the positions he had just acquired in the Politburo at a party conference in August, on account of his "military adventurism." Together with a small guerrilla army he withdrew into the Jinggang Mountains, where he continued mobilizing the peasants. With his guerrilla tactics, he remained in conflict with the views of the Central Committee of the party in Shanghai under the leadership of Li Lisan, recently returned from Moscow. In November 1931 the first Chinese Soviet Republic, with Mao Zedong as its leader, was proclaimed. The Moscow-oriented group around Wang Ming set the actual tone in this Soviet Republic in the province of Jiangxi, however. The Communist guerrillas were forced into their Long March in October 1934, and in January 1935 Mao gained control of the party at the Zunyi Conference, in Guizhou Province, where he became the secretary in the Central Secretariat. He also assumed the chairmanship of the Party Military Committee, which had command over the Red Army, became a full member of the Politburo, and established himself as primus inter pares[10] in the party leadership. Mao was also acknowledged by Moscow as the leader of the CCP as early as 1938. Even after Zunyi, however, Mao Zedong still had to overcome internal rivals, such as Zhang Guotao, before he could consolidate his leadership in Yanan. There, in 1943, he formally became chairman of the Politburo and the Central Committee. In the series of conflicts that ensued after 1935,[11] Mao decisively gained the upper hand over the international faction in mid-1945, at the Seventh Party Congress. At the Seventh Plenum of the Sixth Central Committee on April 20, 1945, the party leader had put through his own view of party history in the "Resolution Concerning a Few Historical Questions."

In the Yanan years (late 1937 to March 1947) Mao was finally able to devote himself to a more thorough study of the writings of Marxism and Leninism in translation, and he entered a fruitful period as an author, mainly on military and political topics. The rectification campaign[12] of 1942-44 definitively established Mao's ideological leadership and laid the foundations for the later orthodoxy of the CCP. It also established the unequivocal subordination of writers and intellectuals to the party leadership. Seen from a later vantage point, this campaign actually anticipated the practices attendant on Mao's ideological leadership in the People's Republic in the years after 1949.

2. INSTITUTIONALIZATION OF MAO ZEDONG THOUGHT

Mao's ideological aspirations grew gradually. In 1942, for example, the term "Maoism"[13] began to appear in the party newspaper. The actual formalization of this trend occurred at the Seventh Party Congress in April-June 1945 when the new party constitution was drafted, the preamble of which states that the party was under the great leadership of "Mao Zedong Thought." This constitution, binding for 1.2 million party members, replaced one that dated from the Sixth Party Congress of 1926 (and thus had been in force for seventeen years) which did not focus on a single leader. At the 1945 Party Congress, Liu Shaoqi, later to be president of the state, functioned as Mao's authoritative interpreter with his comprehensive "Report on the Revision of the Party Constitution."[14] The new constitution stated: "The thought that unifies the thoery of Marxism and the praxis of the Chinese Revolution..., Mao Zedong Thought, has become the guideline for all [the party's] own work."

Liu interpreted this key sentence in the preamble in extravagant Stalinist language, asserting that Mao Zedong Thought is "Chinese Communism," "Chinese Marxism," the "Sinicization [zhongguohua] of Marxism." It is "the only correct theory and policy for saving China." Mao Zedong Thought is based on Leninism and Stalinism, and Mao is a disciple of Stalin and the other classics:

> Our comrade Mao Zedong is not only the greatest revolutionary and political leader in Chinese history, he is also the greatest theoretician and scholar in Chinese history....
>
> Our comrade Mao Zedong is the brilliant representative of our heroic proletariat, he is the brilliant representative of the most noble traditions of our great people. He is a creative Marxist of genius. He has linked together this highest ideology of mankind, the universal truth of Marxism, and the concrete praxis of the Chinese Revolution; he has raised the thought of our people to heights of reason never before attained.... He has shown the Chinese people the only correct complete and clear way to a thoroughgoing liberation, the way of Mao Zedong.

The best leadership cadres gathered around Mao, according to Liu, "armed with Mao Zedong Thought." At the same time, Liu Shaoqi officially corrected party history so that now Mao Zedong Thought suddenly turned out to have been the sole guiding principle for the last twenty-four years, i.e., since 1921, the year the party was founded. The long passage in Liu's speech paying ideological homage to Mao concluded with a call to all party schools, party propaganda sections, general propaganda training groups, and party newspapers to use Mao's "works" as a foundation and as teaching material and to disseminate Mao Zedong Thought — which had inspired and purified the party since the rectification movement of 1942-44 — in a mammoth wave of study activity.

3. THE EARLY CANON

The precursors of the first editions of Mao's selected works were early volumes of collected essays containing numerous individual writings for propaganda work, such as Mao Zedong's Treatises of 1937, the collection Mao Zedong on the Sino-Japanese War from the same year, or the Selected Speeches of Mao Zedong for the Salvation of the Country[15] printed in 1939 in Chongqing.

Early editions of Mao's selected works had appeared between 1944 and 1948 in several different and independent editions. We should like to discuss six of these, which appeared at roughly one-year intervals. The first edition of Selected Works of Mao Zedong,[16] edited by the gifted writer Deng Tuo, later a prominent victim of the Cultural Revolution, was published in 1944 in Yanan in five volumes. In 1945 a one-volume edition appeared, while in Dalian (Dairen) another edition went into circulation in 1946. The 1947 edition in six volumes plus supplement, from the Xinhua Publishing House (which appeared in the United States in 1970 in a limited reprint), is better known. In 1948 a one-volume edition appeared in Harbin, and we know of other parallel Selected Works of the same year. This short list of some editions of Mao Zedong's Selected Works is hardly complete, but we do not intend here to go beyond the year 1948 to the publication of the actual canon, which took place after the founding of the PRC.

The 1947 edition, to take one of the aforementioned collections as an example, may be regarded as a prototype of the later canonical selection. The texts were brought up to date to include the most recent period, but there was no commentary. An official photograph of Mao was inserted at the front. Some sources were given, but these were later edited out of the canon for political reasons.

The preface to the later, canonical Selected Works of 1951 had the following to say about these earlier editions:

> A number of Chinese editions of [Mao's] works have appeared in various places, but none of them had been gone over by the author; their arrangement was haphazard, there were errors in the text, and certain important writings were omitted.[17]

This comment notwithstanding, at least some of the early editions must have been authorized Selected Works. For example, among those listed between 1944 and 1948, the 1947 edition of the Central Office of the Shanxi-Chahar-Hebei CCP as well as a 1948 edition of the Central Office of the Shanxi-Hebei-Shandong-Henan CCP were official party publications. These precursors, which had a central function in party schooling as decided at the 1945 Party Congress, must therefore be regarded as important sources for the actual development of the personality cult and the establishment of the Mao canon after 1949.

3

Establishment of the Canon of Selected Works *in the Early 1950s*

1. FUNCTION AND SPHERE OF INFLUENCE OF THE CANON

After the Chinese Communists' victory in the civil war and their seizure of power, sealed by the establishment of the People's Republic in October 1949, Mao Zedong, now the undisputed leader of the revolution and the whole of China, felt it his duty to "unify" the political thought of the population and to steer it into new channels, using the techniques he had come to regard as most fruitful during the years of struggle. One such means was the establishment of a cult around his own person; the Marxism-Leninism that had entrenched itself as the ruling ideology in the USSR, and hence also the cult around Stalin's person, was taken as a model (the Stalin cult was reaching its height in these years, the last before the Soviet dictator's death). But the elevation of Comrade Mao Zedong to monumental stature above man and mankind was by no means achieved forceably, through the brutal terror of purges such as occurred in the Soviet Union in the 1930s. Mao had as his collaborators competent people who acknowledged his charisma, willingly subordinated themselves to him, and gave him their firm support in his conviction of the necessity of an autochthonous Chinese personality cult. And certainly the ideal of a First Emperor with a legitimate claim to the people's exaltation and adoration, the founder of a dynasty — an ideal familiar to all Chinese from their two thousand years of dynastic history — was also implicitly at work here, albeit in new forms. The earlier ideological conflict with the Guomindang led by Chiang Kai-shek, who for years had been celebrated to no less degree, betokened a struggle between Mao and Chiang for the establishment of a valid, modern orthodoxy, more befitting the times, to replace Confucianism. On the other hand, no attempt to forswear such political orthodoxy has ever had any notable support in China, either at that time or today.

An important ingredient in the expanding Chinese personality cult was the elevation of Mao's writings to the status of a canon. Here, Soviet orthodoxy and Stalin's claim to infallibility, together with the Confucian classics, the intellectual basis for all political activity in the Chinese Imperial Kingdom, set the tone. A few figures covering almost three decades of the PRC's existence and illustrating the outward dissemination of Marxism-Leninism in China will give some idea of the dimensions of this cult of Mao's writings. Taking the notion of an ideological canon in the broadest sense, it has been estimated that a total of 5.2 billion copies of the five classics — i.e., the works of Marx, Engels, Lenin, Stalin, and Mao — were distributed between the end of 1949 and mid-1976, with 400 million before 1966 and 4.8 billion after. If the Chinese propaganda machine churned out 400 million copies in the sixteen years up to 1966, that means there was an eightfold increase in volume in the following decade. In terms of Mao's writings alone, the official PRC figures (which we reproduce only to provide some idea of the order of magnitude) are shown in the table below.

Figures on the Publication of Mao Zedong's Writings

Period covered	Title	Number of copies
1949-1965	Selected Works, 3 (4) volumes	11.5 million copies
1966-1968	Selected Works, 4 volumes	150 million copies
1949-1976	Selected Works, 4 volumes	225.8 million copies
1966-1968	Selected Readings from the Works of Mao Zedong	140 million copies
To 1968	Red Book	740 million (all editions)
To 1968	Poetry	96 million
To 1968	Individual brochures	2 billion (all editions)[18]

As is evident, the Mao cult reached a crescendo during the Cultural Revolution, which is not surprising when we recall that it was the leadership's express will that literally every person in the People's Republic should have a copy of the Red Book in his possession, while every household was to own an edition of Mao's Selected Works.

The impression that an enormous tidal wave of paper must

have totally inundated the population, especially in the cities, is further reinforced when one notes the extraordinarily efficient propaganda methods used to ensure that these writings were studied by all layers of the population in a succession of mass campaigns, as indeed they were.

The Mao personality cult varied in intensity over the different phases of development of the PRC; likewise, the functions served by the use of this instrument also varied in the importance ascribed to them in any particular situation. From the standpoint of the leadership, its primary function was unquestionably the achievement of a unified ideological orientation among the Chinese population after a century of unparalleled decay of both state and nation. Mao's writings were intended to point out the path of future development clearly and unambiguously. The then nascent ritual of quoting Mao, later symbolized by the use of boldface type in printed works, inevitably became a device for legitimating political action in the most general sense of the term. Mao's words acquired a universally valid, almost legislative force. A further function of the cult was, we must presume, the desire of the CCP chairman to achieve some sort of historical immortality for his own person as the leader of the Communist movement. The occasional words of modesty or ostentatious avowals of dismay about the excesses of the cult should not be taken too seriously in view of this fundamental attitude of Mao Zedong — the most forceful example of this being the party chairman's opposition to the hasty dismantling of the Stalin cult. Finally, the charisma of the Chinese leader, enthralled by the cult around his person, came to be used as a direct weapon in power struggles (struggles between two lines — luxian douzheng) to defeat a strong, often even a superior opposition. This was especially true of the late Maoist phase, from the 1960s on, when Mao felt constrained to proceed ever more mistrustfully and more tyranically against his closest colleagues. The troubled judgment of Lin Biao's son in 1971 on the results of the Mao cult brings this out forcefully: "Nothing is predictable. The chairman commands such high prestige that he need only utter one sentence to remove anybody he chooses."[19]

This last function of the cult, like its later hypostatization, was hardly foreseeable at the beginning of the 1950s. However, we are not so much interested in all the many forms of the cult as in the more central issue of the canon — that is, in the political editing of Mao's writings, which played such a crucial role in the establishment of the canon.

2. THE NEW CANON: GENERAL EDITING PRINCIPLES

By 1949, Mao at fifty-five had already produced a considerable volume of texts dealing with political theory and military tactics. These texts came to be used as ideological guidelines for propaganda schooling by the CCP; they became the raw materials of the canon once the decision to edit the *Selected Works* was taken within the party leadership. The definitive Chinese version of the canon was established in two phases during Mao's lifetime. Between 1951 and 1953 the first three volumes, covering the history of the Chinese Communist movement up to the end of the war against Japan in the autumn of 1945, appeared in rapid succession. Publication of the fourth volume was delayed until 1960, seven years later, when Mao first considered it opportune. The third phase, a posthumous continuation of the canon, began with the appearance of the fifth volume in April 1977, a year after Mao Zedong's death.

The Chinese version of the first three volumes underwent a further minor revision a few months after the initial publication. Thus, the publication dates for the canon of the *Selected Works*[20] may be set down as follows:

First Publication	New Printing
Vol. I, October 1951	Vol. I, July 1952
Vol. II, March 1952	Vol. II, August 1952
Vol. III, February 1953	Vol. III, May 1953
	First Publication
	Vol. IV, September 1960
	Vol. V, April 1977

Note: The bracketed publications comprise the edited version of the not yet completed five-volume canonical selection as of 1982.

As is made clear in the preface to Volume I of the canonical *Selected Works*, Mao Zedong himself directed the editorial work (which was not the case for the pre-1949 editions of selected works) and went over his own writings once again, line for line! "The author has read all the articles, made certain verbal changes and, in isolated cases, revised the text."

It is not to be ruled out that Chen Boda, Mao's devoted propagandist and later chief ideologue (albeit with no real power base of his own), was among those responsible for this editorial work. Chen's position as official interpreter was consolidated in the first years of the PRC by publications such as the brochure with the descriptive title Mao Zedong Thought Is a Unification of Marxism-Leninism and the Chinese Revolution (1951).[21]

Mao's writings were revised extensively. Stuart Schram, for example, came to the conclusion that "one cannot accept even a single sentence as being identical with what Mao had actually written without checking it against the original version."[22] In 1970 the versatile Japanese scholar and Mao specialist Minoru Takeuchi put out a ten-volume edition of Mao's writings[23] in Chinese which covered the same period as the four volumes of the canonical selection up to 1949. This edition made clear the scope of the omissions Mao himself had made as well as the innumerable editorial discrepancies between the Selected Works and the earlier published texts. There have been numerous different versions of many of the texts written before 1949. The text "On Coalition Government" of April 1945, Mao's main contribution at the Seventh Party Congress, to cite only one example, exists in four versions:[24] first, as a stenographic record of what Mao actually said at the Party Congress; second, as a version meant only for party members; third, as a public version for worldwide distribution, published in 1945 after the Party Congress; and finally, fourth, a reedited version of this last text for inclusion in the appropriate volume of the canonical Selected Works.

To anticipate somewhat, we should mention that the canonical Selected Works did not, of course, get through the Cultural Revolution with their originally established form completely intact; for example, a sixty-page summary of the official party history up to 1965 was removed without comment from the Selected Works.

Mao Zedong's own editorial revision of his writings around 1950 consisted, as far as the concrete wording of texts is concerned, in deletions, alterations of passages, and of course the insertion of belated additions of his own. As regards the wider-ranging editorial decisions, he excised whole texts, included only certain sections of some texts, and so on. Many of the peculiarities of the Selected Works may also be owing to the fact that when this editorial work was under way, in the wake of years of war, a number of writings had in fact not yet been recovered.[25]

The annotated critical Takeuchi edition, a good aid for a comparative reading of the texts, enables one to follow in minute detail the general editorial principles as well as the tendencies which the political editing of the canon ultimately reflected. The writings took on a more official character, achieved through stylistic refinements and the reformulation of passages whose clarity left something to be desired. An example of such emendations is Mao's conversation with the American journalist Anna Louise Strong in August 1946.[26] In the Selected Works version the entire introductory portion of the account, a description of the external circumstances of the interview and of the general atmosphere, was omitted from this conversation in which Mao made his now famous observation that reactionaries are paper tigers. Passages describing how Mao, in his cave at Yanan with his daughter on his lap, encircled the American reactionaries with wine glasses to illustrate his point, are left out. As a result, the edited versions of the writings appear diplomatically more reserved and politically more responsible, as for example when the author lets China's rather controversial claims on former vassal states such as Bhutan, Nepal, and Annam fall by the wayside. In addition to reasons of state, sociopolitical considerations were given their due. Official puritanism — almost on the order of a restoration of the Confucian social ethic — necessitated certain revisions in the Selected Works canon wherever Mao had originally ventured more liberal views on life between the sexes.[27]

3. THE NEW CANON: PRINCIPLES OF POLITICAL EDITING

In addition to the greater general coherence achieved in the writings intended for the canon, subsequent comparison of the early and the edited versions of the canon brought out a dominant tendency in Mao's own editing, namely a smoother integration of his writings with the Stalinist version of Marxism-Leninism current at that time. Mao had consciously brought his writings more closely into line with Soviet ideology, and in making such revisions was largely acknowledging Moscow's ideological leadership. Thus, quotations from Stalin were incorporated into the canon and persons who were in political disfavor with Moscow were painted in more negative terms. This focus of Mao's political editing generally required a broader terminological dependence[28] on the Soviet model as well: instead of "democracy" the party leader uses the term "people's democracy" in the Selected Works canon; "Marxist-Leninist truth" replaces "truth," etc.

Passages addressing the Chinese context which placed more emphasis on the revolutionary experiences of China than on those of the Soviet Union were transformed into their exact opposites, and the singularities of the Chinese way were played down. In addition to this appreciation of the Soviet Union and of Stalin, Mao particularly reassessed the historical role of the Communist Party and organization. The CCP was mentioned more frequently and the qualifying phrase "under the leadership of the Communist Party"[29] was tacked onto the recurrent references to "the bourgeois democratic revolution."

In addition to this retroactive upgrading of the role of the CCP we find a drive toward ideological assimilation, likewise aiming at greater orthodoxy. Mao Zedong consistently downgraded the real significance of the peasants and poor peasants in the revolution and inserted statements about the leading role of the working class. The Soviet scholarly polemicists of the 1970s were therefore quick to reproach Maoism for introducing Marxist positions into the canon only in 1950, when the text was reworked, to replace "anti-Marxist concepts that had to be removed."

Otherwise, the general aim of Mao's editing in the early 1950s was to give a greater consistency to the Communist movement; written documents were needed in support of a greater unity and consistency of political development. To this end, for example, historically necessary verbal concessions to the Nationalists, such as Mao's approving words with regard to Chiang Kai-shek in 1938 or in the report to the Seventh Party Congress of 1945, were carefully removed from the edited version.[30] Against this background, therefore, we should not be surprised to see essentially the same general political editing principles in the posthumous edition of Mao's writings. Hua Guofeng and his allies had no trouble at all invoking Mao's editing practices to defend Volume V of the Selected Works canon.

4

Supplementary Editorial Activity Paralleling the Canon of Selected Works *in the 1960s*

1. PROVISIONAL COMPLETION OF THE MAO CANON IN 1960: THE PUBLICATION OF VOLUME IV

In September 1960 another volume of the Selected Works canon appeared after a seven-year pause; this volume concluded the chronological coverage of the period up to the founding of the PRC in 1949. Politically, the appearance of this fourth volume[31] was attuned to the slogans urging perseverance in the difficult years after the Great Leap Forward (that is, if one overlooks for the moment the intent to produce an official history of this period, which of course was paramount). But even after the study campaign waged in connection with these additional Mao writings had subsided, ideological pressures to continue the canon into the years after the founding of the PRC continued practically unabated, the goal being at last to provide the population and grass-roots cadres with more relevant texts interpreting contemporary developments. It also became clear that some sectors of society — for example, the military, the education system — urgently needed study and propaganda texts that were relevant to the present day. However, because bitter debates within the leadership concerning the alternative of a more pragmatic bureaucratic model of development or Mao's more radical orientation toward mass campaigns flared up anew in the wake of the Great Leap Forward, the party leader initially withheld his approval for the publication of Volume V, which would cover the first years of the PRC. For this and other reasons publication of Volume V would in the end be put off until 1977, almost two and a half decades later. From this perspective, therefore, the sixties may be regarded as an interim phase in which, although the canon was not continued, the leadership nonetheless countenanced the publication of official supplemental writings parallel to the canon (over and above the publication of separate pamphlets containing important individual texts, which continued independently of this process) in anticipation of Volume V, the result being the appearance of further volumes of collected Mao writings as a temporary measure.

2. INTERIM TYPE I: THE WHOLE OF MAO ZEDONG THOUGHT IN ONE VOLUME

The most important collections were the Selected Readings From the Works of Mao Zedong,[32] which appeared in 1964 in Beijing in two parallel editions having the same title but different contents. Edition A was intended for study by "normal cadres," as explained in the preface. Edition B was abridged to barely half the size of edition A; significantly, it was published by the Youth Press, whereas edition A was published by the People's Press of Beijing. The abridged version was meant for the general public. This edition B of the Readings was accompanied by a preface in which it is stated that the collection had been edited for worker and peasant youth and could also be used among the broad masses. Both the long version A and the abridged version B were one-volume general overviews of the Mao canon. Most of the texts had been drawn from the four-volume Selected Works canon to 1949. The remainder of the selection, which was quite random, comprised separate texts, from Mao's commentary on the introduction of agricultural cooperatives at the end of 1955 to his February 1957 speech on contradiction. The last text in both volumes is dated May 1963.

For reasons of space, edition B does not contain complete versions of these individual texts of more recent date; only excerpts are given. The Readings in the abridged and long versions were featured prominently in 1964-65 in ideological support of the "socialist education movement in the countryside," which preceded the Cultural Revolution. Otherwise, both versions of the Readings were used throughout the sixties; edition A, rather than the Selected Works canon, was used as a basis for a whole series of further abridged brochures. In 1969 and 1971 an English translation of the long version A was published in China under the title

Selected Readings from the Works of Mao Tsetung.[33] The collection had been compiled by an "Editorial Committee for the Readings," especially created for that purpose. Probably in order to allay the suspicion that these editions were meant as competition to the Selected Works, it was stated explicitly in the prefaces to each volume that the collections A and B were put together under the direction of the editorial committee of the official canon.

3. INTERIM TYPE II: THE OFFICIAL SECTORAL TEXT EDITION

In addition to these collections to be used as handbooks at the basic level, a collection intended for the army, The Selected Military Writings of Mao Zedong, was published. It has been available since 1963 in an official English version, and since 1969, the end of the Cultural Revolution, in an official German version as well.[34] This volume contains an orthodox sectoral collection from the canon; only texts from the four volumes of the Selected Works are included.

Although it is not directly stated in the volumes themselves, these three anthologies must have been influenced considerably by Lin Biao's views on effective propaganda use of Mao Zedong Thought. They were probably even initiated by the then minister of defense; in any case he surely encouraged their publication without reservation. Both the selections for the military sector and the efforts to provide a handbook comprehensible to grassroots cadres and youth are evidence to this effect. Lin's presumed role was confirmed early in the Cultural Revolution. Thus, in the first version of the preface to the Red Book of August 1, 1965, written by the later vice premier, Zhang Chunqiao, we read:

> In compliance with the instructions of Comrade Lin Biao, we must distribute the Selected Readings of Chairman Mao to every soldier in the entire army just as we distribute weapons.[35]

In the polemics of 1978, Lin's connection with the supplementary editions parallel to the canon was mentioned once more. People's Daily wrote, for example:

> [Lin Biao and his supporters] not only sabotaged the publication of the fifth volume of the Selected Works of Mao Zedong, they also abridged the works of

> Chairman Mao from the Selected Works to the Readings, and the Readings they abridged further to the Quotations (the Red Book), until finally all that was left was a handful of sentences to be honored.[36]

Finally, a further feature of the interim editorial phase of the parallel canon were slim brochures containing brief excerpts from Mao's writings, the most widely distributed being Five Philosophical Writings of Chairman Mao, Five Documents of Chairman Mao on Literature and Art, the Three Works and the Five Works.[37] These collections were intended, on the one hand, as the most compendious form of Mao writings (and for that reason became mandatory reading in the schools, from the universities down to the elementary grades); on the other hand, they were put together on a thematic basis as official sectoral text editions, just like the selection of military writings. This editorial activity paralleling the canon came to an end with the publication of nonofficial collections of the so-called internal texts, compiled and disseminated by the activists of the Cultural Revolution, but we will come back to these in another context. They were to strike a telling blow at the orthodoxy of a fixed, consolidated canon.

5

Vice-Chairman Lin Biao as Mao's Interpreter and His Postulate of Unified Thought

1. THE BATTLE FOR POLITICAL AND IDEOLOGICAL LEADERSHIP

Marshal Lin Biao was the first person to thrust himself into the vacuum of Mao's political and ideological succession, which had begun to form even while Mao was still alive. In his own interest Lin had carved out a broad place for himself as Mao's interpreter, standing between the party leader and the Chinese propaganda audience. Indeed, in this respect, one could say that the post-Mao phase had already begun. Lin formulated goals and developed methods with which he seemed to be securing the dual succession for himself quite successfully, his power growing steadily, until Mao shifted course and decided to oppose this trend. In the event, Lin's Mao cult and the cult that was proliferating around Lin's own person were dismantled; ultimately, however, the objective was merely to clear the way for a group of new young cadres who during Mao's last years had also been wrestling in his shadow with the veterans in the Central Committee for the role of legitimate heir to the political and ideological succession.

Mao Zedong came to rely increasingly on his defense minister in the years following the Great Leap Forward, so that during the Cultural Revolution Lin was able to break into the top-level leadership. Lin was indispensable to Mao in executing his plan to put the whole party apparatus to the test and to remove unwanted functionaries from their posts, beginning with Liu Shaoqi, at that time state president and for many years Mao's designated successor, and Deng Xiaoping, at that time party general secretary, down to lower-level cadres in the grass-roots units. At the

Eleventh Plenum of the Eighth Central Committee in August 1966, Marshal Lin Biao moved past Liu Shaoqi into the post of first vice-chairman of the party. Lin became even more firmly entrenched in this position of trust when at the end of the Cultural Revolution the army, then the last instrument of power remaining intact, had to be called in to discipline the warring groups and local factions. The party leader permitted Lin's appointment as "successor to Chairman Mao," a title ratified in the party constitution at the Ninth Party Congress in April 1969 which brought the Cultural Revolution to an end. The draft constitution of the same year, for the Fourth People's Congress, also named Lin Biao as Comrade Mao Zedong's "close comrade in arms and successor."[38]

These formulas indicating Lin's promotion to Mao's political successor, which now recurred continually in the media, were unambiguous enough, but even more so was the cluster of slogans, likewise repeated a thousand times over, which established the ideological succession. This claim was put on record in an article meant to set the tone for any future official biography of Lin Biao — Lin as the only and best interpreter of the state ideology: "Vice-Chairman Lin holds highest the red banner of Mao Zedong Thought; he is a brilliant example of the living study and living application of Mao Zedong Thought. We must follow the brilliant example of Vice-Chairman Lin." Moreover, Lin secured for himself the exclusive rights of interpretation of Maoist ideology: "The method for studying the works of Mao Zedong must be to follow the instruction of Comrade Lin Biao."[39]

Despite his panoply of official posts, the marshal was able to fulfill this claim in practice as well, not least because he had been able to enlist the aid of Chen Boda, Mao's interpreter and chief ideologue for many years, as the efficient controller of the propaganda machinery. Chen was able to steer the Cultural Revolution with authority from his new post as chairman of the "Cultural Revolution Group."

2. SUPERSTRUCTURAL RADICALISM FROM CONVICTION

Lin's general objective in grasping for a monopoly on ideological interpretation above and beyond his position of political power should by no means be dismissed as a sort of automatic, cynical gesture aimed at rounding out the plenitude of the marshal's power. In any number of speeches Lin had time and again, in clear and unmistakable terms, expressed his conviction that a repressive use of the media to achieve an ideological orientation was indispensable in the interest of unity of action by the Chinese nation. In making such statements, however, the marshal, his sights set on total power, showed himself to be much more hidebound than Mao in his faith in the power of ideology to achieve a total influence over the masses:

> Our country is a great socialist state of proletarian dictatorship, and it has a population of 700 million. It requires a unified ideology, a revolutionary ideology, and a correct ideology — Mao Zedong Thought. Only with this thought can a relatively strong revolutionary enthusiasm and a correct and sure political orientation be maintained.[40]

The marshal, immersed throughout his entire career in a military mentality based on law and order, quite certainly overestimated the power of ideology to stimulate and incite to action; by the same token he overlooked the tremendous deadening effect that would result from such intolerance of any sort of unorthodox thinking and from the weariness induced by repetition to the point of satiety.

This basic attitude, which Lin displayed even in the early sixties, also provides a key to understanding the qualitative change that took place in the ideologically exploited writings of state Maoism to the extent that Lin Biao, as interpreter, was responsible for it. It was Lin who set into motion a wave of campaigns of hitherto unimagined scope for the study of Mao Zedong Thought. He directed a propagation and vulgarization that was truly excessive, and he was the prime mover in the veritable quotation mania of those years. The increasing ideological stridency that was to characterize political language in the PRC and would not begin gradually to subside until after 1976 was thus consciously promoted and defended by Lin.

3. LIN'S VULGARIZATION OF MASS INDOCTRINATION

a) Purposes

Lin's career as a political soldier had committed him to quite specific propaganda techniques making use of catchy formulas, allusions, and expressions. He was convinced of their near miraculous powers as political slogans. The rote learning of Mao's writings and handy Mao quotations demanded by his propagandists led to a rampant and excessive use of cliches, fixed formulas, and slogans in the ideological style of the media. It was then only a short step from this predilection for quotation-mongering and political sloganeering to the pious veneration, the moralizing exegesis, and the absolutizing of all of Mao's utterances. Lin propagated a Lin Biao quotation for general study in which he declared Mao Zedong Thought to be the one and only measure of everything: "We must put our firm belief in the thoughts and instructions of Chairman Mao at all times and on all questions without harboring the least doubt."[41]

In the Cultural Revolution these methods and techniques for shaping the Mao cult were used on the whole society. Lin had been testing them out in the People's Liberation Army since the end of the 1950s.

b) Early forms: The Liberation Army as a field for ideological experimentation after 1959

At the stormy Lushan Plenum in the summer of 1959, China's defense minister, Peng Dehuai, was relieved of his post at Mao's urging, on account of his criticism of the excesses of the Great Leap Forward and the precipitous introduction of communes. The aftermath of this altercation gave his successor, Lin Biao, the opportunity to put his own ideas on effective ideological indoctrination to a practical test, working through the General Political Department of the People's Liberation Army (PLA). Whereas Peng had come out strongly in favor of the professionalization of the PLA in the light of the bloody lessons of the Korean War, Lin was intent on shaping the army as a political people's army on the basis of Mao's concept of people's war. On the strength of resolutions passed at a conference of the Central Committee's Military Affairs Committee in 1960 providing for intensified political-ideological work within the armed forces and corresponding instructions from the year 1967,[42] Lin intensified the study of Mao in the army; this, according to one of Lin's many typical slogans, was supposed to leave an indelible imprint on every soldier as "the living study and living application of Mao Zedong Thought."

The publication of the fourth volume of the Selected Works canon in September 1960, the intention of which was to give Mao renewed legitimacy as the irreplaceable leader after the partial setback of the Great Leap Forward, provided a welcome opportunity for Lin to expand this study movement further. In a lengthy article entitled "The Victory of the Revolutionary War of the Chinese People Is a Victory of Mao Zedong Thought,"[43] Lin interpreted and assessed the merits of this addition to Mao's writings, providing as it did an authoritative record of historical developments down to 1949. Breaking with the goal of providing an orthodox view of history, Lin declared that Mao's writings and the fourth volume were valid for both the present and the future; Mao's line would overcome all opportunist tendencies and was just what was needed for combating any and all forms of the ideological deviation of "modern revisionism." In addition to this study of the Mao canon,[44] which was pursued much more intensively in the army than in civilian society, the prototype Red Book, which would capture worldwide attention during the Cultural Revolution, moved to the forefront as an efficient instrument for agitation. The preface of August 1, 1965,[45] signed by the General Political Department of the PLA, noted Lin Biao's leading role in producing this book. First the marshal got the Liberation Army News to print on a regular basis outsize Mao quotations, which were to be memorized by cadres and soldiers. These later gave rise to the Quotations volume, which was designed to fit into every uniform jacket pocket; for the most part the quotations were extracted from their historical context and arranged thematically. The volume had existed since 1961, was printed in a mass edition for the first time in May 1964, and was republished with minor revisions in 1965. Another instrument which Lin introduced for the study of Mao, with a preface expressly recommending it for every soldier, was the Selected Readings from the Works of Mao Zedong, in addition to the special anthology of his military writings, which we have already discussed.

4. THE CULTURAL REVOLUTION: MAO'S THOUGHT BECOMES ABSOLUTE

a) The zenith of Marxism-Leninism in our time

Lin's rise into the inner circle around Mao meant a concurrent extension of his techniques for spreading the Mao canon and the Mao cult to the whole of Chinese society, although to be sure, the seeds of this generalizing process had existed beforehand. Since 1962, exemplary army heroes such as the soldier Lei Feng had been proclaimed as models for the entire nation to emulate; since 1964, and culminating during the years of the Cultural Revolution, there had been a movement calling on the entire country "to learn from the People's Liberation Army." These early manifestations, however, were not yet oriented directly and exclusively toward a study of Mao in Lin slogans. It was not until the Cultural Revolution that the Mao cult, promoted by Lin, achieved hitherto unimagined dimensions, reaching its absolute height in the entire history of the People's Republic. Mao undoubtedly used this idolatry and his elevation to the status of a symbol as political backup in asserting himself over the disenchanted circles of technocrats within the leadership; but he left the task of giving concrete form in the cult largely to Lin and his propaganda aides. First, Lin stressed Mao Zedong's "immortality" by using the man-god paradox in agitational work. The publicity around Mao's sensational swim in the Yangtze River and the metaphor, spread among the masses, of "the good fortune of living under the shadow of such a great tree"[46] were part of this propaganda. Of more central significance, however, was Lin's perspective on Mao's thought in general. Lin's propagandists stylized Mao Zedong Thought into an eternal universal truth, an eternally valid guide for every human action, the common possession of the Chinese people and of all the peoples of the world.[47]

Finally, Lin characterized the chairman simply as the genius of world revolution, a theory which chief ideologist Chen Boda, now clearly favoring the marshal, reinforced in a speech at the critical Second Plenum at Lushan in 1970.[48] Lin proclaimed to the Central Committee, and had the media spread the word, that Marx and Engels were the geniuses of the nineteenth century, while Lenin and Mao were the geniuses of the twentieth century. As the military as well as intellectual commander of the revolution, however, Mao could draw on a completely different store of experience. Moreover, Lenin had died only six years after the October revolution and hence did not have the chance to carry the society forward along the path of revolution after the military victory. Finally, China had the larger population, and for this reason alone the revolutionary experiences of the People's Republic were unexcelled:

Is there anyone higher than Chairman Mao among foreigners or among the ancients? Is there anyone with such a mature thought? A genius such as Chairman Mao occurs only once every several centuries in the world and only once every several thousand years in China. Chairman Mao is the greatest genius in the world.[49]

The central proposition that was advanced in the hymn-like style of those years, with its ritual repetitions and refrains, which in abbreviated form shaped the Red Book, prefaced many Red Guards collections, and in a central passage (in the preface to Volume V) left its mark on the more ritualistic interpretation of Mao after his death, read as follows in expanded Lin-form:

[Comrade Lin Biao says:] <u>Mao Zedong Thought is the zenith of Marxism-Leninism in our time</u>. It is the highest and most creative form of Marxism-Leninism.... Everything that [Mao Zedong] says is the truth; every statement he utters is worth 10,000 sentences.[50]

Thus, not only did Lin banish Marx and Lenin from China's ideological horizon in practice, he also demanded forthrightly that in studying the classical works of Marxism-Leninism, "99 percent of one's efforts" should be devoted to the study of Mao's works.[51] They alone had enduring value as revolutionary textbooks. The writings of Marx and Lenin were too numerous; one could never get through them. Moreover they were too far removed from Chinese reality. Thus Lin elevated Mao to the pinnacle of international Marxism, making clear that ideologically the Soviet Union and all the world's communist parties would have to follow Mao in the end (which contributed to the creation of Maoist splinter parties throughout the world). Although this exaggerated exaltation of the party leader could hardly be justified on the basis of Mao's theoretical writings, Lin further underscored it in his interpretive articles on Mao's concept of a people's war, presenting the Chinese model of revolution as universally valid. With Mao Zedong Thought thus elevated to the status of an absolute, a second level was created on which every Mao utterance was taken up and given a binding force beyond questioning: "As soon as a new instruction of Chairman Mao is issued, [the masses] propagate it and act accordingly. This extremely valuable practice must be retained and fortified."[52]

Using his "powerful" words to back up his rule, Mao was able to guide the Cultural Revolution in the direction he desired and to decide on fundamental questions unopposed until the day of his death, as was demonstrated once again with the second fall of Deng Xiaoping in April 1976.

Even in its verbal formulation, this inflated image of Mao put out by the official interpreter Lin shows parallels with the Stalin cult, which glorified the Soviet leader as the "coryphaeus of sciences," "the great teacher of genius," and the "leader of progressive mankind."

b) Lin's ideal propaganda instrument: the Red Book as a spiritual atom bomb

Externally, the cult Lin Biao molded around Mao took the form of a gigantic movement – given official blessing at the Eleventh Plenum of the Eighth Central Committee Congress – for the study of Mao Zedong Thought on the example of 1961-62, as well as the apotheosis of the abridged Mao canon, the Red Book of Quotations from Chairman Mao Zedong. Accordingly, in his report to the Ninth Party Congress in April 1969,[53] which marked the end of the Cultural Revolution, Lin was able to observe in retrospect that the dissemination of Mao Zedong Thought throughout a country as large as China with its population of 700 million must be regarded as the single most important achievement of the Great Proletarian Cultural Revolution. The Red Book's function during the great campaign – when it moved into stage center and over 700 million copies were distributed – was described as follows in a background report on the party constitution of 1969:

> On [Lin's] urging, the Quotations from Chairman Mao Zedong were first published in 1961 in the army; they circulated rapidly throughout the entire country and even throughout the whole world. This was one of the most important measures undertaken during the preparatory phase of the Great Proletarian Cultural Revolution. This Red Book of wisdom distilled Marxism-Leninism as it had been developed by Chairman Mao and spread Mao Zedong Thought on an unparalleled scale among the entire Chinese people and even among the revolutionary peoples of the entire world. Ideologically it armed millions upon millions of the revolutionary masses. It is the mightiest mobilization of public opinion in support of the Great Proletarian Cultural Revolution, and it has had a far-reaching influence.[54]

The progressive vulgarization of Maoist ideology found reflection in the figurative attributes with which Lin chose to describe Mao Zedong Thought as put forth in the Red Book. Whereas back in 1960 Lin had called Marxism-Leninism-Mao Zedong Thought an "arrow" aimed at the target of revolution, in 1965 the little Mao bible was seen as his mighty "ideological weapon" in the struggle against imperialism, revisionism, and dogmatism — a conventional enough metaphor, which was used in 1975 for example in the preface to the 100-volume Soviet edition of Marx's and Engels's works (MEGA). Finally, in the new preface to the Red Book of December 16, 1966, for the first time personally signed by Lin Biao, Mao's thoughts had grown to the stature of a "spiritual atom bomb"[55] of infinite power — a not exactly felicitous comparison in two respects, considering the destructive potential it evokes.

In the turbulent years of the Cultural Revolution, China's top-level leadership would pull out the Red Book and brandish it on high before the masses, while they in turn had to wave it back a thousand times over. All official publications from the PRC predictably showed Chinese engaged in a ritual study of the little book. Even Chinese statements on the book's effect abroad were not a total exaggeration. Promoted by the student movement in the West, the book met with astonishing acclaim. It went through hundreds of printings and in the Federal Republic of Germany alone was distributed in 140,000 copies, to cite only the best-known pocketbook edition put out by Tilemann Grimm. Imitations were printed not only in North Korea, Albania, and Libya during the Cultural Revolution but also in Taiwan, where the Guomindang put out a little book containing maxims of Chiang Kai-shek as part of a so-called Cultural Renaissance Movement, although the Chiang government made no attempt to mount a study campaign of matching scope.

Lin's intention to make Mao's thought available in handy form to the broadest possible circles even resulted in the little book's having a feedback effect on the *Selected Works* canon. In late 1967 the four volumes of the *Selected Works* were compressed into a one-volume pocket-size edition with a red plastic cover, so that the only thing distinguishing it from the prototype of the little Red Book of Mao quotations was its greater bulk.

With his popular edition of the Mao bible, Lin Biao had fundamentally altered the character of the study of Mao's works. Quotations torn out of context were framed as general thematic statements and presented as universal truths in the moralizing tradition of Confucius quotations. While the *Selected Works* could be regarded as a politically edited (and emended) documentary history of the Chinese revolution, with the Red Book the historical perspective gave way to a hortative litany.[56] Things that Mao had said or written at some time in the past were arranged in a timeless sequence, although 40 percent of the selections, comprising 426 individual passages, were from only nine of Mao's writings. The actual launching of the Red Book took place during the Cultural Revolution with the addition of Lin Biao's preface, mentioned above, which replaced an earlier preface signed by the General Political Department of the PLA. An extract from it was elevated to the position of "The Thirty-Character Classic" as the quintessence of Lin's Mao cult. An exhortation to study Mao's works was added in Lin's own calligraphy. Most significantly, the contents of the second version of the preface extended the effective range of the volume's influence from the army to the entire nation.

As regards its form, the Red Book cannot actually be called Lin Biao's "invention." Regional military commanders in the early days of the republic used to distribute little handbooks of aphorisms or military precepts among their soldiers, and the Nationalists also used this means for the moral rearmament of their soldiers. But Lin Biao was the first to extend the use of this instrument beyond the army to the entire society.

With the appearance of this little book, so popular among China's Red Guards, other attempts in the same spirit which Lin Biao had also encouraged and which were meant as a "shortcut" to the study of Mao quickly faded into the background. For example, a little textbook entitled One Hundred Sayings of Chairman Mao, which had been used within the army during the Cultural Revolution, soon all but disappeared. However, Lin's Three Constantly Read Articles[57] — i.e., Mao's writings "Serve the People," "Yu Gong Moves the Mountain," and "In Memory of Norman Bethune" — were disseminated at the most simplified level of popularization as Lin s minimal vulgate version of the canon.

5. THE CULT AROUND MAO'S "CLOSEST COMRADE IN ARMS"

Lin's Mao cult was only one side of his activity as ideological mentor. An integral part of the measures described was the creation of a cult around his own person — just as Stalin in his time had initiated a Lenin cult, in the wake of which the Stalin cult emerged. Indeed, Lin may very well have appropriated this historical example directly. The thesis of "the three assistants" (Engels for Marx, Stalin for Lenin, and Lin Biao for Mao),[58] propagated by Lin Biao, would tend to bear this out. Since the Lin Biao cult had, as it were, to be borne into Chinese society on the back of Lin's Mao cult, political progaganda slogans became even more complicated and ponderous as they were bent to the task of purveying Lin's exposition and interpretation of Mao's words. The intercession of the interpreter between the exalted Mao and the masses was intended to ensure that the Lin cult would assume an independent existence once Lin had taken over Mao's political functions, whereupon an ideological combination of "Mao canon as eternal truth" with "Lin Biao's writings or instructions as the practical application of Maoism to the changed situation of China and the world" would have set the keynote for political agitation. By that time, newly ordained interpreters would have emerged to present Lin's thought.

The measures taken to promote the nascent Lin cult can be sketched out quickly. For instance, not only did Lin style himself after Mao in his political jargon, but the Mao canon itself was now published in Lin's name. Lin's preface to the Red Book and his calligraphy adorning its frontispiece functioned to the same end: they were the stamp of authority of the designated successor. Second, similar functions were performed by texts such as the 1967 Study Materials on the Works of Chairman Mao,[59] in which two of Lin's texts served as the introduction, and the postscript declared how reliably Lin interpreted Mao. This book included study articles from the time of the Cultural Revolution on some of Mao's writings, which had first been published in People's Daily and Liberation Army News. In some places statements by Lin were prefaced with the phrase [Vice-Chairman Lin] "instructs us" or "teaches us," a formula for the ritualistic buttressing of authority which heretofore had been reserved for Mao alone. In addition to these Lin-inspired study materials, we should mention his article "Long Live the Victory of the People's War"[60] of September 1965. Appearing on the twentieth anniversary of the victory over Japan, this Lin Biao text, distributed in millions of copies as a separate pamphlet for intensive study, definitively established Lin's own theoretical authority as Mao's interpreter, as ideologist of the people's war in China, and as expert teacher of independence movements the world over. His theses maintaining that the rural areas of the world would vanquish the urban areas (i.e., the developed affluent societies) were significant for the mere fact that, in contrast to many other Chinese ideological writings, they attracted international notice and in official circles in the United States were even seen as a threat to the Western world, especially later when the outcome of the Vietnam war seemed to confirm them.

Lin took a further step in building up the cult around his own person with the preparation of an official biography[61] which portrayed him not only as the party leader's worthy heir but as Mao's most intimate and loyal colleague from the very beginnings of the Communist movement. In mid-1969 it could hardly be foreseen that only two years later, after Lin Biao's fall, this refurbishing of Lin's past would be followed by its vilification — first of all internally, within the party, which accused him of being a traitor to Mao and a pseudo-Marxist from the very beginning, and indeed, even in his very own special domain, the military, where he was branded an incompetent. The dissemination of an official biography for the purpose of securing support had been a fixture of the Chinese "cult" arsenal ever since Edgar Snow's biography of Mao was disseminated both within China and abroad. Such precedents induced Mao's wife, Jiang Qing, to undertake an abortive imitation in the early 1970s in anticipation of her later bid for power, when she rather abruptly imposed the role of biographer on the surprised American sinologist Roxane Witke.

Another step on the way toward publication of Lin's work as the preliminary for a future Lin canon was the publication of collections of Mao's writings in which statements and speeches by Lin had been interspersed. Several of the anthologies distributed internally by the Red Guards, such as the Selected Texts of Chairman Mao, were compiled using such editorial devices. The next step was the publication of an imitation of the Red Book, probably with Lin's approval, entitled Sayings of Lin Biao.[62] That further steps toward a Lin canon were in the offing was demonstrated by the publication in Hong Kong of an edition of Selected Works of Lin Biao[63] in which the marshal was hailed as China's future leader.

6. DESTRUCTION OF THE LIN FORMS OF STATE MAOISM AND HIS VILIFICATION IN THE CAMPAIGN AGAINST LIN AND CONFUCIUS

As it turned out, in the eventual campaign against Lin Biao, waged internally from 1971 to 1973 and then publicly after 1974, the launching of the Lin cult and the preparation of a Lin canon were to be roundly condemned. However, within the context of the Cultural Revolution, which saw Lin as Mao's successor, these sallies by the vice chairman cannot but be viewed as logical corollaries of his claim to succession. Assuming for a moment that Lin had been able to carry through his claim successfully — indeed he only failed by a hair's breadth — the question still remains whether Lin could actually have measured up to Mao as a politician and ideologist. Perhaps the aphorism applied to him polemically after his fall was not completely wide of the mark: "Mayflies try in vain to fell the giant tree."[64] Like Hua Guofeng, who in 1976 would be moved to create out of nothing a personality cult of his own, copying the party leader down to the smallest detail, Lin in his time had also ventured down the impracticable path of epigones, as his version of Lin Biao Maoism suggests.

Apart from Lin's statements about Mao Zedong's genius, which were intended for the broad public, there are elsewhere traces of a more sober attitude mingled with sudden flashes of animosity, giving us a glimpse of what Lin's private attitude toward the creation of the Mao cult may have been, and hence, of some of the at first glance unexpected but thoroughly plausible perspectives a Lin government might have offered. The fact that Lin, despite his posture as successor, was tormented by a sense of uncertainty vis-à-vis the party leader was made clear enough by his high-handed decision, circumventing Mao, at the Second Plenum at Lushan in the autumn of 1970. But even Lin's arguments in a talk given before the enlarged Politburo in 1966, on the dangers of a violent shift of course in Chinese politics, testify to a kind of coup mentality.[65] This speech was also haunted by the thought, at that time still regarded as a nightmare, of a "secret de-Maoization report" in the style of Krushchev's de-Stalinization speech at the Twentieth Party Congress on the subject of the Soviet personality cult. Although as source material, the Central Committee's records on Lin's putsch must be used with the utmost caution, from them emerges a picture of Mao as seen by the conspirators, showing him, like Stalin, mistrustfully outmaneuvering his closest comrades in arms, and then, in the third decade of the People's Republic, misusing the trust and the position he had gained, becoming a crude dictator like the First Emperor of the Qin dynasty, or the founder of the Ming empire, Zhu Yuanzhang. Even in this portrayal, however, Mao is allowed to retain his historical role as the person who led the Chinese Revolution and unified China. Thus, under a Lin government, Mao Zedong might perhaps have been quietly cut down to a size more commensurate with his true historical importance, and the cult around the party leader similarly reduced, as indeed happened under the collective leadership after his death.

In the meantime a consensus has been growing among political scientists that Lin Biao's abortive violent bid for power in fact had defensive features. It was not until very late, actually the year 1970, that the party leader decided not to tolerate any further Lin's steadily growing ideological and political power, but we cannot here go into the complex reasons why Mao Zedong took this step. Lin had to react to Mao's turnabout. In any event, Marshal Lin's purported putsch and his attempt to flee the country resulted in a total eclipse of Mao's former interpreter and a dismantling of the specific forms of the Mao cult which had been developed under his hand. An intense struggle over the crucial question of how and to what degree the former Lin exegesis should be condemned took place among the factions in the Politburo as they consolidated their positions; this is perhaps one of the reasons why Lin Biao was first condemned by name at the Tenth Party Congress in September 1973, by Zhou Enlai, fully two years after the crash of his purported escape plane in Outer Mongolia on September 13, 1971. An ominous discussion took place in the media about the nature of his mistakes, Lin being condemned first as an ultra-leftist and then, after some hesitation, as a right deviationist.[66] Mao and the top party leaders do not seem to have seriously considered the possible alternative of a state funeral and a hushing up of the affair, as for instance Hitler decided in the case of Rommel. Instead, the "campaign to criticize Lin Biao and Confucius," which swept over the whole of China, shook the reputation of the party as well as Mao's personal prestige in a devastating way. It was one of the absurdities of the late Maoist phase that Lin's political reputation should be destroyed in such a twisted and perverse manner, coupled with an attack on a distorted picture of Confucianism that embodied all the negative aspects of traditional China. In popular parlance, the pi-Lin pi-Kong [Criticize Lin, Criticize Confucius] campaign was duly ridiculed by the homonymous pun piling pikong, meaning "criticize nil, criticize nothing." The party's claim to infallibility, still insisted upon by the leadership, and the continuous drive toward orthodoxy which is the inevitable consequence of such a claim, required that Lin's career be denigrated from its very beginnings during this campaign. Under such conditions, a more nuanced treatment, portraying him for example as a capable general of the guerrilla Red Army and the PLA who had committed politically serious errors as his power grew, was impossible.

All of this inevitably spelled an end to the Lin-inspired forms of the Mao cult. The entire Mao study system, bearing Lin Biao's signature, disappeared overnight. A secret Central Committee document[67] of November 1971 dissolved the "activist congresses for the living study and living application of the works of Chairman Mao" as well as the institutionalized "assemblies for the exchange of experience in the study of Mao Zedong Thought." The draft constitution — in which, as an addendum to the party constitution, Lin was personally named as successor to Mao — had to be retracted, and the same lot befell the documents of the Ninth Party Congress of April 1969, which Lin had dominated, as well as Lin's pamphlet on the people's war. The Central Committee's anathema extended to all portraits of Lin Biao, the marshal's writings, and any and all materials that had any direct or indirect link to Lin. The Red Book suffered a similar fate. Zhou Enlai, in a drawing up of accounts in his speech at the Tenth Party Congress in August 1973, deliberately ridiculed Lin as someone who "never let his little book of quotations out of his hands and was always breaking out into paeans of praise [for Chairman Mao]...."[68]

However, the Red Book itself could not be summarily withdrawn, given its national and international symbolic value. The Party ideologues chose initially to allow it to be reprinted without Lin Biao's preface, whereafter the Red Book was allowed gradually to recede into the background.

Mao Zedong's displeasure with Lin's practices of Mao study and his interpretation of Marxism-Leninism, which had been growing since the Cultural Revolution, also became public during this phase. In his letter to Jiang Qing of July 1966, which was put into circulation as anti-Lin study material by the Central Committee, the party leader described his own situation as one of coerced acquiescence with the all too rash Lin theses: "It seems that I have to concur with them. It is the first time in my life that I unwillingly concur with others on major questions. I have to do things against my own will!" Thus it would appear that even at the time Mao had only reluctantly tolerated Lin's excesses, and disapproved above all of the reverse side of the peculiar Mao cult of those years, namely the nascent Lin cult. In the same letter he said: "I have never believed that the several booklets I wrote would have so much supernatural power. Now, after he exaggerated them, the whole nation has exaggerated them...." And elsewhere: "My name was then built up with such slogans as 'raise up in a great and special way.' Actually, however, I'm not sure whom he had in mind; to put it bluntly, he built himself up in this way."[69]

Cleansed of the dross of Lin's hermeneutics, for a time Mao's writings once again appeared directly in the ideological field without any interpretive detours. However, Mao, now in his eighties, no longer had the physical and intellectual strength to fill up the vacuum himself. He therefore supported the group of younger radical ideologues who had moved into key positions of power during the Cultural Revolution, so pointedly that they took advantage of the situation to monopolize the entire propaganda apparatus and the media. This meant yet a new stage of Mao interpretation, this time by the ideologues Zhang Chunqiao and Yao Wenyuan. These new forms of the Mao cult and the Shanghai left's radical interpretation of the canon were able to hold their ground, however, only in the most bitter clashes with the faction of moderate senior cadres around Zhou Enlai and Deng Xiaoping, the latter having been rehabilitated in 1973.

Thus with the dismantling of the Lin forms a whole phase in the thirty-year history of the PRC came to an end. Lin Biao had left his mark on an entire decade of the Mao cult: in the first half of this period Lin's influence remained restricted essentially to the military sector, but in the second half of the decade his ideological perspective spread throughout China and in manifold ways to the world outside China as well.

The Radical Shanghai Faction as Mao's Trustees

1. IN THE FOOTSTEPS OF LIN BIAO

From Lin Biao's fall in September 1971 to his political elimination in October 1976, the radical faction in the Politburo, subsequently reviled as the Gang of Four, had set the ideological tone and to a large extent shaped state Maoism. Leaving aside for the moment Jiang Qing, Mao's wife, who was designated to be a legitimizing figurehead, and the youthful Wang Hongwen, party vice-chairman since 1973, who had hardly distinguished himself with any notable propaganda achievements, it was Zhang Chunqiao and Yao Wenyuan who were the real masterminds of ideological radicalism. Zhang, who had been an inspiring mass agitator during the Cultural Revolution, rose to the position of vice-premier in early 1975. The brilliant propagandist and politician Yao became the new chief ideologue, controlling the media, in particular People's Daily, the party's theoretical organ Red Flag, and the official New China News Agency. In addition, the group had created its own, aggressively argumentative theoretical journal, Study and Criticism.[70]

All four of these top-level cadres had made themselves indispensable during the Cultural Revolution when they shaped Shanghai into their power base and center of operations, whence they came to be known as the "Shanghai faction." The group had only limited support in the bureaucratic apparatus of the government or party, since they had decimated this very apparatus during the Cultural Revolution. On the other hand, up to 1976 they had enjoyed Mao's special support in their "march through the institutions" — a step-by-step penetration into key political positions in state offices and departments at both the central and regional levels. For Mao Zedong, the Shanghai faction and its supporters were young revolutionaries devoted to the ideal of a Maoist mass line, "carrying on the revolution" within the higher echelons of the cadres as well as among the youth in general. They had proven their mettle in the Cultural Revolution; the future therefore belonged to them. Yao Wenyuan — who had earned the nickname "the cudgel" by having taken a hard line since the fifties in all important campaigns, his polemical articles laden with ominous consequences for those concerned (indeed one of these articles was the spark that ignited the Cultural Revolution) — essentially took over the position of the former chief ideologue Chen Boda, who had been eliminated with Lin Biao. The 1977-78 political campaign against the Gang of Four might easily give the false impression that the left faction had commanded far-reaching political responsibility and control, at least since the fall of Lin Biao. Such an impression must be corrected: although the group was able to extend its power bases at both the regional and central levels during the violent clashes with the pragmatist faction around Zhou Enlai and Deng Xiaoping, the radicals had uncontested control only of the propaganda apparatus.

The ideological leadership of the Shanghai group, which had the party leader's approval, zealously set out to shape the Mao cult and develop the Mao canon. In essence, then, the Shanghai faction stepped forth as the ideological heirs of the group around Lin Biao. They stuck tenaciously to Mao's radical course of mass campaigns and were explicitly supported in this by the party leader. The Shanghai radicals made every effort to appropriate the interpretation of Mao wholly to themselves as their own monopoly, seeing themselves in particular as the guardians of the Great Cultural Revolution. The second obvious parallel to the Lin Biao period was their battle, using every means at their disposal, to establish themselves in the paralyzing power struggle as the ideological and political heirs of Mao's China.

2. MASTERS OF THE ART OF QUOTATION

Considering this continuity with the years when Lin Biao's ideological perspective prevailed, it is not surprising that the propaganda methods were similar as well. Within this context, however, the Shanghai group developed its own unmistakable style.

Again, the shaping of the Mao canon must be distinguished from the buildup of the group's own ideological authority, which proceeded in parallel. This they accomplished through their control over the media and their sovereign mastery of the instruments of propaganda, for which they had received considerable practical training in the Maoist campaigns. The Shanghai group deliberately developed its own set of slogans built around the concept of "New Socialist Things,"[71] the exact meaning of which was deliberately kept vague and therefore could embrace such varied "achievements" as the Revolutionary Beijing Opera, the barefoot doctor teams, the May 7 cadre schools, the journal Study and Criticism, the institution of the revolutionary committees, the sending of the youth to the countryside, or even the Cultural Revolution itself. The notion thus functioned as a kind of open bank account in which the left faction could register any achievements it chose. At the same time, in a flanking maneuver, heavy use was made of slogans such as "swimming against the current" — called for by Wang Hongwen in his speech to the Tenth Party Congress in 1973 — which quite literally split the society into two warring camps. In addition there was the thesis, which further sharpened such contradictions, of the "new bourgeoisie" (i.e., the members of the moderate faction and their more apolitical fellow travelers) which had to be combated. A distinctive feature of this aggressive sloganeering of the Shanghai group was the almost unparalleled extent of its verbal reliance on Mao's writings, whereas in Lin's political language there had been at least some originality, however limited. The radicals slavishly drew on homilitic slogans from the reservoir of Mao sayings so as to rely completely on the party leader for legitimation of their own political maneuvering. Thus they continued the practice, accepted in all political debates since the Cultural Revolution, of presenting Mao's sayings as absolute truth, driving the "automated language" of the media toward a crescendo of redundancy.

3. THE CAMPAIGN INSTRUMENT AND THE MONOPOLIZATION OF ACCESS TO MAO

However, this sloganeering language of the political struggle did not really come into its own until the launching of a series of minor campaigns in the years to 1976. This is evident in the "criticism of Lin Biao and Confucius" (1974), which apart from its rather labored pseudo-historical schematization of "Legalists" and "Confucianists," was used mainly as a concealed attack on Zhou Enlai and his faction; and further, in the campaign to strengthen the dictatorship of the proletariat and to combat empiricism, launched early in 1975, which also demanded the suppression of "empiricists"; and finally in the critical movement begun in the autumn of 1975 against the classic novel Water Margin,[72] which attacked "capitulationism" but then shifted gears to end up as a criticism of Deng Xiaoping. In addition to the older quotations from Mao, sayings or even fragments of sayings from Mao's most recent writings were used as buttressing, a technique which we will examine later. However, these campaigns, with their assortment of political slogans to drive their points home, had not only the direct goal of weakening the old guard around Zhou Enlai and Deng Xiaoping in the central administration and achieving a reapportionment of cadres in the provinces favorable to the radicals; in addition, the Shanghai faction generally succeeded in creating an intellectual atmosphere that would have justified the necessity of a severe purge for the purpose of seizing and consolidating power. Ghost-writing centers, maintained in strictest secrecy[73] (for example, the mass criticism groups at Beijing and Qinghua universities), prepared hundreds of articles, certain of whose author pseudonyms were known to all as the signature of the left faction. During the spectacular campaigns these were fed into the media to hammer away at the group's defenseless opponents.

A parallel measure was the attempt of the Shanghai faction to monopolize access to the ailing Mao, and in this they were considerably facilitated by their connivings with Mao's wife Jiang Qing and his nephew Mao Yuanxin. Thus, the aged Mao could be influenced and if need be his notes or sayings could be manipulatively interpreted in a slightly altered context, which, of course directly threatened and undermined the moderate faction and its supporters. A court camarilla had formed as the innermost circle around Mao, systematically blocking access to him by others.

4. CAPTURING THE RIGHT TO INTERPRET MAO

Through the rearguard use of well-chosen quotations from Mao's published and unpublished works and the garnering of oral statements from the last days of the party leader, the Shanghai radicals attempted to make themselves the sole authorized editors and interpreters of the Mao canon in its narrower sense, a right which since the early fifties had been reserved to an anonymous editing committee under the Central Committee. Thus it was imperative that they gain control and assume the political leadership of this board. Quite early in the Cultural Revolution the Central Committee had decided to edit further volumes[74] of the Selected Works. In 1969 Mao Zedong encharged Zhou Enlai and Kang Sheng with overseeing the compilation of Volume V (prototypes of Volumes V and VI had been available since late 1967). During the years 1971 through 1976 a stalemate had prevailed as the two factions parried one another with diametrically opposed views on how to edit the most recent past for a long-range perspective. Mao Zedong himself seems to have maintained silence on the topic. A polemical commentary from 1978 had this to say about the actions of the left faction during these years:

> They took advantage of the opportunity to put out articles or editorials altering or falsifying the instructions of Chairman Mao. After Chairman Mao's death, they falsified his "testament," "act according to the principles laid down." To ensure that their deceptions would not be detected and exposed, they tried with all their might to usurp for themselves the right to direct the editing and publishing of the Selected Works of Mao Zedong. They hoped to monopolize the writings and speeches of Chairman Mao that had not yet been officially published so that they could alter them as they saw fit and use them to their own ends.

It does appear that Vice-Premier Zhang Chunqiao gave direct instructions to postpone publication of Volume V for the time being, until his own group would be able legitimately to assume the editorial prerogatives. In order to demonstrate their ignoble objectives for future editions, the following statement of the Four was quoted with polemical intent in 1978: "That is what being effective really means! We will let Volume V appear when we want it to appear! And whomever we want to purge shall be purged [with this volume]."[75]

5. PRELIMINARIES OF A NEW CULT: ZHANG OR YAO?

Just as Lin Biao had attempted to build up a cult around his own person through the specific form he gave to the Mao cult, similar tendencies emerged within the Shanghai faction. First, the group was able to make direct political capital out of the circumstance that during the Cultural Revolution a number of Mao's notes and letters to members of the group, or stenographic copies of talks that the chairman had had with them, had come into circulation via the internal text collections. For example, Mao Yuanxin, the radicals' counsel in Liaoning and nephew of the party leader, reaped unequivocal advantage from several such conversations with Mao that became known to the general public. Chief ideologue Yao Wenyuan and Vice-Premier Zhang Chunqiao each concentrated on fashioning for himself the role of guardian of Mao Zedong Thought and claimant to the succession through a series of articles on basic principles written as part of the Campaign to Strengthen the Dictatorship of the Proletariat. In March 1975 Yao published the article "On the Social Basis of the Anti-Party Clique Around Lin Biao" in the party's theoretical organ Red Flag; a month later Zhang Chunqiao, in an article in the same periodical entitled "On the Complete Dictatorship over the Bourgeoisie,"[76] laid the theoretical foundations for a later purge of the Shanghai group's opponents, which to that end he opportunely classified as the "New Right." Zhang's article was written as an interpretation of Mao's "Notes on the Soviet Textbook on Political Economy" (an essay distributed only internally). Anyone familiar with the Chinese ideological style could hardly fail to see that Zhang was attempting to set himself up as the future interpreter of Mao Zedong Thought.

It was evident from this display of competition between the Shanghai ideologues that no decision had yet been made as to which of the two would assume the role of Mao's ideological successor once they had taken power as intended. Thus, an eventual test of strength between Zhang and Yao was in the cards. Initially, perhaps, precedence had been given to Zhang for the interim period on the basis of his seniority, since in the polemics against the Four in 1977-78 several swipes were taken against foul "Zhang Chunqiao Thought"[77] — which purportedly had perverted Marxism-Leninism in its historical development — while there was no such attack on a Yao ideology.

6. DISINTEGRATION OF THE CANON

Mao Zedong's death on September 9, 1976, at the age of eighty-two and after years of decline, brought to its logical end a process that had begun long before the years just discussed (1971-76), and for the most part had been determined, whether directly or indirectly, by the flagging of the chairman's physical forces (Mao had already been seriously ill on occasion during the Cultural Revolution). While the political efficacy of Mao's own words attenuated, the methods that had been invented to propagate purposefully arranged fragments of his writings and sayings were honed into an ingenious technique in the course of the struggles for his mantle by the successive protagonists Liu, Lin, and the Shanghai radicals. There were several distinct stages, which we can only outline roughly here, to the disintegration of the Mao canon.

The intact cult was premised on the four-volume canon of the Selected Works. Since the founding of the state Mao had also from time to time written basic texts to provide theoretical guidelines for the direction of social developments, such as the July 31, 1955, article "On the Formation of Cooperatives in Agriculture," the speech at the propaganda conference of March 12, 1955, or the February 27, 1957, speech "On Contradiction." These documents were initially published as separate pamphlets for ideological instruction. Since the early 1960s such basic texts had appeared only rarely; Mao was not up to writing such a seminal text on the Cultural Revolution.

The next stage of state Maoism, functionally speaking, was marked essentially by a turning away from the use of the writings of the "theoretician" and toward the use of statements by the "politician." In this stage the propaganda apparatus made use of Mao's numerous political speeches, which in their moody, opinionated tone, abundant quantity, and relatively uncensored form made a profound impression, at least at the highest party levels. The consequence of this was that outwardly the apparatus had to turn to certain edited versions and summaries of individual writings or talks for broad ideological instruction. The best-known text group of this category is probably Chairman Mao Zedong on Imperialism and All Reactionaries Are Paper Tigers, a phrase that has found its way into the international political vocabulary.[78] This was used to launch a propaganda campaign after being published for the first time in the front pages of People's Daily on October 31, 1958. The "paper tiger" texts are a compilation of extracts from a wide range of essays, speeches, and talks of Mao Zedong from 1940 to the late 1950s. Edited passages from speeches, letters, telegrams, and even from a meeting with Chinese students in the USSR, all from Mao's second visit to the Soviet Union in 1957, were similarly published in Beijing-based national newspapers and later as separate pamphlets. Another example was the pamphlet entitled Important Talks of Chairman Mao Zedong with Persons from Asia, Africa, and Latin America,[79] which clarified China's relationship with the Third World and with Japan; this was a compilation of Mao's utterances from various dates, interpolated into a text written by someone else. In a similar way, Mao himself had overseen the drafting of the ideological attacks against the Soviet Union in the early 1960s; he had approved the use of individual quotations from his works and contributed parts of the argument himself.

These stages — first the rearrangement and then the gradual dismemberment of the author's own cohesive lines of reasoning — were still for the most part under the control of Mao Zedong himself. The next stage in the disintegration process, however, gave rise to a less controlled and hence more manipulative textual interpretation in various forms. In the face of the intraparty conflicts consequent to the Great Leap Forward, Mao had grown increasingly reserved about releasing his writings and statements from the period after 1949. As late as 1977, Hua Guofeng still felt it necessary to clarify this position apologetically:

> Chairman Mao always took an extraordinarily serious and cautious attitude toward ideological and theoretical questions; he did not give permission for the compilation of his Selected Works before his writings had been tested in practice for some period.[80]

The loosened discipline and enthusiasm generated by the Cultural Revolution, together with the need of various quarreling factions to have some redeeming and legitimating Mao saying ready for every action, opened up an entirely new dimension — namely, the publication of Mao's writings in nonofficial internal volumes of collected writings or even quite random selections. The Cultural Revolution had only intensified the call for Mao's writings on the concrete situation existing in the People's Republic; the dissemination of mimeographed copies of such collections was a highly creative expression of mass study. This group of texts consisted mostly of transcripts, forming continuous series of relatively complete Mao documents. Initially the dissemination of such texts must have been promoted or at least tolerated by certain members of the leadership, but after the Cultural Revolution, the leadership made haste to confiscate and destroy all materials still in circulation on the strength of a Central Committee order.

The actual study of Mao's writings reached its apogee in the Cultural Revolution; simultaneously, however, control over the orthodox canon was essentially lost in the outpouring of altered and parallel versions and trial runs of not yet officially published works. The prefatory appeals of the Red Guards who edited these internal selections could do nothing to prevent this outcome, no matter how hard they might protest that their Mao texts had only provisional validity and would become obsolete with the publication of official versions. There is no better illustration of the party's diminishing control over Mao orthodoxy than a description of the methods[81] the Red Guards used to compile and publish Mao texts. They profited from the fact that masses of secret or internal party documents had fallen into unauthorized hands during the confusion of the Cultural Revolution.

After the Cultural Revolution it increasingly became customary to string together Mao sayings extracted from their original historical and political contexts, usually without any source reference, for some purpose of the moment. A further stage in the disintegration was the use of whole patchworks of Mao quotations drawn from the complex of Mao's writings on a particular theme; these would be printed over an entire page in People's Daily in support of a new campaign. Such quotation montages were used, for example, in the February 1975 Campaign to Strengthen the Dictatorship of the Proletariat and again in February 1977 during the campaign against the Gang of Four,[82] when a veritable medley of quotations was adduced in support of the leadership's efforts to achieve a more sober political style. Such techniques, however, had already had to be used on occasion in the 1950s, albeit in a less manipulative spirit, whenever no integral Mao text on a particular topic was available. In December 1951, for instance, People's Daily published a montage of quotations[83] condemning corruption and waste, for use as a fundamental study text in the "3-antis" and "5-antis" campaigns which unfolded during 1952.

The logical next stage was the publication of pamphlets and books consisting solely of strings of Mao quotations. The best example remains the Cultural Revolution's Red Book, which does, however, give sources for each quotation. While this book stands as an official text, there also were pamphlets of internal quotations as well as compilations by the Red Guards — for example, Sayings of

Chairman Mao on Education.[84]

In addition, there were texts and pamphlets compiled by stringing together line after line of "veiled" quotations. These were then passed off as coherent Mao texts — as in the case of "Examples of Dialectics,"[85] which during the Cultural Revolution became a new Mao text overnight — and were included as such in foreign translations.

The publication of "open" books of Mao quotations, with their sources documented, is likely to continue as an occasionally useful form in which to present state Maoism. This was obviously the case with the collection Sayings of Chairman Mao on Revolutionary Foreign Policy, which appeared — though it did not go undisputed — in June 1977.[86]

The disintegration process (for clarity's sake we have portrayed it here in a logical sequence; in reality the editorial forms we have distinquished overlapped) reached its culmination during the last stages of the power struggle, with the Shanghai faction's publication in the newspapers of one-line quotations and fragments of quotations. The long, protracted formal process of disintegration of the Mao canon is compelling evidence that the shapers of state Maoism had to resort to such forms because even a decade before Mao's death there already existed an intolerable "vacuum," given China's general, historically molded tendency to conformism and its predilection for orthodoxy. Only this can explain why at least one influential group in the post-1976 leadership wanted to arrest this process of dissolution by reestablishing a refortified orthodoxy, while an opposing group championed a partial dismantling of orthodox Maoism.

7

The Dialectic of the Post-Mao Phase: Beginnings of Dedogmatization, 1977-1978

1. TENDENCIES SUPPORTING STATE MAOISM

The post-Mao phase directed by a collective leadership under Hua Guofeng brought a new policy of order based on a number of difficult compromises. The priority given to the country's technological and economic reorganization and the promotion of the natural sciences as the foundation of this growth signaled the end of the decade-long political paralysis that had obtained while the two major factions grappled for power. The new policy also clearly signified abandonment of the central Maoist concept of the mass line, which had shaped China from the Great Leap Forward to the Cultural Revolution; at least the leadership put away such political techniques of social transformation as an anachronistic product of the revolution which, if continued, would have hindered development in the seventies and eighties.

The abrupt shift in perspective, which, following a two-year planning stage, began to show practical results after 1978, was not introduced quite so abruptly at the rhetorical level. The collective leadership came to a consensus that the outward forms of state propaganda had to create the appearance of the broadest possible continuity. Not only was this a diplomatic stance, it was also dictated to a certain extent by circumstances. The Politburo had as an admonitory example the internal instability that had ensued after the Soviet Union's sudden shift of course in 1956, and obviously they were wary of further eroding the CCP's already shaken authority by indulging such verbal openness as Khrushchev had dared. Still, the tightly unified stance of the new leadership could in no way gloss over the fact that alongside the forces of the pragmatist faction linked to Zhou Enlai, with Deng Xiaoping as its guiding light, there were Politburo members around Hua Guofeng and Wang Dongxing, head of the Central Committee's General Office, who had been very close to the deposed radicals or at least had entered into far-reaching compromises with them.

a) The victorious moderate faction's decision to continue a revised Mao cult

The special situation created by an abrupt shift of course, clothed nonetheless in familiar forms, cast the further development of the Mao canon and Mao cult in the same dual mold. The endeavor to maintain ideological continuity seems primarily to have been dictated by a short-term perspective focused on strengthening the stability of the new leadership, while in the background, the long-term tendencies of a new policy of order were already discernible. Thus it was inevitable that contradictions should emerge in state propaganda, and for that matter in other domains as well. In the short-term perspective of months and years, the policy of continuing and fortifying the Mao cult and reviving and continuing the canon, in tandem with a trend toward limited de-Maoization, a pruning of the hyperbole and overstatement that had been customary since the Cultural Revolution, would bring about a contradiction in Maoist ideology.

Let us first take a look at the posthumous consolidation of the Mao cult in forms chosen by the new moderate leadership for the immediate purpose of maintaining a semblance of continuity. After October 6, 1976, an immediate decision had to be made as to Mao's political successor, in order to fill the post of party chairman. Initially the new political constellation had at its disposal a number of options with respect to the future ideological course. The leaders of the moderate faction had the choice of an open break with the Maoist legacy, an explicit toning down of the cult and canon, or maintenance of an external continuity. For several reasons, this last option prevailed. Mao's writings still seemed a useful ideological connecting link, while Mao himself, as the irreplaceable symbol of the Chinese Revolution, had to remain unassailed; the new leadership constellation had first and foremost to effect a prompt show of stability.

It is perhaps one of the imponderables of this particular political constellation and moment that Hua Guofeng gained the post of party chairman, on the basis of his sudden decision to join in the expulsion of the left faction; the manifold legacy of Mao Zedong seems truly to have dropped in Hua's lap, as if this were a result of the more or less automatic functioning of the apparatus. It is easy to overlook the fact that at least the post of premier would certainly have gone to Deng Xiaoping, had the April 1976 disturbances in Tiananmen Square not put him out of the running, and we can easily imagine a scenario in which, had Zhou Enlai lived longer, the party chairmanship might have gone to him (or another leading member of of the old guard), without Hua Guofeng's having had any chance at all at these top posts. Hua was chosen as premier because he was acceptable to both right and left as a compromise candidate at the crucial moment after Zhou's death in 1976 and because he was in favor with Mao. After he took power as party chairman in addition to his premiership — a move ratified only "after the fact"[87] by the Third Plenum in July 1977 — it was necessary to give public legitimacy to Hua's assumption of office. Institutional authority, undermined in the Cultural Revolution, was not enough to consolidate Hua Guofeng in his role as successor, especially since he was not in any way a historical figure like the old leaders. He therefore had to find a basis for legitimacy in Mao and the canon itself. This he did in a legitimation ritual based on not much more than six Chinese characters scribbled by Mao (an indication of the enduring political power of the Mao cult), instead of taking the route of discussions within the leadership followed by ratification in a party vote and acclaim at mass rallies. As can happen only in a dynastic dictatorship, a fragmentary, cryptic, and at that time undated statement of Mao's — "With you in charge, I'm at ease!" — would serve as the connecting link between the Mao and the post-Mao periods. Of course, this legitimation ritual was played out in almost apologetic fashion, in consideration of the radical Shanghai faction's recent effort to smooth their way to power by invoking immediately after Mao's death the slogan "Act on the principles laid down,"[88] also taken completely out of context. After the October 1976 rout of the left, the first slogan was used exclusively with reference to the political course taken by the newly unified leadership around Hua Guofeng, to whom Mao had purportedly given his blessing as his successor. Thus the last instructions of Mao Zedong, susceptible of any number of interpretations, became the focal point of the media in the months after October 1976. The fragmentary quotes from Mao used in this ritual of

ASIAWEEK, February 16, 1979

legitimation were supplemented by graphic symbols. Illustrations of the statement about the new party chairman, who was now "in charge," show Hua Guofeng at Mao's feet — as it were, receiving from him the sceptre of power. After Hua was thus enthroned as the guardian of Mao's legacy and as such, borne up by the rest of the collective leadership in an astonishing, emergency display of unity, the old mechanism began to operate anew: Hua Guofeng assumed the role of interpreter of the Mao cult ex officio and post festum, so to speak, and reminiscent of the Lin Biao period, a new Hua Guofeng cult emerged in turn.

b) A new cult is created around Hua Guofeng

Hua Guofeng had proven himself to be a capable organizer at the regional level in the province of Hunan for many years before his rise to the position of minister of public security, but he was almost unknown among the general population. While Western analysts laboriously reconstructed Hua's career from the Chinese local press, the Chinese leadership and above all Hua himself were working assiduously to fill in the biographical vacuum of a too-young authority figure as swiftly as possible. Pamphlets appeared bearing the titles Chairman Hua Is Our Good Leader and Stories on Chairman Hua in Xiangyang,[89] in which impressive details about the life and works of Hua were laid out. The forms in which the new cult was molded were not evolved from the personality of Hua himself; nor did they draw on any other possible prototypes. On the contrary, Hua endeavored to adopt Mao's ways down to the last detail. For example, he went on inspection tours, often to places Mao himself had once visited to the same purpose, as was expressly pointed out. These inspection tours generated photo exhibitions, including one held in September 1977 in Liaoning following Hua's inspection tour[90] through the three northeast provinces in April of that year. In other external features as well, Hua Guofeng cleaved to the familiar elements of the Mao cult. For example, he had himself photographed working in a train, in emulation of a well-known Mao photo, and changed his hairstyle to match that of the deceased party chairman.

A quite effective publicity medium, and indeed a stamp of Mao Zedong's authority, had been his calligraphy, which was reproduced a thousand times over. Mao's penstrokes embellished the front pages of innumerable newspapers and periodicals, from People's Daily down to the local press, and bold calligraphic versions of his poems were hung wherever Chinese political propaganda was disseminated. Now Hua Guofeng made a frantic attempt to invest his own powerful but angular and labored hand style with a comparable function. First it was used in general rallying phrases of two lines or a sentence, for example for the newly revived periodicals People's Literature and the local Hubei Daily, and for slogans promoting rapid development of the electronics industry. Even more important, however, were calligraphic texts for monuments, such as the inscriptions on the Mao Mausoleum in Beijing's Tiananmen Square and on one of Mao's former residences which had been converted into a memorial hall. Many newspapers and periodicals began to appear with their logos in Hua's calligraphy, among them Hunan's journal Science and Technology, the PLA Ji'nan units' publication Vanguard, and the Kunming units' National Defense, and other local military periodicals such as Shandong Militia and Yunnan-Guizhou Militia. Further, the Hua cult attended to usage in the newspapers of obligatory formulas such as "the brilliant example of our wise leader Chairman Hua" or "the wise leader Chairman Hua and the Central Committee of the Party," with Hua's every word referred to as an "important instruction."

Even Mao's practiced ritual of modesty and a closeness to basic-level cadres was duly carried on by Hua Guofeng, as for example when he journeyed with other central leaders to the Miyun Dam[91] and took a shovel in his own hands, as Mao had done in his time. Such events were of course documented in People's Daily with appropriate photographs, broadcasted over the central radio network, and acclaimed by regional activists throughout the provinces. Hua Guofeng presented basic policy statements at important party and government events such as the Ninth Party Congress in 1977 and the Fifth People's Congress in Spring 1978 and at all important planning meetings, for example the National Agricultural Conference and the National Science Conference. Thus, within a very brief time quite a considerable collection of Hua texts had been assembled — the building blocks, perhaps, for a future edition of the works of Chairman Hua. Although no steps in this direction had been taken by 1978-79, the press regularly published – sometimes even as the newspaper banner – inspirational quotations from Hua alongside quotations from Mao or the other Marxist classics. To be sure, in 1977 the new party chairman allowed some of his own writings[92] from 1963, originally published in a local Hunan newspaper, to be rescued from oblivion and printed in People's Daily for his greater glory. But the notion of a "Hua Guofeng Thought," which could well have been the goal of this ideological buildup of the personality cult in 1978, seems to have been unimaginable for official propagandists, nor did it occur to anyone in the West to speculate about the birth of "Huaism."

Thus this personality cult was created suddenly and had little about it that was original. Its strained promotion was accepted by the leadership, though not without some embarrassment, after the October 1976 rout of the Gang of Four. As a result, the way was paved for a recognition of Hua's authority as the guarantor of a continuation of the Mao cult, so that Hua indeed became the first official interpreter of Mao Zedong Thought after Mao's death. Of course, one must assume a prior consensus among the collective leadership in the Politburo favoring perpetuation of the Mao cult. The formal authority of Mao interpretation, which fell to Hua by virtue of his position as party chairman, was thus officially decreed, almost overnight. It did not evolve as it would have had the left faction taken power, that faction having viewed the ideological sector as its own particular domain since the Cultural Revolution. Hua's appropriation of this field occurred quite abruptly on October 8, 1976, two days after the left faction had been eliminated, in a "decision on publication of the Selected Works of Mao Zedong and preparatory work for publication of the Collected Works of Mao Zedong by the Central Committee of the CCP." In this decision Hua confirms his role:

The work on the editing of the Selected Works of Mao Zedong and the Collected Works of Mao Zedong is under the direct leadership of the Politburo of the Central Committee of the CCP with Comrade Hua Guofeng at its head.[93]

It soon became evident that the éminence grise behind this Mao interpretation was to be Wang Dongxing, director of the powerful General Office of the Central Committee and after 1976 party vice-chairman.

The fifth and succeeding volumes of the Selected Works were to be published as quickly as possible. To give Volume V of the Selected Works its final form, a new "Committee for the Editing and Publication of the Works of Chairman Mao Zedong" was constituted under the Politburo of the Central Committee in October 1976. Pursuant to the Central Committee decision of 1976, the Bureau of the CCP Central Committee was designated keeper of the archives of all original Mao documents, which were being assembled in more or less complete form for the first time.

A Central Committee decision of April 7, 1977, appealed to the population to undertake a campaign for study of the volume, which was produced in the record time of only six months[94] (an official English version setting the standard for all translations appeared scarcely half a year later). The October decision of the Central Committee deliberately and solemnly proclaimed the current as well as the historical significance of Mao's writings for China. The decidedly political editing of the Selected Works canon, resumed again after many years of interruption, will therefore be dealt with in more detail.

In a parallel effort to reinforce the continued Mao cult, a considerable number of previously unknown Mao writings were now published; this measure was prompted also by the newly established leadership's need for legitimation. This flurry of new publications abated once the new political course had been secured and state Maoism had reassumed a definitive ideological form.

c) Legitimation of the new Realpolitik by publication of some Mao Zedong texts (Series A)

If for the moment one disregards the legitimation formulas discussed above — phrases culled from Mao Zedong's last years, torn from their contexts and used both by the Shanghai faction and by the Hua leadership — we find that within the 18-month period

New Mao Texts (Series A)
(December 1976–July 1978)

	Publication date	Title	Date of Mao text
1.	RMRB, December 26, 1976	On the Ten Great Relationships	April 25, 1956
2.	RMRB, March 22, 1977	Instruction for the Factory Charter of the Anshan Steelworks	March 22, 1960
3.	April 15, 1977	Vol. V of the Selected Works	1949-1957
4.	RMRB, July 30, 1977	Letter of Chairman Mao to the Communist Workers' College at Jiangxi	July 30, 1961
5.	RMRB, September 11, 1977	Learn More from One Another, Don't Mark Time, Overcome Arrogance and Self-Complacency	December 13, 1963
6.	RMRB, September 11, 1977	On the Question of Imperialism and All Reactionaries Are Paper Tigers	December 1, 1958
7.	RMRB, December 26, 1977	China Will Make a Great Leap Forward	December 13, 1964
8.	RMRB, December 26, 1977	A Letter on the Mechanization of Agriculture	March 12, 1966
9.	RMRB, July 1, 1978	Speech at the Expanded Work Conference of the Central Committee	January 30, 1962

RMRB – People's Daily.

(1977-78)[95] we shall examine here there were six occasions for the new leadership to publish in the newspapers eight individual Mao texts. We shall call these texts "Series A" (to distinguish them from another group of Mao texts to be discussed later). In addition Volume V had appeared, expanding the still incomplete Selected Works canon. The fact that such publications were undertaken was something unusual in itself, although to be sure, sparing use had been made of this instrument in the last six years of the mounting power struggle as well as in the five years preceding the Cultural Revolution (if one overlooks some fragmentary, often undated quotations). No such abundance of new Mao writings as appeared in 1977-78 had been published officially within China in a comparable period since the early 1960s, except of course during the Cultural Revolution. Both the date of each new publication and the content of each text or excerpt were keyed to the policy of the day. Thus the writings assumed a new function, quite separate from the historical importance of any particular text.

The first individual text, "On the Ten Great Relationships," appeared on Mao's birthday, December 26, 1976, about two months after the left faction was expelled. Publication coincided with the Second National Agricultural Conference, which put forth a long-term basic plan for agriculture. Hua Guofeng had for years demonstrated his competence in this field. The text, written by Mao Zedong in April 1956, was acclaimed by the Hua government as a guideline for future social development and hence for its own course. Accordingly it showed up once again as a key text in Volume V, published a few months later. The effect of this text was to thrust the radical Mao of the Great Leap Forward and the Cultural Revolution completely into the background and to focus attention instead on the more pragmatic phase of construction of the 1950s.

There had been some pointedly sarcastic comments to the effect that the new leadership had swept away not only a Gang of Four but a Gang of Five, one that included Mao; but the publication of this text within China made it absolutely clear that the moderates had no intention of undertaking a total de-Maoization in the style of Khrushchev. In the Soviet Union after March 1953, the official edition of Stalin's Collected Works was cut short at Volume XIII, and the already completed Volume XIV[96] had to be destroyed, since even then no one in the leadership was willing to write an article marking Stalin's death. Now there was no mistaking the fact that China would not travel that same road. Moreover, attentive readers could not fail to notice that, in contrast to the unauthorized version of the April 1956 "Ten Relationships" speech which had been circulated during the Cultural Revolution, there now appeared in the text passages critical of Stalin and the successes of Soviet construction; obviously these references had previously been omitted in consideration of the friendly relations with the USSR.

The ostensible reason for the publication of Mao's commentary on the model factory charter of the Anshan Steelworks was a commemorative date, the passage of exactly seventeen years since the document had been signed by the party leader. Anniversaries of celebrated speeches were a favorite pretext in the Mao study movement both during and after the Cultural Revolution for bringing a text to the center of media attention and making it a touchstone for lengthy exegeses. Mao's March 1960 commentary on the Anshan Steelworks factory charter directed the attention of the reader of 1977 to a model of socialist factory management which was to point China down the pathway of technical and economic development as laid out by the Hua leadership. Clearly the publication of the text was intended as a gesture in support of the National Industrial Conference which met in April to discuss the long-term planning of industrial development. But while the text suggested a formal continuity, in the historical context it should not be forgotten that the Anshan charter was in fact a model for the Maoist mass line, whereas China's new leadership favored a functional, hierarchically organized and rigidly administered factory management and downplayed the mass line, which tended to interfere with production.

After Volume V of Mao's Selected Works was published in mid-April 1977, establishing Hua's authority as the officially legitimated interpreter of the Mao legacy, Mao's letter to the Jiangxi Workers' College was published at the end of July 1977, on the sixteenth anniversary of its writing; this obviously was intended to coincide with the Academy of Sciences Work Conference held in July, at which new incentives were announced for the development of Chinese science and technology in accordance with the priorities established by the moderate leadership. Again, publication of Mao's letter gave the appearance of a formal continuity; but closer examination reveals a discrepancy between the achievement-oriented technological emphasis which Deng Xiaoping especially championed and Mao's concept of mass study at workers' colleges as elucidated in this letter.[97] Indeed, in 1961 Mao was describing schools that were to be responsible for their own upkeep and would train students committed to the half-work, half-study principle. Moreover, Mao's letter, as internal sources were quick to explain, was addressed to none other than Wang Dongxing, then director of the Jiangxi Workers' College; certainly the Hua Guofeng-Wang Dongxing group wanted to use this connection to strengthen its position vis-à-vis the pro-Deng group within the new leadership.

The second anniversary of Mao's death was used by the leadership as the occasion for an impressive demonstration of loyalty to the deceased party chairman. At the beginning of September, the Mao Mausoleum at the Tiananmen Square was dedicated. To mark the occasion, Hua Guofeng had two new Mao texts published in the newspapers, one legitimating Hua as a leading cadre and the other supporting the general course of accelerated modernization. In the first text, from 1963, Mao praised Hua Guofeng, then leader of the provincial party committee at Hunan, for his modest eagerness to learn and his involvement in the agricultural successes of another province. The second text, from 1958, dealt with the "paper tiger" of imperialism. This may have been an allusion to the visit of U.S. Secretary of State Cyrus Vance in late August 1977. The talks with Vance, which concerned the Taiwan problem as an obstacle to a final normalization of relations between the two countries, bore but little fruit at that time. On the other hand, Mao had also attacked "false tigers," referring to the obstacles encountered by party activists in industry and agriculture, which had to be overcome with enthusiasm.

A second pair of texts was published in the newspapers on Mao's birthday, December 26, 1977. The first, an excerpt from a text of 1964, explained what was meant by a "great leap forward." Here Mao does not lay out the foundations of mass campaigns, as might have been expected, but focuses his discussion on the purposeful development of science and technology. The second text, dated March 1966 and devoted to the mechanization of agriculture, was linked to the two National Agricultural Conferences[98] held in September–October 1975 and December 1976. Hua had dominated both conferences, which were intended to ensure energetic achievements in that field. Mao's rejection of the Soviet solution to agricultural development was an important subtheme.

The last new text, Mao's speech before 7,000 cadres at a Central Committee Work Conference in January 1962, was published on a formal commemorative date, January 7, 1978, the fifty-seventh anniversary of the founding of the CCP. To be sure, the text had been widely available for years, even abroad, in pocketbook editions. This extensively detailed speech of Mao's was on a level comparable to the text "On the Ten Great Relationships." Its call for more intraparty democracy and genuine democratic centralism was being adduced in support of the purge and personnel renewal now under way within the administration, the party, and the army, which had provoked considerable unrest. According to People's Daily, the article was a potent ideological weapon in the movement for rectification of the party organs; only in this way could "chaos be defeated and order restored," it said, because a "reactionary fascist dictatorship" had rooted itself in the party and a "white terror" had undermined the socialist legal system under Lin Biao and the Gang of Four.

Since the hundreds of thousands of now-rehabilitated victims of the great campaigns — the Hundred Flowers, the Cultural Revolution, or the factional power struggles of 1971-76 — expected the guilty to be punished, which was quite unrealistic given the scale of things, reference to Mao's speech could also be used to suggest (if one chose so to interpret it) that even the most passionate intra-Chinese conflicts might be resolved in a peaceful way as "contradictions among the people."

During the period we are analyzing there was one situation of note that no single Mao text could cover, and which thus occasioned a sort of "quotation emergency." In its official reply to the unexpectedly violent attacks by the PRC's once intimate ally Albania on Mao's "three worlds theory," and hence on the policy of the Hua leadership, which the Albanians saw as right-wing revisionism, the leadership had to make do with a patchwork of quotations,[99] primarily because Mao's statements on the subject lacked the requisite consistency for an effective refutation of the Albanian criticism.

Clearly the political function of the carefully selected Mao texts of series A was to lend support to the new policy. By means of pragmatic political sophistry, Chinese readers were to be persuaded of a continuity in state objectives before and after the October 1976 power shift, though in reality there was no such continuity. The chosen texts were used as an instrument of legitimation, now that Mao's successor Hua Guofeng had permitted himself to be designated interpreter of the canon as well as a competent agricultural expert. Likewise, Wang Dongxing's fidelity to Mao's educational goals was documented, while individual texts were also used to support the goals of the "four modernizations" in industry, defense, agriculture, and science and technology. Significantly, it was largely internal developments that guided the selection; foreign policy was almost entirely excluded from the picture as China's leadership focused on putting its own house in order.

d) Return to the Mao canon: Resumption of publication of the *Selected Works*, Volume V

The editing of a 500-page work such as Volume V of the *Selected*

Works must be seen as signaling the leadership's deliberate resumption of the Mao cult once they had consolidated their positions in 1976. This compilation was an appreciably more complex process than the selection of individual topical writings for publication. Since all the major currents of the changed political direction were in one form or another reflected in this volume, the editing of Volume V, like that of Volume IV before it (which brought the canon up to 1949), can hardly be said to have been based on any fundamentally scientific conception of history. Nevertheless, the term "falsification" is as little applicable to the editorial process for Volume V as to that for the four preceding volumes; given the political constellation in 1976-77, it would be more appropriate to speak of a "political editing" or of "history as the present projected into the past."

The pressures that produced an edition defined by political rather than historical and scholarly criteria derived more from the nature of the system itself than from any national peculiarities. It was the system of socialist party dictatorship that shaped the editorial process, rather than anything peculiar to modern China. Indeed, this "political editing" displayed characteristics strikingly similar to those that mark the new history of the German Democratic Republic's Socialist Unity Party, which came out in 1978.[100] Our analysis of the development of the Mao canon has up to now concentrated on the more formal aspects of the process; we should now like to turn to Volume V of the Selected Works canon, which appeared in April 1977, and deal with it at more length, considering it a model case of Chinese editorial practice.[101]

Publication of the Chinese edition of Volume V of Mao's Selected Works was China's literary event of 1977. Seventeen years had passed since the last volume of Mao selections had come out, describing the history of the Communist movement down to the founding of the PRC. Furthermore, twelve years had passed since publication of the two collected volumes of Selected Readings from the Works of Mao Zedong, which contained some of Mao's more recent post-1949 writings. Publication of Volume V, made possible only by the defeat of the left faction, was the first groping attempt to come to terms with the past embracing the years from the founding of the PRC to the end of the Hundred Flowers campaign (China's version of The Thaw) in 1957. The centerpiece of this 500-page book, produced so abruptly and initially available only in the Chinese language, was the April 1956 speech "On the Ten

Great Relationships," which the new leadership had made into a blueprint for their pragmatic conception of social development; the left had omitted this speech from their draft of Volume V.[102]

The current import of the new writings could hardly be overlooked. They rehabilitated fallen functionaries, bestowed on the late premier Zhou Enlai the tribute he deserved but which had initially been withheld, and consolidated the new collective leadership. The preface made specific reference[103] to the representatives of the radical faction (including Mao's wife, Jiang Qing, a would-be legitimation symbol and successor to Mao), singling them out for destruction, as could be inferred from apposite parallels in Volume V. In the ensuing campaign directed against them in 1977-78 they would be pilloried as the "Gang of Four." Indeed, in a truly audacious terminological about-face, these radicals so long supported by Mao were pronounced "right-wing" revisionists by the erstwhile pragmatist faction. Suddenly everything acquired a meaning that implicated the Gang of Four — Mao's text against opponents of the regime[104] from the time of the Hundred Flowers campaign and statements made during the campaign against liberal writers, cultural figures steeped in American liberalism, neo-Confucianist philosophers, and bourgeois literary scholars. Party Chairman Hua Guofeng, now Mao's successor, under whose nominal editorship Volume V was published, prudently refrained from impressing his name on the preface or in the text as had Lin Biao.[105] This probably is an example not only of Hua's already demonstrated political cleverness but of the concessions he was more or less forced to make to the factions of the collective leadership.

As the official fuss over this event amply demonstrated, China's leadership believed that for the foreseeable future it would have no ideological alternative to continued use of Mao's writings as an instrument of integration with respect to the broad perspective of historical identity and as a legitimation of current policy. Mao himself had viewed the destruction of the Stalin cult and the abrupt abandonment of further publication of Stalin's works in the USSR as flagrant disregard of just such considerations; nor were his successors disposed to allow any overt dismantling of the Mao legacy,[106] in view of the USSR's "negative" example. Now, within the documentary framework of Volume V, the task of filling the interpretive vacuum of the past ten years could begin in earnest. Yao Wenyuan's drafts for a radical version of the party's history had been disposed of, clearing the way for discussion of a new party history; after years of turmoil, the museums of the revolution would now be able once again to present to the public a coherent, unified interpretation.

In terms of content the publication of Volume V did not add much that was dramatically new, with the exception of three particulars. The violent and bitterly debated revolutionary process of collectivizing agriculture into production cooperatives was portrayed in brighter terms, as precursory to the communes.[107] The first political convulsion of a revolution that would begin to devour its children at a growing rate, namely the expulsion in 1954 of the cadres in charge of the planning apparatus and the industrial centers, Gao Gang and Rao Shushi, as well as the course taken by the Hundred Flowers movement when it turned into a campaign against the right, had to be redescribed from a new vantage point in light of the documents in Volume V.[108]

In those years Mao Zedong was not concerned with writing abstract philosophical treatises. The party chairman's real contribution was the uniquely Chinese form of the peacetime "continuing revolution" as it evolved during the Hundred Flowers period[109] — the archetypal Maoist mass campaign, with wall newspapers, militant criticism assemblies, and the vanquishing of political opponents by means of mass mobilization. The experience gained in the hunt for "ox demons and serpent ghosts"[110] in 1957 was improved upon by Mao in the Cultural Revolution, which came within a hair's breadth of civil war, and later taken to absurd forms by his Shanghai-faction disciples in their ever more impetuous campaigns.

A new dimension stylistically distinguished Volume V from its predecessors documenting the years of struggle. A sovereign "internal" Mao, the party chairman freely holding forth, unrestrained, made a sudden appearance in the official canon — Mao without the expletives deleted, so to speak. His abrupt shifts in mood, from jovial pleasantry to demonic outbursts of rage, are stylistically the high points of the volume, putting it on a par with the famous 1959 Lushan speech against the opponents of communes.[111] In linguistic terms alone this must be viewed as something quite extraordinary on the monotonous landscape of China's media in the decade since the Cultural Revolution.

The Chinese leadership's bitter debates on how to evaluate the recent past, both in factual terms and with regard to the individuals involved, made the editing of Volume V — which had already been attempted several times — a kind of balancing act. Mao himself had apparently "held out" on the further publication of his works. He was just as unwilling to furnish the cue for the "correct" editing of the projected volume as he was to utter the word that would resolve the decade-long factional struggle within the party. This may have been the wisdom of old age or it may have been an appreciation of his waning ability to stay on top of things in his last years of physical decline. Perhaps too, Mao Zedong shared the attitude of Ho Chi-minh, who politely put off foreign visitors thirsting for biographical details until the time when he would be no more.

Thus this version of Volume V remained in crude form, almost without commentary, much like the rudimentary Mao canon of the forties and in contrast to the four heavily annotated volumes preceding it.[112] Attempts were made to edit Volume V on three separate occasions, concerning which pieces of information, and even tables of contents have leaked out. A draft dating from before the Cultural Revolution and prepared under the direction of chief ideologue Chen Boda, who was later to fall with Lin Biao, became obsolete in 1967-68 when the top leadership of the party came apart at the seams. A second radical version, prepared shortly thereafter by the left faction under the direction of the feared propaganda chief Yao Wenyuan,[113] would have glorified the Great Leap Forward and the Cultural Revolution (and probably have best reflected Mao's own views), creating at the same time, however, a personal monument to the rising generation of revolutionaries in the Shanghai faction. But the grappling of the two major factions within the leadership stalemated the editing of Mao's writings, so that an evaluation of the past via commentaries, annotations, text selections, and text editing was impossible down to the end of 1976. The third version, finally published under Hua, which was completed in early 1977 after only three months of preparation,[114] essentially rejected the proposed commentaries and the editorial guidelines of the first two drafts. The responsible editors, having indirectly established normative guidelines through the text selection itself, chose to leave room for later interpretations. Official texts taken from newspapers or individual pamphlets and thus susceptible of cross-checking were left unaltered, while drafts of internal texts underwent some drastic editing.[115]

Let us review the principal guidelines followed in the Hua edition.

Presentation of the period of steadfast Sino-Soviet friendship obviously caused the greatest headaches. This was an editorial problem of long standing, the subject of rumors for a decade past. During the Cultural Revolution, the editors of the much heralded "radical" version came up with the idea of postponing Volume V, which would have covered these years of friendship with the USSR, and moving on to publication of Volume VI with its focus on the Great Leap Forward, the greatest mass campaign of all aside from the Cultural Revolution.[116] The solution finally adopted in the editing of Volume V was simple. The principal documents attesting to Beijing's then customary subordination to its northern neighbor and the role of Soviet aid in developing the country during those years were omitted — for example, texts dealing with Mao's first visit to the Soviet Union and his audience with Stalin as well as his 1953 obituary for the Soviet dictator. Mao's unofficial, critical comments — which at the time, in accordance with the rules of the Chinese information hierarchy, had been accessible to only the inner circle — were now featured as central documents.[117] This technique was applied so unreservedly that even the official welcoming speech at the CCP's Eighth Party Congress in 1956, friendly to the Soviets, was left out, while Mao's acid remarks made during the planning of the Party Congress were included.

The Hundred Flowers movement — which eventuated in a hard-fought campaign against right deviationists who, taking their cue from the party's encouragement of criticism, had then overstepped the bounds — was portrayed in a manner that deliberately disregarded its initial, liberal phase. This reweighting of emphasis creates the impression that what occurred was a carefully planned measure against guileful critics of the regime rather than a contradictory reversal of course by the CCP after the failure of its liberalization effort.

Finally, the status accorded key political figures in Volume V was of particular interest. The rehabilitation of Deng Xiaoping, who had been twice deposed by the left,[118] was effected "between the lines." As "Comrade Xiaoping," or "our [Party] General Secretary Comrade Deng Xiaoping," he was referred to once again in Mao's familiar terms of address. Nonetheless, in accordance with the inner logic of the power struggle of 1976, those pragmatists and party bureaucrats slated for posthumous rehabilitation, such as the former state president, Liu Shaoqi, were sacrificed on the altar of unity and abandoned to merciless condemnation as personifications of all evil. Every positive reference to them was carefully pruned from the texts.[119] In a hopelessly confused depiction of history, Liu, who had not been deposed until the Cultural Revolution, was portrayed as an opponent and enemy of the party since 1948, a convenient scapegoat for all those mistakes committed in the three decades of Communist power which no official history could pass over in silence.

The decision in favor of a highly political editing made the prospective compilation of an official complete edition[120] an undertaking fraught with difficulties. The rejected alternative was a more objective approach by the party to its own past, one bent not merely on rehabilitating its damaged self-conception and making the projection of the present onto the past a task of historiography and an ideological function. That sort of editing would not have camouflaged the extant contradictions or the now evident mistakes made in party resolutions; rather, it would have entailed a more historical treatment of the expediencies of the day, and in this sense might have become a representative documentation.

The editorial labors that went into the selections for Volume V did have a guiding principle, for the purpose that lay behind all the cosmetic embellishments was a modulation of the leadership's abrupt shifts of course, which had actually taken place *more sinico*, in the time-honored style of Chinese governments. Indeed, this had been the basic tendency as well in the editing of the first four volumes, in which Mao himself had participated.

The party, we learn from Volume V, was almost always correct: actually, the Soviet Union had never really been trusted over the long haul, the opponents of the regime had all along been destined for ouster in 1957, and the party leader had always been clear about those archenemies Liu Shaoqi, Lin Biao, Marshal Peng Dehuai, and others. In the end, Mao Zedong's image was inevitably tarnished by the repeated appeals to political expediency and reasons of state. Still, Hua's editors referred to Mao as "the greatest Marxist-Leninist of our times"[121] and called Volume V an immortal Marxist-Leninist document, going overboard in their reversion to the turgid political language of the years of the Cultural Revolution.

The appearance of Volume V was much celebrated in the

People's Republic. It also marked the start of a "study movement" of these writings, as had happened in 1960. The publication was announced over the radio on the evening of April 14, 1977; the next day, flags were flying over public buildings and fireworks were set off in many places. Factory workers were presented free copies of the volume in a solemn ritual. Banners were hung in many factories to announce an "Assembly to mark the triumphant publication of Volume V of Mao Zedong's Selected Works.[122] By the end of April, according to Beijing statistics, 28 million copies had been distributed. The study campaign was launched in a Central Committee decision of April 7, 1977,[123] and a concise interpretation was provided in the form of a general introduction distributed by "The Editorial and Publishing Committee of the Central Committee of the CCP for the Works of Chairman Mao Zedong." Specific goals were spelled out for the study movement. A circular from the Hubei Provincial Committee, for example, stipulated that all leading cadres at the regional (county) level and above had to have read the volume within two and a half months; for the lower levels, only a selection and a few key articles required study.

The media presented study articles by leading cadres, with a long treatise by Party Chairman Hua Guofeng[124] heading the list. In addition, the newspapers printed series presenting philological and practical explanations, for example "Reference Materials for the Study of Volume V of Mao Zedong's Selected Works" in People's Daily and "Guidelines for the Study . . ." in Guangming Daily. An official English translation was published as the "model version" for other foreign-language editions; Hua honored foreign translators and colleagues at a reception given especially for the occasion.[125] For months the newspapers recorded positive reactions from abroad to the publication of Volume V. Not surprisingly, the East European media also took note of the publication and reproved the Chinese for falsifying history[126] by suppressing the era of friendship with the Soviet Union in the 1950s.

These many modes of presentation of the expanded Selected Works canon only serve to demonstrate once more that of all the socialist countries, China has probably carried furthest the ritual surrounding the orthodox writings of its leader; accordingly, it stands quite apart from the road on which, for example, the Eurocommunist parties have set out.

2. TENDENCIES CONSTRAINING STATE MAOISM

a) Dedogmatization and the curtailment of the Mao cult

In light of the link that still is maintained between the Chinese nation and the father figure Mao, any analysis of the changes that have taken place in the ideological domain since 1976 ought to avoid use of the term "de-Maoization," patterned after the term "de-Stalinization." It would be closer to the mark to speak of a withdrawal of the Mao cult from untenable positions, a qualified dedogmatization, with Mao receding to the horizon to become a manageable symbol of modern China's identity. The limited dedogmatization toned down the exaggerated claim that Mao was the most prestigious (and only genuine) theoretician of Marxism-Leninism since Stalin; it defined the PRC's first party chairman as a respected leader of the Chinese Revolution and the driving force of China's post-1949 social transformation, without claiming eternal and universal validity for Mao's every word.

Since 1977 there has been no doubt that in principle the leadership had reached agreement on the necessity of curtailing the Mao cult. Nonetheless, this decision, which entailed abolition of specific external forms of the Mao cult, was not as systematically publicized by the propaganda apparatus as was Hua Guofeng's dogged adherence to the rituals of state Maoism. The general consensus in favor of dedogmatization was reflected, however, in some measured statements that appeared in the media. For example, an editorial in People's Daily argued as follows, using quotations from the deceased party leader himself:

> With regard to the study of Marxist-Leninist theory Chairman Mao said: "The theories of Marx, Engels, Lenin, and Stalin are universally applicable. We should not see them as dogma, but as guides to action. . . ." Chairman Mao criticized certain people who regarded "isolated quotations from Marxist-Leninist works as ready-made panaceas that need only be applied to cure any disease forthwith. Such people betray a childish ignorance, so we must explain this to them."

> These words are equally applicable to our present study of Mao Zedong Thought. . . . Chairman Mao's position on a particular question at a particular

time and under particular circumstances is correct, as is his position on the same question but at another time under other circumstances. Nonetheless, the positions taken on a particular question at different times and under different circumstances may well differ in degree, in points of emphasis, and even in formulation. For this reason, when we are dealing with problems bearing on a specific aspect or a particular area, we should strive to understand correctly Mao Zedong Thought as a whole. This is how all party members and cadres should study the writings of Chairman Mao. Middle-level and top-level cadres, certainly, must study Marxism-Leninism-Mao Zedong Thought as a whole, and not piecemeal.[127]

Deng Xiaoping gave this attitude a more concrete formulation applying to the entire propaganda apparatus quite generally in his widely regarded and intentionally laconic speech at the Eleventh Party Congress on August 18, 1977, when he presented his motto for China's new stage of development (thereafter a key slogan), "Seek the truth in facts":

...the very least one must demand from a Communist is honesty, honesty in words and honesty in deeds. Words and deeds must agree, theory and practice must be closely linked. We reject bombast and any exaggeration; what we need is less empty chatter and more hard work.[128]

The first step in this new attempt to rein-in ideology was a general dedogmatization in nearly every realm of intellectual activity. People's Daily reinterpreted Mao's slogan "red and expert," which had stressed political consciousness over technical specialization, accordingly. Now it was said that anyone who had mastered his own specialized area was on that account "red" and dedicated to the cause of socialism:

With regard to the "red and expert" problem, we must specify different requirements for different groups of the population. Scientific and technical work differs from political work, and hence we cannot demand from scientific and technical workers what we require of political workers. Scientists should devote the major portion of their energy and time to research and other professional activities. They need not read so many books about political theory and should not use up so much time for social political work as do political workers.[129]

This, however, was a 180-degree turn, a redefinition of all previous standards. The hitherto prevailing view, which gave the political orientation of intellectuals priority over scientific training, bold creativity, and scientific results, was now disavowed as an intellectual confusion traceable to the expelled radicals (and implicitly, to Mao as well).

Deng set forth the need for a dedogmatization of state Maoism in even sharper terms in his speech at the Conference on Political Work in the Army on June 2, 1978. The left-wing Hong Kong newspaper Ta Kung Pao ran its commentary under the revealing headline "Deng Xiaoping Explained How Mao Zedong Thought Should Be Interpreted." Thus it would seem that at this point Deng and the army were appropriating for themselves the right to interpret Mao Zedong, with the intention of dismantling the excesses of the Mao cult, while Hua assumed the role of guardian of the state ideology. This trend toward de-Maoization encountered considerable resistance among party cadres, however. For example, in an allusion to Deng's call "to seek the truth in facts," it was commented:

> When we stress practice . . . and assert that theories must be tested out in practice, aren't we diminishing the importance of theory and casting doubt on the truths of Marxist theory?
>
> Some cadres have posed the following question: If we place practice above all else and view it as the sole criterion, then what good are Mao Zedong Thought and the sayings of Chairman Mao?[130]

When confronted with such questions and doubts concerning the new course, the advocates of dedogmatization adopted a rearguard strategy, intimating that dogmatic Maoism, the "religious doctrine of Marxism-Leninism-Mao Zedong Thought," was a degeneration for which Lin Biao alone was responsible. This line of defense was one of the major reasons for the resumption of criticism of Lin Biao in mid-1978, especially in the army.

The next step in the curtailment of the cult was the party's concession that even such a great leader as Mao Zedong could, and in fact did, make some serious mistakes. The attack on Mao's infallibility was effected through the publication in 1978 of Mao's speech before 7,000 cadres in which the party chairman undertook self-criticism for mistakes he had made during the Great Leap Forward:

> When mistakes are made, self-criticism must be undertaken in every case; people must be induced to speak and to criticize. On June 12 of last year [1961], the last day of the Central Work Conference in Beijing, I spoke about some of my own shortcomings and mistakes. I asked the comrades to go into every province and to every place to make these known. Later I learned that there were still many places where this had not occurred. It would thus appear

that my mistakes might be glossed over. In general I am directly responsible for a mistake made by the Central Committee; moreover, I am also involved indirectly because I am the chairman of the Central Committee. It is not my intention to shift responsibility onto others. Other comrades bear responsibility as well. But I am the one who must bear primary responsibility....

Indeed we lack experience, and as a matter of fact we still do not have such a long-term plan [for the development of China]. The year 1960 was a time in which we encountered many difficulties.[131]

Of central concern in the curtailment of state Maoism was the effort to introduce a more sober mode of argumentation and have done with the hymns of idolatry to Mao and hyperbole around his person; at the same time there was the desire to put an end to the rote learning of extracts from the canon, which had crippled independent political thinking. Moreover, no longer was Mao's every word to enjoy the force of law in political debates and polemics it had had ever since the Cultural Revolution. The overall mentality that reduced social debate to quotation-slinging rather than the probing of each argument for its validity, the whole timorous, servile dependency on Mao's words, had become thoroughly untenable. Finally, Mao had to be scaled down to historical dimensions, which also meant that the study of his writings had to be rooted in their historical context.

The psychological situation within the Politburo as concerns this cautiously formulated partial dismantling of the Mao myth must also be taken into account here. The pragmatist faction led by Deng Xiaoping had been under pressure during and after the Cultural Revolution. Deng himself had suffered criticism during these years for his purported lack of deference toward Mao Zedong. In a "statement of evidence," presented as a matter of routine, Mao in 1966 reproved Deng, saying that he had not discussed any pressing affairs with the party chairman since the Sixth Plenum of the Eighth Party Congress in 1958. Deng no longer called on him, Mao said, or asked for instructions. The party chairman was also indignant over Deng's "Sixty-point Outline for the People's Communes," which made critical modifications in Mao's impetuous Great Leap Forward policy, as Deng had to confess in his self-criticism of December 16, 1966. The polemic reached an extreme in a Red Guards pamphlet addressing those who had differed with Mao in the aftermath of the Great Leap Forward:

> The traitor Deng attacked our Great Leader without restraint and made the absurd claim that Mao Zedong was not free of shortcomings and mistakes, indeed that Chairman Mao was subjective.... He screamed hysterically that the chairman should step down and resign. He said, in an open challenge, that Chairman Mao should be overthrown.[132]

The alienation between these two political figures culminated in Deng's thinly veiled rejection of the Cultural Revolution and his attempt to keep developments under control by suppressing the activist "work groups."

It is thus understandable that several of the moderates in the Politburo after 1976 experienced a certain private satisfaction in seeing Mao Zedong, who had been elevated to mythic proportions during the last decade of his life, scaled down once again to human political dimensions, although reasons of state set certain limits to this process. However, for cadres such as Hua Guofeng, Wang Dongxing, and Wu De — who had initially been allied with the left and indeed, after the left's ouster in October 1976, were themselves forced to engage in self-criticism regarding the positions they had taken in the last phase of the power struggle — the case for curtailment of the cult was convincing only insofar as it facilitated a more flexible implementation of the new policy goals within a more objective, less ideologically charged atmosphere.

Let us illustrate the external forms of the curtailment of the cult as well as the new perspectives on the Mao canon with a few examples. First, the printing of maxims from the classics as banner newspaper headlines and journal frontispieces was reduced to a minimum — on a somewhat surprising pretext. A disingenuous critique published in Guangming Daily observed that the printing of pages upon pages of quotations, often repeated unchanged over several successive issues of a periodical, was a "waste of paper": "Since the beginning of this year [1977] the journal Red Flag has done away with the four pages of Mao quotations at the beginning of each issue; this could save 20 million pages of paper each year."[133]

A second successful step along this line was the leadership's unannounced decision to eliminate the practice of printing quotations from Mao, from other Marxist classics, and even from Hua Guofeng in boldfaced type, and thus to reintegrate them into the text. Red Flag, for instance, without notice simply dropped this convention, a matter of course since the Cultural Revolution, in April 1978.[134]

An inscription, "Beijing Language Institute," penned by Mao in his last years (on September 9, 1974); it was later engraved in gold letters and put up at the entrance to the institute. The calligraphy is blurry and uneven, undoubtedly because several attempts were required to complete each stroke — evidence of Mao Zedong's physical decline. (Photo: China Archive, Martin Krott)

In addition to this quite effective visual downgrading of Mao Zedong, his uncontested authority was reduced in two further areas — verse and calligraphy. Once the reproduction of Mao's poems, in his own calligraphy, became a means for enhancing his image as poet and statesman (indeed, some of his poems had even been used to attack the pragmatists in factional disputes), no junior or senior party functionary dared to publish his own poetry for fear of *lese majesty*. The taboo was broken after Mao's death. Poems by several party leaders,[135] among them Marshal Ye Jianying, Zhu De, and the former foreign minister Chen Yi, appeared in the newspapers and in anthologies. A similar fate awaited the party chairman's calligraphy, which had also assumed a political function and served as Mao's seal of authority. After Mao's death this effect was diluted as the calligraphy of not only Hua Guofeng but most of the other party leaders appeared in the press in political contexts. All these measures served visually and graphically to reabsorb Mao Zedong into the ranks of the party leadership.

This following up of short-term efforts to achieve legitimacy with some steps toward dedogmatization acquired a dynamic of its own. This is made clear in a secret Central Committee decree[136] which amnestied and rehabilitated over 100,000 intellectuals who had been branded right-wing elements in the anti-rightist movement following the Hundred Flowers period. What this amounted to was a complete reversal of the attitude that had guided the political editing of Volume V of Mao's writings the previous year; Volume V had given disproportionate space to the resolutions condemning the "rightists" during the campaign and moreover had affirmed them. In his widely read study article on Volume V, "The Continuing Revolution," Hua Guofeng had stressed that the specifically Maoist instrument of mass campaigns had been born of this campaign against the right. Until the appearance of the official de-Maoization document of 1981, there was probably no more spectacular example of the abrupt eclipse of the Maoist notion of the campaign instrument, and of the effects of Deng's efforts to curtail the Mao cult, than these rehabilitations.

More time had to pass before it was clear whether the divergent views concerning Mao ideology for which Hua Guofeng and Deng Xiaoping threw their political authority in the balance were merely clever theater, with roles assigned, or whether behind them lay a serious political disagreement that could be papered over only with difficulty in official proclamations. That the latter was the case was convincingly proved only in the course of the step-by-step ouster of Hua's group, and finally of Hua himself, from the top leadership. By the same token, one should guard against any presumption that these dissonant notes were the echoes of a conflict between fierce enemies of orthodoxy, or even ideological iconoclasts of the Solzhenitsyn type, and radical Maoist advocates of perpetual cultural revolutions. In the light of his entire past, Deng Xiaoping, as a symbolic figure, was rather the sponsor of a new, and by no means unopposed, intellectual orientation whose goal was the establishment of a "neo-Maoist orthodoxy more attuned to reality," if we may venture a definition. Deng's move against the tiny group of dissidents in 1980-81 and his reestablishment of party "law and order" in the cultural realm would seem to corroborate this interpretation.

8

The First Phase of De-Maoization: From the Central Committee Work Conference and the Third Plenum in 1978 to 1979

1. THE DE-MAOIZATION DISCUSSION ON THE OFFICIAL LEVEL

In the latter half of 1977 the Deng group began an uncompromising drive to achieve a redefinition of basic ideological and practical political questions. There ensued a heated debate which continued through 1978 within the Politburo and among leading cadres and other official political groupings. For the first time since October 1976 the existence of two factions struggling for control in the post-Mao leadership was clearly apparent. Simply stated, these groups can be called the "pragmatists" and the "leftists." The pragmatists were former supporters of Zhou Enlai who were now backing Deng's majority position. The group opposing them, which included Hua Guofeng and Wang Dongxing among others, had been promoted into leadership positions during the Cultural Revolution and in the years following. As former allies of the Shanghai faction (the Gang of Four), these leftists now represented a minority opposition.

By January 1978 the debate between the two factions began to take on unmistable, if somewhat muted contours in the press. In mid-year the ideological conflict intensified as Deng Xiaoping pushed ahead with his concept of de-Maoization despite considerable resistance, and the debate came to its first climax in November 1978 with the convening of a Central Committee Work Conference, to the accompaniment of a wall poster campaign. Then in December the Third Plenum of the Eleventh Central Committee settled accounts, effecting new ideological unity along with an extensive reshuffling of personnel and positions. Against the background of the contradictory efforts at de-Maoization described in the previous chapter, this period (mid-1978–1980) must be regarded as the first phase of de-Maoization.

Early 1979 was marked by a backlog of problems left unsolved in the clashes at the plenum and the preparatory conference; thus began a new stage of Mao interpretation, under Deng's auspices. During this phase the rehabilitation of prominent victims of the Cultural Revolution and earlier campaigns continued apace. In addition, through a series of audacious strokes, the history of the party and along with it the official self-image of the People's Republic were recast. Coming onto the horizon was a second, more energetic de-Maoization phase, intended to be the final stage in the process of redefining China's political, ideological, and economic orientation for the remainder of the century.

a) The debate between the majority faction of Deng Xiaoping and the radical minority around Wang Donxing: Ideology is reinterpreted in support of the new policy

The debates in the press in 1978 took the following form. Articles emanating from the Deng faction guardedly attacked its (unnamed) ideological opponents. Meanwhile, the orthodox Maoist group around Party Vice-chairman Wang Dongxing — who, as director of the powerful Party General Office, had considerable control over propaganda and the media — impeded the spread of Deng's ideological reorientation discussion. As in earlier controversies, the split in the Politburo was reflected in threatening gestures by the majority faction, conveyed via the formula: "There are persons among the cadres, especially among the leading cadres, who ... [are guilty of such-and-such error]."

From veiled exchanges such as these may be culled the arguments of the Wang faction (which ultimately was defeated) against key aspects of Deng's policies, arguments that took the distilled form of an "intellectual current" (sichao), according to officious Deng apologists. It is significant that Party Chairman Hua Guofeng was clearly disposed to support the views of Wang Dongxing's orthodox left-wing position in a number of important arguments and that he was tolerated by the Deng group only temporarily and after face-saving compromises.

Initially the Deng faction's attacks were directed at political opportunists who "resisted with all their might" the effort to "set the record straight" on the past. In January, from Deng's own power base in the army, significantly, attacks were mounted (in the army newspaper) against the "wind faction" (fengpai), the "drifters" (liupai), and the "earthquake faction" (zhenpai), later broadening out to include a polemic against the "insurrectionary faction" and those who were trying to "hold the lid down." In other words, among the intended targets were those leading cadres and military personnel of the former Zhou Enlai group who had switched over to the left faction out of their instinct for self-preservation and their designs on power — General Chen Xilian for example, and "drifters" such as Beijing's Mayor Wu De, who opposed every attempt at self-criticism and a reinterpretation of the Tiananmen affair. Also targeted, though more as an object lesson, were those cadres who specialized in "political earthquakes," i.e., who had been used by the left faction to engineer violent shakeups in leading groups during the major and minor campaigns prior to October 1976, for example Shanghai's top functionary Ma Tianshui, among others.

The arguments of the Hua/Wang faction were directed against Deng's policies in general. In its pursuit of a pragmatic course, it was charged, the Deng group was committing "crimes that cried out to high heaven." Deng was continuing down the road to revisionism and, as the Gang of Four's old anti–Deng slogan put it, was an "unrepentant" capitalist-roader.

The Wang faction (including Hua Guofeng) opposed first and foremost Deng's uncompromising approach to de-Maoization, which Deng had articulated in discussions on the theme "seek the truth in facts." The Wang group argued that one had strictly to adhere to Mao's writings, i.e., to the fundamental concepts of Maoism. Deng's position, they said, amounted to "an abstract affirmation but a concrete rejection" of the Maoist heritage; Deng was "tearing down the red flag." Implied here as well was a rejection of the "division-into-two method" (liangfen fa — that is, "one divides into two," or yi fen wei er), according to which all things and persons may be viewed from two aspects: all have their shortcomings as well as their merits. It was with this slogan that Hong Kong's pro-Deng left press had opened its de-Maoization debate and begun to criticize Mao more directly.

Wang's faction also strongly opposed any resumption of criticism of Lin Biao or a fusion of such criticism with the campaign against the Gang of Four. Further, the Wang faction accused Deng of completely negating the Maoist line, and raged against his depoliticization of the personnel evaluation process, especially as it affected cadres, and the stress now put on demonstrated competence in certain specialities. In Maoist terminology, "politics" should remain "in command," whereas Deng had "abandoned politics." Deng was guilty of "giving priority to questions of technical expertise" in the "red and expert" discussion when he proposed that a technically flawless performance should be considered "red," "patriotic," and "ideologically correct" — an institute of the Academy of Sciences had even held a conference on this question in mid-1978. Deng's attempts in this way to induce a process of fundamental ideological rethinking met resistance from the Wang faction, particularly in connection with Deng's reassessment of agrarian and industrial models and of "progressive units" in general so as to reshape the concrete goals of future policy. Wang's own commitment to specific models such as Dazhai (agriculture), Daqing (industry), and Anshan (factory and plant management) stood in direct opposition to the Deng group's attempts to downgrade these models and to reinterpret them in their concrete details.

In the economic domain the Wang group attacked Deng's efficiency-oriented notion of "distribution according to performance"; the Deng group countered in kind, arguing that neither had the classics of Marxism-Leninism laid down a doctrine of "distribution according to performance and political line." Further arguments of the orthodox Wang Dongxing faction were directed against the policy of granting extensive autonomy to intellectuals with the goal of encouraging scientific and technological advancement, as well as against the increasing reliance on foreign technology and the probable implication of such a policy.

How are we to evaluate the character and the significance of this debate? We can be certain that it was not merely an orchestral accompaniment to yet another life-or-death power struggle. This is clear from the objection raised by the left press in its discussion of this question — namely, that had there been any actual plot to overthrow the Deng faction, the perpetrators would have been removed forthwith from the political scene. Why, then, go to the trouble of "criticizing without naming names" in proceeding against the Wang group? The apologetic form of the Deng majority faction's counterarguments in the official media made it clear that this debate at the top, with all its ideological as well as personal implications, was precisely intended to penetrate the Wang-dominated media and thus to reach the attention of the basic level, so as to blunt the edge of the Hua/Wang group's orthodox Maoist arguments. This was a campaign of persuasion, a "panel discussion" designed to justify the new policy directly and to put an end to the half-compromise of late 1976, which had sought to throw an ill-fitting Maoist mantle over the pragmatic policy. Thus it was intended to combat the "ideological current," the "residual poison" of the Shanghai left, and last but not least, to exert pressure against the strong though unarticulated resistance of bureaucrats who feared for their privileges. People's Daily spoke quite openly of the fact that the poison and the spirit of the "four" were still present, and that that poison had infected not only their one-time adherents but "several of our own comrades as well." On the other hand, the polemical tirade that the Deng group directed against the Hua/Wang minority faction was justified with the argument that the notorious radical line had to be completely stamped out both ideologically and politically, so that it would be impossible for "leftist theoreticians" to organize a comeback at some future date.

b) Deng forces a discussion of de-Maoization, originating in the army and the provinces and directed against the center, using the theme "practice is the sole criterion for gauging the truth"

By 1977-78 the majority faction around Deng Xiaoping was openly engaged in a dispute with the Maoist minority opposition over how far the criticism of Mao Zedong and the redefinition of the ideological system should or could be permitted to go. Deng's preferred strategy was to start from the general position that even the highest leaders should not be regarded as infallible, and then proceed to more concrete examples of obvious mistakes made by Mao on essential questions of China's development over the past decade. Thus would be laid the groundwork for a future discussion of responsibility for the political line in mass campaigns during the Great Leap Forward and the Cultural Revolution as well as the series of lesser campaigns since 1970. The charge against the Hua/Wang opposition therefore was dogmatism, because they proposed to remain faithful to the Mao heritage more or less down to the letter; this prompted an attack from the Deng group against what was now dubbed the "whatever faction" (fanshipai). The origin of this label is to be found in an unsigned editorial written during the early period of compromise following expulsion of the Shanghai faction in February 1977. In this article Li Xin, one of Wang Dongxing's men in the party's General Office, insisted that whatever Mao had written, said, or suggested was under no circumstances to be "tampered with." The highly charged atmosphere of the time marked a critical phase in the discussion of Deng's rehabilitation and the priorities of the new leadership.

During the planning of the de-Maoization discussion in 1978 the Deng faction did not control the Propaganda Department of the Central Committee; moreover, the General Office under Wang Dongxing was opposed to any discussion of Mao in terms of the slogans "seek the truth in facts" and "practice is the sole criterion for gauging the truth." Thus Deng was forced in mid-1978 hurriedly to gather support for his campaign in the army and at the local provincial level in order to prevail in the Central Committee and the Politburo. Formally this was done by organizing meetings of provincial party committees, their propaganda departments, and other special assemblies. The party first secretaries would give a talk — usually amounting to a personal endorsement of the "truth discussion," and hence a declaration of loyalty to Deng, which expanded on Deng's line of reasoning and thus prepared the basic levels for specific limited criticisms of Mao. While the party's theoretical organ Red Flag, controlled by Wang, remained silent on this theme, and the national press took stands on the controversy only very irregularly, a few provincial papers and local radio stations covered these appearances of the party secretaries and their public remarks in detail. The controversy reached a climax in November 1978 when Hu Sheng, a propaganda specialist and follower of Wang Dongxing, made a speech in which he reproached the provincial party secretaries for making public their views concerning this issue when the Central Committee had not yet taken a clear stand. From this he moved on to the argument now being used to condemn Deng's pragmatism, namely that if practice were the sole criterion for gauging the truth, the October revolution would have never taken place, the People's Republic would not have been proclaimed, and the Gang of Four could never have been stripped of their power.

Nonetheless, the Deng group succeeded in putting through its own view at the Central Committee Conference, and Party Chairman Hua Guofeng was even forced to concede self-critically that he had not adequately supported the praxis discussion.[137] The road was now clear, and in December and January the media joined unconditionally Deng's de-Maoization campaign.

i) Legitimating the praxis discussion. In order to understand the legitimation of the "praxis" viewpoint, hereafter the keynote of state ideology, it will be helpful to review the use of this term[138] historically in the Communist movement as well as the historical perspective within which the party leadership presented its own pragmatic line in 1978-79. (We might note that China specialists in the West had adopted this "new" perspective years before it could be broached in China itself.)

Mao was now to be portrayed as having led the struggle against left opportunism since the party's founding, as in the case of Wang Ming. In abandoning the Soviet model of revolution in the cities and concentrating instead on the peasant revolution,[139] Mao, it was claimed, had given the first graphic demonstration of the principle of testing truth in practice. The next milestone of the pragmatist line was Mao's 1956 speech "On the Ten Great Relationships," which since 1976 had served as the blueprint for the four modernizations policy. The real keystone of this edifice, however, was a precursor of the praxis discussion, the "year of seeking truth in facts" proclaimed in 1961 by the Ninth Plenum of the Eighth Central Committee. Mao's self-critical speech delivered before 7,000 cadres at the expanded meeting of the Central Committee in January 1962 was seen as a logical culmination of this year of praxis. The readjustment policy of Liu Shaoqi and Deng Xiaoping, who had assumed the task of setting aright the catastrophically bad results of the Great Leap Forward mass campaign, had been implemented at that time. Thus allusions to party history were once again being brought to bear, this time to push the radical Mao and his mass line into the background and to highlight instead instances of his opposition to left radical deviations.

Backing up this legitimation of the praxis discussion was the publication of a fragment of a report made by Zhou Enlai at the First National Youth Congress in May 1949, giving a general perspective on Mao personally as well as on the newly consolidated state Maoism.[140] This text literally invoked the praxis slogan and moreover took issue with the exaggerated "superstition" of the burgeoning personality cult.

The most important arguments put forward by the pragmatist side against the orthodox Maoists can be summarized as follows. Mao Zedong Thought is an objective truth which has been tested in practice. It must continue to be susceptible of testing. To hold Mao Zedong Thought as the sole criterion for gauging the truth, as the Gang of Four and Lin Biao, in their total degeneracy, had done, is completely wrong. Mao Zedong Thought must be seen as a revolutionary science, not a religious dogma; it is both absolute and relative in nature (thus it is subject to change). The revolutionary teachers all revised and rewrote their works continually; Mao Zedong Thought should likewise be able to sustain alterations. It must be "further developed" and "enriched" (*fazhan* and *fengfu*) in the future. This in no way means a fettering or a decimation of Mao ideology. The goal of the discussion is and remains the "elimination of chaos and the reestablishment of order" in the ideological domain and the relieving of anxieties "still troubling the air" among the people and cadres. (Indeed it was quite clear to what extent this discussion was aimed at a broader audience that for a decade had been submerged in radical Maoism.)

Thus, with the new "magic formula" of "further development" of Mao Zedong Thought, the historical Mao and his methods were neatly separated from state Maoism, which would continue to exist and change. Deng gingerly shunted aside radical Maoism, allowing Mao his place in revolutionary history yet giving the leadership the latitude to undertake whatever measures it considered necessary as part of the new policy.

c) Publication of individual new texts (Series B): Collapse of the Hua/Wang editorial line on the Mao writings and the switch to Deng's more critical approach to Mao

Although the party controversy over just how much Mao criticism should be allowed moved in favor of Deng Xiaoping's interim solution, Deng's supporters continued outwardly to pursue Mao's edification in areas that did not appear to be controversial, using the official publication of previously unknown individual Mao texts as a means in the process. For half a year the Deng ideologists engaged in a heated internal party debate with the Maoist minority faction over how such texts should be used, during which time the journalistic waters were calm. Mao's birthday on December 26, 1978, served as an occasion for the appearance of a rapid succession of additional previously unpublished individual texts, hereafter referred to as series B. The nature of this second phase (beginning in December 1978) was, however, completely different from the transitional period between 1976 and mid-1978 which had produced text series A, discussed above.

Let us take a brief look at the components of series B, edited to support Deng's modernization policies, in order to identify its political function:

— Letters written by Mao in 1941 to his sons and to other young people, including a son of Liu Shaoqi. These were basically appeals to children of Chinese leaders studying in the Soviet Union to devote serious attention to their scientific studies; as such they fit in nicely with the modernization policy. Of paramount importance in this text, however, was the first indirect reference to Liu Shaoqi as a "leading cadre" since his condemnation during the Cultural Revolution. Moreover, on the general theme of the rehabilitations, it was understood that the practice (dating to the Cultural Revolution) of wholesale arrest of a victim's entire family followed by political trials anathematizing them, was to be abolished.

— A poem written by Mao praising Peng Dehuai's service as an army commander during the Long March. This poem was published as part of Peng's rehabilitation and underscored the resolve to honor representatives of the old revolutionary leadership group.

— Mao's text "On How to Conduct a Study in the Countryside" conveyed to the reader of 1978-79 that in the future, in consonance with Deng's pragmatic approach, political actions were to be based not on a "theology" but on an exact "study" of the concrete situation. A further and more important function of the text was the parallel intended between the 1978-79 developments and the rectification movement in Yanan which eliminated the so-called Wang Ming

New Mao Texts (Series B)
(December 1978–January 1979)

	Publication date	Topic	Date of Mao text
1.	RMRB, December 1, 1978	Calligraphy on the sixtieth birthday of Zhu De	December 1, 1946
2.	NCNA, December 12, 1978 (from the journal Chinese Youth, two slightly modified versions)	Two letters to Mao's sons, Liu's son, etc.	January 31, 1941 January 8, 1946
3.	RMRB, December 13, 1978 (also printed as a pamphlet in other languages)	On How to Conduct a Study in the Countryside	September 13, 1941
4.	RMRB, December 26, 1978 (from the journal Chinese Woman, 1978, No. 6, bearing a Mao inscription)	On the Continuing Revolution	January –, 1958
5.	RMRB, December 27-28, 1978 (the journal Philosophical Studies, 1978, No. 12, published facsimiles)	Three letters to Li Da	March 27, 1951 September 17, 1952 December 28, 1954
6.	NCNA, December 27, 1978	Conversations with railroad employees on the forms of the Mao cult and the Cultural Revolution	September 26, 1967 July –, 1969
7.	RMRB, December 30, 1978 (from a special volume dedicated to the hundreth birthday of Wu Yuzhang, Beijing, 1978)	Letter of congratulations on the sixtieth birthday of Wu Yuzhang	December 30, 1938; celebrated on January 15, 1940
8.	RMRB, January 1, 1979	Letter to Guo Moruo	November 21, 1944
9.	RMRB, January 3, 1979 (also published in the journal Lyric)	Poem in praise of Peng Dehuai	— –, 1935, during the Long March

RMRB — People's Daily. NCNA — New China News Agency.

line. The Deng faction's maneuvers within the party in 1978, leading to the December plenum, prepared the way for a thoroughgoing reinterpretation of party history since the late 1950s, on the basis of which the great mass campaigns could be condemned as "left-deviationist" — an effort that culminated in the official de-Maoization document of 1981. The significance of this text became clear in late December 1978 when it was distributed in pamphlet form and translated into foreign languages. Mao had delivered his speech at the Women's University of Yanan, which was headed by

Wang Ming, thereby sealing Wang's political removal (the 1941 Yanan rectification campaign had been directed against Wang Ming, who was accused of "dogmatism, subjectivism, and formalism" in the women's movement). The parallel to the suppression of the orthodox Maoist opposition around Wang Dongxing was obvious. In addition, a declaration by the official news agency specified that this speech made by Mao in 1941 had endorsed "the concept of the primacy of praxis" and held that the "truth is to be sought in facts."

— The publication of still another text on the "continuing revolution" served as a political signal. This text title was obviously not Mao's but rather a shrewd choice on the part of the editors, for in fact the text is but a segment from "Sixty Points on Work Methods." In the interpretive speech delivered by Hua Guofeng[141] on the occasion of the publication of Volume V of the _Selected Works_ in 1977, the anti-rightist campaign of 1957 was called the prototype for subsequent mass campaigns and an example of the "continuing revolution" (_jixugeming_); the entire editing of Volume V was to underscore this idea. Now a complete reinterpretation of the concept of continuing revolution was in the works. The fact alone that this excerpt had been lifted from an integral text suggests the extent of the liberties taken by the editors. In short, it was no longer mass campaigns but rather the drive for technological modernization that was to come under the title "revolution." This reinforced the Third Plenum's appeal to put an end to the "campaign against the Gang of Four" and "mass campaigns" and instead to direct all efforts toward building up the country. Finally, a criticism of the Great Leap was implied, since Mao wrote this passage before the Great Leap but in fact had directed subsequent events along an entirely different path.

— Three letters written by Mao in 1951 to the Marxist ideologist and Mao interpreter Li Da were selected for the purpose of relativizing the established Mao canon, since the letters made reference to the practice, never before publicly acknowledged in the PRC, of continually reediting and emending texts (this confirms one of the major contentions of the Mao scholars Schram and Takeuchi). Li Da belonged to the circle of prominent intellectuals who had fallen in the Cultural Revolution, and he had been rehabilitated posthumously only a short time before (1978). He was the author of a standard commentary on Mao's well-known essays "On Practice" and "On Contradiction," which were the subject of these Mao letters. An official 1978 commentary to the letters pointedly noted that both of Mao's texts had undergone "a process of continuous development and gradual perfecting." "From Mao's 1937 speech to the Anti-Japanese Military-Political Academy down to the Selected Works as published after the establishment of the PRC, the two works "On Practice" and "On Contradiction" underwent a series of revisions and amendments, not only in the choice of words and in the presentation but also in the crystallization and formulation of certain truths. Each new revision made the two works still more precise and perfect!" Yet Mao was not quite satisfied, it was claimed, and even in the sixties had toyed with the idea of rewriting both works in the light of new experiences. Thus in 1978-79 Mao is portrayed not as a dogmatist, but as a questioning thinker and a politician. Most important here, however, was the departure from the adulatory rituals of Maoist orthodoxy, with its fixation on supposedly inviolate writings.

— Even Mao memorial literature, usually highly hagiographic, was turned to the editors' purposes. One prominent example, a conversation between Mao and some railway workers, was used to show how much the chairman allegedly regretted that there were simply no books left to read, because the outstanding works of literature had all been discarded as "poisonous weeds" during the Cultural Revolution. Mao was aggrieved that most operas had been forbidden; he actually preferred the original versions, later repudiated, of the model films on the Cultural Revolution. In short, Mao was shown to be a concerned critic of the Cultural Revolution!

— Finally, a letter from Mao Zedong to Guo Moruo suggesting the party chief's deep admiration for Guo's scientific accomplishments signaled an appeal to scientists in 1978-79 to become productive again, to write books, and thereby to ensure themselves the support of the leadership. Yet another important reason for publishing the letter was the fact that it was one more instance of Mao's remarking on some of his own political mistakes, as at the conference of 7,000 cadres.

To sum up, we can say that publication of the series B individual texts was meant as a further, and in this instance quite emphatic, legitimation of Deng's new pragmatic policies. Texts were selected and edited with an eye to the pragmatic strategy of economic development under the rubric "seek the truth in facts," and hence toward an accelerated expansion of scientific research and appropriation of the most modern technological know-how.

A "purification" process was waged in the ideological superstructure whereby, first, Mao Zedong was separated from the later Mao cult (the various forms of leftist idolatry); second, an attempt was made to restore a basic trust in publication practices by releasing facsimile versions of texts that implied Mao's own opposition to this cult; and third, the publication of his writings was portrayed as a process reflective of changing editorial considerations rather than adherence to the orthodoxy of a few rigid phrases.

With Mao now described as just one leading figure among others in the party, surrounded by other capable top-level functionaries, it became feasible to publish in assorted periodicals and individually a series of new Mao texts and writings of secondary importance, without the national press being compelled to trumpet every text as if it were the latest gospel of the party. Only the most important texts were published in Red Flag, the party's theoretical organ. In this manner Mao's statements were incorporated into a series of posthumously published statements of other leading cadres, which were now also cited in the press as the legitimating wellsprings of Deng's policies.

The initial attempts to legitimate the pragmatic road required a redefinition of the concept of "continuing revolution"; to wit, Mao's central concept of the mass campaign was to be transformed into a formula for technological modernization. This turnaround, which could hardly be justified in the historical context, was intended to imply a retroactive condemnation of the Cultural Revolution and to mark out the proposed new line in party history, one that condemned the mass campaigns after late 1957 as left-deviationist and sought historical parallels in Mao's defeat of the left-deviationist Wang Ming in the thirties.

In keeping with this "purification" process, those leading cadres of the older generation who had withdrawn into semi-obscurity or whom Mao had expelled were honored in various ways, and the party as a whole was moved into the spotlight. Those who had been brought low during and after the Cultural Revolution were duly rehabilitated. In addition, leading intellectuals (and the intelligentsia in general as a social stratum) had their good names restored and were administratively promoted into new positions, after years of immobility.

A comparison of phases A and B of these Mao text publications shows that the political sophistry described in Chapter 7, by which the new coalition tried to create an illusion of continuity with the radical politics of the past (though this was undermined by the minority opposition faction's resistance to Deng's course), had now given way to a straightforward legitimation of the pragmatist position. The first series of texts took a toll on the historical Mao, since the radical Maoism inherent in a number of them was quite at odds with the pragmatic new politics they were supposed to condone. A contradiction emerged in the second phase as well, with Mao now portrayed as a scientific pragmatist in accord with Deng's new policies. Basic Maoist conceptions such as the mass campaign and the Cultural Revolution were relegated to the sidelines while Mao's activities in his last years were passed over in silence. Ironically, Western Mao scholars found that they too had to shift gears, this time to preserve the radical Mao from being buried under this new interpretation!

Once the new course had been consolidated in 1981, the political use of individual Mao texts became less problematic; given a general dismantling of the Mao cult and a dying down of controversy over the new political course, the practice of publishing such texts lost much of its significance. It remains to be seen whether a diminishing need to legitimate the new policies will eventually lead to a phase of growing realism with regard to Mao's historical image as it is shaped by future publication practices.

d) Clear sailing for a Deng version of Mao's Selected Works? Commotion over Volume VI

The Politburo's decision shortly after the Shanghai radicals' October 1976 defeat to publish additional volumes of the *Selected Works*, with Hua Guofeng as nominal editor and Wang Dongxing in *de facto* control, had entailed the formulation of an interim interpretation of the events of 1949-1957 for the new Volume V. However, owing to the shift in course after the Central Committee Work Conference and the Third Plenum in late 1978, that interpretation had become obsolete and required revision. The official dedogmatization of the Mao cult, and further, the fulminating unofficial criticism of Mao both in the Hong Kong left press and in

Chinese wall posters (whose themes found an echo in the official press as far as evaluation of the general foundations of radical Maoism was concerned), had by late 1978 created a climate that was decidedly inauspicious for the publication of a Volume VI,[142] which the Hua/Wang editorial staff had already completed and had translated. The 1979 plenum's decision to downplay the political purge and to focus all efforts on building the economy had the clear implication that some time would elapse between the publication of Volume V and the subsequent volumes of Mao's Selected Works. The disbanding of the editorial committee of the Selected Works and the appointment of Deng's close associate Hu Qiaomu (whose posts included the directorship of the Academy of Social Sciences in Beijing) to head the committee[143] made the hiatus even more conspicuous. Hua's outlines for Volume VI and subsequent volumes were discarded, much as the radicals' had been. Meanwhile, the Selected Works editorial committee developed a new profile, more to Deng Xiaoping's liking, for future volumes. Indeed, the Hua outline of 1978-79 for Volume VI included the Great Leap Forward, now undergoing a major reinterpretation, and the readjustment period in the early sixties, for which Liu Shaoqi and Deng Xiaoping had been responsible. The question of how to evaluate Mao's mass campaigns during the Great Leap Forward and the Cultural Revolution, and the readjustment period between them, had been a subject of controversy. It was due to the need for a new official interpretation of these events that Volume VI and the outlines for subsequent volumes which Hua and Wang were in the midst of preparing had to be discarded.

The basic contours of a possible new "Deng" Volume VI had been established by December 1978. Important aspects, if not all, of both movements were treated as left-deviationist, while the period of readjustment was depicted as a necessary policy of recuperation. Thus, in subsequent volumes, the launching of the Cultural Revolution would appear as a highly incriminating repetition of previous left-radical errors.

Two central events may serve here to illustrate the striking array of versions of the PRC's history and of Mao's role in it, as well as the tension between the repudiated Hua version of Volume VI and an interpretation that might be anticipated under Deng's influence. At the Lushan conference in 1959, Marshal Peng Dehuai had spoken out against the excesses of the Great Leap Forward, and for this he lost his post as defense minister after a Politburo struggle in which Mao prevailed over the majority. In Peng's rehabilitation at the Third Plenum in December 1978, the documents of the case at first omitted mention of this clash. However, from the overall context of the discussion, and in particular from an official Peng-rehabilitation article published in 1979 by Lu Dingyi,[144] another victim of the Cultural Revolution, it became clear that the position taken by Peng in 1959 was approved by the Deng editors and that Peng's criticism of the Leap might even appear as an addendum to a future Selected Works VI. This meant in fact a transparent criticism of the political maneuverings of Mao Zedong and his colleagues at the Lushan Plenum and a complete transposal of political right and political wrong, which cast doubt on the wisdom of any further publication of the Mao canon. Indeed, the continuing attempts of Deng's propagandists to clear the ideological waters only made Mao's late writings more vulnerable to criticism as examples of the party leader's mistakes, so that at best, further publication of Mao's writings would be but a historical documentation of his errors and mistakes, and hardly an instrument in the services of state Maoism.

A second important example of the successive shifts of direction was the treatment of the case of Liu Shaoqi[145] and political Liuism. Hua's Volume V portrayed Liu as a negative figure who early on had advocated a false line. This position would hardly be tenable in any prospective Volume VI, since a new evaluation of Liuism, Liu's role, and his partial rehabilitation had already been initiated at the Work Conference and the Third Plenum. Liu would be officially rehabilitated at the Fifth Plenum in February 1980.

Thus, in contrast to the period from 1951 through 1953, when three volumes of Mao's Selected Works appeared in rapid succession presenting a unified perspective, at the end of 1978 it was clear that the interpretation of Mao's writings would continue to be be a hotly disputed political issue as would the final definition of the canon, inasmuch as the interpreters had already managed to produce two diametrically opposed interpretations in the brief time that had elapsed since Mao's death.

e) The technique of "immunity formulas": Mao is temporarily spared direct responsibility for mistakes

From late 1977 until the period immediately following the Third

Plenum, criticism of Mao in the official media remained indirect and rather mild. Even Mao's most obvious political errors were carefully side-stepped. This contrasted sharply with the vehement criticisms and condemnation of Mao's basic political decisions then appearing in Hong Kong's left press, which was sympathetic to Deng, and in wall posters within the PRC.

Mao's mistakes had been given only indirect airing, in allusions to the 1962 speech to 7,000 cadres, published in mid-1978 and quoted repeatedly in the press, and in the above-mentioned 1944 letter to Guo Moruo,[146] which was released late in 1978. In the wake of the Work Conference and the 1978 plenum, pressure intensified to deal head-on with the ultra-leftist mistakes made during the anti-rightist campaign that followed the Hundred Flowers, during the Great Leap Forward, and during the Cultural Revolution, and quite generally to take issue with the ultra-left line that had done such obvious harm to China's economic and political development. This narrowed the focus of criticism more and more to Mao personally as one of those chiefly responsible for many obviously damaging political errors. The sweeping rehabilitations that took place between 1978 and 1979, and the concomitant condemnation of the thousands of leading cadres who were either directly or indirectly sacrificed to the Deng group's struggles against leftist radicalism, indeed invited attacks on the party leader as the person chiefly responsible and demanded an official reassessment of earlier struggles over the political line. However, Deng Xiaoping's official propagandists stopped short of a full-scale de-Maoization on the order of the de-Stalinization drive that had taken place in the Soviet Union. In order to fend off direct attacks on Mao, the center came up with a simple ideological device. The newspapers published assessments of past controversial incidents that incorporated what we shall call "immunity formulas"; that is, every explanation included a rather transparent excuse exempting Mao from any responsibility for the actions being condemned. Expedient statements were issued, transparently false interpretations were devised, and on the whole a flimsy mantle was thrown over Mao's controversial decisions or his involvement in events that were now under a cloud of suspicion. In the furious wall poster attacks that ensued, this tactic was assailed as a "smokescreen." Below are but a few examples showing how these immunity formulas were used; the list could be lengthened at will.

— In connection with the hundreds of thousands of rehabilitations carried out under Deng's auspices, People's Daily observed[147] that there was no way around the fact that innocent people had been wrongly condemned. In the same breath, however, the party paper dismissed the question of the party chairman's responsibility, asserting that if Mao were still alive he himself would have taken on the task of righting these wrongs.

— In late 1978, after the April 1976 Tiananmen incident was reclassified from a "counterrevolutionary" intrigue to a "revolutionary" mass uprising (this of course was tantamount to a rehabilitation of Deng Xiaoping and his policies), an explanation was needed for Mao's involvement in the incorrect Politburo decision that had led to the second dismissal of Deng and his closest colleagues. Deng, as everyone remembered, had been removed on Mao's own urging. Now, in 1978, Deng was saying that Mao had already been seriously ill at the time of the Politburo's wrong decision, when Hua Guofeng had been in charge of the Central Committee. Indeed, not even Hua had been able to see Mao personally at the time; the only person who had access to him was a member of the Shanghai faction. The chairman was so ill that he could neither speak coherently nor make sound judgments. "Had Mao been in a position to form his own views about things, he certainly would not have made such a decision. He was, after all, the one who had protected me [Deng] during the Cultural Revolution."[148]

— The case of the deliberate attack (which touched off the Cultural Revolution) levied by Yao Wenyuan against Wu Han for his play "Hai Rui Dismissed from Office" was a bit too complicated to be explained away by such a facile excuse as "a wrong decision attributable to illness." Indeed, there were statements by Mao personally urging Yao to write the article. In November 1978, after condemning Yao's 1965 diatribe as a bungled piece of slander, Guangming Daily felt compelled to add that the late Mao had in no way ordered the publication of the controversial shot that started the Cultural Revolution, maintaining instead that the blame lay solely with Mao's wife, Jiang Qing, who with chief party ideologue Chen Boda and Zhang Chunqiao had herself fabricated the widely publicized instruction to Yao.[149]

— The media used a similar tactic to explain Mao's association with the five Red Guard leaders who in late December 1978 were condemned by the Beijing City Party Committee as counterrevolutionaries responsible for acts of "sabotage during the Cultural Revolution." An existing protocol[150] of a conversation between

Mao and these "little generals," though it shows Mao attempting to exert a moderating influence on the Red Guards, otherwise serves merely to highlight Mao's strategy of mobilizing an army of young activists. Beijing's Party First Secretary Lin Hujia, Deng's replacement for the already compromised and dismissed Wu De, declared at a mass rally that Mao had on many occasions criticized the careerists and ex-Red Guard leaders Nie Yuanzi and Kuai Dafu and had given instructions that they were to be severely punished, but that the Gang of Four had prevented this from happening.

— The resumed campaign attacking Lin Biao culminated in a condemnation of the forms taken by the Mao cult and Mao canon during the Cultural Revolution. One commentary asserted that in 1967 Mao had energetically rejected the formula then in wide use in the personality cult characterizing him as the "great teacher, great leader, great commander-in-chief, and great helmsman."[151]

— Finally, Mao's personal responsibility for the controversial decision to dismiss Marshal Peng Dehuai at the Lushan conference in July 1959 was passed over in silence, although Peng had been rehabilitated at the Third Plenum and was explicitly praised for his objection to the precipitate introduction of communes during the Great Leap Forward. Guangming Daily[152] took pains to deny that Wu Han's historical play on the dismissal of Hai Rui contained an allegory on the fate of Defense Minister Peng, although it was common knowledge in China that the play had particularly enraged Mao because of its indirect but unmistakable appeal for Peng's rehabilitation.

It does not require much imagination to surmise how someone who had lived through the Cultural Revolution would react to such immunity formulas. At any rate, in mid-December 1978 the wall posters attacked Deng Xiaoping directly for his role in covering up Mao's responsibility for the Tiananmen incident. One poster commentary concluded that it would be a good idea for "Vice-chairman Deng to come here and read the wall posters, instead of making excuses for Mao's mistakes."[153]

When one considers the history of the campaign device as used in the CCP, it is not at all surprising that tactical dodges and subterfuges such as these should initially be played out on the battlefield of reinterpretation. The individual incidents for which Mao was patently responsible had to be handled impersonally and one by one before Deng Xiaoping and his ideologists would be prepared to mount their major attack on Mao for his failed policy during the Great Leap Forward and the Cultural Revolution and for his later support of the Shanghai radicals. Of course, one might as easily invoke a simpler explanation: that such maneuvers were necessary if Mao was to be granted immunity, and that reasons of state required his protection from any probing criticism in the future as well.

f) Stalin and Khrushchev: Deng's "lessons" from the Soviet classics and from the history of the USSR

"Lessons" from the history of the Soviet Union, and especially, selected parallels to Stalin and his policies, figured as a counterpoint to the internal ideological debate in China. Since the Sino-Soviet split China had held Stalin in high esteem, partly out of protest against the "revisionist" Soviet leadership; still, the issue of Stalin had not been specifically addressed in some years. Now texts of his were printed in Chinese newspapers to be used for study purposes, serving the same legitimating function as the series of new Mao texts.

i) The publication of annotated Stalin texts parallel to the publication of new Mao texts: Themes. In late 1978 three documents (or excerpts) by Stalin plus appropriate interpretations were printed in Chinese national circulation newspapers. Additional commentaries on them appeared in the press on a number of occasions. In addition, individual articles dealt with specific Soviet political experiences or with Stalin's political approach.

— The first text, published in early November 1978, was an extract from a speech made by Stalin to the Comintern in which he criticized Zinoviev as a "revisionist leader, a bourgeois conspirator, and a traitor to the CPSU(B)," and contemptuously dismissed Zinoviev's notion of "revisionism." According to Zinoviev, Stalin maintained, every improvement, every refinement in old formulations or particular ideas of Marx and Engels, and especially, their replacement with formulations adapted to changed circumstances, was revisionism. Stalin cited numerous examples of Lenin's creative emendations of theory which would not have been permissible according to Zinoviev's criteria. This line of argu-

Texts on Stalin and the Soviet Union

Article	Stalin texts (excerpts)
1. RMRB, September 25, 1978 (individual thematic texts)	1. GMRB, November 12, 1978. December 13, 1926, Stalin's Works, Chinese edition, Vol. 9, pp. 86-90. Stalin's ridicule of Zinoviev's understanding of revisionism, Summary of the Seventh Expanded Meeting of the Executive Committee of the Comintern.
2. RMRB, November 20, 1978; PR, December 19, 1978, No. 50, pp. 10-12 (abridged). Attack on Wang's opposition to rehabilitations; comparison of the purges, the Cultural Revolution, and the Yan'an movement; comparison of Khrushchev and Wang Dongxing.	2. RMRB, November 24, 1978, and November 26, 1978. April 23, 1920, Stalin's speech on Lenin's fiftieth birthday, Stalin's Works, Chinese edition, Vol. 4, pp. 280-82. Political leaders acknowledge their mistakes; an attack on such mistakes does not destroy their reputation!
3. NCNA, January 2, 1979. Article by Huang Kecheng from Liberation Army News, January 1, 1979. De-Stalinization–de-Maoization; Peng (Deng) opposes Mao's wrong policies.	3. GMRB, December 23, 1978. January 26, 1934, Report to the Seventeenth Party Congress of the CPSU, Stalin's Works, Chinese edition, Vol. 13, pp. 316-18. An attack against the purported left-wing line and the view that poverty is socialism.

RMRB — People's Daily. NCNA — New China News Agency. GMRB — Guangming Daily. PR — Beijing (Peking) Review.

ment fitted neatly into the Chinese ideological debate. It was clear that the expression "old formulations" (jiu gongshi) was meant to refer to Wang Dongxing's argument that Mao's teachings must not be distorted.

— A second text of Stalin's was published to set forth this argument in even more concrete terms, relating it directly to Mao and his politics. In late November China's national newspapers published a speech Stalin gave on the occasion of Lenin's fiftieth birthday in 1920. In it Stalin praised "Comrade Lenin" for his modesty and courage to admit his own mistakes. Stalin pointed to two episodes, one in 1905 and one in 1917, during the course of which Lenin had revised some of his own incorrect views.

— A third text of Stalin's which had been delivered at the Seventeenth Party Congress in 1934 criticized the "ostensibly left-wing but in reality rightist" views of leading cadres on the poverty and wealth of collectivized workers and peasants: certain leftist blockheads had idealized poverty as the eternal bulwark of Bolshevism and socialism. The task of Leninists, Stalin continued, was not to perpetuate and preserve poverty, for "who would want that sort of so-called socialism?" Here was another attack on the dogmatic Maoist ideologists around Hua Guofeng and Wang Dongxing who disapproved of Deng's new pragmatic economic course as a betrayal of Maoism.

These and similar themes appeared time and time again in articles dealing with Stalin and the Soviet Union. The whole of the argument contained in the three articles reappeared in a commentary published as a special article in both national newspapers simultaneously in late September 1978. In them the commentator argued that politics and ideology had to be further developed, new theses had to replace old ones, Marxism had to be "developed" and "enriched." Marxism's inherent relation to practice had to be maintained and any leadership cult rejected, because a "Marxist scientific attitude" requires a deep respect for objective reality and "not for individual opinions or persons." In his Economic Problems of Socialism in the USSR Stalin had already established that the economic laws of socialism are independent of man's will, and that therefore they cannot be created, changed, or eliminated. "We should not expect that a revolutionary party can be 100 percent correct in its daily struggles, it can only be correct on the whole and in essence. For this reason Comrade Mao Zedong stressed that no political party or person is infallible."

The text went on to say that the principle "one divides into two" applies to every party and every person, and that anyone who believes a political party or a person to be outside the compass of critical analysis is guilty of "metaphysics" or "historical idealism." One should expect that a party or a person can and will make only small mistakes and that they will correct these as soon as possible.

A second article which also appeared in People's Daily drew striking parallels between the purges in the Soviet Union and the Great Proletarian Cultural Revolution along with the rehabilitations that became necessary after these events. One of the chief arguments of the Hua/Wang faction in the ideological struggle of 1977-78 centered on opposition to a sweeping rehabilitation of the victims of the Cultural Revolution and the 1957 anti-rightist campaign and to the indulgent treatment of intellectuals in general.

The major parallels between the Cultural Revolution and the Stalin purges were drawn in a commentary written for People's Daily in late 1978 entitled "A Historical Lesson on Correcting Unjust Verdicts." The article stated that Stalin's purges prior to 1937 were thoroughly correct because the party was in need of a cleansing and "counterrevolutionaries" had to be defeated. It went on to say that the purge had unfortunately led to some unjust verdicts as Stalin himself had observed in his report to the Eighteenth Party Congress in March 1939, whereupon some of these "mistakes" were corrected. It was pointed out, however, that in contrast to what had occurred in the Soviet Union, Mao's conduct of purges and the repression of counterrevolutionaries had been in accordance with the principle "kill no one and imprison only few."

As the Chinese media portrayed it, guilt for the Soviet Great Purge and the Gulag lay not with Stalin, curiously, but with individual "careerists" within the party. Khrushchev had simply used the Soviet people's outrage over the injustices of the Stalin era to his own advantage and had stirred up unrest by attacking Stalin and defaming the socialist system and the dictatorship of the proletariat in the Soviet Union. But Khrushchev himself had behaved as a ruthless tyrant in Moscow and the Ukraine during the Great Purge. He had won Stalin's trust as a hardliner during the purges — which is precisely how he was able to reach such a high position. His later de-Stalinization policy had exactly the same purpose — to establish himself firmly in power.

With this argument the Deng ideologists executed a remarkable maneuver by which the obvious parallels between Deng's de-Maoization and Khrushchev's de-Stalinization were neatly circumvented. In the internal party debate in 1978 Deng obviously had been accused of Khrushchevism, as had Liu before him; indeed, this had been part and parcel of the radical argument since the Cultural Revolution. Now the Deng group devised an analogy that deflected the charge of Khrushchevite revisionism onto their opponent Wang Dongxing; they also established an effective distinction between de-Stalinization and de-Maoization, showing that de-Stalinization had been wrong, if for no other reason than that the official criticism of Stalin had gone too far.

Another nuance, one with ominous implications for the future assessment of the Cultural Revolution, was an additional parallel drawn to the Stalinist purges. Not only the Cultural Revolution but also the Yanan rectification movement was analyzed in the light of Soviet events. The Chinese commentator argued that rehabilitations were to be different in cases of injustice that occurred while the leadership was following a correct line as compared with a period when an incorrect line was being pursued. In the former case, e.g., the Yanan movement, it was to be expected that political amends would be made, as indeed they were. If the leadership was pursuing an incorrect line (as in the Cultural Revolution), however, then those who represented the correct line would have to take action to correct the mistakes, "seizing the appropriate opportunity" — an allusion to and a legitimation of the October 1976 routing of the Gang of Four.

ii) The Chinese perspective for 1979: What is the difference between de-Maoization and de-Stalinization? In early 1979 the Chinese press took up the problem of de-Stalinization versus de-Maoization in another parallel to the Soviet Union, which was developed via an elaborate multi-leveled system of symbolic references. An argument between Soviet and Chinese top-level cadres in 1956 was cited in which the Chinese expressed their indignation over the nature of de-Stalinization, which they felt was going too far. On April 6-8 of that year (the year of the Twentieth Party Congress) a Soviet government delegation headed by A. I. Mikoyan, first vice-chairman of the Council of Ministers of the USSR, was in Beijing, and Mikoyan was received by Mao. The next day, the two sides issued a communique that glossed over their differences. In the 1979 review of these events, China's news agency published a report prepared by former General Chief-of-Staff Huang Kecheng concerning the role of his immediate superior, Defense Minister Peng Dehuai, who, along with Huang, was to fall in 1959. Peng, it may be remembered, was removed from all of his offices by Mao for his criticism of the Great Leap Forward, and later met an unworthy end during the Cultural Revolution; he was not rehabilitated until after Mao's death (as was Huang), by Deng Xiaoping at the Third Plenum in late 1978. Huang's report said:

> The old soldier Peng [Dehuai] especially despised the sort of know-it-all cadres who always played it safe, shifting with the wind, paying no heed to principles, and making no distinction between right and wrong. He bitterly hated the two-faced types whose appearance belied their thoughts and who said one thing but did another. We recall that in 1956, while a Soviet delegation was visiting

> our country, the old soldier Peng asked Mikoyan the following question point-blank: "Stalin made his mistakes. Why didn't you express your views about his mistakes while he was alive? Now you are going all out in opposing him after his death!" Mikoyan answered: "We didn't dare to state our views at the time. If we had, we would have lost our heads!" The old soldier's reply left no room for misunderstanding: "Anyone who is afraid of death shouldn't call himself a Communist!" That's the kind of person our old soldier Peng was! When the interest of the party and the people was at stake, it was impossible for him to keep his views to himself. As he once said: He would have his say, even if it meant death![154]

The point of this story, which was partly aimed at the radical Maoist opposition still putting up resistance within the party, was its clear line of demarcation between Soviet de-Stalinization and China's de-Maoization campaign, which had already started up some time ago in Hong Kong's left press under the rubric "a reassessment of Mao." As the Chinese portrayed it, in the Soviet Union spineless opportunists under party leaders such as Khrushchev had bloodied their hands in Stalin's purges and then went overboard in their criticism of the Soviet leader, whereas in China, one was to infer, a bold but limited criticism of the personality cult was called for, and indeed had begun, because mistakes that had been made had to be straightened out. Peng Dehuai's opposition to Mao on the issue of the communes, which he had voiced at the 1959 Lushan conference without any regard for personal loss or gain, was an example of an early stand against Mao's impetuous leftist mass campaign line.

Another implicit parallel may be drawn between Peng's fearless protest — which, to be sure, had to wait twenty years for vindication in the PRC — and the implementation of Deng Xiaoping's new modernization policy after Mao's death. Deng, who twice had risked everything, in opposing the Cultural Revolution and the radical Shanghai faction (the Gang of Four), had simply had the good fortune, unlike Peng Dehuai, not only to survive but to emerge the victor in the end. This attack on de-Stalinization thus not only served as a symbolic legitimation of Deng Xiaoping's moderate criticism of the late Mao, and hence of Deng's pragmatic new policy, but also helped to discredit the radical Maoist rearguard.

To sum up, a review of the quotations from Stalin and of commentaries on Stalin and the Soviet Union that appeared in the Chinese press shows that they were all used against the Maoist minority opposition, under attack since November–December 1978; these same materials undoubtedly were also used as study texts at the grass-roots level. The charges of revisionism against Deng's line were held up to ridicule, while the radical Maoism of the Hua/Wang opposition was shown to be a dogmatic doctrine, far removed from reality, that could promise only a leadership of toadying cadres, incapable of political action. The Hua/Wang faction's resistance to Deng's sweeping rehabilitations had to be broken, just as the radical Maoist violations of the most elementary economic principles had to cease. The specious left-wing line glorifying the collective poverty in agriculture and industry had to be combated. On the other side of the coin, Deng's line of "development" and "enrichment" of the state ideology and his emphasis on practical political goals now appeared to be necessary and correct since even great leaders like Mao had made mistakes, and to correct their mistakes was not at all to deny their greatness. Stalwart dissidents like Deng Xiaoping and Peng Dehuai were the new heroes of the party, the only persons with the authority to carry out a limited de-Maoization, which had nothing in common with Khrushchev's cowardly and intemperate assault on Stalin's stature as a political leader (Khrushchev, of course, being equated with Wang Dongxing, via the implication that Wang was just as involved in the purges of the Cultural Revolution as Khrushchev had been in Stalin's purges).

In a broader sense, what these homilies about Stalin and the USSR amounted to was yet another form of "shadow boxing," with historical parallels and lessons being drawn so as to sway the middle- and lower-level leadership and the public at large to Deng Xiaoping's new political course, which was still on a rather shaky ideological footing.

But many of these newly conceived parallels were quite dubious and far-fetched — for example, the portrayal of Stalin as the guarantor of a nondogmatic political atmosphere and an opponent of the personality cult. The distortion of Khrushchev's role and the downplaying of Stalin's responsibility for the Gulag compel one to draw some rather unflattering conclusions about the proponents of the new course in China. Rather than dispensing altogether with such hopelessly convoluted analogies (the parallel between the Cultural Revolution and the Stalinist purges is the only one that could be considered apt) and instead, legitimating the new course in terms of its own objectives, the new leadership chose to make a pretense of orthodoxy. The "classic" statements they invoked, like the parallels, held up only as long as one did not inquire into the context or historical background. Their egregious but cleverly fashioned distortions of the past display such an appalling contempt of truth as to cast even their soundest assertions under a cloud of suspicion. What is perpetuated here is a tradition of historical exegesis which treats the past as a storehouse of "cases" that can be used to interpret and influence action in the present; this of course invites manipulation of the historical facts so that they can be fitted into a preordained system that radiates certainty and harmony.

In addition to its rebuttal of the radical left's case against the new leadership, this discussion of the Stalin theme contained an implicit attack on the mounting trend toward a reassessment of Stalin in the Soviet Union. Back in 1969 the Institute of Marxism-Leninism in Moscow had planned a special session in honor of Stalin on the occasion of the dictator's ninetieth birthday, and the party newspaper Pravda had prepared a special editorial for this date — which, however, never did find its way into print on account of Polish and Hungarian objections plus the anticipation of protests from other communist parties and world public opinion. The problem came up again with renewed sharpness in 1979.[155] The first sign that the Soviet leadership had decided to rescue Stalin from his historical limbo as a "nonperson" was the quasi-official publication of a short biography of Stalin that included a portrait of the dictator; the book recounted Stalin's career in a bare, matter-of-fact chronology without invective, once again referring to him as the eminent leader of the CPSU and the Soviet state, the international Communist movement, and the labor movement, and as a theoretician and propagandist of Marxism-Leninism. The tone of earlier Stalin criticism was absent until the last sentence, where we read: "In addition to these positive aspects, Stalin's activity was marred by political and theoretical errors. The party has emphatically condemned the cult around Stalin's person . . . and stamped out its vestiges." Thus, the appearance in People's Daily of Chinese parables about Stalin contained as well an implicit rebuke of the Soviet leadership, one that took into account their moves toward a more positive reassessment of Stalin; to wit: You once condemned Stalin too harshly, so today you are forced to renounce your renunciation. Since 1956 we have consistently maintained a positive attitude toward this Soviet leader, and now you are compelled by the course of events to tacitly accept our (unchanged) assessment of Stalin.

This sidelight on a phase of Chinese neo-Maoist orthodoxy, with all its many ramifications on the question of de-Maoization, cannot be pursued in further detail here, but it should give some insight into the psychology of the CCP propagandists and shed some light on the ideological climate of the years 1978-79.

2. OPEN CRITICISM OF MAO ON WALL POSTERS IN THE PRC AND IN HONG KONG'S LEFT PRESS

a) The external course of events

The Deng faction decided to take over the device of wall newspapers from the radical arsenal of the Cultural Revolution and to adapt and apply it to their own purposes. This is clear from the massive amount of propaganda that began to appear on wall posters in November 1978. In addition to being directed at the Hua/Wang minority opposition, which had been boxed into a corner since the Third Plenum, the poster campaign raised demands for more freedom, civil rights, democracy, and an orderly legal system. All this was traceable to the Deng leadership — his critics within the party elite had almost no voice in the wall posters — so it was the Deng faction tooting its own horn when the posters proclaimed, correctly, that it had the full support of the people. Another medium the Deng faction used to raise issues without going through official channels was the Hong Kong left press, which sported a growing number of pro-Deng publications. In both these forums — the wall posters and the Hong Kong left press — an extraordinarily lively, not wholly coordinated campaign of open criticism of Mao was conducted throughout 1978-79. The arguments used in it merit our attention, first because the central problems were specified and publicized with a refreshing directness and without all the glosses that are the stock in trade of professional political ideologists, and second because they set the stage for the later, official campaigns of Mao criticism.

One difference between the campaign in the boisterous and aggressive Hong Kong left press and the wall poster campaign was that the latter really lasted only for about a week in Beijing, with but an occasional echo in a few cities such as Shanghai and Hangzhou; after the turbulent week of November 19-26, 1978, and through

January–February 1979, wall posters criticizing Mao appeared only sporadically in the PRC.[156] By contrast, from late 1977 the Hong Kong left press carried on its Mao critique as a general policy (the first high point being the call for a "campaign for a reassessment of Mao" in late-1978).[157] When the wall poster attacks in China stopped, the Hong Kong papers pushed on with their criticism of Mao and even served up spicy new details, which contributed greatly to swelling their circulation.

For the Deng group the use of the wall posters, which attracted lively popular participation, remained a ticklish affair. The PRC's official press treated the wall posters as a "nonevent" as far as their content was concerned, but did find grounds for tolerating this form of expression of opinion sanctioned by Mao himself. The wall posters found considerable echo via international press coverage as well as their feedback effect (intended by Deng) in the party's own internal information apparatus. Then, suddenly, a formal resolution adopted by the party leadership to curb the criticism of Mao brought all this to an abrupt halt. The reason for the retreat is not far to seek. A poster by some anonymous "party members" which appeared in early December suggests just how concerned certain leading party cadres must have been about some possible repercussions of the wall poster campaign. In this case, the complaint was about "false reporting by foreign journalists": "You are friends of the Chinese people, and therefore it is imperative that you understand the situation. The people are making their voices heard in China. What we want is democracy. You ought to be aware of all this and stop writing about demonstrations or about conflicts between Chairman Hua and Vice-chairman Deng, because they are in full agreement with one another."[158]

The wall newspaper campaign (in which the criticism of Mao was but one of several burning issues) was orchestrated to coincide with the crucial discussion at the expanded Central Committee Work Conference, which began in early November 1978. Deng Xiaoping was thus able to marshal from the streets some additional arguments with which to put pressure on his opponents, the shifty Hua and the cornered Maoist minority faction.

b) Criticism of internal developments in the PRC

i) May Chairman Mao be criticized at all? In view of the unassailable public stature Mao had attained during the Cultural Revolution if not earlier, even the question as to whether Mao might have made some mistakes, the expression of doubts as to his infallibility, or the simple placing of his person, the Mao cult, and the Mao canon in any sort of critical light, presented a very difficult threshold to cross. Two official steps that had been taken toward breaking this taboo were the release in mid-1978 of the text in which Mao admitted to personal mistakes and the attack on Lin Biao's dogmatization of Mao's teachings. The question of Mao's vulnerability to criticism (now suddenly become rhetorical) was first translated into political terms in Hong Kong's left press, which opened its Mao debate in 1977 with the slogan "one divides into two."[159] Without any mention of Mao by name, the question as to whether the actions of "great" or "heroic" personalities could be critically evaluated was answered with a clear yes: Mao himself, despite his deep admiration for Stalin, had judged the Soviet dictator in the spirit of this maxim when he concluded in 1956 that Stalin could look back on a record of "70 percent positive achievements and 30 percent failures." This had been the Chinese leadership's hesitant response to the de-Stalinization debate in the Soviet Union at the time.

In the context of 1978, revival of the notion of complexity in the assessment of political personalities (de Gaulle and Tito had been so viewed in the PRC) raised the question as well of how to regard the "bad eggs," i.e., politically malignant figures, such as the leaders and followers of the Gang of Four? The view that ultimately prevailed was that the differentiating dialectic of the maxim "one divides into two" could not be applied to enemies of the people and that accordingly, they could continue to be painted in wholly negative terms. In any event, the establishment of these fine distinctions did not have much immediate effect. A few halting steps were taken toward a specification of Mao's errors, but these were rather inconsequential and isolated instances and stress was always laid on the fact that Mao himself had made efforts to correct his wrong decisions.

In the summer of 1978, however, the Hong Kong left press reported that massive criticism of Mao had already begun within the party and that a major controversy was being fought out. The reports matched up with what we know of the disagreement between the Deng faction and the Hua/Wang group, especially in discussing what was behind the Deng slogan "seek the truth in facts." The expressions used in these sources to refer to criticism of Mao are themselves interesting. The straightforward "criticism of Mao" (pi Mao) was considered too extreme and was generally avoided. For a while the Hong Kong left press made cautious use of "devaluation of Mao Zedong" (biandi), and then finally settled on "movement to reassess Mao" (ping Mao yundong). From time to time, the shorthand expression that was almost universally used in translations of Western reports — the term "de-Maoization" (fei Mao hua) — also appeared.

ii) Mao's cardinal political error: The mass campaigns. Once the Mao discussion was unleashed in the Hong Kong left press and then in the wall poster campaign in the PRC, criticism focused on the policies of the two decades since 1957 and became especially fierce with reference to the last decade before Mao's death. The wall posters confronted Mao with a catalogue of sins[160] and posed a series of leading questions. "Ask yourselves: How could Lin Biao have accumulated such power unless Mao had given his approval?" And further: Why didn't Mao see through Lin Biao, Jiang Qing, or the vice-premier and left ideologue Zhang Chunqiao? How could the Tiananmen incident have been labeled "counterrevolutionary"? How was it that Deng was expelled from office for a second time? How could a "campaign against the rightist wind" have been initiated in 1975-76? Other penetrating questions in the interrogatory asked whether Liu Shaoqi and other leading cadres of the "bourgeois headquarters" who were attacked during the Cultural Revolution had really "intended to lead China into darkness," or whether they simply had a difference of opinion with Mao. Was not the Cultural Revolution perhaps but an impetuous experiment? Was Mao unaware that other persons also knew how to use their heads and did not like to be regimented? And, if Mao were alive today, would he in fact welcome these questions? "A Marxist certainly would!"

A wall poster sharply critical of the system as a whole reproached Mao for having forced his developmental model on the nation without regard for the circumstances that obtained in the country, and for persisting in ruling through mass movements rather than by legal means even after 1957.

This raised the issue of the Hundred Flowers campaign, which was originally intended to enhance intellectual freedom but later evolved into a campaign against the right that condemned hundreds of thousands of people as "rightists."

The next mass campaign, the Great Leap Forward, was attacked head on as a politically meretricious failure, a scramble after delusory goals; the conventional euphemism of "the three difficult years" was thus exposed for what it was. On November 26, 1978, standing before the poster wall in Beijing, a cadre gave a bold speech calling for the rehabilitation of Marshal Peng Dehuai (heretofore a taboo subject): "Peng Dehuai was completely correct, the Maoist policy of the Great Leap Forward was an absurdity."

The Cultural Revolution was condemned in the wall posters as a national calamity, a great leap backward, the greatest setback China had suffered in its entire history: its only value was as a "lesson by negative example." One student wall poster proclaimed Mao's responsibility for the armed clashes that occurred during the Cultural Revolution, for the chaos in the country, for the decline in the nation's economy, and for the excesses of the personality cult.

Naturally, a favorite theme was Mao's close cooperation with the Shanghai faction (the Gang of Four), official "immunity formulas" notwithstanding: "Because he had begun to think metaphysically in his old age and for all sorts of other reasons," Mao supported and helped to power the Gang of Four, including his own wife, Jiang Qing. Here again, Deng's reference to Mao's illness was cited as a mitigating factor.

Finally, a central point in the attacks was Mao's "misjudgment" of the Tiananmen incident, causing a "popular uprising" to be condemned as "counterrevolutionary," and his responsibility for the second expulsion of Deng Xiaoping and his now ascendant group.

The left press and the wall posters brought Mao to account for his domestic policies; his foreign policy never figured as a central theme in either of these forums. However, from time to time criticism of Mao's attitude toward the Soviet Union and of his profligate, ideologically motivated developmental aid policies was heard. In the aforementioned speech by a cadre at a demonstration in Tiananmen Square, Mao's one-sided policy toward the Soviet Union, his "leaning to one side," was condemned. China, it was charged, had to wait until 1972 to establish diplomatic relations with the United States although the U.S. State Department had shown a willingness to do so as early as 1949: "Over twenty years were lost." "We were stupid to imitate the Soviets; that was the cause of all of China's mistakes and all of China's ills. The Russians are autocrats, they are tsars." So went the criticism, with a backhanded swipe at Mao's style of leadership as well. Mao's policies of generous economic aid to Third World countries also came in for some harsh treatment. One wall poster complained: "While people in many parts of China went begging on the streets, the dictator of our country distributed Chinese money to his dictator comrades in Vietnam and Albania." Here we have an airing of the disappointments occasioned by the Beijing leadership's ill-fated policies vis-à-vis Vietnam, which would lead to the invasion of that country in January 1979 along with the consequent Chinese refugee problems, Vietnam's invasion of Cambodia, and unrelenting media attacks from Albania, which continued to accuse China of betraying socialism.

c) A nepotistic dictatorship

The Maoist exercise of power became a hot issue in the wall poster debate. Overnight, the Chinese social order was given the label "social feudalism," which was compared to "national socialism." In Mao's last decade (1966-76), it was claimed, a "fascist regime" was in command. Premier Zhou Enlai had been the lone defender of the little man. Mao had permitted chaos to reign, so that a "democratic group" (the pragmatists) had had to wage a bitter struggle against the "fascist family dictatorship" (the radicals). This accusation of nepotism undoubtedly referred to the way Mao had come to rely on his wife Jiang Qing in Beijing, his nephew Mao Yuanxin in the northeast provinces, his niece Wang Hairong in the Foreign Ministry, and on other family members.

The old image of China's imperial despotism was conjured up from various perspectives. The First Emperor, Qin shihuang di (221–206 BCE) — to whom Mao Zedong, in a reevaluation of Confucian historiography, liked to be compared — although praised in the wall posters for his progressive role in "uniting the country" was also condemned for having "repressed the people and burned books." China, they said, had been under feudal rule for more than 2,000 years, including "the era of Mao Zedong." Under the heading "We have had enough of dictatorship," one wall poster cried out:

"Chinese, rise up. It is time to resist all dictators, whoever they may be. We must bring them to trial and pass judgment upon them!"

Speakers who appeared before the poster wall to address the demonstrators explained that leaders had to be criticized during their lifetimes. "We must not wait until emperors are dead to judge them; nor must we await the verdict of history. Only those leaders who allow themselves to be criticized are good leaders." Implicit here is a judgment on the legitimacy of the seizure of power in 1976, and on the handling of power in general.

One Beijing wall poster blamed Mao for having made the state into his personal property as had the feudal rulers before him, and asked how this could be reconciled with the constitution and with Marxism-Leninism. Another wall poster, referring to Marx's essay on the Paris Commune, said that the people must always be able to elect and remove their representatives, that this is a fundamental right of the people, and that this alone could prevent "the advance of opportunists and plotters."

Finally, the one known expression of self-criticism deserves mention in this context: it raised the question of conformity and opportunism, and the popular lack of will to resist certain repressive practices of the regime. The simple fact is that whatever was the current line was always what the people followed; the most generous judgment is that rebellion was always precluded by the regime's refined methods of repression. Nevertheless, self-criticism, e.g., for a lack of civil courage, was as good as absent from the wall poster discussion. However, in the last days of November 1978, during an officially organized demonstration of solidarity for Hua Guofeng, who was already under heavy pressure from the Deng group within the leadership, absolute silence set in when a member of the air force rather sarcastically asked bystanders if indeed it was so praiseworthy that people who during the Cultural Revolution had nothing short of hooted Deng Xiaoping to his fall were now, after the defeat of the Gang of Four, thronging the streets at the bidding of Vice-premier Deng without misgivings.

d) An outrageous personality cult

The theme of late Maoist depotism led into an attack on the cult surrounding Mao's person using terminology borrowed from the Soviet criticism of the Stalin personality cult (in Chinese: geren chongbai).

Acceptance of the Soviet model, it was said, had merely produced a Soviet-style dictatorship and perpetuated a thousand years of Chinese feudalism, for which Mao had to be held responsible. In a surprising detour around the analogy "revisionist: Deng the de-Maoizer equals Khrushchev the de-Stalinizer," the Hong Kong press paired Lin Biao with Khrushchev, since these two had built up the respective personality cults around Mao and Stalin and thence around their own persons. (It should be remembered that the official press had equated Wang Dongxing and Khrushchev with the same intention, i.e., to parry the Deng-Khrushchev revisionism parallel.) Of course, this equation was in many respects a rather high-handed way of relieving both Mao and Stalin of responsibility for the cults. But in spite of sporadic attempts to smooth things over, the discussion around the personality cult produced some hard conclusions in the wall posters. For example: "Chairman Mao is a human being and not a god. It is time we put him in his proper place. Only then will it be possible to uphold Marxism-Leninism-Mao Zedong Thought."

The wall posters and the left press adduced numerous examples of how much the "personality cult," the religious mystification of the leader as perpetrated by the Gang of Four, had weighed down upon the people and how any cadre who even suggested the possibility that Mao may have made mistakes was promptly branded a "counterrevolutionary" or "splitter." With the wisdom of hindsight, the wall posters picked up Deng Xiaoping's call for greater attention to the party rather than just its leadership figure, and to the contributions of veterans of the revolution and the period of construction (in an interview Deng had remarked that Mao had been a great strategist who accomplished great things, but that he had also made mistakes and was "not the only person" who had led China's revolution).

e) The controversy over the Mao mausoleum

The imagination of the wall poster writers was understandably fired by the latest symbol of the Mao cult, the mausoleum of the deceased party chairman on Tiananmen Square. There Mao's body was laid out in a crystal coffin past which the faithful filed in imitation of the Soviet and Vietnamese ritual, with some even permitted to bow during a solemn visit. The grandiosity of this hall was in no small part a reflection of the Hua faction's legitimation anxieties, as it was built before Deng Xiaoping had assumed political control. The commentaries on this topic in the wall posters undoubtedly echoed the controversy going on within the leadership and were enflamed by the comparative modesty of the tribute paid to Zhou Enlai. In late November 1978 several wall posters suggested that a memorial hall and bronze statue be erected in honor of Zhou Enlai on the same Tiananmen Square. The authors of the wall posters took some symbolic steps to raise the money for construction costs from public donations. They even went so far as to suggest names for a preparatory construction committee, including Deng's protégé Hu Yaobang, general secretary of the party.

In early January 1979 a nineteen-point human rights manifesto called for a Zhou memorial, but linked this petition with the unheard-of demand that Mao be removed from the mausoleum. Such a step would be completely justified, it said, from a "Marxist standpoint," for it would put an end to "feudal superstition." However, these radical cult wreckers were stumped by an ancillary problem: where then should the casket of the deceased chairman be placed?

Ceremonies held on January 7, 1979, to commemorate the third anniversary of Zhou Enlai's death confirmed that a process of rethinking was under way within the leadership. After that date[161] the Mao mausoleum remained closed for four months, until May. On the eve of the observance, workers erected scaffolding over the two entrances to the memorial hall and removed one of the two large marble plaques bearing the inscription "Memorial Hall for Chairman Mao" in the calligraphic script of Hua Guofeng. Word went around that the building would be rededicated to both Mao and Zhou. This did not come to pass. After the removal of Wang and Hua in 1981, Deng Xiaoping would shift to law and order policies and a reinforcement of the status quo. Zhou Enlai got publication of an edition of his _Selected Works_, but neither his own monument in the square nor a place of honor beside Mao in the mausoleum.

f) The ideology of Mao Zedong Thought

Despite the sharp criticism directed at the Mao dictatorship and

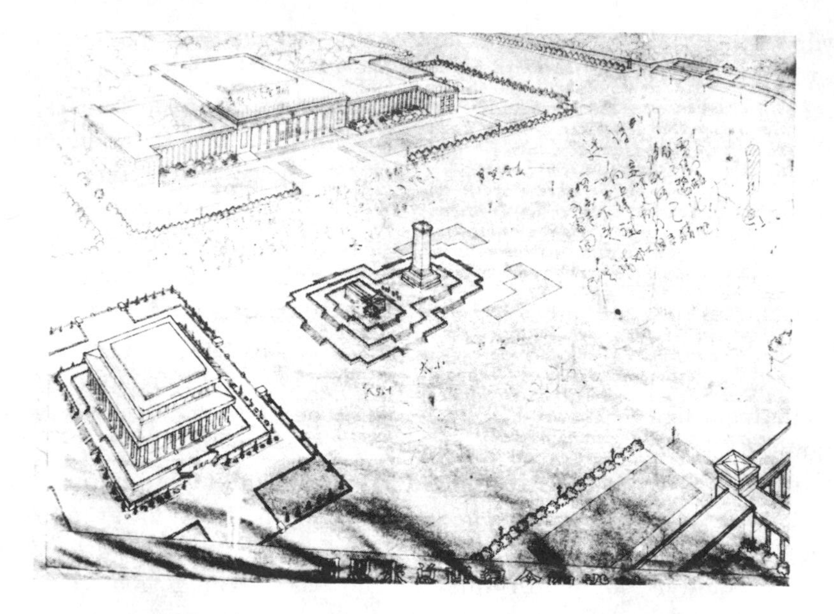

A Beijing wall poster from February 1979 showing the Mao Mausoleum (left) in Tienanmen Square with a (nonexistent) Zhou Enlai Mausoleum next to the column in the center. The handwritten commentary of a still dissatisfied wall poster reader on this "Plan of a Memorial Column for Premier Zhou": "It looks too small!" During this period of criticism of Mao some leading functionaries in the Politburo were convinced that the grass roots could be induced to find a rollback of the exaggerated Mao cult attractive by the simple ploy of an additional Zhou cult. This solution might not have pleased Zhou, who foresaw the coming conflict and dodged it by ordering that his ashes should be scattered over Chinese soil from the air. (Photograph: M. Morgenstern)

the cult surrounding the chairman, the question of state ideology was kept almost completely out of the official discussion, and for good reasons. Although the wall posters charged that the Cultural Revolution had engendered total ideological confusion so that no one knew any longer what was meant by Marxism and what was not, in November there appeared wall posters calling upon the Chinese people to "rise up and free themselves from all ideological yokes." One wall poster produced by a group from Guizhou stated: "To achieve human rights and democracy, we have to condemn and crush the dictatorship. We must smash the superstition of the past, we must destroy the great ideological wall of several thousand years of dictatorship."

Nonetheless, the discussion did not probe into the Mao ideology, and only in the Hong Kong press were there any indications[162] as to the nature of the controversy within the leadership concerning the continuing practice of publishing individual texts as well as Mao's Selected Works. The Hong Kong press pointed out that Mao's thought was by no means the exclusive product of an omniscient Mao, but rather a distillation of the general experience of the Chinese revolution and the Chinese path of development. Mao, in collaboration with high-ranking party cadres, had brought together the insights of many, and had "processed" them and raised them to a theoretical level. Even some of the texts in Mao's famed Selected Works had come also from the pens of Mao's colleagues. Finally, Mao's own writings had been revised and emended by many hands before being incorporated into the canon of the Selected Works. For example, the guideline of the new course, the "Ten Great Relationships" text, had been discussed within the party and revised before it acquired its final form, a process in which ideologist Hu Qiaomu had "performed a very meritorious service." In this respect, Mao Zedong Thought was not the product of a single person but rather the crystallization of the whole of the party's accomplishments and the wisdom of the entire Chinese people.

Once again, Deng's efforts to deflate Mao's accomplishments are apparent, as is an attempt to view the writings as collections of objective party documents, a history of the decisions reached at political meetings and conferences. This perspective was officially underscored after the plenum by the publication of Mao's letters to his commentator, the philosopher and ideologist Li Da.

g) The party resolution concerning the suspension of wall criticism of Mao

The outbreak of wall criticism of Mao initially evoked no voice of protest. Apparently, the party leadership thought it necessary to make a quick decision on how to respond to this situation at the Central Committee Work Conference then in session. On November 23, some five days after the outbreak of criticism, the first wall poster in defense of Mao appeared, bearing the title "If we want a proletarian democracy, we need a dictatorship of the proletariat."

According to the poster: "Chairman Mao was great, Premier Zhou Enlai was honest and frank, Chairman Hua Guofeng is wise. Whoever opposes Chairman Mao will come to a bad end, whoever opposes Premier Zhou will come to a bad end, and whoever opposes Chairman Hua will come to a bad end." This blanket statement, a patchwork of compromises, was not well received by the readers; a fistfight broke out in front of the poster wall when a youth who called out slogans in support of Mao was trounced by an angry crowd of about fifty persons.

On November 26 Deng personally announced the leadership's decision to halt the Mao campaign; the attacks had been a mistake, he said, and were not approved by the leadership. At a reception for a Japanese delegation in the Great Hall of the People, Deng declared that the mass campaign for a reassessment of Chairman Mao was being conducted without official party support; at the same time he absolved both Mao and Hua Guofeng of any responsibility for the Tiananmen incident.

The authorities then issued instructions to campaign activists to cease explicit criticism of Mao by name and to tone down their agitation around the rash demand for democracy. The front-page coverage of the campaign in the international press obviously made the leadership nervous, since activists were expressly warned not to speak about internal affairs with foreign journalists. A nineteen-point document issued by the Central Committee was read and studied within work groups; temperate in tone, the document concluded that while the merits of Chairman Mao should not be exaggerated, his mistakes were really comparatively minor.

New wall posters in defense of Mao now appeared bearing the long customary ritual portrait of the chairman. They praised Mao as a "modern Lenin" and called the dispute over Mao's status a battle between "two armies." Critics of Mao Zedong were warned to expect bitter defeat in the not too distant future. People who attacked Mao were once again called "bothersome fleas."

The pro-Mao wall posters proliferated into a sort of counter-campaign invoking Deng's statement that the Party Central Committee and the Chinese people would "never act like Khrushchev," i.e., China would not follow the example of Khrushchev's de-Stalinization. A Red Guard-style wall poster which warned "If the people who want to put up wall posters criticizing Mao Zedong will just let us know who they are, we will smash their dog heads in," included formulations reminiscent of Lin Biao: "Chairman

Mao is the red sun that shines in our hearts." These wall posters maintained that the task of the present generation was not to examine the shortcomings of Chairman Mao but to make the "four modernizations" a reality. Yet Deng's slogan "seek the truth in facts" also came under fire, with the argument that Mao's alleged mistakes and the Cultural Revolution had not yet been adequately tested by time and practical experience.

And then, around November 29, yet another round of wall posters began to appear, this time to denounce Deng's ban on attacks naming Chairman Mao. One poster declared that if Mao had made mistakes, then one ought to be able to criticize him openly: "You [Deng] can force the people back into silence, but that won't solve anything."

In any event, the party had wasted no time in squelching the first articulated criticism of Mao in the PRC that went straight to the heart of the problem. Later developments, such as the silencing of dissident papers, and finally in 1981 the official warning to foreign newsmen in Beijing to stop any reporting on "illegal" activities of one-time poster authors and dissidents ("They did not represent the views of the Chinese government," declared the Foreign Ministry) made things even clearer. The poster campaign of 1978 may have been silently backed by the Deng Xiaoping group, though officially Vice-chairman Deng had to restrain it; however, the moment the last of his opponents within the leadership was eliminated, i.e., after Hua's removal from the party chairmanship in 1981, the old ideals of governmental orthodoxy and intolerance quickly got the upper hand.

h) Is the judgment on Stalin — "70 percent positive achievements and 30 percent failures" — also applicable to Mao?

Now that we have described this dispute of 1978-79, which ended in a stalemate, we shall conclude by examining some of the forms into which the overall assessment of Mao has crystallized at the official level.

The expectation that criticism of Mao would evolve into a "movement of Mao criticism"[163] embracing the entire Chinese people, as demanded by a bold editorial in a pro-Deng Hong Kong journal in early December 1978, was ended by the party resolution. The rather vague general formulas that were proposed for the criticism ranged from the statement that Mao's "crimes had been consequential and serious" to the verdict that he had made "relatively serious mistakes."

But in the meantime, the ritualistic "70–30" formula had become entrenched as a correct and workable provisional motif for the official overall assessment of Mao; it was the same formula the CCP leadership had used twenty years earlier to weigh Stalin's "merits and mistakes" in counterposition to Khrushchev's de-Stalinization, which they considered excessive and politically ill-timed. The formula was applied quite generally to mean that Mao was "70 percent good and 30 percent bad," while alternate versions added qualifiers. For example, a 30-meter-long wall poster near the Mao mausoleum declared that "70 percent of what Chairman Mao did in the Cultural Revolution was to his merit, while 30 percent was in error," a judgment that accorded with the current assessment of the Cultural Revolution, although the latter avoided the question of Mao's responsibility for this campaign. Thus, in a curious contradiction (i.e., despite Stalin's positive image in the PRC), the Gulag dictator cast a dark shadow over Mao Zedong, so that people could now be heard to say in the new popular shorthand, "Mao was 30–70, like Stalin."

Deng Xiaoping made a visible effort to stick to this general assessment (after all, one could file an impressive number of accusations under the rubric of "30 percent failures" if need be). He did not distance himself from this line even in an interview with the American journalist Robert D. Novak in late November 1978; indeed he reinforced it with a superficially conciliatory and humorous self-critical comment on his own person, to wit: "I myself am only 60–40."[164] On his own account Deng marked out the far boundary of Mao criticism with his statement that "there would have been no new China without Mao Zedong," but even this claim came under attack in a Hong Kong left journal in March 1979.

In order to portray the Mao criticism formula as one "approved" by the chairman himself, the left press cited a humorous quotation from Mao in which he mused over how posterity would regard him. In one of his last years he was supposed to have remarked to a top-level official: "The life of someone like you is probably divisible into 30–70 percent. But don't be dissatisfied with this. Let me tell you, if it should come about that after my death I am assessed at 30–70, I'll be quite satisfied."[165]

3. THE INTERNAL PARTY DISCUSSION ON MAO ZEDONG AND THE SUPPRESSION OF THE MAOIST MINORITY

a) The Central Work Conference and the Third Plenum, November-December 1978

The full range of ideological issues along with some derivative questions were the subject of the Central Committee Work Conference held in November and the Central Committee Plenum held in December 1978, both in Beijing. The participants were leading cadres from the provinces, cities, and autonomous regions, commanders from the regional People's Army units, and cadres from the central party and government apparatuses as well as the mass organizations. The debate between the Deng group and the Maoist opposition around Wang Dongxing and other Deng opponents was extremely heated; the work conference, originally scheduled for three days, in fact lasted more than a month, from early November to mid-December. After a pause to review the results of the discussion, the Third Plenum of the Eleventh Party Congress met from December 18 to December 22. An official communique, quite detailed by the standards of earlier years, reported on the topics and results of both the conferences.[166] But for the most part the actual course of events at the meetings was not divulged; indeed, there was little indication of who had what to say on which topics.

The work conference and the plenum were accompanied by some confusing tunes played on the most varied instruments. In the first place, the well-orchestrated wall poster campaign, already discussed above, created an audience for itself in Beijing, while selected news items were leaked to the Hong Kong left press and individual Chinese leaders made themselves available for interviews that were carefully calibrated for internal or foreign consumption. The description that follows, where it goes beyond the text of the communique or is not based on specified official documents, is essentially a conspectus of these materials.

The international press played up the obvious tensions of the conference discussions in a less than responsible manner, despite — or indeed, because of — the general reserve of the Chinese media. While *Pravda* produced reports of a power struggle and an organic crisis of Maoism, the Hong Kong newspaper Mingbao, usually well-informed, speculated that Deng Xiaoping would become party chairman and premier, while Hua Guofeng would be forced to resign, a conjecture which leading Western newspapers including the New York Times passed along to their readers.[167] Deng Xiaoping felt himself compelled to give reassuring interviews to Japanese and Americans, declared his support for Hua Guofeng, and explained that he had no ambitions to become premier since he had already declined the post once before. He stated repeatedly that the political situation in China was stable and that there would be no shakeups within the leadership group. There is little doubt that the sense of uncertainty was rife also within China, since official versions of Deng's remarks were made public and became the principal study texts of a discussion on "stability and unity." Be that as it may, these assurances from the man who had by now become the leading figure in China were true only to the extent that no one in the Politburo or among the vice-premiers had yet been purged. What had happened, however, was that the Deng faction had succeeded in wresting key offices and functions out of the hands of the Hua/Wang group.

b) The conferences

As the communique stated, the plenum and the preparatory conference dealt with important problems of domestic and foreign policy; in line with the modernization efforts special focus was placed on general economic planning and the discussion of pressing questions in the agricultural sector. We shall pass over these topics for the present and concentrate on the ideological discussion of Maoism as well as the personnel shakeups that took place in the aftermath of these rearguard factional struggles.

"Ten Major Incidents"[168] were apparently dealt with at the conferences:

1. The Tiananmen incident
2. The January Storm
3. The February Countercurrent
4. The clique of the sixty-one traitors
5. The case of Peng Dehuai
6. The case of Tao Zhu
7. The case of Kang Sheng
8. The case of Xie Fuzhi

9. The case of Yang Shangkun
10. The "army's support of the left"

Some radical reassessments, both positive and negative, lay behind such an agenda. With the exception of the new light shed on the Tiananmen incident, which essentially amounted to a rehabilitatory readjustment of Deng Xiaoping's second fall in 1976, all the other items pertained to the Cultural Revolution — a clear sign that this, the greatest of all of Mao's mass campaigns, had already been subjected to an extensive reassessment at the two conferences, although the Third Plenum had decided to postpone an accounting for this campaign. In addition to the Cultural Revolution, the other mass campaigns of the past two decades and the concept of class struggle itself came in for discussion. Especially notable is the raising of the issue of the Great Leap Forward (since Peng Dehuai's resistance to the precipitous establishment of the communes had to be addressed). Here was the opening wedge for a complete reinterpretation of party history since the late fifties.

The discussion was dominated by the debate on the status of state Maoism as conceptualized in the pragmatism debate launched by Deng ("seek the truth in facts") and vigorously opposed by the Wang group. Another major topic was a critical reevaluation of Mao Zedong's role as a political leader which included a direct criticism of his mistakes, a subject kept out of the public discussion until 1981.

The individuals criticized at the conference included, aside from Mao, all the important members of the Hua/Wang faction, for example, Beijing's former mayor Wu De, and General Chen Xilian, denounced as an opportunist. These leading figures had to undertake a self-criticism. Even Chairman Hua Guofeng — who had profited from Deng's second fall, had been involved in the Tiananmen incident as the Minister of Public Security, and had opposed the Mao reinterpretation of 1978 — did not escape; he too presented a self-criticism which later circulated among party cadres. The late chief of intelligence and left-wing party theoretician Kang Sheng, who had been responsible for a good number of cadre purges during the Cultural Revolution, and former Security Minister Xie Fuzhi were also vehemently criticized.

Rehabilitation questions were the official focus of the plenum, particularly with respect to Marshal Peng Dehuai, who had lost the Defense Ministry to Lin Biao in the aftermath of the Great Leap Forward, and Tao Zhu, a former first secretary of the Guangdong

Provincial Party Committee and vice-premier. The rehabilitation of former Beijing mayor Peng Zhen was discussed but not implemented, since that would have entailed an unearthing and perhaps a reevaluation of the Liu Shaoqi affair. Peng Zhen had in fact once presented himself as one of Liu's close colleagues to Wu Han, author of the play "Hai Rui Dismissed from Office," which the left-wing party theoretician Yao Wenyuan, on instructions from Mao's wife, Jiang Qing, and Mao Zedong himself, had chosen as the target for the attack that precipitated the Cultural Revolution. Both Peng Zhen and the deceased Wu Han would soon be rehabilitated once the plenum broke the lingering resistance.

The "clique of the sixty-one traitors," also linked indirectly to Liu, counted both Bo Yibo (former vice-premier), and Yang Shangkun, officially rehabilitated at the plenum, among its ranks. During the Cultural Revolution an incident from the thirties had been disinterred and made into a pretext for criticizing and imprisoning a number of high-ranking cadres around Liu Shaoqi. The January Storm, in which the radicals seized power in Shanghai with the help of the Red Guards, was now painted in wholly negative terms, which was tantamount to a verdict against the Red Guard leaders and the Red Guards in general; in turn, the February Countercurrent of resistance to the cadre purges of the Cultural Revolution was now placed in a positive light.

However, given the communique's asseveration that the time was not ripe for an official reassessment of either the Cultural Revolution or the Liu Shaoqi affair, the one tangible result of the plenum and the conference (aside from the above reinterpretations) was the suppression of the Wang faction, which had to pay for obstructing the de-Maoization process. Deng achieved this by isolating (kaobianzhan) the most important cadres. They were nominally allowed to keep their positions in the Politburo and as vice-premiers; however, they found themselves hedged in from all sides by upstart members of the Deng group, and their influence was radically curtailed since they were stripped of their most important functions. The influence of Wang Dongxing in the ideological and propaganda domain was thus reduced to a minimum. Finally, a few military posts in the sensitive Beijing garrison and in the special 8341 bodyguard section for the Central Committee leadership were placed firmly in the hands of the Deng group.

c) The orthodox Maoist Wang Dongxing group is outmaneuvered

The opposition group around Wang Dongxing, with Chairman Hua as protector, found its power effectively reduced by the decisions made at the conference and the plenum on Deng's initiative. This was also the case with the party chairman personally, who in his self-criticism was obliged to advocate a more collective leadership and to stress the merits of the veteran party cadres, thus abandoning the imitative Hua cult. The practices of one-man rule and of circumventing the party hierarchy with "instructions of the chairman" were condemned.

In the Politburo Standing Committee (26 members before the plenum) the Deng group had to deal with a considerable number of functionaries who in the end had to swallow a drastic diminution or even loss of their power. These included Saifudin, who had been relieved of his regional functions in Xinjiang before the conference; Wu De, already removed as Beijing party first secretary; the utterly compromised Hua Guofeng; and Ni Zhifu, who lost his position as party second secretary at Shanghai. Wu De was accused of opposing Deng's return to power, misgoverning the city of Beijing, and being guilty of crushing the Tiananmen demonstration. Ni Zhifu, as commander of the Beijing militia, was charged with having provided 100 tanks for the Gang of Four's planned coup. The model farmer Chen Yonggui, symbol of the Dazhai spirit in agriculture, lost his influence on agricultural development and resigned from the leadership of the agricultural commission in the State Council. Although Chen, a Politburo member and vice-premier, had at one time come out in favor of Deng's return to the Politburo, later, in mid-1978, he had opposed the "truth" discussion. Vice-premier Ji Dengkui lost his position as political first commissar of the Beijing military region. General Chen Xilian remained in the Politburo and retained his vice-premiership, although he had already de facto had to relinquish the command over the Beijing military region.

Wang Dongxing was formally allowed to remain in his office as party vice-chairman (since August 1977), but he lost his most important position as director of the General Office of the Central Committee, his control of the Central Committee's Propaganda Department (through the removal of Zhang Pinghua) and of the theoretical monthly Red Flag (through the removal of the editor-in-chief Xiong Fu), and finally the editorship of Mao's works, nominally in the hands of Hua Guofeng. He was also stripped of his command over the elite unit 8341 and his directorship of the party school.

d) New posts for the Deng Xiaoping faction

The composition of the Politburo had not been entirely to Deng's liking, so it too was reshuffled and augmented with loyal adherents of the vice-premier. First Deng maneuvered his former colleague, the agriculture and finance expert Chen Yun, into a powerful position as member of an expanded Politburo, member of the Politburo's Standing Committee, and party vice-chairman, which ranked him above Wang Dongxing. Second, the Deng group got Zhou Enlai's wife Deng Yingchao, his close collaborator Hu Yaobang, and Wang Zhen into the Politburo.

Yao Yilin took over from Wang Dongxing the direction of the Central Committee's General Office. Supervision of cadre affairs was taken from the General Office and placed under the control of a newly created Central Committee for the Inspection of Discipline, directed by the permanent secretary, Huang Kecheng, Peng Dehuai's now rehabilitated former general chief-of-staff. Yang Yong, the first deputy general chief-of-staff, took over the command of the Beijing garrison and the mysterious unit 8341 (formally among Wang Dongxing's numerous official functions), which was downgraded to an ordinary unit of the People's Liberation Army and placed under the command of the Beijing military region.

Hu Yaobang, former vice-chairman of the party school and director of the Organizational Department of the Central Committee, rose to extraordinary prominence. He became a member of the Politburo and received the newly reinstituted post of party general secretary (*mishuzhang*); this key position of power within the party, which Deng Xiaoping himself had held before the Cultural Revolution, was at that time abolished and its functions transferred to Wang Dongxing's General Office. Deng now reinvested this post with significance and installed in it a trustworthy junior functionary of his own persuasion as a sort of crown prince. Indeed, in 1981 it was Hu Yaobang who would take over the party chairmanship from Hua Guofeng.

The directorship of the Central Committee's Organizational

Department went to Song Renqiong, a general of the old guard and one of Deng's trusted adherents. Hu Yaobang in addition took over the key ideological position of director of the Central Committee's Propaganda Department from Hua Guofeng's demoted colleague Zhang Pinghua. One of the first tasks Hu took on after his appointment was to restore the good name of this department, which Mao during the Cultural Revolution had derided as "the Palace of Hell." Hu had been one of Deng's mainstays even before his promotion to such a wealth of official posts. In 1978 he had organized the campaign of Mao criticism and initiated the campaign for more democracy and the rule of law. Without his authorship becoming known, while head of the Youth League he had submitted to the newly revived periodical _Chinese Youth_ an article ("On Getting Rid of Modern Superstition") which was so explosive that the Wang faction moved to halt distribution of the publication in order to keep Hu's attacks on Mao out of the public eye.[169] As early as 1975–76 Hu Yaobang had gone into battle alongside Deng in an attempt to introduce a rudimentary version of the modernization policy, prompting the radical Shanghai faction to target attacks on the "two Hu's" (including ideologist Hu Qiaomu). In his former capacity as _de facto_ president of the Academy of Sciences, Hu Yaobang had been an originator of the so-called "three poisonous weeds," the programmatic core of the current modernization program.

e) _A new style of conflict resolution_

The manner in which the conflict between the Deng faction and the Maoist minority was played out differed sharply from the campaign style of personal humiliation and threats that had been typical since the Cultural Revolution. To be sure, it cannot be said that there was no vengeful tinge to the pragmatist group's drive for a reassessment of the Cultural Revolution; nevertheless the victor did try to keep the conflict within bounds. Indeed, _People's Daily_ made explicit mention of the restraint characterizing the conduct of the factional dispute and the exercise of "criticism and self-criticism."[170] During the Cultural Revolution this ritual had been turned into a license for "merciless attacks" that were unrelenting until an adversary was reduced to self-derision and even self-destruction, whereupon the public would be brought in "to criticize on call." The conduct of the recent plenum, however, showed that under party discipline, criticism need not spell the immediate downfall of an official; nor were cadres necessarily ruined or completely discredited by having to engage in self-criticism. Moreover, by abjuring the use of bellicose mass criticism sessions and wall poster attacks to demolish censured cadres, the plenum also showed that now that the post-Mao leadership had assumed power, even leading Central Committee members could endure criticism. Thus, according to People's Daily, a spirit of democracy had been revived at these conferences, the like of which the party had not seen for many years.

f) Topics of the discussions

Through the internal channels of communication, the Chinese people were kept much more informed of the suppression of the Maoist opposition, from the details of the preliminary discussion contributions down to the subsequent reshuffling of positions,[171] than one might suppose from the communique. One thing at least is clear: at these meetings the Wang Dongxing faction had fought the de-Maoization discussion that had been forced on them. Hu Sheng, who before the Cultural Revolution was assistant editor-in-chief of Red Flag and since 1973 had again been entrusted with certain tasks, argued in his speech at the work conference that the provincial cadres who had all given lip-service to the maxim "practice is the sole criterion of truth" had done so mechanically, and that therefore the actual views of the provincial first secretaries were unknown. Further, Hu Sheng continued, this sort of political campaign, which essentially glossed over the real theoretical questions, was hardly designed to motivate dissenters to undertake a rethinking of their views. The media expert Wu Lengxi argued in his speech that the new ideological directions departed from Marxism-Leninism-Mao Zedong Thought. The new course was attacked in more general terms by Xiong Fu, editor-in-chief of Red Flag, who warned against another backslide into revisionism. Within the party, he said, there were still unrepentant devotees of the capitalist road (i.e., Deng), and they had to be tossed out. This caused an uproar at the conference; a number of cadres jumped up to demand that Xiong Fu specify exactly whom he had in mind.

Economic expert Chen Yun gave the principal talk in support of de-Maoization. He posed three questions: Was Mao Zedong a man or a god? Was Peng Dehuai a good or a bad cadre? Was Kang Sheng a human being or a devil? The questions directed attention toward three central points. The last implicitly condemned secret service head Kang Sheng as the prosecutor of respected cadres during the Cultural Revolution and the second supported an official rehabilitation of Peng Dehuai. The first, however, could be construed as a license to criticize Mao Zedong and his "mistakes," since not only was it clearly he who had violated the spirit of "seeking truth in the facts" but he was directly named. The full dimension of this sharpest of all official steps toward de-Maoization was spelled out by Chen Yun: If the chairman had died in 1956, without a doubt he would have remained the great leader in the memory of the Chinese people and would have been respected and loved throughout the world as a genuinely great personality in the proletarian revolutionary movement. If he had died in 1966, his great merits would have been diminished a bit (on account of the Great Leap Forward). "However, since he died in 1976, there is nothing we can do to change the situation!"

This speech — Chen had delivered it boldly and emotionally, and then stormed out of the conference without giving the opposition an opportunity to debate his judgment — was rebutted by Wang Dongxing as leader of the opposition faction. Wang reiterated his belief that the chairman's words and his policies should be followed to the letter. He proudly invoked his authority as an interpreter of Mao Zedong Thought — after all, he said, he had worked longest at Mao's side and hence had the right to deliver opinions on his thought. Wang was supported by Zhang Pinghua, director of the Propaganda Department, who argued in more theoretical terms.

The speakers of the Deng faction insisted that Mao Zedong Thought had to be "developed further." Indeed, that is precisely what Mao had done with Marxist theory, they argued; otherwise he would never have been able to carry off a peasant revolution against the cities. Deng's ally General Xu Shiyou delivered a harsh denunciation of the radical opposition. He rejected the possibility that Wang's supporters could function credibly as guarantors of the new course and cultivate a new loyalty to Deng. Both Party Vice-chairman Marshal Ye Jianying and Deng Xiaoping himself had risked their lives in the 1976 debates and the preceding factional fight, and it was for this reason, said Xu Shiyou, that the populace held them in such high regard. However, in their ranks they had a "Khrushchev" (meaning Wang Dongxing) who nursed evil designs and undoubtedly would launch a counterattack as soon as the opportunity presented itself, because he wanted to return to the old revisionist road of the Gang of Four.

The Wang opposition's front quickly collapsed, whereupon Deng's supporters demanded and secured a self-criticism from all quarters. After Party Vice-chairman Wang Dongxing, General Chen Xilian, and former Beijing mayor Wu De had delivered their self-criticisms, Liao Zhengzhi, who had worked closely with Zhou Enlai in matters of foreign policy, dealt them a further blow. He asserted that their declamations were just as dishonest and dishonorable as the self-criticism of Mao's rival Zhang Guotao had been back in November 1937 in Yanan (in April 1938 Zhang deserted to Chiang Kai-shek's Guomindang, becoming a party renegade).

If these few references are any indication, the Deng faction's strategy of containment and suppression of the left, and the pivotal significance assigned to the de-Maoization debate, had indeed ignited a spark. In this context Chen Yun's attack came closest of all to being the CCP's functional equivalent of Khrushchev's secret speech denouncing Stalin's personality cult at the CPSU's Twentieth Party Congress.

9

The Next Stages of De-Maoization and the Prospects for the Development of State Maoism

1. TOWARD A SECOND STAGE OF DE-MAOIZATION: OPEN CRITICISM OF THE CHAIRMAN IN BEIJING

"I'm waiting for my flight in the hall of the Beijing airport. Tourists from Miami are amusing themselves with Mao — they hang a cane from the arm of the plaster-of-paris statue and try to perch a canary-yellow cap on its head. No Chinese takes notice. That's how quickly things have changed."[172] This chance observation by a German journalist visiting China in February 1979 demonstrates one thing: The leadership discussion on Mao's ideological legacy and the ideological debate that it fueled in the official media had reverberations in daily life that were much more profound than could have been surmised even from the attacks on Mao in the wall posters or the Hong Kong left press. The situation in the PRC now seemed ripe for a second stage of de-Maoization that would have the following hallmarks. First, the media would no longer use "immunity formulas" to set up a protective wall around Mao, and second, direct and specific criticism of Mao's previously inviolable figure would now be permitted within predefined limits. It was hard to see how the Deng Xiaoping group could take such a step without its having ominous implications for the radical opposition around Wang Dongxing and ultimately for Hua Guofeng, nominally Mao's successor, who had so far ranked himself with Deng.

However, the rather sweeping changes wrought in the climate of Chinese society during March 1979 seemed initially to contradict such a turn of events. The party now took firm steps to silence the call for more democracy in the country. The excesses of the liberalization experiment were stopped, critical wall posters were removed by the authorities, and contacts between foreigners and Chinese once again became difficult and problematic; self-appointed spokesmen demanding human rights — such as the now prominent Wei Jingsheng, editor of the wall newspaper Tansuo (Exploration) which had begun appearing in November 1978 — were abruptly arrested. It was clear that it was Deng who took the lead in terminating the "Beijing Spring." In a speech given before the National People's Congress on March 16, 1979, which marked the end of the incursion into Vietnam, Deng delivered instructions supplementing pronouncements issued by regional security authorities at the beginning of the month. Restrictions were placed on freedom of assembly, freedom of expression, and the pasting up of posters, with an explicit prohibition on "slogans, announcements, wall newspapers, books, periodicals, pictures, photographs, and other publications" that "attacked socialism, the dictatorship of the proletariat, the Communist Party leadership, Marxism-Leninism, and Mao Zedong Thought."[173] The April edition of Red Flag featured an essay that strained to draw a rather unconvincing black-and-white distinction between "bourgeois human rights" (renquan) as touted in the "abstract empty slogans" of a "minority," and the commendable call for a "democracy" (minzhu) subserving the modernization of China. There followed a polemic against anarchism, disturbance of the peace, misuse of the freedom to assemble and to demonstrate, obstruction of traffic, and violent attacks on public officials and buildings. Despite what one might easily conclude at first glance, these were not retaliatory measures initiated by the Wang group against the Deng faction in response to a destabilization of the internal political situation and hence of the PRC's new political course (i.e., a resurgence of the left). Rather, this was the net outcome of Deng's experimental open-door policy: the setting of certain necessary limits to the new "Hundred Flowers."

Quite apart from these retrenchments, the approach of a second open phase of de-Maoization had already been foretokened in 1979. Since 1977 there had been occasional glimpses of a large-scale persuasion campaign in all the areas of social life that Deng and his supporters controlled, including the army. For example, the party committee of the Guanzhou military region together with the Guangdong provincial party committee had made the following internal proclamation on the subject of "assessing Chairman Mao":

> The founder of our party, our army and our state, Mao, is undoubtedly one of the greatest proletarian revolutionaries in the history of mankind. His enormous contributions to the revolution in our country and in the world must not be dismissed, nor can they be, by anyone. However, over the long period in which Mao performed the offices of leader of our party, commander of our army, and chief of our state, he was certainly not free of shortcomings and mistakes, as we have indeed constantly stressed. If we continue to deny his shortcomings and mistakes, and do not have the courage to undertake a thorough review, this can only do harm to the cause of revolution and bear no good fruit. The eye of the people sees clearly; everyone has kept his own ledger of Mao's merits and shortcomings. If the Party Central Committee continues to hush up Mao's errors and shortcomings not only will it become impossible to uphold the authority of the party among the masses, it will also have further negative consequences for the party.[174]

An opinion survey conducted in the PRC in late 1978 by the Hong Kong left-wing publication Dongxiang — which, although not necessarily representative, was the first of its kind to be conducted officially in the People's Republic — provided a rough picture of the impact of such admonitions: "98.7 percent" of those questioned had come to the opinion that "all the words and theories of the great leader" had to be "subjected to the test of practice."

2. *PEOPLE'S DAILY* USES THE TERM "DE-MAOIZATION"

A key sign of a sharpening of the Mao criticism was the use — for the first time officially (albeit still defensively) — of the term "de-Maoization" (fei Mao hua), a neologism that first appeared in a translation in People's Daily on March 9, 1979. Lead articles in more moderate Hong Kong left publications then went a step further by using the more sweeping term "de-Maoization movement" (fei Mao hua yundong)[175] to describe the ideological situation in the People's Republic. The above-mentioned article in People's Daily made reference to "well-intentioned" and "evil-intentioned" critics abroad who were following the process of de-Maoization. The Chinese term fei, used in the translation, implies a complete negation, and thus conveys something rather stronger than the word "de-Maoization." Therefore, the paper maintained, most foreign critics grasped that there was no de-Maoization taking place in China, but rather a "restoration of the original face of Mao Zedong Thought" after the distortions that had taken place, a "confirmation of Mao's merits," "a defense of the core" of his teachings, and a pruning of certain mistakes or "overblown incidents." Nonetheless, in abandoning nebulous circumlocutions such as "seek the truth in facts," People's Daily had for the first time gotten a full bead on the problem terminologically: since no "negation" in the manner of "de-Stalinization" was meant in China, the way was indeed clear for adoption of the term, also used in this article, of a "reassessment" (pingjia) of Mao.

3. A TEMPERING OF THE "IMMUNITY FORMULAS" EXONERATING MAO

A second sign was the increasing dilution of the "immunity formulas" that had been used to evade or gloss over the real sore points whenever a critical examination of incidents led to a clear implication of Mao's responsibility or co-responsibility. In April 1979, informed Chinese commentators outside the PRC had called the treatment of certain unambiguous issues in the Beijing press (including the rehabilitation of the essayists Deng Tuo, Wu Han, and Liao Mosha) a "direct-indirect criticism" of Mao.[176] In his June 12, 1961, self-criticism for the misplanning of the Great Leap Forward (the literal text of which has still not been made public), Mao had promised more diversity of opinion and tolerance of critics in the future, but later, far from keeping the promise, had taken bitter revenge. The "rehabilitation" of the "February countercurrent" was also seen in the same light. In a top-level meeting in mid-1967, seven vice-premiers and vice-chairmen of the military commission (including Foreign Minister Chen Yi and Deng's later minister of defense Xu Xiangqian) had attacked the radical Cultural Revolution Group (which included the ideologist Chen Boda, Mao's wife Jiang Qing, Yao Wenyuan, and Zhang Chunqiao) for their wholesale purging of respected party cadres, for which they in turn were accused of being opponents of the "revolutionary line of Chairman Mao," and their actions labeled a "countercurrent."[177]

Of course, though the leftist Hong Kong commentators now played the game of hauling out relevant Mao sayings to show that in every case Mao Zedong had invariably been on the "wrong" left side — including when he had denounced the Ministry of Culture during the Cultural Revolution and had personally overseen the downfall of Peng, the minister of defense, and of his rival, State President Liu Shaoqi — this was still not an unequivocal abandonment of the use of "immunity formulas" on Mao's behalf. For that, China's official press had to address directly the question of Mao's personal responsibility for these incidents.

4. OFFICIAL CRITICISM OF HUA GUOFENG'S EDITING OF VOLUME V AND EARLIER MANIPULATIVE EDITORIAL PRACTICES

A third and somewhat elusive sign was the first direct criticism (in People's Daily, March 13, 1979) of the editing of Mao's works, in particular Volume V (published in 1977 under the editorship of Party Chairman Hua Guofeng) but also the previous volumes of the Selected Works. Although the criticism was outwardly directed only at the editors and publishers, on closer look there was no mistaking the allusions to Mao's politics as well. However explosive the effect of these arguments, appearing as they did in China's official press, a feeling of déjà vu was unavoidable: Western political commentators had raised them when the volume first came out.

It was admitted for the first time in People's Daily that "many parts" of the four-volume Selected Works had been "revised" in reprintings since the Cultural Revolution. The one-volume pocket edition of 1967 and the sixth printing of Volume I of the four-volume edition of June 1969 were especially criticized.[178] Entire documents, it was claimed, had been dropped out under the editing of "Lin Biao and the Gang of Four"; footnotes had been eliminated, and passages mentioning Liu Shaoqi by name had been arbitrarily removed. Such manipulations were now called an "extremely harmful practice" and evidence of a "frivolous attitude toward historical documents" that was tantamount to a deliberate attempt to revise party history. Semi-illiterate peasants had been deceived. Historical documents had been used primarily for the purpose of attacking political figures regarded as enemies. Further (to round out this involuntary reprise of some principles of traditional historiography), it was stated that certain people had usurped for themselves an absolute dictatorship over life and death: "What a misuse of power and a violation of history!" Such manipulations were also linked to the incessant reorganizations of museums and memorials of the revolution which had gone on everywhere in the past decade.

The attack on the editing of Volume V under Hua Guofeng and

Wang Dongxing was aimed particularly at the editors' "technical corrections" (as they were called in the preface of the volume). Cadres who were in the process of being rehabilitated (such as the former vice-premier Bo Yibo, Yang Shangkun, and eventually State President Liu) had been dealt with unfairly in Volume V, the Maoist title of address "comrade" had with malice aforethought and "without authorization" been eliminated from references to them, and Liu's activities even in the early sixties had retroactively been depicted in a negative light. Such "technical corrections" (the need for which even the pro-Deng critic in People's Daily would endorse under other circumstances) were in the final analysis nothing other than a carte blanche to manipulate — "to leave out something here, to add something there, and to make a few general emendations."

The argument of those such as Hua and Wang who defended this technique — to wit, that it was the only way to let people know "who should be loved and who should be hated" — was rejected in the name of historical truth. "If additions and omissions continue to be made, when can Mao Zedong's writings and party documents be regarded as final and unalterable?" asked the critic, in an unthinking nostalgic reversion to the notion of an orthodox state Maoism.

The Hong Kong criticism of the Hua/Wang editing of Volume V then took up some of the key problems involved in the interpretation that this edition sought to present. Volume V had highlighted Mao's Hundred Flowers initiative,[179] and in particular its transformation into the inquisitorial anti-rightist campaign in 1957. However, as became known in April 1979, between June 14 and June 22 (1978) a debate had taken place between the Wang Dongxing opposition and the Deng faction at the Central Committee Work Conference in Yantai (Shandong Province) as to how far the rehabilitation of the victims of the 1957 campaign could go and under what conditions it should take place. A compromise had been consigned to writing in Central Committee document No. 11 (drafted beforehand) and Central Committee document No. 55 (1978) of this conference. The Wang group had backed up their editorial interpretation in Volume V with the argument that the campaign against the right, which according to official statistics affected between 520,000 and 600,000 persons, had still to be regarded as correct and lawful althought a few mistakes had marred it in the execution, which of course were grounds for certain rehabilitations. The counterargument of the Deng group was that the editorial selection of documents for Volume V of the Selected Works had distorted the actual events, and that the editorial committee had edited "to suit its own needs." A dozen Mao documents from the period leading up to the liberalization policy of the Hundred Flowers had been suppressed in order to mute the abruptness of the about-face, which at the time had cost the CCP an enormous loss of popular trust. Here again, the criticism of the editorial practices shifted almost imperceptibly into a criticism of Mao and the general political line he had defended.

Against this background of stepped-up attacks on Mao, in March 1979 serious discussions resumed within the party and the leadership on the general theme of direct criticism of Mao and how a limited campaign of criticism could be most skillfully carried out — a question on which the Central Committee ended up holding a secret meeting.[180]

5. "HISTORICAL TRUTH" INSTEAD OF THE CULT AND CANON OF STATE MAOISM?

This sharpened tone in dealing with Mao's mistakes generated the terminology and the arguments for a second stage of de-Maoization in mid-1979. From 1957 on, claimed Red Flag,[181] Mao had swept China with campaigns that followed one another like waves, and in this made himself guilty of a headstrong, obstinate "left opportunism" that had had tragic repercussions for over 100 million (!) people. The radicals of the Gang of Four were not, as initially claimed, guilty of an "extreme right-wing line," or of "ostensibly left-wing, but in reality right-wing politics"; the essence of their errors was a "left-opportunist" line, through and through. This barely disguised attack on Mao by the party's theoretical monthly was mitigated only to the extent that in internal grassroots discussions the entire party was held jointly responsible — a point that could not be denied by any amount of arguments.

The more general trends in the development of state Maoism were shaped to a large extent by the growing criticism of Mao which even forced its way into the official media. The wall poster attacks on the cult of personality were formalized and given consummate form in March 1979 in the national newspapers.[182] "The phenomenon of exalting individuals and the worship of certain persons among our ranks" goes back to the worship of the emperor as the "son of heaven" in traditional society, observed Guangming Daily. Official party interpreters of state Maoism such as Lin Biao, Chen Boda, and the former secret service head, the late Kang Sheng, were condemned as modern "idol-builders" (initially Kang remained nameless as the media referred to him as a "theoretical authority") and allusions were made to negative points of similarity between the Mao cult and the Stalin cult. The attack against cult forms was followed up with a condemnation of political leaders who had bound every Chinese to "unqualified loyalty to individuals"; this, it was said, was at variance with the principles of a functioning party organization. The warning for the future, which made direct reference to Mao, charged that certain leaders had brushed aside party control to become "special personalities" who consciously or unconsciously placed themselves over party and state and abused their authority by acting solely in accordance with the motto "only what I say counts."

Presumably with an eye to the specific forms of Mao worship that had emerged since the death of the party chairman (e.g., the ritual publication of new individual texts), newspaper critics of the personality cult pointed to one-time party rules which prohibited formal observance of the birthdays of party leaders. The ideologues around Deng demanded an end to manipulations of Mao's legacy by interpreters, a renewed respect for the "historical truth"[183] of party documents and party history, and that Mao's writings be divested of their status as "supreme instructions" — which did not augur well for further publication of Mao's works. The dilemma of how to assess the Lushan Conference and the Great Leap Forward was thus left for a future volume of Selected Works. If Defense Minister Peng was correct in his criticism, Mao's elimination of the Peng opposition could hardly be depicted as "a lesson by negative example." What the Deng ideologues were aiming for was a documentation of party history based on historical facts, in which writings and statements of other prominent party leaders, for example, the literary legacy of Zhou Enlai, would have their rightful place alongside the Mao texts. Indeed, the Central Committee announced (on the occasion of Zhou's eighty-first birthday) that Zhou's writings would be compiled;[184] they were made publicly available by early 1980.

A comparison of the sharply accented reinterpretation and redefinition of state Maoism with the existing record of political events of the recent past clearly shows that even the avowal of these new principles did not completely eliminate the problem of "political editing" of Mao's writings. The Deng historians would in any event have had to come up against the dictates of party secrecy. If a broad openness and a sober view of wrong turns in the past were to be maintained, the appeal for "historical truth" would make such a definition of history a severe taskmaster for the party in the future. To wit: "Certain comrades currently think that the second decade after the founding of our state did not go as well as the first and that the third was even worse than the second decade, and that hence we have gone backward. We cannot say that such arguments and views are completely unfounded."[185] This is a burdensome retrospective indictment for a party attempting a new start!

Let us now take a look at the most essential aspects of de-Maoization as it developed up to the Fifth Plenum (February 23-29, 1980). The events leading to the plenum included a revival of the theoretical discussion on "practice as the sole criterion for gauging the truth" — a sort of "remedial session" for the slow learners, as the Hong Kong left press called it — and by a self-criticism from the party organ Red Flag for its earlier suppression of this theme in September 1979. The Fifth Plenum thus constituted the keystone in the long-imperiled archway begun by the Third Plenum: it drew the personal implications of the political reorientation, implications that would have been inescapable from the start had everything gone Deng's way. The "new Gang of Four," as the Maoist opposition was now called (Party Vice-chairman Wang Dongxing, Vice-premier Ji Dengkui, Politburo member Wu De, and Marshal Chen Xilian), having undertaken another self-criticism and asked Deng Xiaoping's pardon at a Central Committee Work Conference in late 1979 was removed once and for all from all party and government posts. The creation of a strong Central Committee Secretariat (headed by Hu Yaobang and including eleven Deng supporters) to take care of current affairs of the party put the seal on the expulsion of the residual opposition from the Politburo. Personnel reshufflings could henceforth take place without any disputes over party line and with a view toward ensuring the best possible implementation of the new policy. It would seem that the position of Deng and his group must have still been remarkably weak in 1978 if he required two full years to effect this purge!

Thus the plenum effected the encirclement and isolation of the Party Chairman and Premier Hua Guofeng. It put party affairs largely in the hands of Hu Yaobang, while government business was overseen by Zhao Ziyang, who had risen to membership in the Standing Committee of the Politburo. The press launched transparent attacks on the use of Mao's words to legitimate Hua ("with you in charge I'm at ease"). A People's Daily editorial of March 10, 1980, declared that the top leadership was a collective from whose midst a leader "with the highest authority, greatest influence, and most experience would be chosen." "Successors" would emerge only gradually, and not "by the sort of sudden high-handed maneuver by which anyone might grab another's position."

The elimination of the loyal Maoist "whatever faction" at the Fifth Plenum opened the way for a further reorganization of the regional leadership and basic-level cadres, whose passivity or even passive resistance — whether stemming from fears over one's own past, disillusionment, or the anticipation of a possible return of the left — was hindering implementation of the new course. The Fourth Plenum in the fall of 1979, featuring the rather unflattering speech written by Hu Yaobang and delivered by Marshal Ye Jianying on the occasion of the thirtieth anniversary of the founding of the PRC, had to be considered the greatest exercise in party self-criticism since the assumption of power. Now there was an attempt to enhance the party's authority with a propagandistic discussion of the "crisis of confidence" (xinren weiji). Such a discussion was probably thoroughly necessary, if the critical statements made by one disillusioned student, who had been sent abroad to study in Belgium and sought political asylum there in late 1979, are at all representative: "In 1976 we were confident; now that we had a new good leadership, everything was going to improve. But three years have gone by, and I find no great change in any of the basic things."

However, the painstakingly prepared official rehabilitation of former president Liu Shaoqi at the February 1980 plenum was of decisive importance in paving the way for an open criticism of Mao. Instead of continuing and completing the canon of the Selected Works of Mao as announced, party ideologists were now fully occupied with the preparation of Liu's Selected Works. Liu's rehabilitation, as stated in the Fifth Plenum's communique, not only brought justice to the party's second most prominent leader (and his family members), whom the Cultural Revolution had swept away and buried for a decade. In addition, a political line and a general conception for the building of Chinese society which had been set down at the Eighth Party Congress in 1956, but reviled as the worst sort of revisionism since 1966, was now rehabilitated — and with it the thousands of party cadres and others who had been brought to ruin by the Cultural Revolution. However, Mao's obvious responsibility for Liu's tragic political fate was left unspoken, to the great disapprobation of many, especially the young. For reasons of state, observed Hong Kong's left-wing monthly Dongxiang in its analysis, "the degree to which people within the country and friends around the world absorb these things" (jieshou chengdu) had to be taken into consideration.

Mao Zedong Thought was now redefined as a collective good of the party, and thus shielded against the impending criticism of Mao himself. In this case Mao Zedong Thought was only conditionally regarded as commensurate with Mao's political ideas: it transcended Mao as an individual. Ye Jianying declared it to be the crystallization of the collective wisdom of the CCP: "Of course Mao Zedong Thought is not exclusively the product of Mao's personal wisdom; it is just as much the product of the wisdom of his close comrades in arms, the party, and the revolutionary people." This redefinition — which explicitly called for the "further development" and integration of Mao Zedong Thought into the modernization efforts, since otherwise the "salvaging of Mao Zedong Thought" would unquestionably become impossible (People's Daily editorial of October 3, 1979) given the political and ideological reorientation — gave rise to a cynical comment in party phrasing: "Mao's policy is again valid."

Meanwhile, behind the scenes, a full settling of accounts with Mao was already under way in preparation for open criticism, although with the repeatedly stressed proviso: "The assessment of Mao must not be construed as de-Maoization" (ping Mao bushi fei Mao). In a detailed secret report at a Central Committee Work Conference in late 1979, Wang Ruoshui, one of Deng Xiaoping's "theoretical advisers" and deputy editor-in-chief of People's Daily, catalogued all of Mao Zedong's mistakes for the first time. In these statements we meet, in official and weighed tones, all the arguments that had appeared on the wall posters during the Beijing Spring. A central issue was Mao's responsibility for the tragedy of the Cultural Revolution, the unparalleled intellectual and cultural suppression and the elimination of all independently thinking politicians and personages such as Marshal Peng Dehuai. This was followed by an attack on the cult of personality and the rank simplification of ideology, and reproaches for Lin Biao's promotion to the highest party and state posts. Mao was held to account for his close collaboration with the Gang of Four, for an almost immoral oppression of the altruistic Premier Zhou Enlai, and finally for the nepotism of his last years (Zhongguo shibao, January 1, 1980). Wholly in this spirit of Mao criticism were "reports" from within the hierarchy, for cadre consumption, of an imminent transfer of Mao's body to a more remote resting place (presumably desired by Deng but opposed by Marshal Ye) and even rumors that the hastily erected Mao mausoleum on Tiananmen Square in Peking would be torn down.

Thus was the groundwork laid for the Twelfth Party Congress scheduled for 1980-81, which would bring a reshuffling of the entire Central Committee and definitive reappraisal of the Great Proletarian Cultural Revolution. (The media had already observed that the Cultural Revolution needed to be renamed, for not only did the destructive influence of this mass campaign reach far beyond the domain of culture, more, it had brought discredit to the very term "revolution.") Likewise, some decisions had to be made about the impending trial of the Gang of Four, announced by Hua Guofeng at a press conference on October 7, 1979. Apparently, the youthful former Party Vice-chairman Wang Hongwen had so fully cooperated with the pretrial investigations as to put himself forward as a rueful witness for the prosecution, thus smoothing the way for this controversial event.

The Mao canon was also affected by these developments. There was no longer any talk of Volume VI of the Selected Works; moreover, the alleged "false editing" (Zhengming, October 24, 1979) of Volume V under the direction of the discredited Hua Guofeng and Wang Dongxing prompted calls for an entirely new edition. It was charged that the Eighth Party Congress had not been accurately reported (Mao's opening speech had been omitted), that the preface, with its emphasis on "continuing revolution," was ideologically misleading, etc. People's Daily reserved its strongest condemnation (January 7, 1980) for the Red Book. The quotations were taken out of their contexts in space and time and were used to vulgarize Mao's thought, it was charged; they continued the worst traditions of quotations from the Analects of Confucius or from the book of quotations of the neo-Confucian philosopher Zhu Xi of the Song period. The little Mao bible served as a warning that the Chinese "must never again give in to their obsessive reverence for quotations." "Such practices have now become an object of derision, but they have not yet completely disappeared."

Certainly the approach to the state Maoism question was, all things considered, an ambitiously conceived, serious attempt to come to terms with the past. However, questions bearing on the future (e.g., the ability of even a restructured Maoist state to successfully modernize a developing country) were still far from playing the role they warranted in the public discussion. Not by chance did demonstrators against Deng's new course at Beijing's Democracy Wall in early May 1979 distribute pamphlets that compared the economic modernization policy with the ill-fated radical Maoist Great Leap Forward of the late fifties.[186] To what extent could even a disembodied, increasingly ritualized state Maoism, still relied upon as the mainstay of national identity, be of any future use in the face of such an unsettling modernization experiment?

Even in the wake of Liu Shaoqi's official rehabilitation, the trial of the Gang of Four, and Hua's removal from the party chairmanship, the fate of Mao's ideological legacy was not yet finally determined. The official document that addressed the issue of Mao, the resolution "On Questions of Party History" adopted by the Sixth Plenum of the Eleventh Central Committee in June 1981, did, however, present a carefully balanced summation of the arguments we have encountered along the tortuous way to a limited critique of Mao's rule, the compromise upon which the leadership finally settled. It is this document which concludes what we have termed the second phase of de-Maoization.

Our look back over the almost four decades of development of state Maoism, the Mao canon, and the personality cult around the chairman himself must perforce stop here. But in order to suggest a larger context for the above analysis, we shall conclude our presentation with a brief comparative assessment of the development of state ideology outside of China.

Canonical Writings and Forms of the Personality Cult at China's Periphery

The nature of Chinese state Maoism and the changes it underwent become clearer if we examine this ideology not just in isolation but also in comparison with Soviet ideology and with other Asian versions of communism. The way the Soviet ideological canon took shape, especially under Stalin, had a manifold influence on CCP ideology before the revolution and on state Maoism in the years after 1949. A comparative survey of the development of canonical forms in the countries of "real socialism" (though here we shall have to limit ourselves to the Soviet Union, Vietnam, and Korea) should both reveal any uniform tendencies of development and at the same time bring into relief the distinguishing features of state Maoism.

1. THE USSR: CHANGES IN THE PERSONALITY CULT AND THE DEGENERATION OF SOVIET IDEOLOGY TO AN INSTRUMENT OF SELF-JUSTIFICATION

a) Four levels of Soviet ideology

We shall begin with the Soviet Union, the first country of "real socialism" and the first to develop a state ideology in terms of the principles laid down by Karl Marx and Friedrich Engels, a country that has never abdicated its self-proclaimed role as spokesman for the world communist movement. The establishment of an ideological canon and a cult of the political leader in the Soviet Union was to have reverberations far beyond that country's borders — and of course, the model was directly imposed on the

Eastern European countries within the Soviet Union's postwar sphere of influence. Let us broadly outline the development of both cult and canon in the Soviet Union.

The shaping of the canon of Soviet ideology over the period of a half-century was a far more complex process than its counterpart in the younger PRC. One is immediately struck by the sheer abundance, intricate pattern, and versatility of the fabric of ideological writings that has been woven to meet the ever-changing ideological requirements of nation and state. We can distinguish four successive stages in the development of the canon, each with its own dynamic. The first stage is the reworking of the Marx–Engels writings and their canonization under Soviet auspices. Second, there is the canonization of Lenin's writings in the context of the posthumous Lenin cult promoted by Stalin, and the forging of these two into Marxism-Leninism. Third is the stage of Stalin's cult around his own person, the party leader laying claim to the same reverence accorded the deceased Lenin. Investing his cult with yet another dimension of hyperbole, Stalin then added to his assertion of political leadership a further claim to ideological infallibility, stamping his every writing with the seal of orthodoxy. This claim to dual authority breaks down at the fourth stage, represented by Khrushchev and Brezhnev; though during the tenure of each, political custom required ubiquitous citation of their writings, neither leader purported to be a fountainhead of dogmatic truth.

In any case, it cannot be said that the classics, even in their popularized versions, have set the ideological tone in the Soviet Union. Not only the very bulk of these works but their diversity and subtlety ill suit them for direct use as propaganda; indeed, any number of seminal texts quite simply contradict current political dogma. Since the rise of Stalin a panoply of official, authoritative ideological treatises have been assigned a place alongside the canonical classics, but these have had to be revised or replaced with each major policy shift. The classic canonical works have themselves been moved to the back shelves; their primary function is as a source of quotations for use in official tracts pronouncing on every conceivable domain of social life (Lenin on Education, Lenin on the Art of Warfare, etc.).

b) The Marx–Engels writings and their canonization in the Soviet Union

The canonization of the Marx–Engels writings in the Soviet Union was certainly not something that might have been wished by the founders of Marxism, if one recalls that as early as the 1870s they had resisted their followers' tendencies to reduce scientific socialism to a dogma, Marx saying "I am not a Marxist." In no uncertain terms Marx took his stand against any "superstitious belief in authority," i.e., any dogmatic orthodoxy or "monolithic thought" legitimated by the invoking of quotations. Not by any means can Marx be considered a model for Stalin's later claim to infallibility. The sort of workers' party championed by Marx and Engels had no license to pronounce on every facet of social life. No party arrogating to itself the power of total censorship over literature, art, and the press finds legitimation in their works; in the opinion of Marxism's founders even party newspapers ought to be independent of the party leadership.[187]

Certainly, publication of the writings of Marx and Engels, and even a systematic effort to publish them in their entirety, need not have led to their canonization under state auspices. But, as it happened, the plan for full publication of the Marx–Engels writings originated in the Soviet Union, thus shifting the center of editorial activities to that country; there the necessary research institutions were set up with state support, and there the potential audience was great. Since the founding of the German Democratic Republic (GDR) its SED party institute has been an active participant in this project, ratifying, as it were, Soviet appropriation of the right to interpret the Marx–Engels legacy. The first fruit of the movement toward canonization was a Russian edition (the second) of Marx–Engels Works[188] prepared under the direction of the Central Committee of the CPSU; this appeared between 1955 and 1966 in thirty-nine volumes (forty-two books), and later was expanded by another eleven volumes. Also available are a thirty-nine-volume German edition (MEW)[189] and a thirty-nine-volume Chinese edition published in the PRC between 1956 and 1974; both are based on the second Russian edition. A fifty-volume English edition now being prepared under the direction of Moscow will mirror the Russian edition of thirty-nine plus eleven supplementary volumes.

c) Two starts on a complete edition

The Marx–Engels Institute founded in 1921 in Moscow under the direction of D. B. Riazanov and later V. V. Adoratskii undertook a complete edition of the works of Marx and Engels (MEGA), to be published in the original German. The first seven volumes, which appeared between 1927 and 1935, were printed in Frankfurt and Berlin. There is little doubt that the abrupt decision to discontinue this edition was in some measure prompted by a realization on the part of the Soviet leadership that between the basic political conception of Marx and Engels and the Stalinist system in the USSR there was a rapidly widening gulf; significantly, Riazanov was to be a victim of Stalin's purges. The official reason later given for discontinuing the MEGA opus was Hitler's seizure of power.[190]

In recent years the idea of a MEGA edition has been revived. Since 1975 the institutes for Marxism-Leninism under the central committees of the CPSU and the SED have been engaged in the joint publication of a grandly conceived MEGA edition (a projected 100 volumes) to be compiled on a dual principle — organized partly by subject and partly chronologically.[191] This critical historical edition of the Marx–Engels collected works includes the preparatory notes for different versions of texts, the correspondence and the excerpts, notes, and marginalia of the authors, in addition to their finished writings. The principle of completeness has been carried so far that in certain contexts the letters of other persons to Marx and Engels and even the letters of third parties to one another have also been included. The scholarly commentary on the individual volumes is bound separately — a prudent decision, given the revisions such interpretations tend to undergo over time. This ambitious effort has produced an ideological canon of abstruse completeness, which is intended to serve as the basis for various editions of selected works. The canon has probably been over-inflated: strictly speaking, all of Marx's and Engels's statements on the political conception of scientific socialism would barely fill two volumes, and of course this monumental 100-volume canon is outside the purview of the general propaganda audience. In fact, editions of selected works are ordinarily used for actual study and series of short pamphlets have been prepared for ideological indoctrination purposes. Thus, the MEGA has become exclusively the tool of official ideologists.

Nonetheless, even this scholarly edition is bound to a clear political objective as outlined in its preface. The MEGA is to serve as an ideological weapon buttressing the orthodoxy of the one and only scientific world outlook, in the spirit of "revolutionary partisanship" (partiinost'). The MEGA canon is seen as a bulwark against "bourgeois ideologists" and "Marxologists" who, it is alleged, have capitalized on the demand for the classics and published biased selections of texts along with "anti-Marxist prefaces and commentaries." Trends of interpretation singled out for attack are the contrasting of the works of the young Marx with those of the mature Marx, the comparison of Marx's writings and Lenin's writings, and the "erroneous thesis of the pluralism of Marxism"; moreover, the MEGA preface takes special aim at the "attempts of bourgeois and revisionist ideologues to reduce Leninism to a national, specifically Russian phenomenon."[192]

Alongside the Marx–Engels canon, the works of Lenin and Stalin were enshrined as a "Soviet addition to Marxist orthodoxy." Lenin's writings appeared between 1941 and 1950, and an authorized German version was published in East Berlin between 1956 and 1960. An (incomplete) edition of Stalin's writings was issued in Moscow between 1936 and 1951, with a German edition published between 1951 and 1955 in East Berlin.

d) Leninism and Stalinism

Although Lenin in his lifetime was early recognized as an eminent ideological and political leader (as was grudgingly noted in his dossier by the Tsarist secret police), and certainly the fame of his person and his work grew dramatically in the period between October 1917 and his death in 1924, the actual Lenin cult was Stalin's invention. In his day Lenin was not the party's one and only "chief ideologist"; Trotsky, Bukharin, and Plekhanov also figured as leading propagandists.

At a more general level, however, it was Lenin who laid the groundwork for a Soviet orthodoxy, which perforce gave rise to a leadership cult and an ideological canon. The theoretical formulation and practical shaping of a "crack" party weapon was certainly Lenin's contribution in the adaptation of Marxism to Russian conditions; likewise the call for "partisanship" in art and science, later to prevail throughout the Soviet sphere of influence under the doctrine of socialist realism. Lenin also defended partisanship in the media, although on this point his statements vary and in some cases are contradictory. Furthermore, Lenin had overseen the initial crystallization of the actual Lenin canon. Lenin himself appointed Kamenev as the editor of his Collected Works and an authorized ideological interpreter; later, Kamenev became the founder and first director of the Lenin Institute, which was responsible for the new canon.

Stalin, deterred not at all by Lenin's rejection of him in the letter known as Lenin's Testament, entrenched himself more and more firmly in the leadership and deliberately created the Lenin cult. With the latter came a new, turgid style of political language on the example of Stalin's invocation at Lenin's grave, nothing short of an homage in prayer form[193] (to be echoed in the sixties by Lin Biao). Stalin replaced the revolutionary figure with the figure of the high priest in a church hierarchy. He "chopped up Lenin's thoughts into phrases that could be quoted in mendacious sermons, to confuse and intimidate the masses with illiterate pap,"[194] in Trotsky's disdainful evaluation. Stalin's Lenin cult (again in Trotsky's words) brought lowered theoretical standards, political stupefaction, and a rhetoric of reactionary triviality.

Stalin, over the opposition of many high-ranking Soviet leaders, originated the tradition, later adopted in Vietnam and China, of interring the leader in a mausoleum. Official books on Lenin (which Trotsky considered unworthy and insulting) became just as much a part of the party sepulchre as the mausoleum on Red Square. A few months after Lenin's death and the creation of the Lenin cult, Stalin fashioned his own monument as the "continuer of Lenin's cause" with his lectures on the Foundations of Leninism, which for twenty-five years would be acclaimed as a great theoretical work. Trotsky, for one, ridiculed the Foundations as a hash, a bungled attempt[195] to celebrate the theoretical traditions of the party, a work full of errors, the offering of a dogged empiricist lacking any creative imagination.

The Lenin cult received its ultimate ideological validation in the proclamation of Marxism-Leninism in 1938. At the same time, a Lenin canon was defined under Stalin's auspices; since then it has been replaced by an enlarged forty-volume edition, published in a multitude of languages.

e) Forms of the Stalin cult

Stalin's personality cult hailed him not only as vozhd', i.e., the absolute leader, but also as a theoretician. He proclaimed his own theoretical canon, though after his death, publication of his writings was broken off at Volume XIII. The enormous authority of Lenin, or later, Mao, which predated their revolutionary victories, did not fall automatically to Stalin; only after he had gained power was Stalin able to build up the cult around his writings. Not surprisingly, these texts were by and large expositions of particular policies rather than of theoretical considerations prefatory to political action; that is, they present the political views of someone wielding power, as scornfully portrayed in Solzhenitsyn's The First Circle. Trotsky similarly derided Stalin's later writings, conceived and disseminated in a sultry atmosphere of infallibility; of course, for Stalin's aggressive rival even the early texts were but banalities that merely wrapped up the reflections of others, while Stalin's writings on the October Revolution were little more than a "dull commentary on brilliant events."[196]

A second seminal work for the cult was the Short Course on Soviet party history, published in autumn 1938; in general outline it is a factual account of the development of the Bolshevik party from Stalin's point of view. As all of Mao's writings testify, this Course played a decisive role in shaping not only Mao's view of Soviet history but also his conception of ideology and the more formal elements of his political style. The Soviet canon was also supplemented with the official Short Biography of Stalin published in 1948, an unexcelled exercise in idolatry. Trotsky's writings have proved an enduring corrective to the inflated claims of this official biography, which backdated Stalin's record of revolutionary activities and put him on more intimate terms with Lenin. As the crowning glory to this cult around his own person, Stalin had his name immortalized in the text of the new national anthem introduced in 1944. The writings of Marx and Engels paled before this new corpus of Stalinist canon. Moreover, Stalin's system of bureaucratic terror used his cult and canon as yet another tool of conformity: any criticism, even of but a single sentence of the dictator's infallible writings, carried a sentence of mandatory imprisonment or worse.

f) De-Stalinization and the reconstruction of the canon

Yugoslavia's 1948 rebuff to the Cominform was an early step

toward the dismantling of Stalinism. That breach was to have significant consequences in Yugoslavia; it led to curtailment of the role of the Yugoslavian Communist Party and retraction of the demand for a partisan bias in art and science. In 1951, notions of orthodoxy were cut down another peg when the Central Committee declared that the party leadership's writings were no longer absolutely binding. In their party program of 1958 Yugoslavia's communists discarded the Soviet thesis of the Communist Party's leading role; and, having renamed their party the "League of Communists," they renounced its ideological monopoly as well.

In the Soviet Union the rollback of the Stalin cult and abandonment of the Stalin canon began immediately after the dictator's death in March 1953. The years preceding the period of open criticism of Stalin ushered in by Khrushchev's secret speech have been called the quiet phase of de-Stalinization. The publication of Stalin's works was stopped abruptly upon his death. The funeral ceremonies were restrained, and even Stalin's closest associates abstained from the sort of eulogies one might have expected of them. This radical change of mood in the USSR stood in glaring contrast to Mao's bombastic praise of the Soviet dictator on the occasion of Stalin's death. On the whole, the 1953–1964 Khrushchev period — like the period following Mao's death in China — was one of political thaw, the leadership venturing out on the path toward de-Stalinization step by step, with a call for true "socialist legality" in sharp contrast to the former reign of terror, an attempt to break out of isolationism, and removal of the exaggerated party tutelage over the economy and science. A perceptible effort was also made to get rid of the "spirit of monotony in the newspapers,"[197] i.e., the imprint of Stalinism on the language of propaganda.

The open campaign for de-Stalinization, which began with Khrushchev's secret speech on "The Personality Cult and Its Effects," delivered at the Twentieth Party Congress on February 25, 1956, triggered the Polish and Hungarian uprisings and a general destabilization in Eastern Europe. In the Soviet Union the incomplete dismantling of Stalinism — an explanation of the faults and failures of the past being sought in Stalin's own person rather than in the system itself — contributed directly to Khrushchev's fall in 1964, after which the process gave way to a phase of renewed, if cautious, re-Stalinization. Resistance to the de-Stalinization course — signs of which had been evident even as early as the

Twenty-second Party Congress in 1961, which under Khrushchev's leadership had decided on the removal of Stalin's body from the Lenin mausoleum — grew steadily in momentum, until at the Twenty-third Party Congress in 1966 it was quite unmistakable.

The zigzag course taken in the dismantling of Stalinist orthodoxy — from the hammering out of a new ideological consensus under Khrushchev to the partial re-Stalinization — is faithfully mirrored in successive efforts to conceptualize and disseminate newly revised canonical textbooks defining party doctrine. Indeed, it was in the midst of this ideological shilly-shallying that Mao Zedong moved to publicly condemn Khrushchev's course — an ideological rupture that opened the floodgates to the political conflict that has split China and the Soviet Union to this very day. One consequence, hardly welcomed by Moscow, was the fact that in a clear and unmistakable affront to the Soviet leadership, the Stalin cult and the propaganda use of his writings were kept alive in Korea to support Kim Il Sung's dictatorial regime, and in Beijing as a pointed weapon against Moscow's "revisionism."

With the crumbling of Stalinist orthodoxy, the _Foundations of Leninism_, which had been used as a textbook, and the _Short Course on the History of the CPSU_, which had been a mandatory indoctrination text even in the countries of Eastern Europe, were moved to the back shelves; now new orthodox texts had to be compiled. In August 1956 the Central Committee of the CPSU passed a resolution commissioning the preparation of an ideological textbook under the direction of Otto Kuusinen; this book, the _Foundations of Marxism-Leninism_, was published in October 1959. The partial shift of course and re-Stalinization after Khrushchev's fall made the arduous task of revision necessary once again. Late in 1966 the _Foundations of Scientific Communism_ was published as an official textbook, and by the summer of 1968 over a million copies had been distributed — it had been made mandatory party reading and was used in colleges and universities as well. This strategy of canonical textbooks brought to an end the third stage of canonical development, in which the political leader, directly conscious of his ideological mission and his role in pointing the way, was held up as a theoretical authority. Silence reigns over Khrushchev's theoretical contribution, and Brezhnev's writings, though credited with valuable political insights, are not classified as part of the canon of Marxist classics.

g) Soviet ideology and state Maoism

The development of a leadership cult and of ideological orthodoxy in the USSR, with Lenin as their focus, amounted to an adaptation of Marxism to subserve national aims. The multiple levels of the official ideological writings — ranging from the Soviet version of the Marx–Engels canon down to the works of Lenin and Stalin and, in a separate category from the true classics, the works published by later heads of state — has made for a motley foundation From the vantage point of the seventies, one notes a tendency toward progressive contraction of the sphere of Soviet ideological hegemony to the country's own national borders; only within them can orthodoxy be maintained. The swelling stream of critical theoretical works written from a Marxist perspective (and unofficially circulated in Eastern Europe) and also the first stirrings of Eurocommunism are part of this phenomenon, but the trend is evident even in the documents of the international communist party conferences organized on Moscow's initiative.[198] In November 1957, at the first world communist conference following de-Stalinization and the Hungarian and Polish uprisings, the leading role of the Soviet Union was still acknowledged, but the Sino-Soviet conflict troubled the air of the second world conference in late 1960. At the third conference — which did not meet until 1969, having been postponed on account of the invasion of Czechoslavakia — Eurocommunist ideas gained some partial acknowledgment; conspicuous in the documents are certain formulations implying that communism no longer had a presiding center. The culmination of all this was the so-called European summit conference held in East Berlin in June 1976, at which Moscow struggled to regain control over the ideological line. However, the conference was unable to agree on a unified Marxist-Leninist platform; nor did it issue a condemnation of Maoism. It thus marked the end of a uniform conception of European Communism with Moscow as its acknowledged point of reference.

The growth and development of Chinese orthodoxy, grounded in Stalinism, has taken a similar turn. Since Mao's death the leadership has refrained from holding up Maoism as the sole continuation of orthodox doctrine and from denouncing all other currents or tendencies outside of China as revisionism. On the international scene, since the Cultural Revolution little progress has been made in the creation of pro-Chinese splinter parties or the establishment of fraternal alliances (alongside such heavyweights as Albania, whose friendship has cooled). Hua Guofeng, as an interim figure, had little prospect of attaining to Mao's international stature as an ideological leader. Since the October 1976 fall of the Gang of Four, Maoist policies of the previous decade — indeed two decades, back to the Great Leap Forward — have been ever more firmly disavowed at the level of actual policy, though at the rhetorical level the tendency has been to avoid the sort of tempestuous formal ideological housecleaning that followed Stalin's death. Still, the message of the official condemnation of persons from Mao's most intimate circles was unambiguous enough, encompassing as it did Mao's personally appointed successor Lin Biao, Mao's chief ideologist Chen Boda, and the leading figure of the left faction (and Mao's wife) Jiang Qing, as well as the leaders of the radical Shanghai faction, whose actual influence was certainly exaggerated in the campaign against the Gang of Four.

Thus China too has ideologically withdrawn behind its own national frontiers, without, however, wishing completely to forgo the establishment of a new orthodoxy, as is evident from the molding of the Mao canon and the reconstitution and propagation of the histories of the party and the army. Hua's less than inspiring writings, which figured as a sort of brief intermezzo between late Maoism and the post-Mao era symbolized by Deng, could not become part of the canon. Like the official documents recording the views of Zhou Enlai or Deng Xiaoping[199] over the years, they are but "objective" milestones of party history and Chinese developments, part of the official records on various subjects concerning the People's Republic in general rather than the personal legacy of some outstanding political figure.

2. VIETNAM: A HO CHI MINH CULT WITHOUT AN ORTHODOX CANON

Vietnam, like China, adopted as its state ideology a version of Marxism-Leninism that centered on a figure personifying national unity — in Vietnam's case, Ho Chi Minh. Has the Vietnamese political ideology likewise produced forms of orthodoxy analogous to the Chinese? Have a cult of Ho and a corresponding Ho canon been the focal point of state propaganda?

In simplified form the answer might be that, yes, Vietnam's state ideology does entail a Ho cult, but it has not developed a "Ho-Chi-Minhism" comparable to Maoism (Mao Zedong Thought). While to some extent the state ideology does highlight Ho's person, it is not fixated on it. One indication of this is the obvious fact that Vietnam's Marxist-Leninist state ideology does not incorporate Ho's name in its self-definition. Having borrowed freely from the theory and practice of Moscow and Beijing alike, the Vietnamese have not gone on to style their eclectic mixture of forms as a universally valid body of Marxist-Leninist doctrine. Vietnam makes no claim to national originality in the ideological domain, unlike China, which has asserted its ideology energetically and left its mark on the international scene, or North Korea, which has done so doggedly, albeit to little effect. A more unpretentious, more flexible ideological instrument has been evolved in Vietnam rather than another new dogma to join the ranks of Leninism, Stalinism, and Maoism. As is evident in the following description of Vietnam's educational policy by a minister of education, there is a fundamental difference between the Vietnamese ideology and orthodox Maoism.

> Even if the general line remains unchanged, the forms and ways in which it is applied are constantly being modified so that we can respond to the needs emerging at every new stage in the revolution. On the one hand, our education has evolved in response to the concrete needs of a colonial nation that has waged a heroic struggle for its liberation.... On the other hand, its forms and methods are the result of a continual application of Marxist-Leninist doctrine in the field of education. Though we do have a clear and precise doctrine, we by no means pretend to have found any magic formulas that will solve all problems. We have sought, explored, and felt our way around, and we shall continue to seek, explore, and feel our way around.[200]

The flexibility of this ideological instrument, with its drastically scaled down claim to orthodoxy, stems from Ho Chi Minh's pragmatic understanding of ideology, which was passed on to the party. Party ideologist Truong Chinh, who worked at Ho's side for forty years, once observed that Ho "despised theory" and abhorred "arid pedantic quoting" from the classics of Marxism-Leninism.[201] Ho held on to this credo after the establishment of the North Vietnamese state. His dim view of the Sino-Soviet conflict is quite understandable in the light of such a root attitude. At the Congress of the Eighty-one Communist Parties held in Moscow in 1960, Ho did everything he could to prevent the break between Moscow and

Beijing. The subject came up again in December 1965, during Ho Chi Minh's last visit to Mao. Ho's position was given its clearest expression in his so-called Testament of May 10, 1969,[202] in which the Vietnamese leader deeply lamented the political and ideological split between China and the USSR and called on his own party to step up its efforts to mend the rift.

Another good example of this fundamentally pragmatic attitude is the Vietnamese response to the Cultural Revolution. Ho and his party firmly rejected the exaggerated Mao cult of that period with all its ramifications, perhaps anticipating that what had been built on sand would soon have to be pulled down — as indeed it was after 1976.

A natural consequence of Ho's aversion to theoretical debates, whether at home or abroad, and of his contempt for the conventionally monotonous language of functionaries was his willingness to let subordinate party leaders author important ideological documents of the Vietnamese revolution, without considering this any threat to his own position. For example, Truong Chinh, former general secretary of the Communist Party of Indochina, wrote the 1947 pamphlet Resistance Will Triumph, which became the handbook of the Vietnamese guerrillas. Another such figure was the brilliant polemicist Le Duc Tho; likewise General Giap and Le Duan[203] authored significant political documents. Thus Ho often left writing to others, preferring instead to concentrate attention on his role as an initiator of action, his organizational work, and the maintenance of close contact with the people.

a) Forms of the Ho Chi Minh cult

Ho's reserve, as compared to the ever prolific Mao, proved no obstacle to the emergence and promulgation of a Ho cult in Vietnam. But the cult of Ho was as different from that of Mao as the leaders were from one another; most notably, Ho was never apotheosized in the manner of the Mao cult. Of course Ho, like Mao, undoubtedly saw himself as a figure of unity and a symbol of national liberation, which is probably why he offered no resistance to the spread of a Ho cult. Esteemed by the people for his good nature, his amiable and sentimental manner, in their eyes he was not the "Great Helmsman" but rather "Uncle Ho." Just as Mao's reputation as a poet, reinforced by state propaganda, was a part of the Mao cult, so was Ho known as a writer of verse and in fact, even as a playwright;[204] yet, the Vietnamese honored the man more than his work, and the Ho cult did not incorporate the party leader's numerous writings. Ho issued no "guiding principles"; he did not aspire to be the omnipresent and paramount ideological inspiration of his people or to create "new men" by controlling and shaping the superstructure as had Mao Zedong.

Even after Ho Chi Minh's death in 1969, this modest Ho cult underwent no qualitative change or wild inflation. Whereas in China the embattled Hua faction, anxious to legitimate its succession, had within a year of the chairman's death erected a grandiose mausoleum for the veneration of his remains, Ho's successors had built for him a mausoleum modeled on Lenin's, which was opened on August 29, 1975, fully six years after his death. Although in the interim the Hanoi leaders briefly toyed with the idea of forging a "Ho Chi Minh Thought" out of the Ho cult, they soon discarded the idea.

b) Noncanonical Ho writings

Ho's numerous writings, which, like Mao's *Selected Works*, were first published in a four-volume set that was translated into foreign languages, could not be compared with Mao's in either content or political function. Ho's writings have been called poor material for literary anthologies. Indeed, Lacouture described many of Ho's texts — his moral sermons, his exhortations to children, his appeals to the troups in combat, his expressions of gratitude to his fellow citizens — as frankly stupefying: "One sometimes gets the impression that the author or speaker is a country preacher or a rather mediocre village schoolteacher."[205] In editing the four-volume selection, which ran the gamut from the early anticolonial writings, unpolished and emotional, to the more prosaic documents of the Hanoi government and the Vietnam war, it would have been an easy matter to make some cosmetic improvements on Ho's texts. The editorial committee did not do this, undoubtedly at the party leader's own wish. The important point, however, is that Ho's *Selected Works* were never intended for use as an ideological canon for propagandistic indoctrination. This was clear from their outward appearance alone. Indeed, conventional errata inserts — which would have been unthinkable for the editors of an edition of Mao's works — were used to remedy the many errors attributable to careless typesetting and slapdash proofreading. In short, neither the four-volume selection nor a one-volume selection of writings from 1920 through 1969 (published in 1971 and translated into English) was treated as holy writ. There was no mention of any special Central Committee board that assumed formal responsibility for the Selected Works; they were presented as the writings of a leading revolutionary, that was all. This approach spared the party a great deal of worry, since there was no formal editorial apparatus to suggest that the party was putting its stamp on an orthodox unified picture of the history of the revolution and the epoch — a consideration that delayed CCP publication of Mao Zedong's post-1949 writings until 1977, almost thirty years.[206] On the contrary, the four-volume Ho selection published in 1961-62 included all of Ho's writings to that date; likewise, the one-volume 1971 selection contained documents right up to Ho's death in 1969.

Thus, Ho Chi Minh's life and works have never served as a cornerstone of state ideology; nor have they been presented as the one and only orthodox basis for the indoctrination of the Vietnamese people. By and large, official assessments of Ho's accomplishments have maintained this low key. There has been no attempt to generalize theoretically and dogmatically the Vietnamese way as shown by Ho. The party made no audacious demand that Ho's teachings should be placed at the summit of the edifice of Marxist-Leninist doctrine: Vietnam had simply made a national application of the basic tenets of Marxism-Leninism, and did this without adding many specifically national modifications to the ideology (less, for example, than Yugoslavia).

c) Differences in the use of cult and canon in Vietnam and in China

We have already outlined some of the reasons for the profound differences between the Chinese and the Vietnamese ideological attitudes toward cult and canon. Hanoi's ideological modesty is undoubtedly to be explained at least in part by Vietnam's relatively subordinate position in the international concert, where it figures only as a regional power, and should by no means be ascribed solely to Ho's distaste for dogma. Clearly, without the help of the Soviet Union and China, the Vietnam war could hardly have been sustained to its termination in 1975.

Ho's aversion to a cult around his own person, and especially around his writings, may be traced to certain peculiarities of his personality; but it is also the case that Ho's long commitment to internationalism helped him to see his own achievements in a far broader, and hence a far more relative perspective than did Mao. It was said about Ho that he had a wonderful way of not taking himself seriously,[207] which was only underscored by his frail build and the almost comical figure he cut, reminiscent of Charlie Chaplin. He had the unworldliness of the wise, and this was never more true than in the last and most successful years of his life, when he chose to reside in a small garden house rather than the presidential palace. One can hardly imagine a greater contrast to the imposing figure of Mao Zedong, particularly the mature Mao proclaiming the Cultural Revolution before hundreds of thousands of Red Guards in Beijing, and all the Byzantine ritual that attended his public appearances.

Mao's basic disposition, which was at least tacitly approving of his glorification by the nation, offers a striking contrast to the more self-critical urbanity of Ho Chi Minh. The latter had seen much of the world while still a young man, had frequented all the Mediterranean harbors for two years as a ship's kitchenhand, passed five years in Paris, spent time in Moscow, and lived some years in China. Ho, who esteemed French as a universal language of culture and was thoroughly conversant with French literature, had written many of his early works in that language. Within the world communist movement as such he was from the beginning a more internationalist figure than Mao Zedong. By the end of World War I he was a fully accepted figure in the French Socialist Party hierarchy[208]; his activities in the anticolonial movement were hardly confined to his own country; nor, of course, was his Comintern work. Indeed, Ho's profoundly international outlook may be exemplified by his early writings on repression in the United States.

d) Ho's attitude toward Mao

This major difference in inclination and early experience may well have shaped the attitudes of these two men toward one another. In Ho's view Comrade Mao Zedong had correctly applied the ideology of Marx, Engels, Lenin, and Stalin to the practical situation in China and led the Chinese revolution to total victory. He was thoroughly aware of the significance of Mao Zedong's ideas for the Vietnamese revolution,[209] although in his writings Ho never went beyond the simple assertion of this fact. Mao's mass campaigns after the founding of the PRC fell outside the bounds of Ho's appreciation both practically and theoretically. He never permitted the term "greatest Marxist of our time" to be applied to Mao, and in this way politely but unambiguously undercut Mao's claim to ideological hegemony. On occasion Ho could not resist a bit of discreet sarcasm on the subject of Mao. A foreign visitor once asked him bluntly whether he did not want to publish any articles or books, as Chairman Mao had done and was still doing. Ho reportedly replied with a twinkle in his eye: "If something still remains about which Chairman Mao hasn't written, then tell me and I'll try promptly to fill up this gap."[210]

Ho's occasionally pointed reserve was matched by a measured aloofness on Mao Zedong's part. The record holds nothing more than the sort of routine exchanges one would expect to find in the telegrams between the leaders of closely allied parties. When Ho died there was no obituary forthcoming from Mao to join his deeply adulatory essays about Stalin and Sun Yat-sen.[211]

3. NORTH KOREA: AN INFLATED CULT AROUND KIM IL SUNG AND THE "JUCHE" IDEOLOGY

There is also a personality cult around North Korea's leader Kim Il Sung — one of absurd proportions — with a canon of Kim Il Sung's works comprising an integral part of the cult. This North Korean cult, the "Stalinism of the East," is distinguished by its fixation on the person and on the official biography of the "esteemed and beloved leader." The exaggerated celebration of leader Kim's "genius" and of Korean ideological creativity make a vivid contrast to the Vietnamese situation, while in the over-inflation of the cult to the point that it is potentially a destabilizing force, we find something of a quite different order from Mao's cult and canon and the way state Maoism has been used in the PRC.

The climate in the People's Democratic Republic of Korea is suffused by the personality cult around Kim Il Sung, which in its intensity is comparable only to the Stalin cult or possibly the Mao cult during the Cultural Revolution. Indeed, the affinity to Stalinism is not denied; Stalin has been ceremoniously hailed as the "Great Leader" to whom the Soviet Union owed the building of socialism and who thereby became the most celebrated teacher of Marxism, surpassing Lenin, Marx, and Engels.[212] The Korean cult whose roots reach back to Korea's highly centralized version of the Confucian system of ranks, that is, its tradition of bureaucratic centralism — would lead one to suppose that the country belongs to Kim, and not Kim to his country.[213] A unique feature of the state propaganda of the Kim Il Sung cult is its veneration of the entire Kim clan as a holy family; they are honored with countless monuments and even a small collection of relics, and Kim's mother has been glorified as the "Mother of Korea."

In emulation of the catchwords of Mao Zedong Thought, North Korea's state ideology was defined as a system of "Kim Il Sung ideas" and credited as the major component of the "three great revolutions" in the ideological, cultural, and technical domains. Its central ideological concept is "Juche," or the creative application of Marxism-Leninism to the realities of the Korea,[214] along the lines of Stalin's formula that culture must be "national in form and socialist in content." The Korean constitution of December 1972 refers specifically to this key concept, but not Kim's name or Kim's thought; here we find a difference from China, where allusions to Mao Zedong Thought in successive versions of the state and party constitutions provide a sort of barometric reading of the degree of "Maoist radicalism" in a particular period.

Again on the Chinese example, Korea's party ideologists have fashioned a canon of Kim's writings. The initial version was a six-volume collection of writings from the years 1946 through 1959, and there is a new edition that updates the first; both have been translated into foreign languages.[215] These Kim writings were published officially by the Central Committee's Institute for Party History as a canonical selection. As in China, the canon is paralleled by countless individual pamphlets and, since the Cultural Revolution, even a Red Book of excerpts from Kim's writings. Unlike the situation in China, however, Kim's writings are not invoked by the various political currents within the leadership as a means of legitimation, and therefore the practice of more or less automatically publishing current Kim texts provokes no controversy.

Also in contrast to the Chinese case, an official hagiography in the form of a party biography of Kim[216] has been given a central function in the canon; anyone who does not know the history of the Korean leader, it is held, cannot understand the country. Hence, in the schools, children from the age of four must learn to recite stories about the leader in simple sentences and recount the Kim myth with the help of picture posters; older schoolchildren must learn the leader's biography by heart. The ideas of the leader Kim are likewise the focal point of higher education, which entails extensive memorization of Kim texts. Korean party cadres take pride in their ability to repeat flawlessly whole speeches and party reports by leader Kim. The only thing comparable to this is the Mao cult at its most intense, under the direction of Lin Biao during the Cultural Revolution. Korea's Kim cult, however, lacks the ingredient of genuine mass participation, while Kim himself lacks the charisma and natural authority of an independent revolutionary leader.

In light of its extreme over-inflation, the prospects for long-term stability of the Kim cult and endurance of the canonical writings of "state Kimism" would seem doubtful, an impression supported by the difficulties that have been encountered during a series of efforts to set up Kim's son as his eventual successor. The Kim myth is fatally undermined by the well-known fact that his regime was established in North Korea only with the help of the Soviet Army. Moreover, Kim's claim to have made an independent Korean contribution to the development of Marxism-Leninism is not well supported. The "Juche" concept is quite as vague and amorphous as Sun Yat-sen's "Three People's Principles" were during pre-revolutionary China's republican period. Despite vigorous official propagation of the writings of "Kim Thought" both at home and abroad, the ideology has made little headway outside Korea; in contrast to the international influence of Maoism, or the prestige of Ho Chi Minh as a symbol of the revolution in Vietnam, a small regional power, the Kim canon has had about as much international impact as Albania's two dozen volumes of the Enver Hoxha canon.

Thus, the canon and cult of North Korea's revolution — a revolution "from above and from without," as opposed to the revolutions in Vietnam and China, which spread from below and within — may well be permanently dismantled and demolished after Kim Il Sung's death, more along the lines of the destruction of the Stalinist edifice after 1953 than the cautious de-Maoization that has been under way in China since 1976.

Notes

1. Publication of a more definitive version of the collective writings of Mao Zedong remains a task for the future, so we do not yet have a documentary record of Mao on the order of the 40-volume Lenin edition or the projected 100-volume Marx–Engels edition (MEGA). The seven-volume bilingual collection edited by Helmut Martin with Gerhard Will entitled Mao Zedong Texte: Schriften, Dokumente, Reden, Gespräche. Deutsch-Chinesisch, Munich, Hanser Verlag, 1977-1982, is but a step in this direction. A first draft of the present study was written as part of this project. See Helmut Martin, Kult und Kanon. Entstehung und Entwicklung des Staatmaoismus 1935–1978, Hamburg, 1978, and China ohne Maoismus, Reinbek/Hamburg, 1980.

2. China's term for Maoism, Mao Zedong sixiang, rendered as "Mao Zedong Thought" in official translations, may also be translated as "ideology."

3. This is illustrated, for example, by Mao's statement of displeasure in 1966 with regard to Lin's excessive Mao cult, which Mao was unable to curb because he himself had to make use of the cult to achieve his own objectives during the Cultural Revolution. See Text, July 8, 1966, Mao Intern (see below, note 6), pp. 205-208.

4. Stuart R. Schram, The Political Thought of Mao Tse-tung (hereafter Thought), New York, 1963.

5. Minoru Takeuchi, Mao Zedong ji (Collected Texts of Mao Zedong) (hereafter Mao ji), Tokyo, 1970-72, 10 vols.

6. Compare, for example, the collections containing references to the Chinese texts, translated into several languages: Jerome Ch'en, Mao Papers. Anthology and Bibliography, New York, 1970; Stuart R. Schram, Mao Tse-tung Unrehearsed. Talk and Letters: 1956-1971 (hereafter Unrehearsed), Harmondsworth, 1974; Helmut Martin, Mao Intern. Unveröffentlichte Schriften, Reden und Gespräche Mao Tse-tungs 1949-1971 (hereafter Mao Intern), Munich, 1974.

7. The phrase "the great, glorious, and correct party" (weidade, guangrongde, zhengquede dang) is to be found, for example, in the preamble of the party constitution of April 1969 and that of August 1977. For a comparison of the constitutional texts of 1956, 1969, 1973, and 1977 see Oskar Weggel in the German monthly China aktuell (hereafter C.a.), October 1977, pp. 692-735.

8. The following terms have been used interchangeably for the two factions

of the Politburo of 1971–1976: radical Shanghai faction, left (Shanghai) faction, Shanghai left; right faction, pragmatists, moderates. We have omitted from our terminology the term "palace faction" (gongting pai) and "old cadre faction" (yuanlao pai), which have been used in analyses outside the PRC. In our terminology the left–right paradigm is used only in reference to intraparty struggles within China during this period, i.e., it indicates the relative positions taken by these groups on all questions, whether verbally or in their concrete political actions. Furthermore, this paradigm largely reflects how the persons concerned viewed themselves during this period; for example, the radicals considered themselves "left" and struggled against the "rightist tendency..." (youqing fan'anfeng) of the moderates. The moderates, on the other hand, were constrained to remain silent in the media with respect to their own position; however, they did attempt to attack the position of the radicals as ultra-left, particularly after the fall of Lin Biao. After the October 1976 defeat of the radical Shanghai faction, which was promptly condemned as a rightist putsch by foreign devotees of the Maoist left, the victorious moderates polemized against their former archenemies, calling them "right wingers" masquerading as leftists, without, however, expressly calling themselves "leftist." The Deng group has since 1979 settled on a more appropriate terminology in criticizing the Gang of Four for "left opportunism."

9. The original version is found in Takeuchi, Mao ji, Vol. 1, pp. 207-49. See also Mao Tse-tung, Ausgewählte Werke (the official German translation, referred to hereafter as AW, I–IV), Beijing, 1968, pp. 21-63.

10. See Wu Tien-wei, Mao Tse-tung and the Tsunyi Conference, Washington, 1974.

11. On this period see Benjamin I. Schwartz, Chinese Communism and the Rise of Mao, Cambridge, Mass., 1958, and John E. Rue, Mao Tse-tung in Opposition, 1927-35, Stanford, California, 1966.

12. See Boyd Compton, transl. and introd., Mao's China. Party Reform Documents, 1942-44, reprinted Seattle, 1966.

13. See Schram, Thought, p. 80.

14. Liu's "Report on the Revision of the Party Constitution" appears in Liu Shaoqi xuanji (Selected Writings of Liu Shaoqi), Tokyo, 1967, pp. 135-223. This text dates from June 1945; it also includes passages from the party constitution. Liu, who assumed the office of state president in April 1959 and until his fall in the Cultural Revolution had been recognized as Mao's official successor, appeared several times after 1945 as the authorized interpreter of Mao Zedong Thought. Only in the course of Liu's rehabilitation did we learn that he had been in charge of the official editorial committee for the Selected Works. During the Great Leap Forward it was Liu who articulated Mao's so-called theory of continuing revolution (buduan geming), since there were no cohesive texts by the party chief available on this topic. See Liu's speech of May 5, 1958, at the Second Session of the Eighth Party Congress, printed in Renmin ribao (People's Daily – RMRB) on May 27, 1958; the German text is found in Stuart R. Schram, Die permanente Revolution in China. Dokumente und Kommentar, Frankfurt, 1966, pp. 87-88. Schram's analysis is an informative case study on the elaboration and presentation of a central Maoist concept by authorized interpreters.

15. Mao Zedong lunwen ji (Mao Zedong's Treatises), n.p., Dazhong Press, 1937; also Mao Zedong lun Zhong-Ri zhanzheng (Mao Zedong on the Sino-Jap-

anese War), n.p., Shanxi People's Press, 1937; and Mao Zedong jiuguo yanlun xuanji (Selected Speeches of Mao Zedong on the Salvation of the Country), Chongqing, 1939.

16. Mao Zedong xuanji (Selected Works of Mao Zedong), Yanan, 1944, 5 vols.; Mao Zedong xuanji, n.p., Suzhong Press, 1945, 1 vol.; Mao Zedong xuanji, Dalian, 1946; Mao Zedong xuanji, n.p., Xinhua Press, 1947, 6 vols. and supplementary volume (xubian), edited by Zhongguo gongchandang jinchaji zhongyangju. A reprint by the Center for Chinese Research Materials appeared as Selected Works of Mao Tse-tung, Washington, D.C., 1970, in 2 volumes. See also Mao Zedong xuanji, Harbin, 1948, 1 vol.; and Mao Zedong xuanji, n.p., edited by Zhongguo gongchandang jinji luyu zhongyangju, 1948. Deng Tuo was editor of the 1944 version.

17. Mao Zedong xuanji (hereafter Xuanji); this is the one-volume edition of the four-volume Selected Works canon, Beijing, 1969. Preface; cf. AW, I, p. 5.

18. This survey is based on official PRC statistics. See Peking Rundschau/ Peking [Beijing] Review (hereafter PR), January 14, 1969, No. 2, p. 3, and PR, June 1, 1976, No. 22, p. 3. Both of these figures should be understood propagandistically with reference first to the success of the Cultural Revolution and second to the left faction; according to the list of mid-1976, 236.6 million copies of the four-volume edition of the Selected Works were printed, of which 10.8 million were printed before the Cultural Revolution and 225.8 million copies in the ten-year period after 1966. That it is only the order of magnitude which is relevant here is also shown by comparison of figures from the two sources: according to the 1969 figures, there was a total of 11.5 million copies of the four-volume edition of the Selected Works from 1949 to the end of 1965, while according to later statistics it was 10.8 million. For the distribution of the Red Book and the Selected Works, see also PR, June 1, 1976, No. 22, p. 3.

19. In the purported program of the failed coup d'etat of Lin Biao, "Outline of 'Project 571' "; see the most complete compilation of Chinese sources, Michael Y. M. Kau, The Lin Piao Affair: Power Politics and Military Coup (hereafter Lin Affair), White Plains, N.Y.: M. E. Sharpe, 1975, p. 92.

20. In 1978 there also existed an internal edition of Mao's Selected Works edited by the General Political Department of the PLA, mentioned in Summary of World Broadcasts, Part III, The Far East (hereafter SWB), May 15, 1978, according to a report in Jiefang jun bao (Liberation Army News); however, it is unclear to what extent it differs from the generally available five-volume edition.

21. Xuanji, Preface: AW, I, p. 5; Chen Boda, Mao Zedong sixiang shi Makesi Liening zhuyi yu Zhongguo geming de jiehe (Mao Zedong's Thought Is a Unification of Marxism-Leninism and the Chinese Revolution), Shanghai, 1951; Chen Boda, Lun Mao Zedong sixiang (On Mao Zedong Thought), Beijing, 1952; Chen Boda, Mao Tse-tung's Theory of the Chinese Revolution, On Reading Mao Tse-tung's "Report on the Peasant Movement in Hunan," Beijing, n.d. (written in 1944); see Chen's biography in Donald W. Klein and Anne B. Clark, Biographical Dictionary of Chinese Communism 1921-1965, Cambridge, Mass., 1971.

22. Schram, Thought, p. 92.

23. Takeuchi, Mao ji (see note 5). Takeuchi did not include in his edition all the texts that appeared only in the official four-volume edition. An English translation of these ten volumes is in preparation.

24. See, for example, P. P. Vladimirov, Osobyj rajon Kitaja 1942-1945 (The Special Region of China), Moscow, 1973, p. 525, 636, 651-52. The "Resolution Concerning a Few Questions of the History [of Our Party]" of the Seventh Enlarged Plenum of the Sixth Central Committee, issued on April 20, 1945, and published in the Selected Works canon as an appendix to the Mao text of April 20, 1944, was removed from the Chinese-language edition; see for example Xuanji, III, Beijing, 1964; the resolution is on pp. 955-1002. In the later 1-volume edition Xuanji, Beijing, 1969, the text is missing. In the official German translation, AW, III, Beijing, 1969, it is also omitted. However, an unauthorized translation of the resolution was published in Mao Tse-tung. Ausgewählte Schriften, Berlin/E, 1956, Dietz Verlag, Vol. 4, pp. 222-85.

25. Xuanji, Preface; and AW, I, p. 5: "Since revolutionary documents were destroyed by the Guomindang reactionaries and were scattered and lost during the long years of war, we were unable to bring together all the writings of Comrade Mao Zedong; in particular, many letters and telegrams, which make up a considerable portion of his writings, are missing."

26. On the Strong interview of 1946, compare Takeuchi, Mao ji, Vol. 10, pp. 47-55; Xuanji, pp. 1087-92, and AW, IV, pp. 97-102. The Takeuchi version is from the Hong Kong journal Qunzhong (Masses) of June 5, 1947, and is based on an English version.

27. For the following examples see Schram, Thought, passim. Cf. Text of December 15, 1939, and Takeuchi, Mao ji, Vol. 7, pp. 97-135; cf. Text of March 28, 1927, and Takeuchi, Mao ji, Vol. 1, pp. 207-49.

28. In consideration of Moscow's condemnation, remarks made by Mao in recognition of "Comrade Browder" of the Communist Party of the United States were omitted. Text of July 29, 1945, Takeuchi, Mao ji, Vol. 9, pp. 303-304; cf. Schram, Thought, pp. 285 and 292. "National bourgeoisie" instead of "liberal bourgeoisie," Text of April 1, 1948, Takeuchi, Mao ji, Vol. 10, pp. 127-41; "people's democracy" instead of "democracy," Text of February 25, 1947, Takeuchi, Mao ji, Vol. 10, pp. 97-116; "Marxist-Leninist truth" instead of "truth," Text of February 8, 1942, Takeuchi, Mao ji, Vol. 8, pp. 89-108. For a longer omission to achieve greater ideological coherence, compare Texts May 26–June 3, 1938, Takeuchi, Mao ji, Vol. 6, pp. 49-145.

29. Text passages that gave the revolutionary experiences of China priority over those of the Soviet Union were transformed into their opposites: Text — –, 1936, Takeuchi, Mao ji, Vol. 5, pp. 83-168. The unique features of the Chinese path were downplayed in Mao's report on April 2, 1945, Takeuchi, Mao ji, Vol. 9, pp. 183-275. A more emphatic mention of the CCP: Text of December –, 1929, cf. Takeuchi, Mao ji, Vol. 2, pp. 77-125. Several additions of the phrase "under the leadership of the Communist Party," see Text April 2, 1945, Takeuchi, Mao ji, Vol. 9, pp. 183-275.

30. Several changes downplayed the role of the peasants, especially of the poor peasants: Text of March 28, 1927, Takeuchi, Mao ji, Vol. 1, pp. 207-49. Insertion of the phrase "leadership of the working class," Text of February 1, 1926, Takeuchi, Mao ji, Vol. 1, pp. 161-79. Youth and intellectuals were no longer mentioned as the leading force of the revolutionary movement: Text of May 4, 1939, Takeuchi, Mao ji, Vol. 6, pp. 325-37. Soviet polemicists generously overlook the fact that Mao himself made these changes. Extensive examples of such changes are also found in the analysis of Maoism as a political

ideology in Idejno-politicheskaja sushchnost' maoizma (The Nature of Maoism as a Political Ideology), Moscow, 1977, pp. 25-31. For Mao's praise of the Guomindang and Chiang Kai-shek in 1938, see Text of October 12-14, 1938, Takeuchi, Mao ji, Vol. 6, pp. 163-240, or the Report of the Seventh Party Congress, Text of April 2, 1945, Takeuchi, Mao ji, Vol. 9, pp. 183-275.

31. Volume IV appeared without an interpretative preface. New China News Agency (NCNA — September 29, 1960) gives a rundown on the publication of Volume IV: see also Survey of China Mainland Press (hereafter SCMP), October 6, 1960, No. 2353. The lead article of RMRB (September 30, 1960) on this event is contained in SCMP, October 7, 1960, No. 2353. Study articles after its publication treated the period from the end of the war with Japan to the establishment of the PRC, with a particular stress on events that had relevance to the situation of 1960. See, for example, a collection of the "Results of Study" of Volume IV in translation: Current Background, December 7, 1960, No. 641, with articles from central as well as local newspapers and periodicals. Such analyses emphasized that perseverance in the face of difficulties after the Great Leap Forward was made easier by the study of Mao's texts: these difficulties are nothing, it is claimed, in comparison with the tribulations of the revolutionary period. See, for example, a study article in Gongren ribao (Workers' Daily), October 7, 1960. A conference for upper-level cadres which focused on the study of Mao's writings had a more radical tone of self-assertion; Gongren ribao of October 6, 1960, also stressed that Volume IV ought to be seen as a potent ideological weapon for accelerating the socialist revolution.

32. In June 1964 two volumes of selections from Mao's works were published in addition to the Selected Works to provide support for the "Socialist Education Movement in the Countryside"; these were entitled Mao Zedong zhuzuo xuandu (jia) (yi) zhongben (Selected Readings from the Works of Mao Zedong, Editions A and B), Beijing, 1964. The preface to Edition A was dated May 1964, and a second printing came out in April 1965; Edition B appeared in June 1965 in a second edition, with a preface dated March 1965. A fourth (unaltered) printing of Edition B appeared in 1969.

33. Edition A was the basis for an official English translation of Selected Readings from the Works of Mao Tse-tung, Beijing, 1967. Another English edition from Beijing (1971) was referred to as the "first edition" (new orthography for the name "Mao Tsetung").

34. Selected Military Writings of Mao Tse-tung, Beijing, 1963, and Mao Tsetung, Ausgewählte Militärische Schriften (Selected Military Writings), Beijing, 1969. In 1978 a new expanded edition of Mao's military writings for the army had been prepared, as Ye Jianying reported in a speech before the Academy for Military Science; see PR, March 28, 1978, No. 12, pp. 6-9: "Chairman Mao's works on military theory are models of Marxist-Leninist military theory. We must study them assiduously. A multitude of instructions, orders, articles, and programs of Chairman Mao on building an army and on conducting war are a living embodiment of his great military ideals and his military praxis. We must gather these together as rapidly as possible, compile them, and study them conscientiously." See another collection, Mao zhuxi lun qingnian ji qingnian gongzuo (Chairman Mao on Youth and Work), Beijing, 1964.

35. Quoted according to the first version; see also Stuart R. Schram, ed., Quotations from Chairman Mao Tse-tung (hereafter Quotations), New York,

1968. Zhang's editorial role and authorship of the preface are confirmed in Guangming ribao (Guangming Daily – GMRB), May 18, 1978.

36. RMRB, May 8, 1978.

37. Mao zhuxi de wupian zhexue zhuzuo (Five Philosophical Writings of Chairman Mao), Beijing, 1970. These are the Texts of July –, 1937, August –, 1937, February 27, 1957, March 12, 1957, and May –, 1963. These texts were taken from the Readings (A), and not from the Selected Works canon, and were accompanied by calligraphy by Lin Biao, excerpted from the preface to the Red Book. Here compare the exegetical literature: Mao zhuxi de wupian zhexue zhuzuo zhong de lishi shijian he renwu jianjie (A Short Commentary on the Historical Circumstances and Personal Clarifications of Persons Mentioned in the Five Philosophical Writings of Chairman Mao), Beijing, 1972. A precursor from the time of the Cultural Revolution was Mao zhuxi de sipian zhexue lunwen (Four Philosophical Treatises of Chairman Mao), Beijing, 1966, also selected from the second edition of the Readings (A); the text of March 12, 1957, was omitted. Mao zhuxi guanyu wenxue yishu de wuge wenjian (Five Documents of Chairman Mao on Literature and Art), Beijing, 1967. Three Works, called, in the political language, the Laosanpian (Three Constantly Read Articles): "Serve the People," September 8, 1944; "Yu Gong Moves Mountains," December 21, 1939; "In Memory of Norman Bethune," June 11, 1945. The PRC also published a bilingual edition, Mao Tsetung, Serve the People, In Memory of Norman Bethune, The Foolish Old Man Who Removed the Mountains, Beijing, 1972, taken from the second edition of Readings (A). Five Works: in addition to the above three articles, "Against Liberalism," September 7, 1937, and "On the Correction of False Views in the Party," January 18, 1948.

38. "Mao Zedong tongzhi de qinmi zhanyou he jiebanren" (cf. the bilingual reprint of the party constitution in C.a., October 1977, p. 718). See also the "Discussion Materials for the Study of the Constitution of the CCP" in Yuan Rui, ed., Lin Biao shijian yuanshi wenjian huibian (A Compilation of Original Documents on the Lin Biao Affair) (hereafter Lin huibian), Taipei, 1973, pp. 1-5. See also the draft constitution prepared after 1969 and adopted at the Second Plenum of the Ninth Central Committee on September 6, 1970 (Preamble and 1, 2), in Edgar Tomson and Jyun-hsyong Su, Regierung und Verwaltung der Volksrepublik China (Government and Administration of the People's Republic of China), Cologne, 1972, pp. 495-96.

39. In the draft of an official Lin Biao biography of June 1969, Mao zhuxi de jieban ren: Lin Biao fu tongshuai (The Successor of Chairman Mao: Vice-Commander Lin Biao), n.p., 1969; the second quotation is in RMRB, October 10, 1966.

40. The quotation comes from Lin's letter on the study of Mao Zedong Thought, March 11, 1966, in RMRB of June 19, 1966, "Letter on the Living Study and Living Application of the Work of Chairman Mao on the Industry and Transportation Front." Compare similar versions: "There are always differences in thought; different levels of human knowledge and consciousness cannot be unified. But we need unification. Mao Zedong Thought can give that unification," in "Talk at the Reception for Some Delegates from Hunan, Guizhou, and Szechuan at the Ninth Party Congress," May 2, 1969, in Wenhua dageming wenjian huibian (A Compilation of Documents on the Great Cultural Revolution), n.p., 1970, No. 3-4, pp. 1-5. The same thought occurs in Lin's

"How to Raise the Study of the Writings of Chairman Mao to a New Level," September 18, 1966, in Mao Zhuxi wenxuan (Selected Texts of Chairman Mao) (hereafter Wenxuan), n.p., n.d., pp. 99-102. Lin Biao's daughter reported on the marshal's habits in her article "On Writing"; see Kau, Lin Affair, pp. 472-84. In a March 20, 1967, speech to leading cadres in the army Lin noted that one should hang ideological slogans on the wall and look at them day and night until one could say them by heart; see Zhonggong nianbao 1971 (Yearbook on Chinese Communism) (hereafter Yearbook), Taipei, VII, pp. 25-28.

41. Lin Biao yulu (Sayings of Lin Biao), Kunming, 1967, p. 9.

42. In 1960 Lin chaired an expanded conference of the Military Committee of the Central Committee which drew up the "Resolution on Strengthening Political Ideological Work among the Troops." In January 1961 Lin issued "An Instruction on Strengthening Political and Ideological Work among the Troops"; see Kau, Lin Affair, p. 46. A fascinating documentation of this period of schooling within the army can be found in the internal army bulletin Gongzuo tongxun (Work Reports) (copies available in the archives of the Institut für Asienkunde, Hamburg); see Chester J. Cheng, ed., The Politics of the Chinese Red Army, Stanford, California, 1966.

43. Selected Works of Lin Biao (hereafter Works of Lin), Hong Kong, 1970, pp. 233-61.

44. See Lin's instructions on the study of the Volume IV within the army, December 17, 1960, and December 30, 1960, in Works of Lin, pp. 268-69 and p. 275.

45. Cf. Schram, Quotations, pp. xxxi-xxxii.

46. Lin used the metaphor of the shadow in his speech of May 18, 1966, at an expanded session of the Politburo of the Central Committee: "Chairman Mao is still alive, therefore we can rejoice under the shadow of such a great tree. Chairman Mao is now over seventy years old and still very healthy; he can live to be over one hundred." See Yearbook 1970, VII, pp. 50-56.

47. In the speech of May 18, 1966 (see note 46).

48. Mentioned in Mao's "Open Letter to the Whole Party" in Central Committee Document No. 57 of September 14, 1971; see Kau, Lin Affair, p. 68. In his speech before the Eleventh Plenum of the Eighth Central Committee of August 1, 1966, Lin called Mao the genius of world revolution: "The chairman is the genius of world revolution. There is a great distance between him and us; we must quickly correct the mistakes we have made." See Wenxuan, pp. 95-97. The genius theory is also taken up in Lin's speech before the Politburo of April 18, 1966 (see Note 46).

49. Lin's instructions of September 18, 1966; see Wenxuan, pp. 99-102.

50. Wenxuan, p. 87; see also p. 91. The Red Guards collection of readings, WS 69, bore a slightly altered version of this sentence on its title page: "Comrade Mao Zedong is the greatest Marxist-Leninist of our time." This was the first sentence in Lin Biao's preface to the Red Book. It was also contained in the preface to Volume V of the Selected Works (see note 121).

51. Speech of September 18, 1966 (see note 49).

52. Lin huibian, p. 37.

53. Report at the Ninth Party Congress of the CCP of April 1, 1969, in Hongqi (Red Flag) (hereafter HQ) 1969, No. 5, pp. 7-48. On the significance of the Eleventh Plenum see Lin's speech of September 18, 1966 (note 49).

54. Lin huibian, pp. 1-5.

55. Lin used this metaphor, for instance, on December 17, 1960, in his political-ideological instruction of leading army cadres. See Works of Lin, p. 269. The metaphor of ideology as an "arrow" was quite common before 1949 in the CCP. For example: "How can Marxist-Leninist theory and the reality of the Chinese Revolution be linked together? Take the expression 'shoot an arrow and have a target.'... The relationship between Marxism-Leninism and the Chinese Revolution is the same as that between an arrow and a target"; Text of February 1, 1942, Takeuchi, Mao ji, Vol. 8, p. 74. Both prefaces are in Tilemann Grimm, ed., Das Rote Buch, Frankfurt, 1977, pp. 15-18; in May 1977, 140,000 copies of this edition, which first appeared in 1967, were sold. On the MEGA see Neue Marx-Engels Forschung, zur Marx-Engels-Gesamtausgabe (MEGA) (New Marx-Engels Research: On the Marx-Engels Complete Edition), Information Report No. 24 of the Institut für Marxistische Studien und Forschungen, Frankfurt, 1976, pp. 27-43. Concerning the one-volume edition of the Selected Works canon in the form of the Red Book, the Xuanji edition, Beijing, 1969, noted that a one-volume edition had already been published in April 1964; the one-volume pocket edition appeared for the first time in November 1967.

56. A detailed analysis of the Red Book was presented in the preface to the English edition edited by Schram (see note 35). On the "Thirty-Character Classic" see RMRB, May 18, 1978; the following sentence was meant: "[The Works of Chairman Mao Zedong] must be studied in connection with practical questions, learned in connection with practice; what is learned must be used in practice; study and practical application must be linked together; one must learn first those things that are urgently needed, so that quick results may be achieved, and the greatest emphasis must be placed on use" (from the preface of December 16, 1966). Slight alterations were made in the text of the Red Book in the various printings before and during the Cultural Revolution (see note 68).

57. The expression zou jiejing may be translated "taking the shortcut." There was a Mao zhuxi yulu yibailu (One Hundred Sayings of Chairman Mao), edited by the Propaganda Office of the General Political Department of the PLA, as mentioned in Lin's instructions of September 18, 1966; in the same speech Lin Biao called for special study of the "Three Constantly Read Articles," see Wenxuan, pp. 99-102.

58. This thesis of the san da zhushou was propagated especially strongly within the army. Lin Biao was purportedly the best of these three assistants. Zhang Chunqiao stressed this in his "Short Report of the Revolutionary Committee of Shanghai on the Revision of the Party Constitution," December 23, 1967, No. 25; cf. RMRB, May 18, 1978.

59. Mao zhuxi zhuzuo xuexi fudao cailiao (Study Materials on the Works of Chairman Mao), Guilin, August 1967, Red Guards Materials of the Revolutionary University of Guilin, preface and p. 454.

60. "Long Live the Victory of the People's War," September 3, 1965, HQ, 1965, No. 10, pp. 1-28. The article was published as a separate brochure: Lin Biao, Long Live the Victory of People's War! Beijing, 1968.

61. On the official biography see Kau, Lin Affair, pp. 5-47.

62. In the collection Wenxuan (Selected Texts of Chairman Mao), for example, texts by Lin Biao were interspersed among Mao's writings, a dozen Lin Biao

writings were added between pages 86 and 120. Lin's Red Book was Lin Biao yulu (Sayings of Lin Biao), Kunming, 1967, a Red Guards publication; for the edition by Lin supporters in Hong Kong, see note 63.

63. Selected Works of Lin Piao, Hong Kong, 1970, from "China Problems Research Center." See the preface of October 1, 1969, by Smarlo Ma, who greeted Lin as Mao's successor. This research center also published a Quotations from Marshal Lin Piao in Hong Kong.

64. See HQ, 1971, No. 12, pp. 7-11.

65. Lin's speech before the expanded session of the Politburo of the Central Committee, May 18, 1966, in Yearbook 1970, VII, pp. 50-56. Lin stated that, during his lifetime, anyone who opposed Mao would be punished by the party and the entire country: "Whoever makes a secret report after his death, as Khrushchev did, must be an ambitious double-dealer and conspirator; he will receive his punishment from the entire party and the entire country." For China's attitude on the Twentieth Party Congress see Helmut Martin, "Stalin, Revisionisten, und die maoistische Strategie der KP Chinas" (Stalin, Revisionists, and the Maoist Strategy of the Chinese CP) in Roy Medwedew, Robert Havemann, and Jochen Steffen, Entstalinisierung. Der XX. Parteitag der KPdSU und seine Folgen (De-Stalinization: the Twentieth Party Congress of the CPSU and Its Consequences), Frankfurt, 1977, pp. 194-209.

66. Although not directly named, Lin was first condemned as an ultra-leftist after September 1971. After January 1973 the media referred to "swindlers like Liu Shaoqi," explaining that "one must recognize that their real mistake was ultra-rightism and not ultra-leftism, although at certain times and in certain questions they promoted left extremism. . . . Those who considered their mistake ultra-leftism failed to grasp the essential thing" (see C.a., April 1973, p. 115 for further references). This discussion was revived after the fall of the Gang of Four, when the radical left was again suddenly condemned as rightwing; see PR, April 18, 1978, No. 15, pp. 6-10, and GMRB, April 30, 1978.

67. "Report of the Central Committee of the CCP on the end of the 'Four Goods and Five Goods' movement and the deliverance of inscriptions and portraits of Lin Biao to the responsible authorities," Central Committee Document Zhongfa, No. 64, November 1971. See Lin huibian, p. 31.

68. In Zhou Enlai's "Report on the Tenth Party Congress," August 24, 1973; see RMRB, September 1, 1973. Lin's preface was now removed from the Red Book, just as earlier Lin had removed from it any traces of Liu Shaoqi. Lin's preface was dated December 1966. A few months later a passage and the title of Chapter 24 — in which Mao quoted Liu in a humorous and approving tone, and used the Liu term "self-cultivation" (xiu-yang) from Liu's well-known essay "On the Self-Cultivation of Communists" of July 1939 — were removed from the Red Book. See Schram, Quotations, pp. 134, 136, and 181.

69. For the letter to Jiang Qing, Text of July 8, 1966, see Mao Intern, pp. 205-208 [see also Kau, Lin Affair, pp. 118-21]. The second quotation comes from the internal Central Committee Document Zhongfa, No. 12, 1972; see Yearbook 1973, VII, p. 6.

70. Xuexi yu pipan (Study and Criticism), Shanghai, founded in late 1973, ceased publication with the September 1976 issue.

71. "Xinsheng shiwu" (newborn things). Peking Review translated this political slogan before October 1976 as "New Socialist Things"; in the years of criti-

cism against the Gang of Four the term was taken up again and formally incorporated into the text "new socialist things." For the term "swimming against the current" in Wang's Report at the Tenth Party Congress, RMRB, September 2, 1973, see C.a. September 1973, pp. 562-66, following PR, September 11, 1973, No. 35/36, pp. 30-37, and explained in GMRB, October 21, 1973. Even clearer is the internal speech of Wang Hongwen of January 14, 1974, against the "prevailing current," in C.a., April 1975, pp. 182-85.

72. The criticism of the campaign against "capitulationism" in the novel Shuihu zhuan (Water Margin; also translated under the title "All men Are Brothers") was directed as early as August–September 1975 against both Zhou Enlai and Deng Xiaoping; see Richard v. Schirach in C.a., October 1975, pp. 635-38.

73. Under the pseudonym "Liang Xiao"; see RMRB, July 13, 1977, RMRB, March 21, 1978, and C.a., December 1976, p. 667.

74. See Mao Intern, "Nachwort zu den Texten," pp. 253-62, and RMRB, May 8, 1978, in an anti-Lin article from the Shenyang troops.

75. RMRB, May 8, 1978, anti-Lin article.

76. Yao's article appeared in HQ, 1975, No. 3, pp. 20-29; cf. PR, March 18, 1975, No. 11, pp. 4-10. This article was attacked in HQ, 1978, No. 6, pp. 16-19. Zhang's article appeared in HQ, 1975, No. 4, pp. 3-12; cf. PR, April 8, 1975, No. 14, pp. 5-11.

77. For example, this term was mentioned in a polemical context in RMRB on May 8, 1978.

78. RMRB, October 31, 1958. The English edition was Comrade Mao Tse-tung on Imperialism and All Reactionaries Are Paper Tigers, Beijing, 1961.

79. For example, as individual brochures: Mao zhuxi zai Sulian de yanlun (Statements of Chairman Mao in the Soviet Union), Beijing, 1957; see also Important Talks of Chairman Mao Tse-tung with Persons from Asia, Africa, and Latin America, Beijing, 1960.

80. HQ, 1977, No. 5, pp. 3-18. In PR, May 10, 1977, No. 19, pp. 15-26 (p. 16).

81. Excerpted translations of these prefaces are contained in Mao Intern, p. 257, in the "Postscript to the Text"; the editorial methods of the Red Guards are also discussed in the introduction. The wealth of materials that came into unofficial circulation during the Cultural Revolution has been the most important source for the new comprehensive German-Chinese bilingual edition of Mao texts cited in note 1.

82. RMRB, February 22, 1975, and RMRB, February 2, 1977.

83. RMRB, December 21, 1951, as in Xinhua yuebao, 1952, No. 1, pp. 5-6.

84. Mao zhuxi jiaoyu yulu (Sayings of Chairman Mao on Education), Beijing, July 1967, a Red Guards publication.

85. "Examples of Dialectics (Excerpts)," WS 67, pp. 123-51. This text contains 33 separate passages from different sources, with dates ranging from October 11, 1955, to December 19, 1958, where they can be identified at all. The WS text dates the "examples" to "about 1959"; in our edition we have dated them — –, 1958 because most of the texts come from this year. In a French translation, Mao Tse-toung, Textes 1949-1958, Edition intégrale, Paris, 1975, pp. 524-563, the text was regarded as excerpts from a single document, see p. 524. An Italian translation by Fernando Orlandi, ed., Mao tse-tung, senza contraddizione non c'é vita, inediti sulla dialettica, Verona, 1976, features this

collection of quotations as the main section of the book, pp. 43-92; however, on p. 42 the editor comments that these are Mao extracts from different sources published as study materials during the Cultural Revolution.

86. See the brochure entitled Mao Zhuxi geming waijiao yulu, Beijing, 1977, purportedly edited by the "Editorial and Publication Committee for the Works of Chairman Mao Zedong of the Central Committee of the Communist Party of China," according to the preface of June 1, 1977. A publication of this type by this committee would seem unusual, especially in light of the fact that it also contains articles by Mao's nephew Mao Yuanxin, one of the militants in the Shanghai faction who had been removed from power (for example, p. 35).

87. See the communique of the Third Plenum of July 21, 1977, in PR, August 2, 1977, No. 31, p. 3.

88. Mao's so-called last instruction, "Act according to the principles laid down" (an jiding fangzhen ban), was used in the media by the left to support their claim to legitimation during September, between Mao's death and the fall of the radicals; thereafter this use of the quotation was considered a falsification. Instead, it was stated that Mao had named Hua Guofeng as his successor when he jotted down on a piece of paper, "With you in charge, I'm at ease" (ni banshi, wo fangxin); see C.a., December 1976, p. 666. However, the context in which this note had been written remains unclear.

89. Compare Michel Oksenberg's and Sai-cheung Yeung's presentation of the work of Hua between 1949 and 1966 in The China Quarterly, March 1977, No. 69, pp. 3-53, and Ting Wang, "A Concise Biography of Hua Kuo-feng," Chinese Law and Government, 1978, No. 1, pp. 3-71. See Chairman Hua Is Our Good Leader (in Chinese), Beijing, 1977; Stories of Chairman Hua in Xiangyang (in Chinese), Beijing, 1977.

90. Examples of such inspection tours are, for example, Hua's visit to the earthquake-damaged city of Tangshan in mid-January 1978 (NCNA, January 14, 1978), or the inspection of the Miyun Dam (NCNA, December 2, 1977), which Mao inspected in 1959, at which time he had taken a swim in the reservoir. Photo exhibitions, such as the one in Liaoning in September 1977, after Hua's April 1977 inspection tour through the three Northeast provinces, were created on the basis of the documentation of these inspection tours; see SWB, September 26, 1977.

91. For the foregoing data see SWB, December 20, 1977 and January 12, 1978. On the calligraphy for the Mao Mausoleum see GMRB, August 30, 1977; on the calligraphy for a Mao Memorial Hall in Shijiazhuang, Hebei, see SWB, December 20, 1977; on the calligraphy for the journal Renmin wenxue (People's Literature), see RMRB, January 17, 1978. For Hua at the Miyun Dam, see NCNA, February 2, 1977; for reports, see RMRB, February 12, 1977; over 1.2 million Beijing-area cadres and commune members heard about it over the radio.

92. A Hua article of April 2, 1963, entitled "Apply Your Strength — That Is Important," originally published in Xin Hunan bao (New Hunan), was republished in RMRB, April 26, 1977; see PR, May 17, 1977, No. 20, pp. 9-10. The reprint was intended as an incentive for raising production in agriculture, according to a statement in the People's Daily.

93. Central Committee decision of October 8, 1976; see PR, October 19, 1976, pp. 3-4.

94. See PR, April 26, 1977, No. 17, pp. 12-14. For the time allotted to the editing, see note 122.

95. More precisely, the period from December 1976 to July 1978; see our list.

96. See Literaturnaia gazeta, January 12, 1956, announcing publication of Volume 14 of Stalin's Works; the volume never appeared. On these questions see Robert H. McNeal, Stalin's Works. An Annotated Bibliography, Stanford, California, 1967, p. 158.

97. Deng Xiaoping's speech at the National Conference on Educational Work on April 22, 1978 (PR, May 9, 1978, No. 18, pp. 6-13) was a good example of how Mao Zedong's quotations were purified of the "false" interpretation given them in more radical times; here Mao's letter to the Jiangxi Workers' College is mentioned. In the education system as elsewhere, efforts were being made to maintain an external continuity with the former mass line. Thus the Ministry of Education instructed industrial plants to continue operation of the so-called July 21 colleges (the name is derived from Mao's directive of July 21, 1968) for the training of technicians. See NCNA, April 20, 1978.

98. On the two National Agricultural Conferences: at the first conference, in September-October 1975, Hua was the chairman, and he gave a speech on principles on October 15, 1975; see excerpts in PR, November 4, 1975, No. 44, pp. 13-17. Hua also gave a speech on December 25, 1976; see PR, January 4, 1977, No. 1, pp. 30-45. See the series of reports on agriculture and mechanization in PR, 1977, Nos. 6-10 and 44, 46, and 47.

99. On the speech to 7,000 cadres, see RMRB, July 1, 1978, and PR, July 11, 1978, No. 27, pp. 6-22. One of the internal text versions is contained in WS 69, pp. 399-423. The speech has been available in the West since 1974 in Schram, Unrehearsed, pp. 158-87. In contrast to the extensively altered version of the official text of "On the Ten Great Relationships," in this case the internal and official texts differ very little. See the People's Daily interpretive article, RMRB, July 2, 1978, and other commentaries in HQ, 1978, No. 7. Mao was said to have circulated this speech in 1966 for internal party reading; a few copies could have gotten into various Red Guards collections, and hence abroad as well. The published defense against the Albania challenge was "The Theory of Chairman Mao on the Tripartite Division of the World — A Significant Contribution to Marxism-Leninism," PR, November 8, 1977, No. 45, pp. 11-43. See also the article by Oskar Weggel in C.a., August 1977, pp. 480-84, on the first public attack by Albania in an editorial in the Albanian Communist Party organ, Zeri i Popullit, on July 8, 1977.

100. An analysis of this new history of the SED of 1978 showed that it was a political rather than a scientific work; to wit, certain periods were suppressed (in this case the Stalin period, while the Khrushchev phase was falsified) and the party's claim to have always chosen the right course was highlighted, etc. See Der Spiegel, May 15, 1978, No. 20, pp. 90-93.

101. I owe thanks to Gerhard Will, Dr. Dietmar Albrecht, and Tienchi Martin-Liao for a number of suggestions for the following analysis. An abbreviated version of my interpretation was published in Der Spiegel, May 16, 1977, p. 129. See also C.a., May 1977, p. 282-89; The Asia Quarterly (Japanese), October-December 1977, pp. 74-83; Zhanwang (Hong Kong), October 1977, No. 377, pp. 4-8; and Mondo Cinese, July-September 1977, No. 19, pp. 27-34. Abroad

there was extensive response to the appearance of Volume V. Some interesting articles were the analysis by Stuart Schram in the Far Eastern Economic Review, October 7, 1977, pp. 57-58, and that in China News Analysis, June 3, 1977, No. 1081, as well as an article by Benjamin Schwartz in the Mainichi Daily of June 6, 1977, and in Chinese, an analysis by the Hong Kong journal Ming Pao, 1977, No. 137, pp. 8-12. Finally, see Thomas Scharping, Mao Tse-tungs Werke 1949-1957, Der V. Band der Ausgewählten Schriften (Berichte des Bundesinstituts für ostwissenschaftliche und internationale Studien), Cologne, 1977.

102. "On the Ten Great Relationships," Text of April 25, 1956, is printed in its official version in PR, January 4, 1977, No. 1, pp. 10-27. An internal version of the speech is contained in WS 69, pp. 40-59. See Schram's comparison of the official and nonofficial versions in The China Quarterly, March 1977, No. 69, pp. 126-35. See also the article on the Gang of Four and Hu Feng by the Criticism Group of Shanghai People's Press. According to this article, Zhang Chunqiao said that this work ("The Ten Great Relationships") was not expressive of Mao Zedong Thought and hence should be omitted (from the draft of Volume V). See Ta Kung Pao, April 21, 1977.

103. To be precise, the preface discusses the "revisionist line of Wang (Hongwen), Zhang (Chunqiao), Jiang (Qing), and Yao (Wenyuan)," i.e., the Gang of Four; the sequence in which they are mentioned corresponds to their ranking in the hierarchy.

104. Concerning the writer Hu Feng, see Volume V, pp. 157-67; the philosopher Liang Shuming, see Volume V, pp. 107-15; the liberal intellectual Hu Shi, see for example Volume V, p. 446; and the literary critic and specialist on the novel Honglou meng (Dream of the Red Chamber), Yu Pingbo, see Volume V, pp. 134-35. See the Central Committee decision of October 8, 1976 in RMRB, October 9, 1976.

105. On Lin Biao's preface to the Red Book, see Schram, Quotations, pp. vii-xxvi.

106. The PRC media reported such Mao criticism in the provinces in Spring 1977; see C.a., May 1977, p. 254.

107. Concerning the introduction of the cooperatives, see Volume V, pp. 168-263.

108. On the Gao-Rao Affair see Volume V, pp. 138-56; on the Hundred Flowers and the campaign against the rightists see Volume V, pp. 419-95.

109. This was stated clearly by Mao in his speech before the Third Plenum of the Eighth Central Committee, Text of October 9, 1957, and at the Thirteenth Supreme State Conference, Text of October 13, 1957; see Volume V, pp. 467 and 480. The term "continuing revolution" is used explicitly only in the preface: "The great theory of the continuing revolution (jixu geming) under the dictatorship of the proletariat." On the prehistory of this concept see note 14. Hua Guofeng chose this term as the title of his major article on the study of Volume V; see PR, May 10, 1977, No. 19, pp. 15-29.

110. This expression, which became known abroad only after the Cultural Revolution, was used by Mao as early as 1957 in his campaign against the right; see for example Volume V, p. 437, and Mao Intern, p. 287.

111. See the Lushan speech, Text of July 23, 1959. Mao's speech to a cadre conference in Shanghai, included in Volume V (Text of July 9, 1957, pp. 440-55),

is just as agitated; in the official edition it has been given the title "Beat Back the Attacks of the Bourgeois Rightists." But in the final analysis one could cite almost all of Mao's statements in the campaign against the rightists. Mao's speaking style is made accessible to Western readers in the volumes edited by Ch'en, Schram, and Martin. See note 6.

112. See, for example, the long pages of commentary in Volume I of the Selected Works in contrast to the almost total lack of commentary in Volume V. The earlier official Mao translations often contain additional explanatory notes interpreting the original Chinese commentary.

113. In the interim there have been numerous allusions in the PRC to the editing done by the radicals; see for example Ta Kung Pao, April 21, 1977 (note 102). The local press has referred to a long and heated struggle over the publication of Mao's works. Zhou Enlai, it was said, intervened in favor of publication of Volume V before his death, but "Liu, Lin, and the Gang of Four" continuously interfered with its preparation, so that the writings could not be made accessible to the masses sooner; see SWB, April 19, 1977. On the preparation of the first and second versions, see "Nachwort zu den Texten," Mao Intern, pp. 253-54. According to Central Committee Documents of late 1967, Volumes V and VI were to appear before the Ninth Party Congress (1969). Some proponents of the more radical version had considered publishing Volume VI (1958 on) first, because the Great Leap Forward was regarded as the more important period and moreover, because the obvious difficulties of the pro-Soviet orientation during the early years of the PRC were an obstacle to the editing of Volume V.

114. On the third version see the Central Committee decision of October 8, 1976, in RMRB, October 9, 1976. The works were to be published by a Committee for Editing and Publishing the Works of Chairman Mao Zedong, newly constituted at that time as an organ of the Politburo with Hua Gufeng at its head. On the preparation time, see note 122. Of course, the scuttling of the first and second drafts does not mean that elements of these earlier compilations did not get in. One carryover from the radical version is the anti-Liu bias; purely formal influences are revealed by a comparison of Volume V with the table of contents of a previous draft edition (published in C.a., September 1974, pp. 569-70 on the basis of an English version); the Chinese version of that prototype accompanies my analysis in The Asian Quarterly (Japanese), October-December 1977, pp. 74-83, and pp. 80-81.

115. Examples of identical reproductions of official texts are, for example, the Texts of September 21, 1949, October 26, 1949, June 6, 1950, June 23, 1950, September 25, 1950, May 20, 1951, and October 23, 1951. Only the recording of applause and references to Liu Shaoqi were omitted (see note 119). The text "On the Ten Great Relationships" may serve as an example of changes made in unofficial versions of a text when the final canonical version of Volume V was compiled (see note 102).

116. References in Mao Intern, p. 254 (see note 113).

117. The Stalin obituary, Text of March 9, 1953 ("The Greatest Friendship") and the opening address to the Eighth Party Congress, Text of September 15, 1956, are omitted. In their place Volume V includes the Text of August 30, 1956 (pp. 293-304), the speech at a preparatory conference for the Party Congress.

118. On Deng, see Volume V, pp. 300 and 357, for typical examples; also pp. 301, 325, 333, 355, and 483.

119. On Liu Shaoqi, see, for example, Volume V, pp. 38, 59, 80, 81, 135. Mention of Liu's name in a positive context was eliminated in the final speech to the Second Session of the Political Consultative Conference, Text of June 23, 1950; compare Volume V, p. 26, and RMRB, June 24, 1950. Another omission is the phrase "a report by Vice-Chairman Liu Shaoqi and . . . ," included in the original version in People's Daily. According to Volume V, Liu had been an antiparty element since 1948; see p. 38. The extremely exaggerated criticism of Liu on p. 80, Text of May 19, 1953, is a three-sentence quotation taken out of context; indeed, Liu's name did not even occur in the text, and had to be inserted in the title given it by the editors.

120. The announcement of the collecting and editing work for the Complete Works was contained in the Central Committee decision of October 8, 1976; see RMRB, October 9, 1976. According to this Central Committee document, these activities were to be pursued during the editing of the Selected Works.

121. Both quotations are contained in the preface to Volume V, pp. 1-2. The sentence served as a title to one of the most important internal collections of Mao material. It was also the first sentence of Lin Biao's preface to the Red Book. This formulation appeared for the first time officially in a communique of the Eleventh Plenum of the Eighth Party Congress on August 12, 1966; see Mao Intern, p. 257, and note 50.

122. German students' eyewitness accounts are found in Das neue China, June 1, 1977, No. 17, pp. 2-3, and in PR, May 3, 1977, No. 18, pp. 12-14. SWB (May 5, 1977) reported that, at the end of April, 28 million instead of the originally planned 15 million copies had been distributed. Hong Kong bookshops were already accepting orders in mid-January. The printing and distribution of the volume were planned at preparatory conferences in the provinces; see for example, SWB, February 19, 1977. Thus the editing work had to be finished by the end of December at the latest, which meant an extremely short time, just about three months, for the editorial work.

123. On the Central Committee decision of April 7, 1977, see PR, April 26, 1977, No. 17, pp. 12-14, and the lead article on this subject in RMRB, April 15, 1977. The general introduction is presented in PR, April 26, 1977, No. 17, pp. 16-33. On the Hubei circular see SWB, April 29, 1977.

124. Hua's article was printed in RMRB, May 1, 1977; see PR, May 10, 1977, No. 19, pp. 15-29.

125. The "authorized" English translation is Selected Works of Mao Tsetung, Volume V, Beijing, 1977. Translations in Mongolian, Tibetan, Uighur, Kazakh, and Korean, as well as in French, Russian, Japanese, and Spanish, were announced at the time the Chinese edition appeared (no German edition was mentioned at this time). On Hua's reception for foreign translators, see NCNA, June 22, 1977. For Chinese reports on the reception of Volume V abroad, see NCNA, May 16, 1977. The Malayan Communist Party promoted Volume V as a guideline for its guerrilla struggle. See other reports from abroad, for example in RMRB, June 4, 1977, and RMRB, August 5, 1977.

126. See, for example, commentary from the Hungarian press in Monitor-Dienst, June 3, 1977.

127. The lead article in RMRB, September 10, 1977, in accordance with NCNA, September 9, 1977.

128. Speech of August 18, 1977; see PR, September 6, 1977, No. 36, pp. 39-41.

129. RMRB, April 20, 1978, NCNA, April 20, 1978.

130. Deng Xiaoping's speech of June 2, 1978, at the Conference on Political Work in the Army (RMRB, June 3, 1978; see PR, June 27, 1978, No. 25, pp. 15-23 and 31) is printed in Ta Kung Pao, June 3, 1978. The front-page headline of this left-wing Hong Kong newspaper, "Deng Xiaoping Explained How Mao Zedong Thought Should Be Interpreted" (literally, "regarded" [kandai]), was followed by the line: "He criticized certain people who always carry on about Mao Zedong Thought...." The principle "seek the truth in facts" (shi shi qiu shi) was the implicit theme here. On the critical voices, see the informative article in Jiefangjun bao (Liberation Army News) of June 24, 1978, also printed in RMRB, June 24, 1978, and later in GMRB. For the renewed criticism on Lin, see the series in Liberation Army News directed against the marshal, following SWB, June 15, 1978, the article of the Shenyang troops in RMRB, May 8, 1978, RMRB, May 10, 1978, and so on.

131. The quotation comes from the Internal Text of January 31, 1962, as found in WS 69, pp. 399-423. On July 1, 1978, People's Daily published the speech of January 30, 1962, given before 7,000 cadres, which was already known in the internal version. The occasion was the fifty-seventh anniversary of the founding of the CCP. The speech contained Mao Zedong's self-criticism for mistakes he had made in the Great Leap Forward campaign. Thus, the policy of mass campaigns was presented as partly mistaken, and an end was made to Mao's infallibility. Such a reassessment was extremely important for the new version of the party history, already prepared, and for the next volume of Mao's writings, Volume VI, which was to cover the Great Leap Forward period and the following difficult years of the readjustment policy.

132. For details, see my biography of Deng Xiaoping in C.a., May 1973, pp. 225-31. On April 9, 1978, Wu De was ridiculed in a caricature posted in Beijing's Tian'anmen Square as part of a campaign begun six days previously. The wall poster depicted the mayor as a bottle bobbing from right to left "without ever losing its contents"; see AFP (English), April 9, 1978.

133. Literally, "40,000 ling" (1 ling = 516 pages); GMRB, February 2, 1977.

134. HQ, 1978, No. 3, still printed quotations from all the classics, including Mao Zedong's, in boldface type; 1978, No. 4, abandoned this practice completely. In Hong Kong's left press this change prompted immediate and detailed comment. See, for example, an article on the "elimination of sentences [quotations from Chairman Mao, Yulu] in boldface type," The Seventies (Qishi niandai), June 1978, No. 101, p. 46. On March 22, 1978, People's Daily and Guangming Daily stopped using boldface quotations; boldface type was still used for stressing important passages, as had been the custom before 1966.

135. The writer Mao Dun points this out explicitly in an article in HQ, 1978, No. 5, p. 51.

136. The secret Central Committee resolution was the Document Zhongfa, No. 11, of April 5, 1978. See C.a., June 1978, pp. 326-32.

137. On the Plenum see the Hong Kong left-wing journal Dongxiang, January 1979, No. 4, 14-17.

138. An article on "praxis" in RMRB of December 26, 1978 gave an important overview.

139. See HQ, 1978, No. 12, 3-10, article by Tan Zhenlin.

140. See the excerpt from a speech of May 7, 1949, published in RMRB, October 8, 1978.

141. On the Hua article, see note 128. The "Sixty Points on Work Methods," February 19, 1968, were spelled out at the Nanning Conference. They have a Mao foreword dated January 31, 1958.

142. According to a verbal communication from German scholars living in Beijing.

143. The left-wing journal Zhengming wrote for the first time on the role of Hu Qiaomu in September 1978 (No. 11, p. 6). Other leading Mao editors were the assistant director of the Marx-Engels-Lenin-Stalin-Mao Zedong Research Institute, Wang Huide (the director was Hu Qiaomu), at the same time director of the Translation Bureau of the Central Committee, and Yu Guangyuan, assistant director of the Academy of Social Sciences. Thus this Academy has played a decisive role in giving shape to and interpreting Mao's legacy.

144. On the rehabilitation of Peng, see NCNA, January 2, 1979; see the article by Lu Dingyi in RMRB, March 8, 1979, in which Peng is clearly depicted as having been correct in the conflict (with Mao hence being the culpable party).

145. See pp. 66-67, above. See also Lowell Dittmer, "Death and Transfiguration: Liu Shaoqi's Rehabilitation and Contemporary Chinese Politics," Journal of Asian Studies, vol. 40, no. 3, pp. 455-79, esp. 467.

146. On the 7,000 cadres speech, see RMRB, July 1, 1978, and note 99. For Mao's letter to Guo Muruo see RMRB, January 1, 1979.

147. On the topic of the condemnation of innocent parties, see for example RMRB, November 16, 1978; RMRB of November 20, 1978, comments on the rehabilitation process as follows: "Mao Zedong and Zhou Enlai were unhappy over the unjust convictions in the Cultural Revolution. For instance, after Lin Biao fell, Mao personally put forth the suggestion that 'Comrade He Long' and other victims be rehabilitated."

148. See Foreign Broadcast Information Service (FBIS), November 27, 1978.

149. See GMRB, November 15, 1978 for a critique of Yao's article. Mao supported Yao's attack on Wu Han and his play Hai Rui Dismissed from Office; see Mao's speech to the Albanian military delegation, May 1, 1967.

150. Mao's talk with the Red Guards leaders of July 28, 1968, in WS 69, pp. 687-716; an abbreviated German translation is in Mao Intern, pp. 180-205.

151. Mao was supposed to have spoken out against the personality cult on September 26, 1967; see NCNA, December 27, 1978.

152. GMRB, December 29, 1978 (cf. note 144).

153. On this wall poster see AFP, December 18, 1978.

154. NCNA, January 2, 1979. Mikoyan was received by Mao on April 6, 1956.

155. A report on changes in the assessment of Stalin in the Soviet Union may be found in the Christian Science Monitor of February 6, 1979.

156. For the appearance in Beijing on November 19 of one of the first wall posters criticizing Mao, see AFP, November 20, 1978. Space does not permit complete documentation of the wall posters discussed here. Our description is based on a collection of wall posters made in Beijing and generously made available to the Institut für Asienkunde. Otherwise, all reports on wall posters during the period under consideration are taken from the New York Times

(hereafter NYT), FBIS, and the SWB. Only the most important posters are quoted individually.

157. The following articles in the journal Zhengming are relevant: Opening of the debate, November 1977, No. 1, pp. 26-28. High points, editorial, December 1978, No. 14, p. 4; see also June 1978, No. 8, pp. 30-31, July 1978, No. 9, p. 19 and pp. 6-9 and 62; August 1978, No. 10, pp. 11-12, September 1978, No. 11, pp. 5-7, and November 1978, No. 13, pp. 40-41. In addition, see the corresponding issues of the journal Dongxiang.

158. According to AFP, December 3, 1978.

159. Zhengming, November 1977, No. 1, pp. 26-28.

160. See AFP, November 22 and November 27, 1979.

161. NYT, January 8, 1979. A photo of a wall poster with a sketch of the construction blueprint of the Zhou Mausoleum to be built on Tian'anmen Square is to be found in Das neue China, 1979, No. 2. Foreign political figures such as the Malaya's Prime Minister Hussein Onn, Prince Sihanouk, as well as numerous Chinese delegations could not visit the Mao Mausoleum again until the beginning of May 1979; see Süddeutsche Zeitung, May 4, 1979. In early March 1979 an editorial in People's Daily stated that "the Central Committee was currently looking for a suitable design for the construction of a memorial hall for Comrade Zhou Enlai and other revolutionaries of the older generation who had contributed significantly to the Chinese Revolution in the Party history" (RMRB, March 5, 1979).

162. Zhengming, August 1978, No. 10, p. 12; and September 1978, No. 11, p. 6.

163. Zhengming, December 1978, No. 14, p. 4.

164. NYT, November 28, 1978; FBIS, November 27, 1978.

165. Zhengming, September 1978, No. 11, p. 6; and July 1978, No. 9, p. 8.

166. The plenum's communique was published in NCNA, December 23, 1978; an important editorial on the plenum appeared in RMRB on December 25, 1978; see also another detailed report in the NCNA on December 23, 1978, with a summary of the personnel changes and short biographies of the new Politburo members as well as the additional Central Committee members and the staff of the Central Commission for Inspection of Discipline; see also Jingbao (Hong Kong), January 10, 1979, No. 18.

167. Pravda, in Tass, December 7, 1978; NYT, November 21, 1978.

168. This list follows Dongxiang, December 1978, No. 3, pp. 4ff; Mingbao of December 22, 1978 gives a similar report; see also Zhengming, December 1978, No. 14, p. 7.

169. The first issue of Chinese Youth was held back by the Wang opposition with four internally presented arguments: first, it contained no articles on the anniversary of Mao's death and no inscription by Party Chairman Hua Guofeng; it should not have published a poem on the Tian'anmen incident, nor glorified one of the "heroes" of that demonstration, Han Zhixiong. Actually, the article by Hu, which criticized Mao indirectly, went too far for Party Vice-Chairman Wang Dongxing.

170. See, for example, the commentary in RMRB, January 13, 1979, on criticism and self-criticism, as well as the RMRB editorial of January 3, 1979, on democratic behavior at the Third Plenum.

171. See Jingbao (Hong Kong), January 10, 1979, No. 18, and Mingbao (Hong Kong), January 15, 1979.

172. Der Stern, March 1, 1979.
173. SWB, April 3, 1979; for other mentions see C.a., March 1979, Übersicht 17; for the essay in Red Flag, see HQ, 1979, No. 4, pp. 16-20.
174. An internal document of February 1, 1977, Zhongyang ribao (Central Daily — Taipei), March 23, 1977. For the opinion survey, see Dongxiang, 1978, No. 4, pp. 35-43; China's internal information bulletin, Cankao ziliao (Reference Materials), for leading cadres printed the results of the survey on January 28, 1979.
175. RMRB, March 9, 1979, and Qishi niandai, 1979, No. 4, pp. 15-18.
176. Qishi niandai, 1979, No. 4, pp. 15-18.
177. On Deng Tuo see GMRB, February 22, 1979; on the countercurrent see RMRB, Februry 26, 1979; on the Ministry of Culture see NCNA, February 28, 1979.
178. For an analysis written shortly after publication of Volume V, see my article in Der Spiegel, May 1977 (cf. pp. 61-68, above). For the critical article in People's Daily, see RMRB, March 13, 1979; this was a reprint ("with omissions"!) of an article from the Jiangxi University News (1978, No. 4) by a certain Huang Shaoqun, so it was published in the form of an individual opinion.
179. Zhengming, 1979, No. 17, pp. 5-8.
180. See, for example, SWB, March 18, 1979.
181. HQ, 1979, No. 4, pp. 21-26; on the 100 million affected, see Zhengming, 1979, No. 17, p. 8.
182. On the personality cult, see an extensive article in GMRB, March 11, 1979.
183. GMRB, March 11, 1979, and RMRB, March 13, 1979.
184. See for example RMRB, March 5, 1979; further mention in C.a., March 1979, Übersicht 12.
185. Internal document of February 1, 1977 (see note 174).
186. Frankfurter Rundschau, May 4, 1979.
187. For details, see, for example, in Wolfgang Leonhard, Die Dreispaltung des Marxismus, Düsseldorf, 1970.
188. The first major Russian-language edition appeared in 28 volumes (33 books) between 1928 and 1941.
189. At the end of the fifties, the Marx-Engels-Werke (MEW) was completed by the Institute for Marxism-Leninism of the Central Committee of the SED in 39 volumes (41 books) plus one supplementary volume in two books. Details on the planning of the MEGA may be found in a publication of the Institute for Marxist Studies and Research (IMSF), Informationsbericht No. 24. Neuere Marx-Engels-Forschung, zur Marx-Engels-Gesamtausgabe, Frankfurt, 1976.
190. Thus Vladimir Sevin, chairman of the Marx-Engels Department and assistant director of the Institute for Marxism-Leninism of the Central Committee of the CPSU in Moscow: see Informationsbericht, p. 18.
191. The preface to the complete edition is reprinted in Informationsbericht.
192. Günter Heyden, director of the Institute for Marxism-Leninism of the Central Committee of the SED, discusses more concretely the "new methods of Marx falsification," singling out for criticism certain Western editions of Marx's works compiled by persons who were considered incompetent if not hostile. This "more refined form of the anticommunist ideological struggle," which "at the same time is a manifestation of bourgeois ideology's forced accom-

modation to the new power relationship between socialism and imperialism in the domain of ideology," is, nonetheless, evaluated to some degree favorably. Heyden lists 30 individual editions, selections, and collections published between 1965 and 1969 in West Germany alone, with special stress on the editions of Günter Hillmann, Hans-Joseph Steinberg, and Maximilian Rubel as well as the eight-volume Marx edition published in Stuttgart by Cotta Verlag. The MEGA, he said, should "do away with further anticommunist manipulation." See Informationsbericht, pp. 11-12. See also Harald Wessel, Marginalien zur MEGA nebst Randglossen über alte und neue "Marxologen," Frankfurt, 1977.

193. Leon Trotsky, Stalin, 1947 (reprint, London, 1968, 2 vols.), Vol. 2, p. 68.

194. Leo Trotzki, Mein Leben, Frankfurt, 1974, pp. 442 and 444.

195. Trotzki, Mein Leben, p. 435.

196. Trotsky, Stalin, Vol. 1, pp. 108-11. After 1956 the cult around Lenin's biography was the successor of the Stalin cult in this respect. For example, early 1979 saw an additional ninth volume of the official Lenin biography (first published in 1970 and now in an edition of 5,500 pages) of the Institute for Marxism-Leninism; several other volumes are supposed to follow. This publication may thus be seen as a symbol of the biography cult.

197. On Chinese developments, see Helmut Martin, "Reformschritte im staatlich gelenkten Pressewesen der VR China," C.a., December 1978, pp. 814-18.

198. See Wolfgang Leonhard, Euro-Kommunismus, Munich, 1978.

199. A useful compilation is Zhou Enlai xuanji (Selected Writings of Zhou Enlai), Hong Kong, 1976, 4 vols. So far there are only a few hastily edited volumes of selections on Deng.

200. See Etudes Vietnamiennes: L'Education en R.D.V., Hanoi, 1965, Vol. 5 (May 1965), p. 4., for the statement by Minister of Education Nguyen Van Huyen.

201. See (with bibliography) King C. Chen, "Ho Chi Minh: The Man and His Ideas," Asian Thought and Society, April 1976, Vol. No. 1, pp. 24-32. In an article on Lenin's nineteenth birthday in 1960, Ho set down his pragmatic attitude toward ideological questions. See Bernard B. Fall (ed.), Ho Chi Minh, On Revolution, Selected Writings 1920-66 (hereafter Revolution), London, 1967, pp. 5-7. In this article, written for a Soviet newspaper, Ho said that the bickering around the International left him cold. What actually finally came of the First International?: "The revolution could be carried out with the second, the second and a half, or the third international. What was the use then of all this arguing?" For Ho it was also of no ideological importance that formulations from the Declaration of Independence of 1776 found their way into the Declaration of Independence of the Democratic Republic of Vietnam of September 2, 1945.

202. Ho Chi Minh, Écrits (1920-1969), Hanoi, 1971, pp. 369-73.

203. See Jean Lacouture, Ho Tschi-minh, Editions du Seuil, Paris, 1967, passim.

204. In 1922, Ho wrote the one-act play The Bamboo Dragon, in which he ridiculed the customs of the Hue court. In 1935 Ho gave talks on the history of Vietnam for students of the Asian Studies Faculty in Moscow in the form of poems. Like Mao, he accompanied political events often with verses; see for example the "New Year Message 1969" in Ho Chi Minh, Écrits, p. 361. However, the best-known was the collection of nearly a hundred poems, Notes from

Prison, which was rendered into Chinese in the style of the Tang lyrics.

205. Ho Chi Minh, Selected Works, Hanoi, 1960-1962, 4 vols. See Fall, Revolution, p.v. ("poor material"); Lacouture, Ho Tschi-minh, p. 170 (reference to village schoolteacher).

206. The 4-volume Selected Works of Ho (1961-62) went up to July 1954 with Volume 3, while Volume 4 covered July 1954 to September 1960. For the one-volume edition see note 202. Not until 1977 did the Vietnamese leadership come out with a plan for publication of the Collected Works of Ho Chi Minh.

207. See for example Lacouture, Ho Tschi-minh, passim.

208. Fall, Revolution, p. viii.

209. See for example Ho's writings of February 1951, April 18, 1955 (Pravda article), September 7, 1957, and November 6, 1957.

210. The quote, slightly edited for style, is in Lacouture, Ho Tschi-minh, p. 184.

211. Mao on Stalin and Sun Yat-sen, see Helmut Martin (ed.), Mao Zedong Texte. Schriften/Dokumente/Reden/Gespräche/Deutsch-Chinesisch, Munich, 1979: the Stalin Text of March 9, 1953, "Die grösste Freundschaft," Vol. I, pp. 89-93; the Sun Text of November 12, 1956, "Rede auf der Gendenkfeier zum 90. Geburtstag von Dr. Sun Yat-sen." Vol. II, pp. 80-82. On September 7, 1969, People's Daily reported only a wreath inscription for Ho written by Mao. The letter of congratulation on the seventieth birthday of Ho Chi-minh, sent on May 18, 1960, was likewise purely formal; see RMRB, May 19, 1960.

212. See Horst Kurnitzky, "Chollima Korea: Ein Besuch im Jahre 23," Kursbuch, December 1972, No. 30, pp. 87-114.

213. Rüdiger Machetzki, "Koreanische Volksdemokratische Republik," in Dieter Nohlen and Franz Nuscheler (eds.), Handbuch der Dritten Welt, Hamburg, 1978, Vol. 4, pp. 337-360.

214. M. Y. Cho, Wirtschaft und Politik in der DVRK, Nordkorea 1974, Hamburg, 1974 (Mitteilungen des Instituts für Asienkunde Hamburg, No. 59), p. 63.

215. The English key edition of Kim Il Sung's Selected Works, published in 1965, was initially based on the 6-volume Korean edition of 1960. The German edition, Ausgewählte Werke, based on the new version of the Korean language Selected Works, had gotten as far as the texts of August 1973 with the printing of Volume 6 in 1977. This German-language single volume reproduced the sixth volume of the Korean edition of 1974.

216. A German-language version was published by the Institute for Party History of the Central Committee of the Korean Workers' Party, Kurze Geschichte der revolutionären Tätigkeit des Genossen Kim Ir Sen, Pjöngjang, 1970.

On Questions of Party History

(Resolution Adopted by the Sixth Plenum of the Eleventh Central Committee of the Chinese Communist Party, June 27, 1981)

Review of the History of the 28 Years Before the Founding of the People's Republic

1. The Communist Party of China has traversed 60 years of glorious struggle since its founding in 1921. In order to sum up its experience in the 32 years since the founding of the People's Republic, we must briefly review the previous 28 years in which the Party led the people in waging the revolutionary struggle for new democracy.

2. The Communist Party of China was the product of the integration of Marxism-Leninism with the Chinese workers' movement and was founded under the influence of the October Revolution in Russia and the May 4th Movement in China and with the help of the Communist International led by Lenin. The Revolution of 1911 led by Dr. Sun Yat-sen, the great revolutionary forerunner, overthrew the Qing Dynasty, thus bringing to an end over 2,000 years of feudal monarchical rule. However, the semi-colonial and semi-feudal nature of Chinese society remained unchanged. Neither the Kuomintang nor any of the bourgeois or petty-bourgeois political groupings and factions found any way out for the country and the nation, nor was it possible for them to do so. The Communist Party of China and the Communist Party of China alone was able to show the people that China's salvation lay in overthrowing once and for all the reactionary rule of imperialism and feudalism and then switching over to socialism. When the Communist Party of China was founded, it had less than 60 members. But it initiated the vigorous workers' movement and the people's anti-imperialist and anti-feudal struggle and grew rapidly and soon became a leading force such as the Chinese people had never before known.

3. In the course of leading the struggle of the Chinese people with its various nationalities for new democracy, the Communist Party of China went through four stages: the Northern Expedition (1924-27) conducted

with the cooperation of the Kuomintang, the Agrarian Revolutionary War (1927-37), the War of Resistance Against Japan (1937-45) and the nationwide War of Liberation (1946-49). Twice, first in 1927 and then in 1934, it endured major setbacks. It was not until 1949 that it finally triumphed in the revolution, thanks to the long years of armed struggle in conjunction with other forms of struggle in other fields closely co-ordinated with it.

In 1927, regardless of the resolute opposition of the Left wing of the Kuomintang with Soong Ching Ling as its outstanding representative, the Kuomintang controlled by Chiang Kai-shek and Wang Jingwei betrayed the policies of Kuomintang-Communist co-operation and of anti-imperialism and anti-feudalism decided on by Dr. Sun Yat-sen and, in collusion with the imperialists, massacred Communists and other revolutionaries. The Party was still quite inexperienced and, moreover, was dominated by Chen Duxiu's Right capitulationism, so that the revolution suffered a disastrous defeat under the surprise attack of a powerful enemy. The total membership of the Party, which had grown to more than 60,000, fell to a little over 10,000.

However, our Party continued to fight tenaciously. Launched under the leadership of Zhou Enlai and several other comrades, the Nanchang Uprising of 1927 fired the opening shot for armed resistance against the Kuomintang reactionaries. The meeting of the Central Committee of the Party held on August 7, 1927 decided on the policy of carrying out agrarian revolution and organizing armed uprisings. Shortly afterwards, the Autumn Harvest and Guangzhou Uprisings and uprisings in many other areas were organized. Led by Comrade Mao Zedong, the Autumn Harvest Uprising in the Hunan-Jiangxi border area gave birth to the First Division of the Chinese Workers' and Peasants' Revolutionary Army and to the first rural revolutionary base area in the Jinggang Mountains. Before long, the insurgents led by Comrade Zhu De arrived at the Jinggang Mountains and joined forces with it. With the progress of the struggle, the Party set up the Jiangxi central revolutionary base area and the Western Hunan-Hubei, the Haifeng-Lufeng, the Hubei-Henan-Anhui, the Qiongya, the Fujian-Zhejiang-Jiangxi, the Hunan-Jiangxi, the Zuojiang-Youjiang, the Sichuan-Shaanxi, the Shaanxi-Gansu and the Hunan-Hubei-Sichuan-Guizhou and other base areas. The First, Second and Fourth Front Armies of the Workers' and Peasants' Red Army were also born, as were many other Red Army units. In addition, Party organizations and other revolutionary organizations were established and revolutionary mass struggles unfolded under difficult conditions in the Kuomintang areas. In the Agrarian Revolutionary War, the First Front Army of the Red Army and the central revolutionary base area under the direct leadership of Comrades Mao Zedong and Zhu De played the most important role. The front armies of the Red Army defeated in turn a number of "encirclement and suppression" campaigns launched by the Kuomintang troops. But because of Wang Ming's "Left" adventurist leadership, the struggle against the Kuomintang's fifth "encirclement and suppression" campaign ended in failure. The First Front Army was forced to embark on the 25,000-li Long March and made its way to northern Shaanxi to join forces with units of the Red Army which had been persevering in struggles there and with its 25th Army which had arrived earlier. The Second and Fourth Front Armies also went on their long march, first one and then the other arriving in northern Shaanxi. Guerrilla warfare was carried on under difficult conditions in the base areas in south China from which the main forces of the Red Army had withdrawn. As a result of the defeat caused by Wang Ming's "Left" errors, the revolutionary base areas and the revolutionary forces in the Kuomintang areas sustained enormous losses. The Red Army of 300,000 men was reduced to about 30,000 and the Communist Party of 300,000 members to about 40,000.

In January 1935, the Political Bureau of the Central Committee of the Party convened a meeting in Zunyi during the Long March, which established the leading position of Comrade Mao Zedong in the Red Army and the Central Committee of the Party. This saved the Red Army and the Central Committee of the Party which were then in critical danger and subsequently made it possible to defeat Zhang Guotao's splittism, bring the Long March to a triumphant conclusion and open up new vistas for the Chinese revolution. It was a vital turning point in the history of the Party.

At a time of national crisis of unparalleled gravity when the Japanese imperialists were intensifying their aggression against China, the Central Committee of the Party headed by Comrade Mao Zedong decided on and carried out the correct policy of forming an anti-Japanese national united front. Our Party led the students' movement of December 9, 1935 and organized the powerful mass struggle to demand an end to the civil war and resistance against Japan so as to save the nation. The Xian Incident organized by Generals Zhang Xueliang and Yang Hucheng on December 12, 1936 and its peaceful settlement which our Party promoted played a crucial historical role in bringing about renewed co-operation between the Kuomintang and the Communist Party and in achieving national unity for resistance against Japanese aggression. During the war of resistance, the ruling clique of the Kuomintang continued to oppose the Communist Party and the people and was passive in resisting Japan. As a result, the Kuomintang suffered defeat after defeat in front operations against the Japanese invaders. Our Party persevered in the policy of maintaining its independence and initiative within the united front, closely relied on the masses of the people, conducted guerrilla warfare behind enemy lines and set up many anti-Japanese base areas. The Eighth Route Army and the New Fourth Army — the reorganized Red Army — grew rapidly and became the mainstay in the war of resistance. The Northeast Anti-Japanese United Army sustained its operations amid formidable difficulties. Diverse forms of anti-Japanese struggle were unfolded on a broad scale in areas occupied by Japan or controlled by the Kuomintang. Consequently, the Chinese people were able to hold out in the war for eight long years and win final victory, in co-operation with the people of the Soviet Union and other countries in the anti-fascist war.

During the anti-Japanese war, the Party conducted a rectification movement, a movement of Marxist education. Launched in 1942, it was a tremendous success. It was on this basis that the Enlarged Seventh Plenary Session of the Sixth Central Committee of the Party in 1945 adopted the Resolution on Certain Questions in the History of Our Party and soon afterwards the Party's Seventh National Congress was convened. These meetings summed up our historical experience and laid down our correct line, principles and policies for building a new-democratic New China, enabling the Party to attain an unprecedented ideological, political and organizational unity and solidarity. After the conclusion of the War of Resistance Against Japan, the Chiang Kai-shek government, with the aid of U.S. imperialism, flagrantly launched an all-out civil war, disregarding the just demand of our Party and the people of the whole country for peace and democracy. With the wholehearted support of the people in all the liberated areas, with the powerful backing of the students' and workers' movements and the struggles of the people of various strata in the Kuomintang areas and with the active co-operation of the democratic parties and non-party democrats, our Party led the People's Liberation Army in fighting the three-year War of Liberation and, after the Liaoxi-Shenyang, Beiping-Tianjin and Huai-Hai campaigns and the successful crossing of the Changjiang (Yangtze) River, in wiping out a total of 8 million Chiang Kai-shek troops. The end result was the overthrow of the reactionary Kuomintang government and the establishment of the great People's Republic of China. The Chinese people had stood up.

4. The victories gained in the 28 years of struggle fully show that:

1) Victory in the Chinese revolution was won under the guidance of Marxism-Leninism. Our Party had creatively applied the basic tenets of Marxism-Leninism and integrated them with the concrete practice of the Chinese revolution. In this way, the great system of Mao Zedong Thought came into being and the correct path to victory for the Chinese

revolution was charted. This is a major contribution to the development of Marxism-Leninism.

2) As the vanguard of the Chinese proletariat, the Communist Party of China is a party serving the people wholeheartedly, with no selfish aim of its own. It is a party with both the courage and the ability to lead the people in their indomitable struggle against any enemy. Convinced of all this through their own experience, the Chinese people of whatever nationality came to rally around the Party and form a broad united front, thus forging a strong political unity unparalleled in Chinese history.

3) The Chinese revolution was victorious mainly because we relied on a people's army led by the Party, an army of a completely new type and enjoying flesh-and-blood ties with the people, to defeat a formidable enemy through protracted people's war. Without such an army, it would have been impossible to achieve the liberation of our people and the independence of our country.

4) The Chinese revolution had the support of the revolutionary forces in other countries at every stage, a fact which the Chinese people will never forget. Yet it must be said that, fundamentally, victory in the Chinese revolution was won because the Chinese Communist Party adhered to the principle of independence and self-reliance and depended on the efforts of the whole Chinese people, whatever their nationality, after they underwent untold hardships and surmounted innumerable difficulties and obstacles together.

5) The victorious Chinese revolution put an end to the rule of a handful of exploiters over the masses of the working people and to the enslavement of the Chinese people of all nationalities by the imperialists and colonialists. The working people have become the masters of the new state and the new society. While changing the balance of forces in world politics, the people's victory in so large a country having nearly one-quarter of the world's population has inspired the people in countries similarly subjected to imperialist and colonialist exploitation and oppression with heightened confidence in their forward march. The triumph of the Chinese revolution is the most important political event since World War II and has exerted a profound and far-reaching impact on the international situation and the development of the people's struggle throughout the world.

5. Victory in the new-democratic revolution was won through long years of struggle and sacrifice by countless martyrs, Party members and people of all nationalities. We should by no means give all the credit to the leaders of the revolution, but at the same time we should not underrate the significant role these leaders have played. Among the many outstanding leaders of the Party, Comrade Mao Zedong was

the most promiment. Prior to the failure of the revolution in 1927, he had clearly pointed out the paramount importance of the leadership of the proletariat over the peasants' struggle and the danger of a Right deviation in this regard. After its failure, he was the chief representative of those who succeeded in shifting the emphasis in the Party's work from the city to the countryside and in preserving, restoring and promoting the revolutionary forces in the countryside. In the 22 years from 1927 to 1949, Comrade Mao Zedong and other Party leaders managed to overcome innumerable difficulties and gradually worked out an overall strategy and specific policies and directed their implementation, so that the revolution was able to switch from staggering defeats to great victory. Our Party and people would have had to grope in the dark much longer had it not been for Comrade Mao Zedong, who more than once rescued the Chinese revolution from grave danger, and for the Central Committee of the Party which was headed by him and which charted the firm, correct political course for the whole Party, the whole people and the people's army. Just as the Communist Party of China is recognized as the central force leading the entire people forward, so Comrade Mao Zedong is recognized as the great leader of the Chinese Communist Party and the whole Chinese people, and Mao Zedong Thought, which came into being through the collective struggle of the Party and the people, is recognized as the guiding ideology of the Party. This is the inevitable outcome of the 28 years of historical development preceding the founding of the People's Republic of China.

Basic Appraisal of the History of the 32 Years Since the Founding of the People's Republic

6. Generally speaking, the years since the founding of the People's Republic of China are years in which the Chinese Communist Party, guided by Marxism-Leninism and Mao Zedong Thought, has very successfully led the whole people in carrying out socialist revolution and socialist construction. The establishment of the socialist system represents the greatest and most profound social change in Chinese history and is the foundation for the country's future progress and development.

7. Our major achievements in the 32 years since the founding of the People's Republic are the following:

1) We have established and consolidated the people's democratic dictatorship led by the working class and based on the worker-peasant alliance, namely, the dictatorship of the proletariat. It is a new type of state power, unknown in Chinese history, in which the people are the masters of their own house. It constitutes the fundamental guarantee

for the building of a modern socialist country, prosperous and powerful, democratic and culturally advanced.

2) We have achieved and consolidated nationwide unification of the country, with the exception of Taiwan and other islands, and have thus put an end to the state of disunity characteristic of old China. We have achieved and consolidated the great unity of the people of all nationalities and have forged and expanded a socialist relationship of equality and mutual help among the more than 50 nationalities. And we have achieved and consolidated the great unity of the workers, peasants, intellectuals and people of other strata and have strengthened and expanded the broad united front which is led by the Chinese Communist Party in full co-operation with the patriotic democratic parties and people's organizations, and comprises all socialist working people and all patriots who support socialism and patriots who stand for the unification of the motherland, including our compatriots in Taiwan, Xianggang (Hongkong) and Aomen (Macao) and Chinese citizens overseas.

3) We have defeated aggression, sabotage and armed provocations by the imperialists and hegemonists, safeguarded our country's security and independence and fought successfully in defense of our border regions.

4) We have built and developed a socialist economy and have in the main completed the socialist transformation of the private ownership of the means of production into public ownership and put into practice the principle of "to each according to his work." The system of exploitation of man by man has been eliminated, and exploiters no longer exist as classes since the overwhelming majority have been remoulded and now live by their own labor.

5) We have scored signal successes in industrial construction and have gradually set up an independent and fairly comprehensive industrial base and economic system. Compared with 1952 when economic rehabilitation was completed, fixed industrial assets, calculated on the basis of their original price, were more than 27 times greater in 1980, exceeding 410,000 million yuan; the output of cotton yarn was 4.5 times greater, reaching 2,930,000 tons; that of coal 9.4 times, reaching 620 million tons; that of electricity 41 times, exceeding 300,000 million kwh; and the output of crude oil exceeded 105 million tons and that of steel 37 million tons; the output value of the engineering industry was 54 times greater, exceeding 127,000 million yuan. A number of new industrial bases have been built in our vast hinterland and the regions inhabited by our minority nationalities. National defence industry started from scratch and is being gradually built up. Much has been done in the prospecting of natural resources. There has been a tremendous growth in railway, highway, water and air transport and post and telecommunications.

6) The conditions prevailing in agricultural production have experienced a remarkable change, giving rise to big increases in production. The amount of land under irrigation has grown from 300 million mu in 1952 to over 670 million mu. Flooding by big rivers such as the Changjiang, Huanghe (Yellow River), Huaihe, Haihe, Zhujiang (Pearl River), Liaohe and Songhuajiang has been brought under initial control. In our rural areas, where farm machinery, chemical fertilizers and electricity were practically non-existent before liberation, there is now a big increase in the number of agriculture-related tractors and irrigation and drainage equipment and in the quantity of chemical fertilizers applied, and the amount of electricity consumed is 7.5 times that generated in the whole country in the early years of liberation. In 1980, the total output of grain was nearly double that in 1952 and that of cotton more than double. Despite the excessive rate of growth in our population, which is now nearly a billion, we have succeeded in basically meeting the needs of our people in food and clothing by our own efforts.

7) There has been a substantial growth in urban and rural commerce and in foreign trade. The total value of commodities purchased by enterprises owned by the whole people rose from 17.5 billion yuan in 1952 to 226.3 billion yuan in 1980, registering an increase nearly 13-fold; retail sales rose from 27.7 billion yuan to 214 billion yuan, an increase of 7.7 times. The total value of the state's foreign trade in 1980 was 8.7 times that of 1952. With the growth in industry, agriculture and commerce, the people's livelihood has improved very markedly, as compared with pre-liberation days. In 1980, average consumption per capita in both town and country was nearly twice as much as in 1952, allowing for price changes.

8) Considerable progress has been made in education, science, culture, public health and physical culture. In 1980, enrollment in the various kinds of full-time schools totalled 204 million, 3.7 times the number in 1952. In the past 32 years, the institutions of higher education and vocational schools have turned out nearly 9 million graduates with specialized knowledge or skills. Our achievements in nuclear technology, man-made satellites, rocketry, etc., represent substantial advances in the field of science and technology. In literature and art, large numbers of fine works have appeared to cater for the needs of the the people and socialism. With the participation of the masses, sports have developed vigorously, and records have been chalked up in quite a few events. Epidemic diseases with their high mortality rates have been eliminated or largely eliminated, the health of the rural and urban populations has greatly improved, and average life expectancy is now much higher.

9) Under the new historical conditions, the People's Liberation Army has grown in strength and in quality. No longer composed only of ground forces, it has become a composite army, including the naval and air forces and various technical branches. Our armed forces, which are a combination of the field armies, the regional forces and the militia, have been strengthened. Their quality is now much higher and their technical equipment much better. The PLA is serving as the solid pillar of the people's democratic dictatorship in defending and participating in the socialist revolution and socialist construction.

10) Internationally, we have steadfastly pursued an independent socialist foreign policy, advocated and upheld the Five Principles of Peaceful Coexistence, entered into diplomatic relations with 124 countries and promoted trade and economic and cultural exchanges with still more countries and regions. Our country's place in the United Nations and the Security Council has been restored to us. Adhering to proletarian internationalism, we are playing an increasingly influential and active role in international affairs by enhancing our friendship with the people of other countries, by supporting and assisting the oppressed nations in their cause of liberation, the newly independent countries in their national construction and the people of various countries in their just struggles and by staunchly opposing imperialism, hegemonism, colonialism and racism in defense of world peace. All of which has served to create favorable international conditions for our socialist construction and contributes to the development of a world situation favorable to the people everywhere.

8. New China has not been in existence for very long, and our successes are still preliminary. Our Party has made mistakes owing to its meagre experience in leading the cause of socialism and subjective errors in the Party leadership's analysis of the situation and its understanding of Chinese conditions. Before the "cultural revolution" there were mistakes of enlarging the scope of class struggle and of impetuosity and rashness in economic construction. Later, there was the comprehensive, long-drawn out and grave blunder of the "cultural revolution." All these errors prevented us from scoring the greater achievements of which we should have been capable. It is impermissible to overlook or whitewash mistakes, which in itself would be a mistake and would give rise to more and worse mistakes. But after all our achievements in the past 32 years are the main thing. It would be a no less serious error to overlook or deny our achievements or our successful experiences in scoring these achievements. These achievements and successful experiences of ours are the product of the creative application of Marxism-Leninism by our Party and people, the manifestation of the superiority of the socialist system and the base

from which the entire Party and people will continue to advance. "Uphold truth and rectify error" — this is the basic stand of dialectical materialism our Party must take. It was by taking this stand that we saved our cause from danger and defeat and won victory in the past. By taking the same stand, we will certainly win still greater victories in the future.

The Seven Years of Basic Completion of the Socialist Transformation

9. From the inception of the People's Republic of China in October 1949 to 1956, our Party led the whole people in gradually realizing the transition from new democracy to socialism, rapidly rehabilitating the country's economy, undertaking planned economic construction and in the main accomplishing the socialist transformation of the private ownership of the means of production in most of the country. The guidelines and basic policies defined by the Party in this historical period were correct and led to brilliant successes.

10. In the first three years of the People's Republic, we cleared the mainland of bandits and the remnant armed forces of the Kuomintang reactionaries, peacefully liberated Tibet, established people's governments at all levels throughout the country, confiscated bureaucrat-capitalist enterprises and transformed them into state-owned socialist enterprises, unified the country's financial and economic work, stabilized commodity prices, carried out agrarian reform in the new liberated areas, suppressed counter-revolutionaries, and unfolded the movements against the "three evils" of corruption, waste and bureaucracy and against the "five evils" of bribery, tax evasion, theft of state property, cheating on government contracts and stealing of economic information, the latter being a movement to beat back the attack mounted by the bourgeoisie. We effectively transformed the educational, scientific and cultural institutions of old China. While successfully carrying out the complex and difficult task of social reform and simultaneously undertaking the great war to resist U.S. aggression and aid Korea, protect our homes and defend the country, we rapidly rehabilitated the country's economy which had been devastated in old China. By the end of 1952, the country's industrial and agricultural production had attained record levels.

11. On the proposal of Comrade Mao Zedong in 1952, the Central Committee of the Party advanced the general line for the transition period, which was to realize the country's socialist industrialization and socialist transformation of agriculture, handicrafts and capitalist industry and commerce step by step over a fairly long period of time.

This general line was a reflection of historical necessity.

1) Socialist industrialization is an indispensable prerequisite to the country's independence and prosperity.

2) With nationwide victory in the new-democratic revolution and completion of the agrarian reform, the contradiction between the working class and the bourgeoisie and between the socialist road and the capitalist road became the principal internal contradiction. The country needed a certain expansion of capitalist industry and commerce which were beneficial to its economy and to the people's livelihood. But in the course of their expansion, things detrimental to the national economy and the people's livelihood were bound to emerge. Consequently, a struggle between restriction and opposition to restriction was inevitable. The conflict of interests became increasingly apparent between capitalist enterprises on the one hand and the economic policies of the state, the socialist state-owned economy, the workers and staff in these capitalist enterprises and the people as a whole on the other. An integrated series of necessary measures and steps, such as the fight against speculation and profiteering, the readjustment and restructuring of industry and commerce, the movement against the "five evils," workers' supervision of production and state monopoly of the purchase and marketing of grain and cotton, were bound to gradually bring backward, anarchic, lop-sided and profit-oriented capitalist industry and commerce into the orbit of socialist transformation.

3) Among the individual peasants, and particularly the poor and lower-middle peasants who had just acquired land in the agrarian reform but lacked other means of production, there was a genuine desire for mutual aid and co-operation in order to avoid borrowing at usurious rates and even mortgaging or selling their land again with consequent polarization, and in order to expand production, undertake water conservancy projects, ward off natural calamities and make use of farm machinery and new techniques. The progress of industrialization, while demanding agricultural products in ever increasing quantities, would provide stronger and stronger support for the technical transformation of agriculture, and this also constituted a motive force behind the transformation of individual into co-operative farming.

As is borne out by history, the general line for the transition period set forth by our Party was entirely correct.

12. During the period of transition, our Party creatively charted a course for socialist transformation that suited China's specific conditions. In dealing with capitalist industry and commerce, we devised a whole series of transitional forms of state capitalism from lower to higher levels, such as the placing of state orders with private enterprises for the processing of materials or the manufacture of goods,

state monopoly of the purchase and marketing of the products of private enterprise, the marketing of products of state-owned enterprises by private shops, and joint state-private ownership of individual enterprises or enterprises of a whole trade, and we eventually realized the peaceful redemption of the bourgeoisie, a possibility envisaged by Marx and Lenin. In dealing with individual farming, we devised transitional forms of co-operation, proceeding from temporary or all-the-year-round mutual-aid teams, to elementary agricultural producers' co-operatives of a semi-socialist nature and then to advanced agricultural producers' co-operatives of a fully socialist nature, always adhering to the principles of voluntariness and mutual benefit, demonstration through advanced examples, and extension of state help. Similar methods were used in transforming individual handicraft industries. In the course of such transformation, the state-capitalist and co-operative economies displayed their unmistakable superiority. By 1956, the socialist transformation of the private ownership of the means of production had been largely completed in most regions. But there had been shortcomings and errors. From the summer of 1955 onwards, we were over-hasty in pressing on with agricultural co-operation and the transformation of private handicraft and commercial establishments; we were far from meticulous, the changes were too fast, and we did our work in a somewhat summary, stereotyped manner, leaving open a number of questions for a long time. Following the basic completion of the transformation of capitalist industry and commerce in 1956, we failed to do a proper job in employing and handling some of the former industrialists and businessmen. But on the whole, it was definitely a historic victory for us to have effected, and to have effected fairly smoothly, so difficult, complex and profound a social change in so vast a country with its several hundred million people, a change, moreover, which promoted the growth of industry, agriculture and the economy as a whole.

13. In economic construction under the First Five-Year Plan (1953-57), we likewise scored major successes through our own efforts and with the assistance of the Soviet Union and other friendly countries. A number of basic industries, essential for the country's industrialization and yet very weak in the past, were built up. Between 1953 and 1956, the average annual increases in the total value of industrial and agricultural output were 19.6 and 4.8 percent respectively. Economic growth was quite fast, with satisfactory economic results, and the key economic sectors were well-balanced. The market prospered, prices were stable. The people's livelihood improved perceptibly. In April 1956, Comrade Mao Zedong made his speech On the Ten Major Relationships, in which he initially summed up our experiences in socialist

construction and set forth the task of exploring a way of building socialism suited to the specific conditions of our country.

14. The First National People's Congress was convened in September 1954, and it enacted the Constitution of the People's Republic of China. In March 1955, a national conference of the Party reviewed the major struggle against the plots of the careerists Gao Gang and Rao Shushi to split the Party and usurp supreme power in the Party and the state; in this way it strengthened Party unity. In January 1956, the Central Committee of the Party called a conference on the question of the intellectuals. Subsequently, the policy of "letting a hundred flowers blossom and a hundred schools of thought contend" was advanced. These measures spelled out the correct policy regarding intellectuals and the work in education, science and culture and thus brought about a significant advance in these fields. Owing to the Party's correct policies, fine style of work and the consequent high prestige it enjoyed among the people, the vast numbers of cadres, masses, youth and intellectuals earnestly studied Marxism-Leninism and Mao Zedong Thought and participated enthusiastically in revolutionary and construction activities under the leadership of the Party, so that a healthy and virile revolutionary morality prevailed throughout the country.

15. The Eighth National Congress of the Party held in September 1956 was very successful. The congress declared that the socialist system had been basically established in China; that while we must strive to liberate Taiwan, thoroughly complete socialist transformation, ultimately eliminate the system of exploitation and continue to wipe out the remnant forces of counter-revolution, the principal contradiction within the country was no longer the contradiction between the working class and the bourgeoisie but between the demand of the people for rapid economic and cultural development and the existing state of our economy and culture which fell short of the needs of the people; that the chief task confronting the whole nation was to concentrate all efforts on developing the productive forces, industrializing the country and gradually meeting the people's incessantly growing material and cultural needs; and that although class struggle still existed and the people's democratic dictatorship had to be further strengthened, the basic task of the dictatorship was now to protect and develop the productive forces in the context of the new relations of production. The congress adhered to the principle put forward by the Central Committee of the Party in May 1956, the principle of opposing both conservatism and rash advance in economic construction, that is, of making steady progress by striking an overall balance. It emphasized the problem of the building of the Party in office and the need to uphold democratic centralism and collective leadership, oppose the personality cult, pro-

mote democracy within the Party and among the people and strengthen the Party's ties with the masses. The line laid down by the Eighth National Congress of the Party was correct and it charted the path for the development of the cause of socialism and for Party building in the new period.

The 10 Years of Initially Building Socialism in All Spheres

16. After the basic completion of socialist transformation, our Party led the entire people in shifting our work to all-round, large-scale socialist construction. In the 10 years preceding the "cultural revolution" we achieved very big successes despite serious setbacks. By 1966, the value of fixed industrial assets, calculated on the basis of their original price, was 4 times greater than in 1956. The output of such major industrial products as cotton yarn, coal, electricity, crude oil, steel and mechanical equipment all recorded impressive increases. Beginning in 1965, China became self-sufficient in petroleum. New industries such as the electronic and petrochemical industries were established one after another. The distribution of industry over the country became better balanced. Capital construction in agriculture and its technical transformation began on a massive scale and yielded better and better results. Both the number of tractors for farming and the quantity of chemical fertilizers applied increased over 7 times and rural consumption of electricity 71 times. The number of graduates from institutions of higher education was 4.9 times that of the previous seven years. Educational work was improved markedly through consolidation. Scientific research and technological work, too, produced notable results.

In the 10 years from 1956 to 1966, the Party accumulated precious experience in leading socialist construction. In the spring of 1957, Comrade Mao Zedong stressed the necessity of correctly handling and distinguishing between the two types of social contradictions differing in nature in a socialist society, and made the correct handling of contradictions among the people the main content of the country's political life. Later, he called for the creation of "a political situation in which we have both centralism and democracy, both discipline and freedom, both unity of will and personal ease of mind and liveliness." In 1958, he proposed that the focus of Party and government work be shifted to technical revolution and socialist construction. All this was the continuation and development of the line adopted by the Eighth National Congress of the Party and was to go on serving as a valuable guide. While leading the work of correcting the errors in the great leap forward and the movement to organize people's communes, Comrade Mao Zedong pointed out that there must be no expropriation of the peasants; that a given stage of social development should not be skipped; that egalitarianism must be opposed; that we must stress commodity production, observe the law of value and strike an overall balance in economic planning; and that economic plans must be arranged with the priority proceeding from agriculture to light industry and then to heavy industry. Comrade Liu Shaoqi said that a variety of means of production could be put into circulation as commodities and that there should be a double-track system for labor as well as for education* in socialist society. Comrade Zhou Enlai said, among other things, that the overwhelming majority of Chinese intellectuals had become intellectuals belonging to the working people and that science and technology would play a key role in China's modernization. Comrade Chen Yun held that plan targets should be realistic, that the scale of construction should correspond to national capability, considerations should be given to both the people's livelihood and the needs of state construction, and that the material, financial and credit balances should be maintained in drawing up plans. Comrade Deng Xiaoping held that industrial enterprises should be consolidated and their management improved and strengthened, and that the system of workers' conferences should be introduced. Comrade Zhu De stressed the need to pay attention to the development of handicrafts and of diverse undertakings in agriculture. Deng Zihui and other comrades pointed out that a system of production responsibility should be introduced in agriculture. All these views were not only of vital significance then, but have remained so ever since. In the course of economic readjustment, the Central Committee drew up draft rules governing the work of the rural people's communes and work in industry, commerce, education, science and literature and art. These rules which were a more or less systematic summation of our experience in socialist construction and embodied specific policies suited to the prevailing conditions remain important as a source of reference for us to this very day.

In short, the material and technical basis for modernizing our country was largely established during that period. It was also largely in the same period that the core personnel for our work in the economic,

*The double-track system for labor refers to a combination of the system of the eight-hour day in factories, rural areas and government offices with a system of part-time work and part-time study in factories and rural areas. The double-track system for education means a system of full-time schooling combined with a system of part-time work and part-time study.

cultural and other spheres were trained and that they gained their experience. This was the principal aspect of the Party's work in that period.

17. In the course of this decade, there were serious faults and errors in the guidelines of the Party's work, which developed through twists and turns.

Nineteen fifty-seven was one of the years that saw the best results in economic work since the founding of the People's Republic owing to the conscientious implementation of the correct line formulated at the Eighth National Congress of the Party. To start a rectification campaign throughout the Party in that year and urge the masses to offer criticisms and suggestions were normal steps in developing socialist democracy. In the rectification campaign a handful of bourgeois Rightists seized the opportunity to advocate what they called "speaking out and airing views in a big way" and to mount a wild attack against the Party and the nascent socialist system in an attempt to replace the leadership of the Communist Party. It was therefore entirely correct and necessary to launch a resolute counterattack. But the scope of this struggle was made far too broad and a number of intellectuals, patriotic people and Party cadres were unjustifiably labelled "Rightists," with unfortunate consequences.

In 1958, the Second Plenum of the Eighth National Congress of the Party adopted the general line for socialist construction. The line and its fundamental aspects were correct in that it reflected the masses' pressing demand for a change in the economic and cultural backwardness of our country. Its shortcoming was that it overlooked the objective economic laws. Both before and after the plenum, all comrades in the Party and people of all nationalities displayed high enthusiasm and initiative for socialism and achieved certain results in production and construction. However, "Left" errors, characterized by excessive targets, the issuing of arbitrary directions, boastfulness and the stirring up of a "communist wind," spread unchecked throughout the country. This was due to our lack of experience in socialist construction and inadequate understanding of the laws of economic development and of the basic economic conditions in China. More important, it was due to the fact that Comrade Mao Zedong and many leading comrades, both at the center and in the localities, had become smug about their successes, were impatient for quick results and overestimated the role of man's subjective will and efforts. After the general line was formulated, the great leap forward and the movement for rural people's communes were initiated without careful investigation and study and without prior experimentation. From the end of 1958 to the early stage of the Lushan Meeting of the Political Bureau of the Party's Central Committee in July 1959, Comrade Mao Zedong and the Central Committee led the whole Party in energetically rectifying the errors which had already been recognized. However, in the later part of the meeting, he erred in initiating criticism of Comrade Peng Dehuai and then in launching a Party-wide struggle against "Right opportunism." The resolution passed by the Eighth Plenary Session of the Eighth Central Committee of the Party concerning the so-called anti-Party group of Peng Dehuai, Huang Kecheng, Zhang Wentian and Zhou Xiaozhou was entirely wrong. Politically, this struggle gravely undermined inner-Party democracy from the central level down to the grass roots; economically, it cut short the process of the rectification of "Left" errors, thus prolonging their influence. It was mainly due to the errors of the great leap forward and of the struggle against "Right opportunism" together with a succession of natural calamities and the perfidious scrapping of contracts by the Soviet Government that our economy encountered serious difficulties between 1959 and 1961, which caused serious losses to our country and people.

In the winter of 1960, the Central Committee of the Party and Comrade Mao Zedong set about rectifying the "Left" errors in rural work and decided on the principle of "readjustment, consolidation, filling out and raising standards" for the economy as a whole. A number of correct policies and resolute measures were worked out and put into effect with Comrades Liu Shaoqi, Zhou Enlai, Chen Yun and Deng Xiaoping in charge. All this constituted a crucial turning point in that historical phase. In January 1962, the enlarged Central Work Conference attended by 7,000 people made a preliminary summing-up of the positive and negative experience of the great leap forward and unfolded criticism and self-criticism. A majority of the comrades who had been unjustifiably criticized during the campaign against "Right opportunism" were rehabilitated before or after the conference. In addition, most of the "Rightists" had their label removed. Thanks to these economic and political measures, the national economy recovered and developed fairly smoothly between 1962 and 1966.

Nevertheless, "Left" errors in the principles guiding economic work were not only not eradicated, but actually grew in the spheres of politics, ideology and culture. At the 10th Plenary Session of the Party's Eighth Central Committee in September 1962, Comrade Mao Zedong widened and absolutized the class struggle, which exists only within certain limits in socialist society, and carried forward the viewpoint he had advanced after the anti-Rightist struggle in 1957 that the contradiction between the proletariat and the bourgeoisie remained the principal contradiction in our society. He went a step further and asserted that, throughout the historical period of socialism, the bourgeoisie would continue to exist and would attempt a comeback and become the source of revisionism inside the Party. The socialist education movement unfolded between 1963 and 1965 in some rural areas and at the grass-roots level in a small number of cities did help to some extent to improve the cadres' style of work and economic management. But, in the course of the movement, problems differing in nature were all treated as forms of class struggle or its reflections inside the Party. As a result, quite a number of the cadres at the grass-roots level were unjustly dealt with in the latter half of 1964, and early in 1965 the erroneous thesis was advanced that the main target of the movement should be "those Party persons in power taking the capitalist road." In the ideological sphere, a number of literary and art works and schools of thought and a number of representative personages in artistic, literary and academic circles were subjected to unwarranted, inordinate political criticism. And there was an increasingly serious "Left" deviation on the question of intellectuals and on the question of education, science and culture. These errors eventually culminated in the "cultural revolution," but they had not yet become dominant.

Thanks to the fact that the whole Party and people had concentrated on carrying out the correct principle of economic readjustment since the winter of 1960, socialist construction gradually flourished again. The Party and the people were united in sharing weal and woe. They overcame difficulties at home, stood up to the pressure of the Soviet leading clique and repaid all the debts owed to the Soviet Union, which were chiefly incurred through purchasing Soviet arms during the movement to resist U.S. aggression and aid Korea. In addition, they did what they could to support the revolutionary struggles of the people of many countries and assist them in their economic construction. The Third National People's Congress, which met between the end of 1964 and the first days of 1965, announced that the task of national economic readjustment had in the main been accomplished and that the economy as a whole would soon enter a new stage of development. It called for energetic efforts to build China step by step into a socialist power with modern agriculture, industry, national defense and science and technology. This call was not fulfilled owing to the "cultural revolution."

18. All the successes in these 10 years were achieved under the collective leadership of the Central Committee of the Party headed by Comrade Mao Zedong. Likewise, responsibility for the errors committed in the work of this period rested with the same collective leadership. Although Comrade Mao Zedong must be held chiefly responsible, we cannot lay the blame on him alone for all those errors. During this period, his theoretical and practical mistakes concerning class

struggle in a socialist society became increasingly serious, his personal arbitrariness gradually undermined democratic centralism in Party life and the personality cult grew graver and graver. The Central Committee of the Party failed to rectify these mistakes in good time. Careerists like Lin Biao, Jiang Qing and Kang Sheng, harboring ulterior motives, made use of these errors and inflated them. This led to the inauguration of the "cultural revolution."

The Decade of the "Cultural Revolution"

19. The "cultural revolution," which lasted from May 1966 to October 1976, was responsible for the most severe setback and the heaviest losses suffered by the Party, the state and the people since the founding of the People's Republic. It was initiated and led by Comrade Mao Zedong. His principal theses were that many representatives of the bourgeoisie and counterrevolutionary revisionists had sneaked into the Party, the government, the army and cultural circles, and leadership in a fairly large majority of organizations and departments was no longer in the hands of Marxists and the people; that Party persons in power taking the capitalist road had formed a bourgeois headquarters inside the Central Committee which pursued a revisionist political and organizational line and had agents in all provinces, municipalities and autonomous regions, as well as in all central departments; that since the forms of struggle adopted in the past had not been able to solve this problem, the power usurped by the capitalist-roaders could be recaptured only by carrying out a great cultural revolution, by openly and fully mobilizing the broad masses from the bottom up to expose these sinister phenomena; and that the cultural revolution was in fact a great political revolution in which one class would overthrow another, a revolution that would have to be waged time and again. These theses appeared mainly in the May 16 Circular, which served as the programmatic document of the "cultural revolution," and in the political report to the Ninth National Congress of the Party in April 1969. They were incorporated into a general theory — the "theory of continued revolution under the dictatorship of the proletariat" — which then took on a specific meaning. These erroneous "Left" theses, upon which Comrade Mao Zedong based himself in initiating the "cultural revolution," were obviously inconsistent with the system of Mao Zedong Thought, which is the integration of the universal principles of Marxism-Leninism with the concrete practice of the Chinese revolution. These theses must be thoroughly distinguished from Mao Zedong Thought. As for Lin Biao, Jiang Qing and others, who were placed in important positions by Comrade Mao Zedong, the matter is of an entirely different nature. They

rigged up two counterrevolutionary cliques in an attempt to seize supreme power and, taking advantage of Comrade Mao Zedong's errors, committed many crimes behind his back, bringing disaster to the country and the people. As their counterrevolutionary crimes have been fully exposed, this resolution will not go into them at any length.

20. The history of the "cultural revolution" has proved that Comrade Mao Zedong's principal theses for initiating this revolution conformed neither to Marxism-Leninism nor to Chinese reality. They represent an entirely erroneous appraisal of the prevailing class relations and political situation in the Party and state.

1) The "cultural revolution" was defined as a struggle against the revisionist line or the capitalist road. There were no grounds at all for this definition. It led to the confusing of right and wrong on a series of important theories and policies. Many things denounced as revisionist or capitalist during the "cultural revolution" were actually Marxist and socialist principles, many of which had been set forth or supported by Comrade Mao Zedong himself. The "cultural revolution" negated many of the correct principles, policies and achievements of the 17 years after the founding of the People's Republic. In fact, it negated much of the work of the Central Committee of the Party and the People's Government, including Comrade Mao Zedong's own contribution. It negated the arduous struggles the entire people had conducted in socialist construction.

2) The confusing of right and wrong inevitably led to confusing the people with the enemy. The "capitalist-roaders" overthrown in the "cultural revolution" were leading cadres of Party and government organizations at all levels, who formed the core force of the socialist cause. The so-called bourgeois headquarters inside the Party headed by Liu Shaoqi and Deng Xiaoping simply did not exist. Irrefutable facts have proved that labelling Comrade Liu Shaoqi a "renegade, hidden traitor and scab" was nothing but a frame-up by Lin Biao, Jiang Qing and their followers. The political conclusion concerning Comrade Liu Shaoqi drawn by the 12th Plenary Session of the Eighth Central Committee of the Party and the disciplinary measure it meted out to him were both utterly wrong. The criticism of the so-called reactionary academic authorities in the "cultural revolution" during which many capable and accomplished intellectuals were attacked and persecuted also badly muddled up the distinction between the people and the enemy.

3) Nominally, the "cultural revolution" was conducted by directly relying on the masses. In fact, it was divorced both from the Party organizations and from the masses. After the movement started, Party organizations at different levels were attacked and became par-

tially or wholly paralysed, the Party's leading cadres at various levels were subjected to criticism and struggle, inner-Party life came to a standstill, and many activists and large numbers of the basic masses whom the Party has long relied on were rejected. At the beginning of the "cultural revolution," the vast majority of participants in the movement acted out of their faith in Comrade Mao Zedong and the Party. Except for a handful of extremists, however, they did not approve of launching ruthless struggles against leading Party cadres at all levels. With the lapse of time, following their own circuitous paths, they eventually attained a heightened political consciousness and consequently began to adopt a sceptical or wait-and-see attitude towards the "cultural revolution," or even resisted and opposed it. Many people were assailed either more or less severely for this very reason. Such a state of affairs could not but provide openings to be exploited by opportunists, careerists and conspirators, not a few of whom were escalated to high or even key positions.

4) Practice has shown that the "cultural revolution" did not in fact constitute a revolution or social progress in any sense, nor could it possibly have done so. It was we and not the enemy at all who were thrown into disorder by the "cultural revolution." Therefore, from beginning to end, it did not turn "great disorder under heaven" into "great order under heaven," nor could it conceivably have done so. After the state power in the form of the people's democratic dictatorship was established in China, and especially after socialist transformation was basically completed and the expoliters were eliminated as classes, the socialist revolution represented a fundamental break with the past in both content and method, though its tasks remained to be completed. Of course, it was essential to take proper account of certain undesirable phenomena that undoubtedly existed in Party and state organisms and to remove them by correct measures in conformity with the Constitution, the laws and the Party Constitution. But on no account should the theories and methods of the "cultural revolution" have been applied. Under socialist conditions, there is no economic or political basis for carrying out a great political revolution in which "one class overthrows another." It decidedly could not come up with any constructive programme, but could only bring grave disorder, damage and retrogression in its train. History has shown that the "cultural revolution," initiated by a leader laboring under a misapprehension and capitalized on by counterrevolutionary cliques, led to domestic turmoil and brought catastrophe to the Party, the state and the whole people.

21. The "cultural revolution" can be divided into three stages.

1) From the initiation of the "cultural revolution" to the Ninth Na-

tional Congress of the Party in April 1969. The convening of the enlarged Political Bureau meeting of the Central Committee of the Party in May 1966 and the 11th Plenary Session of the Eighth Central Committee in August of that year marked the launching of the "cultural revolution" on a full scale. These two meetings adopted the May 16 Circular and the Decision of the Central Committee of the Communist Party of China Concerning the Great Proletarian Cultural Revolution respectively. They launched an erroneous struggle against the so-called anti-Party clique of Peng Zhen, Luo Ruiqing, Lu Dingyi and Yang Shangkun and the so-called headquarters of Liu Shaoqi and Deng Xiaoping. They wrongly reorganized the central leading organs, set up the "Cultural Revolution Group under the Central Committee of the Chinese Communist Party" and gave it a major part of the power of the Central Committee. In fact, Comrade Mao Zedong's personal leadership characterized by "Left" errors took the place of the collective leadership of the Central Committee, and the cult of Comrade Mao Zedong was frenziedly pushed to an extreme. Lin Biao, Jiang Qing, Kang Sheng, Zhang Chunqiao and others, acting chiefly in the name of the "Cultural Revolution Group," exploited the situation to incite people to "overthrow everything and wage full scale civil war." Around February 1967, at various meetings, Tan Zhenlin, Chen Yi, Ye Jianying, Li Fuchun, Li Xiannian, Xu Xiangqian, Nie Rongzhen and other Political Bureau Members and leading comrades of the Military Commission of the Central Committee sharply criticized the mistakes of the "cultural revolution." This was labelled the "February adverse current," and they were attacked and repressed. Comrades Zhu De and Chen Yun were also wrongly criticized. Almost all leading Party and government departments in the different spheres and localities were stripped of their power or reorganized. The chaos was such that it was necessary to send in the People's Liberation Army to support the Left, the workers and the peasants and to institute military control and military training. It played a positive role in stabilizing the situation, but it also produced some negative consequences. The Ninth Congress of the Party legitimatized the erroneous theories and practices of the "cultural revolution," and so reinforced the positions of Lin Biao, Jiang Qing, Kang Sheng and others in the Central Committee of the Party. The guidelines of the Ninth Congress were wrong, ideologically, politically and organizationally.

2) From the Ninth National Congress of the Party to its 10th National Congress in August 1973. In 1970-71 the counterrevolutionary Lin Biao clique plotted to capture supreme power and attempted an armed counterrevolutionary coup d'etat. Such was the outcome of the "cultural revolution" which overturned a series of fundamental Party principles.

Objectively, it announced the failure of the theories and practices of the "cultural revolution." Comrades Mao Zedong and Zhou Enlai ingeniously thwarted the plotted coup. Supported by Comrade Mao Zedong, Comrade Zhou Enlai took charge of the day-to-day work of the Central Committee and things began to improve in all fields. During the criticism and repudiation of Lin Biao in 1972, he correctly proposed criticism of the ultra-Left trend of thought. In fact, this was an extension of the correct proposals put forward around February 1967 by many leading comrades of the Central Committee who had called for the correction of the errors of the "cultural revolution." Comrade Mao Zedong, however, erroneously held that the task was still to oppose the "ultra-Right." The 10th Congress of the Party perpetuated the "Left" errors of the Ninth Congress and made Wang Hongwen a vice-chairman of the Party. Jiang Qing, Zhang Chunqiao, Yao Wenyuan and Wang Hongwen formed a gang of four inside the Political Bureau of the Central Committee, thus strengthening the influence of the counterrevolutionary Jiang Qing clique.

3) From the 10th Congress of the Party to October 1976. Early in 1974 Jiang Qing, Wang Hongwen and others launched a campaign to "criticize Lin Biao and Confucius." Jiang Qing and the others directed the spearhead at Comrade Zhou Enlai, which was different in nature from the campaign conducted in some localities and organizations where individuals involved in and incidents connected with the conspiracies of the counterrevolutionary Lin Biao clique were investigated. Comrade Mao Zedong approved the launching of the movement to "criticize Lin Biao and Confucius." When he found that Jiang Qing and the others were turning it to their advantage in order to seize power, he severely criticized them. He declared that they had formed a gang of four and pointed out that Jiang Qing harbored the wild ambition of making herself chairman of the Central Committee and "forming a cabinet" by political manipulation. In 1975, when Comrade Zhou Enlai was seriously ill, Comrade Deng Xiaoping, with the support of Comrade Mao Zedong, took charge of the day-to-day work of the Central Committee. He convened an enlarged meeting of the Military Commission of the Central Committee and several other important meetings with a view to solving problems in industry, agriculture, transport and science and technology, and began to straighten out work in many fields so that the situation took an obvious turn for the better. However, Comrade Mao Zedong could not bear to accept systematic correction of the errors of the "cultural revolution" by Comrade Deng Xiaoping and triggered the movement to "criticize Deng and counter the Right deviationist trend to reverse correct verdicts," once again plunging the nation into turmoil. In January of that year, Comrade Zhou Enlai passed away. Com-

rade Zhou Enlai was utterly devoted to the Party and the people and the people and stuck to his post till his dying day. He found himself in an extremely difficult situation throughout the "cultural revolution." He always kept the general interest in mind, bore the heavy burden of office without complaint, racking his brains and untiringly endeavouring to keep the normal work of the Party and the state going, to minimize the damage caused by the "cultural revolution" and to protect many Party and non-Party cadres. He waged all forms of struggle to counter sabotage by the counterrevolutionary Lin Biao and Jiang Qing cliques. His death left the whole Party and people in the most profound grief. In April of the same year, a powerful movement of protest signalled by the Tian An Men Incident swept the whole country, a movement to mourn for the late Premier Zhou Enlai and oppose the gang of four. In essence, the movement was a demonstration of support for the Party's correct leadership as represented by Comrade Deng Xiaoping. It laid the ground for massive popular support for the subsequent overthrow of the counterrevolutionary Jiang Qing clique. The Political Bureau of the Central Committee and Comrade Mao Zedong wrongly assessed the nature of the Tian An Men Incident and dismissed Comrade Deng Xiaoping from all his posts inside and outside the Party. As soon as Comrade Mao Zedong passed away in September 1976, the counterrevolutionary Jiang Qing clique stepped up its plot to seize supreme Party and state leadership. Early in October of the same year, the Political Bureau of the Central Committee, executing the will of the Party and the people, resolutely smashed the clique and brought the catastrophic "cultural revolution" to an end. This was a great victory won by the entire Party, army and people after prolonged struggle. Hua Guofeng, Ye Jianying, Li Xiannian and other comrades played a vital part in the struggle to crush the clique.

22. Chief responsibility for the grave "Left" error of the "cultural revolution," an error comprehensive in magnitude and protracted in duration, does indeed lie with Comrade Mao Zedong. But after all it was the error of a great proletarian revolutionary. Comrade Mao Zedong paid constant attention to overcoming shortcomings in the life of the Party and state. In his later years, however, far from making a correct analysis of many problems, he confused right and wrong and the people with the enemy during the "cultural revolution." While making serious mistakes, he repeatedly urged the whole Party to study the works of Marx, Engels and Lenin conscientiously and imagined that his theory and practice were Marxist and that they were essential for the consolidation of the dictatorship of the proletariat. Herein lies his tragedy. While persisting in the comprehensive error of the "cultural revolution," he checked and rectified some of its specific mistakes,

protected some leading Party cadres and non-Party public figures and enabled some leading cadres to return to important leading posts. He led the struggle to smash the counterrevolutionary Lin Biao clique. He made major criticisms and exposures of Jiang Qing, Zhang Chunqiao and others, frustrating their sinister ambition to seize supreme leadership. All this was crucial to the subsequent and relatively painless overthrow of the gang of four by our Party. In his later years, he still remained alert to safeguarding the security of our country, stood up to the pressure of the social-imperialists, pursued a correct foreign policy, firmly supported the just struggles of all peoples, outlined the correct strategy of the three worlds and advanced the important principle that China would never seek hegemony. During the "cultural revolution" our Party was not destroyed, but maintained its unity. The State Council and the People's Liberation Army were still able to do much of their essential work. The Fourth National People's Congress which was attended by deputies from all nationalities and all walks of life was convened and it determined the composition of the State Council with Comrades Zhou Enlai and Deng Xiaoping as the core of its leadership. The foundation of China's socialist system remained intact and it was possible to continue socialist economic construction. Our country remained united and exerted a significant influence on international affairs. All these important facts are inseparable from the great role played by Comrade Mao Zedong. For these reasons, and particularly for his vital contributions to the cause of the revolution over the years, the Chinese people have always regarded Comrade Mao Zedong as their respected and beloved great leader and teacher.

23. The struggle waged by the Party and the people against "Left" errors and against the counterrevolutionary Lin Biao and Jiang Qing cliques during the "cultural revolution" was arduous and full of twists and turns, and it never ceased. Rigorous tests throughout the "cultural revolution" have proved that standing on the correct side in the struggle were the overwhelming majority of Members of the Eighth Central Committee of the Party and the Members it elected to its Political Bureau, Standing Committee and Secretariat. Most of our Party cadres, whether they were wrongly dismissed or remained at their posts, whether they were rehabilitated early or late, are loyal to the Party and people and steadfast in their belief in the cause of socialism and communism. Most of the intellectuals, model workers, patriotic democrats, patriotic overseas Chinese and cadres and masses of all strata and all nationalities who had been wronged and persecuted did not waver in their love for the motherland and in their support for the Party and socialism. Party and state leaders such as Comrades Liu Shaoqi, Peng Dehuai, He Long and Tao Zhu and all other Party and non-Party com-

rades who were persecuted to death in the "cultural revolution" will live for ever in the memories of the Chinese people. It was through the joint struggles waged by the entire Party and the masses of workers, peasants, PLA officers and men, intellectuals, educated youth and cadres that the havoc wrought by the "cultural revolution" was somewhat mitigated. Some progress was made in our economy despite tremendous losses. Grain output increased relatively steadily. Significant achievements were scored in industry, communications and capital construction and in science and technology. New railways were built and the Changjiang River Bridge at Nanjing was completed; a number of large enterprises using advanced technology went into operation; hydrogen bomb tests were successfully undertaken and man-made satellites successfully launched and retrieved; and new hybrid strains of long-grained rice were developed and popularized. Despite the domestic turmoil, the People's Liberation Army bravely defended the security of the motherland. And new prospects were opened up in the sphere of foreign affairs. Needless to say, none of these successes can be attributed in any way to the "cultural revolution," without which we would have scored far greater achievements for our cause. Although we suffered from sabotage by the counterrevolutionary Lin Biao and Jiang Qing cliques during the "cultural revolution," we won out over them in the end. The Party, the people's political power, the people's army and Chinese society on the whole remained unchanged in nature. Once again history has proved that our people are a great people and that our Party and socialist system have enormous vitality.

24. In addition to the above-mentioned immediate cause of Comrade Mao Zedong's mistake in leadership, there are complex social and historical causes underlying the "cultural revolution" which dragged on for as long as a decade. The main causes are as follows:

1) The history of the socialist movement is not long and that of the socialist countries even shorter. Some of the laws governing the development of socialist society are relatively clear, but many more remain to be explored. Our Party had long existed in circumstances of war and fierce class struggle. It was not fully prepared, either ideologically or in terms of scientific study, for the swift advent of the newborn socialist society and for socialist construction on a national scale. The scientific works of Marx, Engels, Lenin and Stalin are our guide to action, but can in no way provide ready-made answers to the problems we may encounter in our socialist cause. Even after the basic completion of socialist transformation, given the guiding ideology, we were liable, owing to the historical circumstances in which our Party grew, to continue to regard issues unrelated to class struggle as its manifestations when observing and handling new contradictions and prob-

lems which cropped up in the political, economic, cultural and other spheres in the course of the development of socialist society. And when confronted with actual class struggle under the new conditions, we habitually fell back on the familiar methods and experiences of the large-scale, turbulent mass struggle of the past, which should no longer have been mechanically followed. As a result, we substantially broadened the scope of class struggle. Moreover, this subjective thinking and practice divorced from reality seemed to have a "theoretical basis" in the writings of Marx, Engels, Lenin and Stalin because certain ideas and arguments set forth in them were misunderstood or dogmatically interpreted. For instance, it was thought that equal right, which reflects the exchange of equal amounts of labor and is applicable to the distribution of the means of consumption in socialist society, or "bourgeois right" as it was designated by Marx, should be restricted and criticized, and so the principle of "to each according to his work: and that of material interest should be restricted and criticized; that small production would continue to engender capitalism and the bourgeoisie daily and hourly on a large scale even after the basic completion of socialist transformation, and so a series of "Left" economic policies and policies on class struggle in urban and rural areas were formulated; and that all ideological differences inside the Party were reflections of class struggle in society, and so frequent and acute inner-Party struggles were conducted. All this led us to regard the error in magnifying class struggle as an act in defence of the purity of Marxism. Furthermore, Soviet leaders started a polemic between China and the Soviet Union, and turned the arguments between the two Parties on matters of principle into a conflict between the two nations, bringing enormous pressure to bear upon China politically, economically and militarily. So we were forced to wage a just struggle against the big-nation chauvinism of the Soviet Union. In these circumstances, a campaign to prevent and combat revisionism inside the country was launched, which spread the error of broadening the scope of class struggle in the Party, so that normal differences among comrades inside the Party came to be regarded as manifestations of the revisionist line or of the struggle between the two lines. This resulted in growing tension in inner-Party relations. Thus it became difficult for the Party to resist certain "Left" views put forward by Comrade Mao Zedong and others, and the development of these views led to the outbreak of the protracted "cultural revolution."

2) Comrade Mao Zedong's prestige reached a peak and he began to get arrogant at the very time when the Party was confronted with the new task of shifting the focus of its work to socialist construction, a task for which the utmost caution was required. He gradually divorced

himself from practice and from the masses, acted more and more arbitrarily and subjectively, and increasingly put himself above the Central Committee of the Party. The result was a steady weakening and even undermining of the principle of collective leadership and democratic centralism in the political life of the Party and the country. This state of affairs took shape only gradually and the Central Committee of the Party should be held partly responsible. From the Marxist viewpoint, this complex phenomenon was the product of given historical conditions. Blaming this on only one person or on only a handful of people will not provide a deep lesson for the whole Party or enable it to find practical ways to change the situation. In the communist movement, leaders play quite an important role. This has been borne out by history time and again and leaves no room for doubt. However, certain grievous deviations, which occurred in the history of the international communist movement owing to the failure to handle the relationship between the Party and its leader correctly, had an adverse effect on our Party, too. Feudalism in China has had a very long history. Our Party fought in the firmest and most thoroughgoing way against it, and particularly against the feudal system of land ownership and the landlords and local tyrants, and fostered a fine tradition of democracy in the anti-feudal struggle. But it remains difficult to eliminate the evil ideological and political influence of centuries of feudal autocracy. And for various historical reasons, we failed to institutionalize and legalize inner-Party democracy and democracy in the political and social life of the country, or we drew up the relevant laws but they lacked due authority. This meant that conditions were present for the overconcentration of Party power in individuals and for the development of arbitrary individual rule and the personality cult in the Party. Thus, it was hard for the Party and state to prevent the initiation of the "cultural revolution" or check its development.

A Great Turning Point in History

25. The victory won in overthrowing the counterrevolutionary Jiang Qing clique in October 1976 saved the Party and the revolution from disaster and enabled our country to enter a new historical period of development. In the two years from October 1976 to December 1978 when the Third Plenary Session of the 11th Central Committee of the Party was convened, large numbers of cadres and other people most enthusiastically devoted themselves to all kinds of revolutionary work and the task of construction. Notable results were achieved in exposing and repudiating the crimes of the counterrevolutionary Jiang Qing clique and uncovering their factional setup. The consolidation of Party

and state organizations and the redress of wrongs suffered by those who were unjustly, falsely and wrongly charged began in some places. Industrial and agricultural production was fairly swiftly restored. Work in education, science and culture began to return to normal. Comrades inside and outside the Party demanded more and more strongly that the errors of the "cultural revolution" be corrected, but such demands met with serious resistance. This, of course, was partly due to the fact that the political and ideological confusion created in the decade-long "cultural revolution" could not be eliminated overnight, but it was also due to the "Left" errors in the guiding ideology that Comrade Hua Guofeng continued to commit in his capacity as Chairman of the Central Committee of the Chinese Communist Party. On the proposal of Comrade Mao Zedong, Comrade Hua Guofeng had become First Vice-Chairman of the Central Committee of the Party and concurrently Premier of the State Council during the "movement to criticize Deng Xiaoping" in 1976. He contributed to the struggle to overthrow the counterrevolutionary Jiang Qing clique and did useful work after that. But he promoted the erroneous "two-whatever's" policy, that is, "we firmly uphold whatever policy decisions Chairman Mao made, and we unswervingly adhere to whatever instructions Chairman Mao gave," and he took a long time to rectify the error. He tried to suppress the discussions on the criterion of truth unfolded in the country in 1978, which were very significant in setting things right. He procrastinated and obstructed the work of reinstating veteran cadres in their posts and redressing the injustices left over from the past (including the case of the "Tian An Men Incident" of 1976). He accepted and fostered the personality cult around himself while continuing the personality cult of the past. The 11th National Congress of the Chinese Communist Party convened in August 1977 played a positive role in exposing and repudiating the gang of four and mobilizing the whole Party for building China into a powerful modern socialist state. However, owing to the limitations imposed by the historical conditions then and the influence of Comrade Hua Guofeng's mistakes, it reaffirmed the erroneous theories, policies and slogans of the "cultural revolution" instead of correcting them. He also had his share of responsibility for impetuously seeking quick results in economic work and for continuing certain other "Left" policies. Obviously, under his leadership it is impossible to correct "Left" errors within the Party, and all the more impossible to restore the Party's fine traditions.

26. The Third Plenary Session of the 11th Central Committee in December 1978 marked a crucial turning point of far-reaching significance in the history of our Party since the birth of the People's Republic. It put an end to the situation in which the Party had been ad-

vancing haltingly in its work since October 1976 and began to correct conscientiously and comprehensively the "Left" errors of the "cultural revolution" and earlier. The plenary session resolutely criticized the erroneous "two-whatever's" policy and fully affirmed the need to grasp Mao Zedong Thought comprehensively and accurately as a scientific system. It highly evaluated the forum on the criterion of truth and decided on the guiding principle of emancipating the mind, using our brains, seeking truth from facts and uniting as one in looking forward to the future. It firmly discarded the slogan "Take class struggle as the key link," which had become unsuitable in a socialist society, and made the strategic decision to shift the focus of work to socialist modernization. It declared that attention should be paid to solving the problem of serious imbalances between the major branches of the economy and drafted decisions on the acceleration of agricultural development. It stressed the task of strengthening socialist democracy and the socialist legal system. It examined and redressed a number of major unjust, false and wrong cases in the history of the Party and settled the controversy on the merits and demerits, the rights and wrongs, of some prominent leaders. The plenary session also elected additional members to the Party's central leading organs. These momentous changes in the work of leadership signified that the Party re-established the correct line of Marxism ideologically, politically and organizationally. Since then, it has gained the initiative in setting things right and has been able to solve step by step many problems left over since the founding of the People's Republic and the new problems cropping up in the course of practice and carry out the heavy tasks of construction and reform, so that things are going very well in both the economic and political sphere.

1) In response to the call of the Third Plenary Session of the 11th Central Committee of the Party for emancipating the mind and seeking truth from facts, large numbers of cadres and other people have freed themselves from the spiritual shackles of the personality cult and the dogmatism that prevailed in the past. This has stimulated thinking inside and outside the Party, giving rise to a lively situation where people try their best to study new things and seek solutions to new problems. To carry out the principle of emancipating the mind properly, the Party reiterated in good time the four fundamental principles of upholding the socialist road, the people's democratic dictatorship (i.e., the dictatorship of the proletariat), the leadership of the Communist Party, and Marxism-Leninism and Mao Zedong Thought. It reaffirmed the principle that neither democracy nor centralism can be practised at each other's expense and pointed out the basic fact that, although the exploiters had been eliminated as classes, class struggle continues

to exist within certain limits. In his speech at the meeting in celebration of the 30th anniversary of the founding of the People's Republic of China, which was approved by the Fourth Plenary Session of the 11th Central Committee of the Party, Comrade Ye Jianying fully affirmed the gigantic achievements of the Party and people since the inauguration of the People's Republic while making self-criticism on behalf of the Party for errors in its work and outlined our country's bright prospects. This helped to unify the thinking of the whole Party and people. At its meeting in August 1980, the Political Bureau of the Central Committee set the historic task of combating corrosion by bourgeois ideology and eradicating the evil influence of feudalism in the political and ideological fields which is still present. A work conference convened by the Central Committee in December of the same year resolved to strengthen the Party's ideological and political work, make greater efforts to build a socialist civilization, criticize the erroneous ideological trends running counter to the four fundamental principles and strike at the counterrevolutionary activities disrupting the cause of socialism. This exerted a most salutary countrywide influence in fostering a political situation characterized by stability, unity and liveliness.

2) At a work conference called by the Central Committee in April 1979, the Party formulated the principle of "readjusting, restructuring, consolidating and improving" the economy as a whole in a decisive effort to correct the shortcomings and mistakes of the previous two years in our economic work and eliminate the influence of "Left" errors that had persisted in this field. The Party indicated that economic construction must be carried out in the light of China's conditions and in conformity with economic and natural laws; that it must be carried out within the limits of our own resources, step by step, after due deliberation and with emphasis on practical results, so that the development of production will be closely connected with the improvement of the people's livelihood; and that active efforts must be made to promote economic and technical co-operation with other countries on the basis of independence and self-reliance. Guided by these principles, light industry has quickened its rate of growth and the structure of industry is becoming more rational and better co-ordinated. Reforms in the system of economic management, including extension of the decision-making powers of enterprises, restoration of the workers' congresses, strengthening of democratic management of enterprises and transference of financial management responsibilities to the various levels, have gradually been carried out in conjunction with economic readjustment. The Party has worked conscientiously to remedy the errors in rural work since the later stage of the movement for agricultural

co-operation, with the result that the purchase prices of farm and sideline products have been raised, various forms of production responsibility introduced whereby remuneration is determined by farm output, family plots have been restored and appropriately extended, village fairs have been revived, and sideline occupations and diverse undertakings have been developed. All these have greatly enhanced the peasants' enthusiasm. Grain output in the last two years reached an all-time high, and at the same time industrial crops and other farm and sideline products registered a big increase. Thanks to the development of agriculture and the economy as a whole, the living standards of the people have improved.

3) After detailed and careful investigation and study, measures were taken to clear the name of Comrade Liu Shaoqi, former Vice-Chairman of the Central Committee of the Communist Party of China and Chairman of the People's Republic of China, those of other Party and state leaders, national minority leaders and leading figures in different circles who had been wronged, and to affirm their historical contributions to the Party and the people in protracted revolutionary struggle.

4) Large numbers of unjust, false and wrong cases were re-examined and their verdicts reversed. Cases in which people had been wrongly labelled bourgeois Rightists were also corrected. Announcements were made to the effect that former businessmen and industrialists, having undergone remoulding, are now working people; that small trades people, pedlars and handicraftsmen, who were originally laborers, have been differentiated from businessmen and industrialists who were members of the bourgeoisie; and that the status of the vast majority of former landlords and rich peasants, who have become working people through remoulding, has been redefined. These measures have appropriately resolved many contradictions inside the Party and among the people.

5) People's congresses at all levels are doing their work better and those at the provincial and county levels have set up permanent organs of their own. The system according to which deputies to the people's congresses at and below the county level are directly elected by the voters is now universally practised. Collective leadership and democratic centralism are being perfected in the Party and state organizations. The powers of local and primary organizations are steadily being extended. The so-called right to "speak out, air views, and hold debates in a big way and write big-character posters," which actually obstructs the promotion of socialist democracy, was deleted from the Constitution. A number of important laws, decrees and regulations have been reinstated, enacted or enforced, including the Criminal Law and the Law of Criminal Procedure which had never been drawn up

since the founding of the People's Republic. The work of the judicial, procuratorial and public security departments has improved and telling blows have been dealt at all types of criminals guilty of serious offences. The 10 principal members of the counter-revolutionary Lin Biao and Jiang Qing cliques were publicly tried according to law.

6) The Party has striven to readjust and strengthen the leading bodies at all levels. The Fifth Plenary Session of the 11th Central Committee of the Party, held in February 1980, elected additional members to the Standing Committee of its Political Bureau and reestablished the Secretariat of the Central Committee, greatly strengthening the central leadership. Party militancy has been enhanced as a result of the establishment of the Central Commission for Inspecting Discipline and of discipline inspection commissions at the lower levels, the formulation of the Guiding Principles for Inner-Party Political Life and other related inner-Party regulations, and the effort made by leading Party organizations and discipline inspection bodies at the different levels to rectify unhealthy practices. The Party's mass media have also contributed immensely in this respect. The Party has decided to put an end to the virtually life-long tenure of leading cadres, change the overconcentration of power and, on the basis of revolutionization, gradually reduce the average age of the leading cadres at all levels and raise their level of education and professional competence, and has initiated this process. With the reshuffling of the leading personnel of the State Council and the division of labour between Party and government organizations, the work of the central and local governments has improved.

In addition, there have been significant successes in the Party's efforts to implement our policies in education, science, culture, public health, physical culture, nationality affairs, united front work, overseas Chinese affairs and military and foreign affairs.

In short, the scientific principles of Mao Zedong Thought and the correct policies of the Party have been revived and developed under new conditions and all aspects of Party and government work have been flourishing again since the Third Plenary Session of the 11th Central Committee. Our work still suffers from shortcomings and mistakes, and we are still confronted with numerous difficulties. Nevertheless, the road of victorious advance is open, and the Party's prestige among the people is rising day by day.

Comrade Mao Zedong's Historical Role and Mao Zedong Thought

27. Comrade Mao Zedong was a great Marxist and a great proletar-

ian revolutionary, strategist and theorist. It is true that he made gross mistakes during the "cultural revolution," but, if we judge his activities as a whole, his contributions to the Chinese revolution far outweigh his mistakes. His merits are primary and his errors secondary. He rendered indelible meritorious service in founding and building up our Party and the Chinese People's Liberation Army, in winning victory for the cause of liberation of the Chinese people, in founding the People's Republic of China and in advancing our socialist cause. He made major contributions to the liberation of the oppressed nations of the world and to the progress of mankind.

28. The Chinese Communists, with Comrade Mao Zedong as their chief representative, made a theoretical synthesis of China's unique experience in its protracted revolution in accordance with the basic principles of Marxism-Leninism. This synthesis constituted a scientific system of guidelines befitting China's conditions, and it is this synthesis which is Mao Zedong Thought, the product of the integration of the universal principles of Marxism-Leninism with the concrete practice of the Chinese revolution. Making revolution in a large Eastern semi-colonial, semi-feudal country is bound to meet with many special, complicated problems, which cannot be solved by reciting the general principles of Marxism-Leninism or by copying foreign experience in every detail. The erroneous tendency of making Marxism a dogma and deifying Comintern resolutions and the experience of the Soviet Union prevailed in the international communist movement and in our Party mainly in the late 1920s and early 1930s, and this tendency pushed the Chinese revolution to the brink of total failure. It was in the course of combating this wrong tendency and making a profound summary of our historical experience in this respect that Mao Zedong Thought took shape and developed. It was systematized and extended in a variety of fields and reached maturity in the latter part of the Agrarian Revolutionary War and the War of Resistance Against Japan, and it was further developed during the War of Liberation and after the founding of the People's Republic of China. Mao Zedong Thought is Marxism-Leninism applied and developed in China; it constitutes a correct theory, a body of correct principles and a summary of the experiences that have been confirmed in the practice of the Chinese revolution, a crystallization of the collective wisdom of the Chinese Communist Party. Many outstanding leaders of our Party made important contributions to the formation and development of Mao Zedong Thought, and they are synthesized in the scientific works of Comrade Mao Zedong.

29. Mao Zedong Thought is wide-ranging in content. It is an original theory which has enriched and developed Marxism-Leninism in the following respects:

1) On the new-democratic revolution. Proceeding from China's historical and social conditions, Comrade Mao Zedong made a profound study of the characteristics and laws of the Chinese revolution, applied and developed the Marxist-Leninist thesis of the leadership of the proletariat in the democratic revolution, and established the theory of new-democratic revolution — a revolution against imperialism, feudalism and bureaucrat-capitalism waged by the masses of the people on the basis of the worker-peasant alliance under the leadership of the proletariat. His main works on this subject include: Analysis of the Classes in Chinese Society, Report on an Investigation of the Peasant Movement in Hunan, A Single Spark Can Start a Prairie Fire, Introducing "The Communist," On New Democracy, On Coalition Government and The Present Situation and Our Tasks. The basic points of this theory are:

I) China's bourgeoisie consisted of two sections, the big bourgeoisie (that is, the comprador bourgeoisie, or the bureaucrat-bourgeoisie) which was dependent on imperialism, and the national bourgeoisie which had revolutionary leanings but wavered. The proletariat should endeavor to get the national bourgeoisie to join in the united front under its leadership and in special circumstances to include even part of the big bourgeoisie in the united front, so as to isolate the main enemy to the greatest possible extent. When forming a united front with the bourgeoisie, the proletariat must preserve its own independence and pursue the policy of "unity, struggle, unity through struggle"; when forced to split with the bourgeoisie, chiefly the big bourgeoisie, it should have the courage and ability to wage a resolute armed struggle against the big bourgeoisie, while continuing to win the sympathy of the national bourgeoisie or keep it neutral.

II) Since there was no bourgeois democracy in China and the reactionary ruling classes enforced their terroristic dictatorship over the people by armed force, the revolution could not but essentially take the form of protracted armed struggle. China's armed struggle was a revolutionary war led by the proletariat with the peasants as the principal force. The peasantry was the most reliable ally of the proletariat. Through its vanguard, it was possible and necessary for the proletariat, with its progressive ideology and its sense of organization and discipline to raise the political consciousness of the peasant masses, establish rural base areas, wage a protracted revolutionary war and build up and expand the revolutionary forces.

Comrade Mao Zedong pointed out that "the united front and armed struggle are the two basic weapons for defeating the enemy." Together with Party building, they constituted the "three magic weapons" of the revolution. They were the essential basis which enabled the Chinese Communist Party to become the core of leadership of the whole nation and to chart the course of encircling the cities from the countryside and finally winning countrywide victory.

2) On the socialist revolution and socialist construction. On the basis of the economic and political conditions for the transition to socialism ensuing on victory in the new-democratic revolution, Comrade Mao Zedong and the Chinese Communist Party followed the path of effecting socialist industrialization simultaneously with socialist transformation and adopted concrete policies for the gradual transformation of the private ownership of the means of production, thereby providing a theoretical as well as practical solution of the difficult task of building socialism in a large country such as China, a country which was economically and culturally backward, with a population accounting for nearly one-fourth of the world's total. By putting forward the thesis that the combination of democracy for the people and dictatorship over the reactionaries constitutes the people's democratic dictatorship, Comrade Mao Zedong enriched the Marxist-Leninist theory of the dictatorship of the proletariat. After the establishment of the socialist system, Comrade Mao Zedong pointed out that, under socialism, the people had the same fundamental interests, but that all kinds of contradictions still existed among them, and that contradictions between the enemy and the people and contradictions among the people should be strictly distinguished from each other and correctly handled. He proposed that among the people we should follow a set of correct policies. We should follow the policy of "unity — criticism — unity" in political matters, the policy of "long-term coexistence and mutual supervision" in the Party's relations with the democratic parties, the policy of "let a hundred flowers blossom, let a hundred schools of thought contend" in science and culture, and, in the economic sphere the policy of overall arrangement with regard to the different strata in town and country and of consideration for the interests of the state, the collective and the individual, all three. He repeatedly stressed that we should not mechanically transplant the experience of foreign countries, but should find our own way to industrialization, a way suited to China's condition, by proceeding from the fact that China is a large agricultural country, taking agriculture as the foundation of the economy, correctly handling the relationship between heavy industry on the one hand and agriculture and light industry on the other and attaching due importance to the development of the latter. He stressed that in socialist construction we should properly handle the relationships between economic con-

struction and building up defense, between large-scale enterprises and small and medium-scale enterprises, between the Han nationality and the minority nationalities, between the coastal regions and the interior, between the central and the local authorities, and between self-reliance and learning from foreign countries, and that we should properly handle the relationship between accumulation and consumption and pay attention to overall balance. Moreover, he stressed that the workers were the masters of their enterprises and that cadres must take part in physical labor and workers in management, that irrational rules and regulations must be reformed and that the three-in-one combination of technical personnel, workers and cadres must be effected. And he formulated the strategic idea of bringing all positive factors into play and turning negative factors into positive ones so as to unite the whole Chinese people and build a powerful socialist country. The important ideas of Comrade Mao Zedong concerning the socialist revolution and socialist construction are mainly contained in such major works as *Report to the Second Plenary Session of the Seventh Central Committee of the Communist Party of China*, *On the People's Democratic Dictatorship*, *On the Ten Major Relationships*, *On the Correct Handling of Contradictions Among the People* and *Talk at an Enlarged Work Conference Convened by the Central Committee of the Communist Party of China*.

3) On the building of the revolutionary army and military strategy. Comrade Mao Zedong methodically solved the problem of how to turn a revolutionary army chiefly made up of peasants into a new type of people's army which is proletarian in character, observes strict discipline and forms close ties with the masses. He laid it down that the sole purpose of the people's army is to serve the people wholeheartedly, he put forward the principle that the Party commands the gun and not the other way round, he advanced the Three Main Rules of Discipline and the Eight Points for Attention and stressed the practice of political, economic and military democracy and the principles of the unity of officers and soldiers, the unity of army and people and the disintegration of the enemy forces, thus formulating by way of summation a set of policies and methods concerning political work in the army. In his military writings such as *On Correcting Mistaken Ideas in the Party*, *Problems of Strategy in China's Revolutionary War*, *Problems of Strategy in Guerrilla War Against Japan*, *On Protracted War* and *Problems of War and Strategy*, Comrade Mao Zedong summed up the experience of China's protracted revolutionary war and advanced the comprehensive concept of building a people's army and of building rural base areas and waging people's war by employing the people's army as the main force and relying on the masses. Raising guerrilla war to the strategic plane, he maintained that guerrilla warfare and

mobile warfare of a guerrilla character would for a long time be the main forms of operation in China's revolutionary war. He explained that it would be necessary to effect an appropriate change in military strategy simultaneously with the changing balance of forces between the enemy and ourselves and with the progress of the war. He worked out a set of strategies and tactics for the revolutionary army to wage people's war in conditions when the enemy was strong and we were weak. These strategies and tactics include fighting a protracted war strategically and campaigns and battles of quick decision, turning strategic inferiority into superiority in campaigns and battles and concentrating a superior force to destroy the enemy forces one by one. During the War of Liberation, he formulated the celebrated 10 major principles of operation. All these ideas constitute Comrade Mao Zedong's outstanding contribution to the military theory of Marxism-Leninism. After the founding of the People's Republic, he put forward the important guideline that we must strengthen our national defense and build modern revolutionary armed forces (including the navy, the air force and technical branches) and develop modern defence technology (including the making of nuclear weapons for self-defense).

4) On policy and tactics. Comrade Mao Zedong penetratingly elucidated the vital importance of policy and tactics in revolutionary struggles. He pointed out that policy and tactics were the life of the Party, that they were both the starting-point and the end-result of all the practical activities of a revolutionary party and that the Party must formulate its policies in the light of the existing political situation, class relations, actual circumstances and the changes in them, combining principle and flexibility. He made many valuable suggestions concerning policy and tactics in the struggle against the enemy, in the united front and other questions. He pointed out among other things:

> that, under changing subjective and objective conditions, a weak revolutionary force could ultimately defeat a strong reactionary force;
> that we should despise the enemy strategically and take the enemy seriously tactically;
> that we should keep our eyes on the main target of struggle and not hit out in all directions;
> that we should differentiate between and disintegrate our enemies, and adopt the tactic of making use of contradictions, winning over the many, opposing the few and crushing our enemies one by one;
> that, in areas under reactionary rule, we should combine legal and illegal struggle and, organizationally, adopt the policy of assigning picked cadres to work underground;

> that, as for members of the defeated reactionary classes and reactionary elements, we should give them a chance to earn a living and to become working people living by their own labour, so long as they did not rebel or create trouble; and
> that the proletariat and its party must fulfil two conditions in order to exercise leadership over their allies: (a) Lead their followers in waging resolute struggles against the common enemy and achieving victories; (b) Bring material benefits to their followers or at least avoid damaging their interests and at the same time give them political education.

These ideas of Comrade Mao Zedong's concerning policy and tactics are embodied in many of his writings, particularly in such works as *Current Problems of Tactics in the Anti-Japanese United Front*, *On Policy*, *Conclusions on the Repulse of the Second Anti-Communist Onslaught*, *On Some Important Problems of the Party's Present Policy*, *Don't Hit Out in All Directions* and *On the Question of Whether Imperialism and All Reactionaries Are Real Tigers*.

5) On ideological and political work and cultural work. In his *On New Democracy*, Comrade Mao Zedong stated:

> Any given culture (as an ideological form) is a reflection of the politics and economics of a given society, and the former in turn has a tremendous influence and effect upon the latter; economics is the base and politics the concentrated expression of economics.

In accordance with this basic view, he put forward many important ideas of far-reaching and long-term significance. For instance, the theses that ideological and political work is the lifeblood of economic and all other work and that it is necessary to unite politics and economics and to unite politics and professional skills, and to be both red and expert; the policy of developing a national, scientific and mass culture and of letting a hundred flowers blossom, weeding through the old to bring forth the new, and making the past serve the present and foreign things serve China; and the thesis that intellectuals have an important role to play in revolution and construction, that intellectuals should identify themselves with the workers and peasants and that they should acquire the proletarian world outlook by studying Marxism-Leninism, by studying society and through practical work. He pointed out that "this question of 'for whom?' is fundamental; it is a question of principle" and stressed that we should serve the people wholeheartedly, be highly responsible in revolutionary work, wage arduous struggle and fear no sacrifice. Many notable works written by Comrade Mao Zedong on ideology, politics and culture, such as The Orientation of the Youth Movement, Recruit Large Numbers of Intellectuals, Talks at the Yanan Forum of Literature and Art, In Memory of Norman Bethune, Serve the People and The Foolish Old Man Who Removed the Mountains, are of tremendous significance even today.

6) On Party building. It was a most difficult task to build a Marxist, proletarian Party of a mass character in a country where the peasantry and other sections of the petty bourgeoisie constituted the majority of the population, while the proletariat was small in number yet strong in combat effectiveness. Comrade Mao Zedong's theory on Party building provided a successful solution to this question. His main works in this area include Combat Liberalism, The Role of the Chinese Communist Party in the National War, Reform Our Study, Rectify the Party's Style of Work, Oppose Stereotyped Party Writing, Our Study and the Current Situation, On Strengthening the Party Committee System and Methods of Work of Party Committees. He laid particular stress on building the Party ideologically, saying that a Party member should join the Party no only organizationally but also ideologically and should constantly try to reform his non-proletarian ideas and replace them with proletarian ideas. He indicated that the style of work which entailed integrating theory with practice, forging close links with the masses and practising self-criticism was the hallmark distinguishing the Chinese Communist Party from all other political parties in China. To counter the erroneous "Left" policy of "ruthless struggle and merciless blows" once followed in inner-Party struggle, he proposed the correct policy of "learning from past mistakes to avoid future ones and curing the sickness to save the patient," emphasizing the need to achieve the objective of clarity in ideology and unity among comrades in inner-Party struggle. He initiated the rectification campaign as a form of ideological education in Marxism-Leninism throughout the Party, which applied the method of criticism and self-criticism. In view of the fact that our Party was about to become and then became a party in power leading the whole country, Comrade Mao Zedong urged time and again, first on the eve of the founding of the People's Republic and then later, that we should remain modest and prudent, guard against arrogance and rashness and keep to plain living and hard struggle in our style of work and that we should be on the lookout against the corrosive influence of bourgeois ideology and should oppose bureaucratism which would alienate us from the masses.

30. The living soul of Mao Zedong Thought is the stand, viewpoint and method embodied in its component parts mentioned above. This stand, viewpoint and method boil down to three basic points: to seek truth from facts, the mass line, and independence. Comrade Mao Ze-

dong applied dialectical and historical materialism to the entire work of the proletarian party, giving shape to this stand, viewpoint and method so characteristic of Chinese Communists in the course of the Chinese revolution and its arduous, protracted struggles and thus enriching Marxism-Leninism. They find expression not only in such important works as *Oppose Book Worship*, *On Practice*, *On Contradiction*, *Preface and Postscript to "Rural Surveys,"* *Some Questions Concerning Methods of Leadership* and *Where Do Correct Ideas Come From?*, but also in all his scientific writings and in the revolutionary activities of the Chinese Communists.

1) Seeking truth from facts. This means proceeding from reality and combining theory with practice, that is, integrating the universal principles of Marxism-Leninism with the concrete practice of the Chinese revolution. Comrade Mao Zedong was always against studying Marxism in isolation from the realities of Chinese society and the Chinese revolution. As early as 1930, he opposed blind book worship by emphasizing that investigation and study is the first step in all work and that one has no right to speak without investigation. On the eve of the rectification movement in Yanan, he affirmed that subjectivism is a formidable enemy of impurity in Party spirit. These brilliant theses helped people break through the shackles of dogmatism and greatly emancipate their minds. While summarizing the experience and lessons of the Chinese revolution in his philosophical works and many other works rich in philosophical content, Comrade Mao Zedong showed great profundity in expounding and enriching the Marxist theory of knowledge and dialectics. He stressed that the dialectical materialist theory of knowledge is the dynamic, revolutionary theory of reflection and that full scope should be given to man's conscious dynamic role which is based on and is in conformity with objective reality. Basing himself on social practice, he comprehensively and systematically elaborated the dialectical materialist theory on the sources, the process and the purpose of knowledge and on the criterion of truth. He said that as a rule, correct knowledge can be arrived at and developed only after many repetitions of the process leading from matter to consciousness and then back to matter, that is, leading from practice to knowledge and then back to practice. He pointed out that truth exists by contrast with falsehood and grows in struggle with it, that truth is inexhaustible and that the truth of any piece of knowledge, namely, whether it corresponds to objective reality, can ultimately be decided only through social practice. He further elaborated the law of the unity of opposites, the nucleus of Marxist dialectics. He indicated that we should not only study the universality of contradiction in objective existence, but, what is more important, we should study the particularity

of contradiction, and that we should resolve contradictions which are different in nature by different methods. Therefore, dialectics should not be viewed as a formula to be learnt by rote and applied mechanically, but should be closely linked with practice and with investigation and study and should be applied flexibly. He forged philosophy into a sharp weapon in the hands of the proletariat and the people for knowing and changing the world. His distinguished works on China's revolutionary war, in particular, provide outstandingly shining examples of applying and developing the Marxist theory of knowledge and dialectics in practice. Our Party must always adhere to the above ideological line formulated by Comrade Mao Zedong.

2) The mass line means everything for the masses, reliance on the masses in everything and "from the masses, to the masses." The Party's mass line in all its work has come into being through the systematic application in all its activities of the Marxist-Leninist principle that the people are the makers of history. It is a summation of our Party's invaluable historical experience in conducting revolutionary activities over the years under difficult circumstances in which the enemy's strength far outstripped ours. Comrade Mao Zedong stressed time and again that as long as we rely on the people, believe firmly in the inexhaustible creative power of the masses and hence trust and identify ourselves with them, no enemy can crush us while we can eventually crush every enemy and overcome every difficulty. He also pointed out that in leading the masses in all practical work, the leadership can form its correct ideas only by adopting the method of "from the masses, to the masses" and by combining the leadership with the masses and combining the general call with particular guidance. This means concentrating the ideas of the masses and turning them into systematic ideas, then going to the masses so that the ideas are persevered in and carried through, and testing the correctness of these ideas in the practice of the masses. And this process goes on, over and over again, so that the understanding of the leadership becomes more correct, keener and richer each time. This is how Comrade Mao Zedong united the Marxist theory of knowledge with the Party's mass line. As the vanguard of the proletariat, the Party exists and fights for the interests of the people. But it always constitutes only a small part of the people, so that isolation from the people will render all the Party's struggles and ideals devoid of content as well as impossible of success. To persevere in the revolution and advance the socialist cause, our Party must uphold the mass line.

3) Independence and self-reliance are the inevitable corollary of carrying out the Chinese revolution and construction by proceeding from Chinese reality and relying on the masses. The proletarian

revolution is an internationalist cause which calls for the mutual support of the proletariats of different countries. But for the cause to triumph, each proletariat should primarily base itself on its own country's realities, rely on the efforts of its own masses and revolutionary forces, integrate the universal principles of Marxism-Leninism with the concrete practice of its own revolution and thus achieve victory. Comrade Mao Zedong always stressed that our policy should rest on our own strength and that we should find our own road of advance in accordance with our own conditions. In a vast country like China, we must all the more rely mainly on our own efforts to promote the revolution and construction. We must be determined to carry the struggle through to the end and must have faith in the hundreds of millions of Chinese people and rely on their wisdom and strength; otherwise, it will be impossible for our revolution and construction to succeed or to be consolidated even if success is won. Of course, China's revolution and national construction are not and cannot be carried on in isolation from the rest of the world. It is always necessary for us to try to win foreign aid and, in particular, to learn all that is advanced and beneficial from other countries. The closed-door policy, blind opposition to everything foreign and any theory or practice of great-nation chauvinism are all entirely wrong. At the same time, although China is still comparatively backward economically and culturally, we must maintain our own national dignity and confidence and there must be no slavishness or submissiveness in any form in dealing with big, powerful or rich countries. Under the leadership of the Party and Comrade Mao Zedong, no matter what difficulty we encountered, we never wavered, whether before or after the founding of New China, in our determination to remain independent and self-reliant and we never submitted to any pressure from outside; we showed the dauntless and heroic spirit of the Chinese Communist Party and the Chinese people. We stand for the peaceful coexistence of the people of all countries and their mutual assistance on an equal footing. While upholding our own independence, we respect other people's right to independence. The road of revolution and construction suited to the characteristics of a country has to be explored, decided on and blazed by its own people. No one has the right to impose his views on others. Only under these conditions can there be genuine internationalism. Otherwise, there can only be hegemonism. We will always adhere to this principled stand in our international relations.

31. Mao Zedong Thought is the valuable spiritual asset of our Party. It will be our guide to action for a long time to come. The Party leaders and the large group of cadres nurtured by Marxism-Leninism and Mao Zedong Thought were the backbone forces in winning great victo-

rics for our cause; they are and will remain our treasured mainstay in the cause of socialist modernization. While many of Comrade Mao Zedong's important works were written during the periods of new-democratic revolution and of socialist transformation, we must still constantly study them. This is not only because one cannot cut the past off from the present and failure to understand the past will hamper our understanding of present-day problems, but also because many of the basic theories, principles and scientific approaches set forth in these works are of universal significance and provide us with invaluable guidance now and will continue to do so in the future. Therefore, we must continue to uphold Mao Zedong Thought, study it in earnest and apply its stand, viewpoint, and method in studying the new situation and solving the new problems arising in the course of practice. Mao Zedong Thought has added much that is new to the treasure-house of Marxist-Leninist theory. We must combine our study of the scientific works of Comrade Mao Zedong with that of the scientific writings of Marx, Engels, Lenin and Stalin. It is entirely wrong to try to negate the scientific value of Mao Zedong Thought and to deny its guiding role in our revolution and construction just because Comrade Mao Zedong made mistakes in his later years. And it is likewise entirely wrong to adopt a dogmatic attitude towards the sayings of Comrade Mao Zedong to regard whatever he said as the immutable truth which must be mechanically applied everywhere, and to be unwilling to admit honestly that he made mistakes in his later years, and even try to stick to them in our new activities. Both these attitudes fail to make a distinction between Mao Zedong Thought — a scientific theory formed and tested over a long period of time — and the mistakes Comrade Mao Zedong made in his later years. And it is absolutely necessary that this distinction should be made. We must treasure all the positive experience obtained in the course of integrating the universal principles of Marxism-Leninism with the concrete practice of China's revolution and construction over 50 years or so, apply and carry forward this experience in our new work, enrich and develop Party theory with new principles and new conclusions corresponding to reality, so as to ensure the continued progress of our cause along the scientific course of Marxism-Leninism and Mao Zedong Thought.

Unite and Strive to Build a Powerful, Modern Socialist China

32. The objective of our Party's struggle in the new historical period is to turn China step by step into a powerful socialist country with modern agriculture, industry, national defense and science and

technology and with a high level of democracy and culture. We must also accomplish the great cause of reunification of the country by getting Taiwan to return to the embrace of the motherland. The fundamental aim of summing up the historical experience of the 32 years since the founding of the People's Republic is to accomplish the great objective of building a powerful and modern socialist country by further rallying the will and strength of the whole Party, the whole army and the whole people on the basis of upholding the four fundamental principles, namely, upholding the socialist road, the people's democratic dictatorship (i.e., the dictatorship of the proletariat), the leadership of the Communist Party, and Marxism-Leninism and Mao Zedong Thought. These four principles constitute the common political basis of the unity of the whole Party and the unity of the whole people as well as the basic guarantee for the realization of socialist modernization. Any word or deed which deviates from these four principles is wrong. Any word or deed which denies or undermines these four principles cannot be tolerated.

33. Socialism and socialism alone can save China. This is the unalterable conclusion drawn by all our people from their own experience over the past century or so; it likewise constitutes our fundamental historical experience in the 32 years since the founding of our People's Republic. Although our socialist system is still in its early phase of development, China has undoubtedly established a socialist system and entered the stage of socialist society. Any view denying this basic fact is wrong. Under socialism, we have achieved successes which were absolutely impossible in old China. This is a preliminary and at the same time convincing manifestation of the superiority of the socialist system. The fact that we have been and are able to overcome all kinds of difficulties through our own efforts testifies to its great vitality. Of course, our system will have to undergo a long process of development before it can be perfected. Given the premise that we uphold the basic system of socialism, therefore, we must strive to reform those specific features which are not in keeping with the expansion of the productive forces and the interests of the people, and to staunchly combat all activities detrimental to socialism. With the development of our cause, the immense superiority of socialism will become more and more apparent.

34. Without the Chinese Communist Party, there would have been no New China. Likewise, without the Chinese Communist Party, there would be no modern socialist China. The Chinese Communist Party is a proletarian party armed with Marxism-Leninism and Mao Zedong Thought and imbued with a strict sense of discipline and the spirit of self-criticism, and its ultimate historical mission is to realize com-

munism. Without the leadership of such a party, without the flesh-and-blood ties it has formed with the masses through protracted struggles and without the painstaking and effective work among the people and the high prestige it consequently enjoys, our country — for a variety of reasons, both internal and external — would inexorably fall apart and the future of our nation and people would inexorably be forfeited. The Party leadership cannot be exempt from mistakes, but there is no doubt that it can correct them by relying on the close unity between the Party and the people, and in no case should one use the Party's mistakes as a pretext for weakening, breaking away from or even sabotaging its leadership. That would only lead to even greater mistakes and court grievous disasters. We must improve Party leadership in order to uphold it. We must resolutely overcome the many shortcomings that still exist in our Party's style of thinking and work, in its system of organization and leadership and in its contacts with the masses. So long as we earnestly uphold and constantly improve Party leadership, our Party will definitely be better able to undertake the tremendous tasks entrusted to it by history.

35. Since the Third Plenary Session of its 11th Central Committee, our Party has gradually mapped out the correct path for socialist modernization suited to China's conditions. In the course of practice, the path will be broadened and become more clearly defined, but, in essence, the key pointers can already be determined on the basis of the summing up of the negative as well as positive experience since the founding of the People's Republic, and particularly of the lessons of the "cultural revolution."

1) After socialist transformation was fundamentally completed, the principal contradiction our country has had to resolve is that between the growing material and cultural needs of the people and the backwardness of social production. It was imperative that the focus of Party and government work be shifted to socialist modernization centering on economic construction and that the people's material and cultural life be gradually improved by means of an immense expansion of productive forces. In the final analysis, the mistake we made in the past was that we failed to persevere in making this strategic shift. What is more, the preposterous view opposing the so-called "theory of the unique importance of productive forces," a view diametrically opposed to historical materialism, was put forward during the "cultural revolution." We must never deviate from this focus, except in the event of large-scale invasion by a foreign enemy (and even then it will still be necessary to carry on such economic construction as wartime conditions require and permit). All our Party work must be subordinated to and serve this central task — economic construction. All

our Party cadres, and particularly those in economic departments, must diligently study economic theory and economic practice as well as science and technology.

2) In our socialist economic construction, we must strive to reach the goal of modernization systematically and in stages, according to the conditions and resources of our country. The prolonged "Left" mistakes we made in our economic work in the past consisted chiefly in departing from Chinese realities, trying to exceed our actual capabilities and ignoring the economic returns of construction and management as well as the scientific confirmation of our economic plans, policies and measures, with their concomitants of colossal waste and losses. We must adopt a scientific attitude, gain a thorough knowledge of the realities and make a deep analysis of the situation, earnestly listen to the opinions of the cadres, masses and specialists in the various fields and try our best to act in accordance with objective economic and natural laws and bring about a proportionate and harmonious development of the various branches of economy. We must keep in mind the fundamental fact that China's economy and culture are still relatively backward. At the same time, we must keep in mind such favorable domestic and international conditions as the achievements we have already scored and the experience we have gained in our economic construction and the expansion of economic and technological exchanges with foreign countries, and we must make full use of these favorable conditions. We must oppose both impetuosity and passivity.

3) The reform and improvement of the socialist relations of production must be in conformity with the level of the productive forces and conducive to the expansion of production. The state economy and the collective economy are the basic forms of the Chinese economy. The working people's individual economy within certain prescribed limits is a necessary complement to public economy. It is necessary to establish specific systems of management and distribution suited to the various sectors of the economy. It is necessary to have planned economy and at the same time give play to the supplementary, regulatory role of the market on the basis of public ownership. We must strive to promote commodity production and exchange on a socialist basis. There is no rigid pattern for the development of the socialist relations of production. At every stage our task is to create those specific forms of the relations of production that correspond to the needs of the growing productive forces and facilitate their continued advance.

4) Class struggle no longer constitutes the principal contradiction after the exploiters have been eliminated as classes. However, owing to certain domestic factors and influences from abroad, class struggle will continue to exist within certain limits for a long time to come and

may even grow acute under certain conditions. It is necessary to oppose both the view that the scope of class struggle must be enlarged and the view that it has died out. It is imperative to maintain a high level of vigilance and conduct effective struggle against all those who are hostile to socialism and try to sabotage it in the political, economic, ideological and cultural fields and in community life. We must correctly understand that there are diverse social contradictions in Chinese society which do not fall within the scope of class struggle and that methods other than class struggle must be used for their appropriate revolution. Otherwise, social stability and unity will be jeopardized. We must unswervingly unite all forces that can be united with and consolidate and expand the patriotic united front.

5) A fundamental task of the socialist revolution is gradually to establish a highly democratic socialist political system. Inadequate attention was paid to this matter after the founding of the People's Republic, and this was one of the major factors contributing to the initiation of the "cultural revolution." Here is a grievous lesson for us to learn. It is necessary to strengthen the building of state organs at all levels in accordance with the principle of democratic centralism, make the people's congresses at all levels and their permanent organs authoritative organs of the people's political power, gradually realize direct popular participation in the democratic process at the grass roots of political power and community life and, in particular, stress democratic management by the working masses in urban and rural enterprises over the affairs of their establishments. It is essential to consolidate the people's democratic dictatorship, improve our Constitution and laws and ensure their strict observance and inviolability. We must turn the socialist legal system into a powerful instrument for protecting the rights of the people, ensuring order in production, work and other activities, punishing criminals and cracking down on the disruptive activities of class enemies. The kind of chaotic situation that obtained in the "cultural revolution" must never be allowed to happen again in any sphere.

6) Life under socialism must attain a high ethical and cultural level. We must firmly eradicate such gross fallacies as the denigration of education, science and culture and discrimination against intellectuals, fallacies which had long existed and found extreme expression during the "cultural revolution"; we must strive to raise the status and expand the role of education, science and culture in our drive for modernization. We unequivocally affirm that, together with the workers and peasants, the intellectuals are a force to rely on in the cause of socialism and that it is impossible to carry out socialist construction without culture and the intellectuals. It is imperative for the whole Party

to engage in a more diligent study of Marxist theories, of the past and present in China and abroad, and of the different branches of the natural and social sciences. We must strengthen and improve ideological and political work and educate the people and youth in the Marxist world outlook and communist morality; we must persistently carry out the educational policy which calls for an all-round development morally, intellectually and physically, for being both red and expert, for integration of the intellectuals with the workers and peasants and the combination of mental and physical labor; and we must counter the influence of decadent bourgeois ideology and the decadent remnants of feudal ideology, overcome the influence of petty-bourgeois ideology and foster the patriotism which puts the interests of the motherland above everything else and the pioneer spirit of selfless devotion to modernization.

7) It is of profound significance to our multi-national country to improve and promote socialist relations among our various nationalities and strengthen national unity. In the past, particularly during the "cultural revolution," we committed, on the question of nationalities, the grave mistake of widening the scope of class struggle and wronged a large number of cadres and masses of the minority nationalities. In our work among them, we did not show due respect for their right to autonomy. We must never forget this lesson. We must have a clear understanding that relations among our nationalities today are, in the main, relations among the working people of the various nationalities. It is necessary to persist in their regional autonomy and enact laws and regulations to ensure this autonomy and their decision-making power in applying Party and government policies according to the actual conditions in their regions. We must take effective measures to assist economic and cultural development in regions inhabited by minority nationalities, actively train and promote cadres from among them and resolutely oppose all words and deeds undermining national unity and equality. It is imperative to continue to implement the policy of freedom of religious belief. To uphold the four fundamental principles does not mean that religious believers should renounce their faith but that they must not engage in propaganda against Marxism-Leninism and Mao Zedong Thought and that they must not interfere with politics and education in their religious activities.

8) In the present international situation in which the danger of war still exists, it is necessary to strengthen the modernization of our national defence. The building up of national defence must be in keeping with the building up of the economy. The People's Liberation Army should strengthen its military training, political work, logistic service and study of military science and further raise its combat effectiveness so as gradually to become a still more powerful modern revolu-

tionary army. It is necessary to restore and carry forward the fine tradition of unity inside the army, between the army and the government and between the army and the people. The building of the people's militia must also be further strengthened.

9) In our external relations, we must continue to oppose imperialism, hegemonism, colonialism and racism, and safeguard world peace. We must actively promote relations and economic and cultural exchanges with other countries on the basis of the Five Principles of Peaceful Coexistence. We must uphold proletarian internationalism and support the cause of the liberation of oppressed nations, the national construction of newly independent countries and the just struggles of the peoples everywhere.

10) In the light of the lessons of the "cultural revolution" and the present situation in the Party, it is imperative to build up a sound system of democratic centralism inside the Party. We must carry out the Marxist principle of the exercise of collective Party leadership by leaders who have emerged from mass struggles and who combine political integrity with professional competence, and we must prohibit the personality cult in any form. It is imperative to uphold the prestige of Party leaders and at the same time ensure that their activities come under the supervision of the Party and the people. We must have a high degree of centralism based on a high degree of democracy and insist that the minority is subordinate to the majority, the individual to the organization, the lower to the higher level and the entire membership to the Central Committee. The style of work of a political party in power is a matter that determines its very existence. Party organizations at all levels and all Party cadres must go deep among the masses, plunge themselves into practical struggle, remain modest and prudent, share weal and woe with the masses and firmly overcome bureaucratism. We must properly wield the weapon of criticism and self-criticism, overcome erroneous ideas that deviate from the Party's correct principles, uproot factionalism, oppose anarchism and ultra-individualism and eradicate such unhealthy tendencies as the practice of seeking perks and privileges. We must consolidate the Party organization, purify the Party ranks and weed out degenerate elements who oppress and bully the people. In exercising leadership over state affairs and work in the economic and cultural fields as well as community life, the Party must correctly handle its relations with other organizations, ensure by every means the effective functioning of the organs of state power and administrative, judicial and economic and cultural organizations and see to it that trade unions, the Youth League, the Women's Federation, the Science and Technology Association, the Federation of Literary and Art Circles and other mass organizations

carry out their work responsibly and on their own initiative. The Party must strengthen its co-operation with public figures outside the Party, give full play to the role of the Chinese People's Political Consultative Conference, hold conscientious consultations with democratic parties and personages without party affiliation on major issues of state affairs and respect their opinions and the opinions of specialists in various fields. As with other social organizations, Party organizations at all levels must conduct their activities within the limits permitted by the Constitution and the law.

36. In firmly correcting the mistake of the so-called "continued revolution under the dictatorship of the proletariat," a slogan which was advanced during the "cultural revolution" and which called for the overthrow of one class by another, we absolutely do not mean that the tasks of the revolution have been accomplished and that there is no need to carry on revolutionary struggles with determination. Socialism aims not just at eliminating all systems of exploitation and all exploiting classes but also at greatly expanding the productive forces, improving and developing the socialist relations of production and the superstructure and, on this basis, gradually eliminating all class differences and all major social distinctions and inequalities which are chiefly due to the inadequate development of the productive forces until communism is finally realized. This is a great revolution, unprecedented in human history. Our present endeavor to build a modern socialist China constitutes but one stage of this great revolution. Differing from the revolutions before the overthrow of the system of exploitation, this revolution is carried out not through fierce class confrontation and conflict, but through the strength of the socialist system itself, under leadership, step by step and in an orderly way. This revolution which has entered the period of peaceful development is more profound and arduous than any previous revolution and will not only take a very long historical period to accomplish but also demand the unswerving and disciplined hard work and heroic sacrifices of many generations. In this historical period of peaceful development, revolution can never be plain sailing. There are still overt and covert enemies and other saboteurs who watch for opportunities to create trouble. We must maintain high revolutionary vigilance and be ready at all times to come out boldly to safeguard the interests of the revolution. In this new historical period, the whole membership of the Chinese Communist Party and the whole people must never cease to cherish lofty revolutionary ideals, maintain a dynamic revolutionary fighting spirit and carry China's great socialist revolution and socialist construction through to the end.

37. Repeated assessment of our successes and failures, of our cor-

rect and incorrect practices, of the 32 years since the founding of our People's Republic, and particularly deliberation over and review of the events of the past few years, have helped to raise immensely the political consciousness of all Party comrades and of all patriots. Obviously, our Party now has a higher level of understanding of socialist revolution and construction than at any other period since liberation. Our Party has both the courage to acknowledge and correct its mistakes and the determination and ability to prevent repetition of the serious mistakes of the past. After all, from a long-term historical point of view the mistakes and setbacks of our Party were only temporary whereas the consequent steeling of our Party and people, the greater maturity of the core force formed among our Party cadres through protracted struggle, the growing superiority of our socialist system and the increasingly keen and common aspiration of our Party, army and people for the prosperity of the motherland will be decisive factors in the long run. A great future is in store for our socialist cause and for the Chinese people in their hundreds of millions.

38. Inner-Party unity and unity between the Party and the people are the basic guarantee for new victories in our socialist modernization. Whatever the difficulties, as long as the Party is closely united and remains closely united with the people, our Party and the cause of socialism it leads will certainly prosper day by day.

The Resolution on Certain Questions in the History of Our Party unanimously adopted in 1945 by the Enlarged Seventh Plenary Session of the Sixth Central Committee of the Party unified the thinking of the whole Party, consolidated its unity, promoted the rapid advance of the people's revolutionary cause and accelerated its eventual triumph. The Sixth Plenary Session of the 11th Central Committee of the Party believes that the present resolution it has unanimously adopted will play a similar historical role. This session calls upon the whole Party, the whole army and the people of all our nationalities to act under the great banner of Marxism-Leninism and Mao Zedong Thought, closely rally around the Central Committee of the Party, preserve the spirit of the legendary Foolish Old Man who removed mountains and work together as one in defiance of all difficulties so as to turn China step by step into a powerful modern socialist country which is highly democratic and highly cultured. Our goal must be attained! Our goal can unquestionably be attained!

Translation from Beijing Review, No. 27
(July 6, 1981), pp. 10-39

About the Author

Helmut Martin is Professor of Chinese Language and Literature with the Ruhr University Bochum and research fellow for China with the Hamburg Institute of Asian Affairs. Since 1980 he has been director of the Institute of Arabic, Chinese and Japanese language (State of North Rhine Westphalia) in Bochum, which provides practical language training for journalists, diplomats, businessmen, students and other interested persons. He has published several books on Chinese literary criticism and Maoist ideology and edited a Chinese-German dictionary of political language in the PRC.